Flowers
on the
Wall

a novel

TANYA MONTÁS PARIS

For my sister

Also by TANYA MONTÁS PARIS

Poetry
Poquito: Unpacking the Memory Jar

Books for Young Readers
A Palace for My Mom
The Runaway Piglet
My Mommy's Hair
Mi mami trabaja mucho
A dormir, mi niña
La cerdita soñadora
La bella en bicicleta

Part One

stand tall, reaching
hoping
the iris holds loosely
uncertain
"let go" says the wind
it sways and latches on
just a bit tighter

THE GIRL SITS IN THE DARK.

The floor of her closet feels cold on her bare legs. The small blade rests in the palm of her open hand like an offering. *Why am I not enough?*

The house is silent, except for the rhythmic scratching of budding branches tapping on the window in the next room. The girl feels the power of the tiny blade calling her name, and she obeys. It grounds her and brings her release.

Mariah stands outside the closed door, remembering, afraid to enter. She touches the inside of her arm and blinks, and the little girl vanishes.

You pulled through, she tells herself, taking a deep breath of relief as she enters the room of sorrows.

"*NEXT IN LINE!*" the cashier called out.

Meg's eyes traveled over the stout man in front of her, observing his silver hair and the annoyance set into his jaw. He wasn't happy to be waiting in line either. Her gaze moved down his back and took in the faded jeans and plaid shirt. She guessed he could have just come from a rodeo—if only he had a Stetson in his hand and worn leather boots on his feet. Just then he turned around; he'd felt her scrutiny. She jerked her head to the right and stared into the crowd to show him he was less than interesting.

The line moved, and the man moved forward with it. Now Meg could see the full length of his arms. He was holding a gallon of milk in one hand and a pack of breath mints in the other. *What an odd combination,* she thought, but decided to release the stranger from her thoughts.

She noticed the sale items displayed along the checkout line. She was tempted to grab the three-piece mini nail lacquer set, a beautiful combination of pastel blues, but the line's progression saved her from the unnecessary indulgence.

The cashier smiled, looked up, and called out, "Next!"

Meg placed the bottle of anti-inflammatory pills on the counter. She reached inside her back pocket for her credit card. "Let's beat cancer together," read the sign next to the signature pad.

"September is Cancer Awareness Month," the cashier said, pointing at the sign. "Would you like to make a donation?" She looked at Meg expectantly.

Meg nodded and the cashier made a comment … or maybe it was a question, but Meg had stopped listening. Her eyes glazed with a cloud of oncoming tears. A monotonous, one-toned symphony pounded her ears.

"How can you stand up against hell?" Meg asked no one in particular. The cashier returned Meg's card and offered a grateful smile. She was one of those cheery types.

"Have a fabulous day," she sang after Meg as she turned to leave.

Meg didn't hear her. She was slipping back to the distant night, a long time ago, when her daughter came into the world. Her premature birth during an emergency Caesarean had saved both her and Meg. Such a miracle, they had thought at the time, not knowing the terror that silently lurked.

"September is Cancer Awareness Month," Meg repeated out loud to herself as she started home.

September is also the month she buried her daughter.

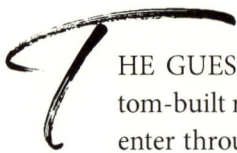

*T*HE GUESTS MEANDER INTO the luxurious, custom-built residence nuzzled in a Boston suburb. Some enter through the front door, but those more familiar with the house take the side garden entrance. A small group talking by the entryway huddles closer against the cold draft as the front door opens. A couple walks in, and the musky scent of oud fills the air. They linger for a bit by the door, finishing a whispered conversation. He helps her out of her tight lilac jacket and gives her braided ponytail a playful tussle. She smiles, bright red lipstick framing the small gap in her front teeth, as she bends down to unzip her knee-high boots. She sets the boots to the side and opens her handbag. Out pops a pair of shoes, just like in a Mary Poppins scene. She neatly arranges them on the floor, side by side, and steps right in.

This girl clearly had dressed for the October New England weather, thinks Mariah, smiling as she realizes who accompanies her. The stout, ginger-haired man in Mariah's group turns around. He, too, has noticed the new arrivals.

"Geez, Max," his raspy voice bounces in unison with his belly pouch. "It's so good of you to show up!" His perfectly round bald spot gleams on the crown of his head like a targeted helipad.

"C'mon Gus, that reputation is getting old!" the newcomer says dryly.

The two old college friends embrace and slap each others' backs.

"This is my friend Luna." Max brings his companion forward, his arm around the small of her back. Her pencil-thin eyebrows line up in alert.

Luna reaches out to shake Gus's hand, but he quickly pulls her over, planting a loud kiss on her cheek.

"So nice to meet you, Luna," Gus says, raising his eyebrows at Max. "I appreciate that your taste in women has been refined, old friend."

Luna smiles shyly, readjusting her glasses to try to hide pink blotches forming on her cheeks, and Max sends Gus a warning gaze.

Mariah steps forward, inserting herself between the two friends. Even though it's been more than a year since they last saw each other, clearly nothing has changed. He may have worked in the grownup job of engineer at a pharmaceutical company since grad school, but clearly Gus is stuck in his college years. She likes to think of him as a radiant sunflower always turning his head upward, searching. She is used to his impertinence and lack of finesse, but she senses Luna's discomfort. She sticks out her hand in welcome.

"Hi Luna, I'm Mariah. I'm so glad to meet you."

She reaches for Max, giving him a gentle hug and whispering, "It's just our old wonderful Gus being himself. Keep breathing and cut him some slack."

If Gus is a vibrant, attention-seeking sunflower, she thinks of Max as a calla lily, requiring minimum upkeep.

"The protector of women's honor," Eleanor, the fourth college friend, had named him.

Mariah takes Luna's arm and sashays her toward the kitchen, deciding she needed a strong cocktail if she is to endure an evening listening to Gus. She maneuvers around the crowded space until she spots the citrusy cocktail dancing in a glass pitcher. She scans the counter for a margarita glass and, seeing none, grabs one of the water tumblers arranged in a neat row by the fridge. Noticing someone had made a spicy mixture of salt and cayenne pepper, Mariah adds a rim on Luna's glass and swiftly pours some of the cocktail. Handing Luna her drink, she reaches for another glass. *Why the hell not,* she reasons, making herself a matching drink.

"To Max," she says, clinking Luna's glass.

Mariah sips the refreshing liquid, savoring the spicy residue dancing on her tongue.

"Thank you," Luna says and takes a long chug. "Tasty." The effect of the extra aged tequila is immediate. The splotches on her cheeks appear again, but this time Gus is not to blame.

Mariah finds a loose corner of cuticle and pulls at it eagerly with her teeth as she watches Luna stare into the crowd. Her large black eyes squint into the sea of faces as if the round, red-framed spectacles were failing to do their job. *She is searching for him,* Mariah smiles into her drink. *Please make him happy,* she pleads silently to the petite figure with the embroidered velvet lace choker.

She had known about Luna for a while now. Max's old room-mate dated her sister a few years back. Max had a big crush on her then, but Luna had been in a relationship at the time. Mariah remembered a few months back when Max called her all excited. He had reconnected with his old roommate soon after moving back to the area. "I asked him about Luna, and what do you know?" Mariah remembered how thrilled he had been to find out Luna was single. "I should give her a call. Right?" he asked.

Luna's bright smile indicates she has found Max. Mariah follows her gaze and watches Max easing his way through the crowd to the kitchen. He had left Gus behind, halfway through a story, she is certain. Max nods at Luna and locks eyes with Mariah.

"Thanks for rescuing Luna," he whispers to her, planting a kiss on her cheek.

He steps away and puts his arm around Luna, who is looking a bit braver and ready to conquer an evening of strangers. He moves a strand of hair hanging loosely over her eye and taps her nose playfully.

"Thanks. That's much better," she says, reaching over for his hand while bringing her drink to his lips.

Mariah notes the tenderness of her gesture.

"Delicious, right? I seem to have fallen into the capable hands of the Margarita Pro, here." She motions to Mariah.

Mariah nods, her ears registering the dry, screechy voice that pauses strategically, enunciating key syllables in each word, demanding the listener's alertness and attention. She repeats this speaking pattern in her mind and wonders whether it would become tiresome for the listener.

Luna's hand gestures become more animated with every statement as if delivering an unspoken message: *Don't let my size or my voice fool you.*

Mariah diverts her attention to the loud clicking of approaching high heels. She recognizes that sound, a proclamation of confidence and demand for attention. She stares into the happy, green eyes of her dearest friend Eleanor, the party host and birthday girl, her "Kiss Me. I'm the Birthday Girl" tiara securely fastened into her expertly styled hair. Her thirty-three-year-old friend looks just as she did when she was eighteen.

"Can I have one of those?" Eleanor motions to the drink in Mariah's hand. She hadn't noticed the man at Mariah's side. When she does, she cries out: "Max! You bastard! You came!" She throws her arms around Max and does a typical Eleanor-excited dance. Without missing a beat, she pulls Luna over and sandwiches her in between, her face lost deeply into the groove of Eleanor's abounding bosom.

"I am so happy you are both here!" She can hardly contain her excitement.

"Mariah, don't you just adore Luna?" she asks breezily.

A pang of jealousy bolts through Mariah. Clearly, Eleanor and Luna had previously met. Her eyes meet Eleanor's, who immediately realizes Mariah's discovery.

"Oh, come on! Stop it Mariah! I bumped into Max and Luna just yesterday at the mall. It's not like Max chose me over you." She sticks her tongue out at Mariah.

"What? I didn't say anything," Mariah replies, feeling relieved. A couple of women make their way into the group. Mariah searches her memory for any recognition, but nothing registers. The oldest woman hugs Eleanor and wishes her a happy birthday. The other woman looks much too young to be drinking, yet she parades her almost empty beer expertly. Mariah directs the young guest toward the beer bucket and then proceeds into the yard, the soft squeak of the glass sliding door muffled by the voices trapped inside.

Mariah takes a full breath of the crisp, clear night and wraps her scarf around her neck, being careful to allow the cascade of her unraveling curls to rest on her shoulders. The stars are out, imposing their presence, forcing her to look up. A small group gathers around the firepit. Eleanor had blankets and cushions out for the guests. That's her friend Eleanor, all details and elegance.

Mariah finds an empty spot on a blanket. She considers getting up and grabbing an extra pillow, but quickly discards the idea as greedy. Her eyes adjust to the darkness, narrowing to inspect the silhouettes around the yard. She registers a sudden sweet earthy scent and is not surprised by the outstretched arm in front of her face. Someone is passing a joint around, but she refuses. The hand ventures over to the man sitting to her right on a beach chair, both legs stretched out resting on not one, but two, large pillows. Mariah notices that he, too, passes on the reefer.

"I haven't touched one of those in a while," the man says.

Mariah realizes his comment is for her benefit. She tilts her head and offers an acknowledging "ah."

"Andrew and I grew up together. I haven't seen him in ages. I moved to New York City right after college and life just got busy." He pauses for a moment, reflecting. "It was Andrew who introduced me to the hallucinatory world of pot," he adds with a chuckle. He pushes the pillows aside and brings his legs closer, knees popped up to the sky.

Mariah listens to this stranger narrate his youthful experimentation.

"Weed and booze, a young man's best bud," he says. He seems to delight at the memories of a younger self. The glow of the fire highlights the twinkle in his eyes and the mischievous smile as he recounts some of his experiences under narcotic influences.

"Riding the Jamaican waves high on pot and magic mushrooms." He stops himself, as if he were going to say something more, but thinks better of it.

Mariah nods but can't relate. She had been a cigarette smoker in college. It had started her junior year in high school as a social activity, but it had escalated quickly into an addiction by her sophomore year in college. *It's my anxiety medicine*, she had called it. Smoking pot was something she chose to avoid out of fear. She knew many kids in college who experimented with recreational drugs, some less harmful like pot, but others as detrimental as heroin or cocaine. Those reckless actions had affected the academic performance of many of her peers.

"It's hard to picture Andrew being the corrupting type," Mariah comments, glancing over at Eleanor's sophisticated and proper husband, his silhouette away from the fire.

"The thing about Andrew," the stranger says, "well, he was a bright kid. He was also very popular, not that he tried to be. Kids just felt comfortable around him. We all went to him for help with the hard courses like Bio and Chem. He was like a big brother to me."

He leans back in his chair and gives a small chuckle. "One day we were hanging out at his house and he just rolled up some grass and lit it up. He handed it to me without even looking. He assumed I knew what to do with it."

"Well, did you?" Mariah asks playfully, fascinated by the story of a younger Andrew.

"I pretended that I did. If he knew my bluff, he didn't call me on it. Then again, that's Andrew." Mariah detects a sense of pride in his smile.

A shower of bright embers crackle, sending shooting sparks into the night. Mariah catches a glimpse of the stranger's face, unprepared for the electric shock that runs unapologetically down the length of her body at the sight of his sensual lips.

Mariah stares back at the fire. She shifts her weight from the left to the right side of her buttocks to relieve the arousal trapped in her pelvic region.

"I'm Jake, by the way." The stranger offers a stretched-out hand, and Mariah feels her heart pounding rapidly. She begs her ribcage to remain silent.

"I'm Mariah. Eleanor and I went to college together."

Mariah watches his mouth move as if he were savoring the syllables that make up her name. "What a beautiful name," he says, his feline eyes scanning her whole.

Mariah offers a silent gratitude to the darkness for hiding the rosy pigment warming her cheeks.

"Well, lady Mariah," Jake bows in reverent fashion. "I'm going in for another drink. May I bring you back a refill?"

Mariah laughs at the title of LADY. She can't remember if anyone has called her that before. She surrenders her empty glass, unaware she had taken her last sip, and stares at the tall figure walking away. She looks at the empty beach chair still surrounded by Jake's mystic aura and considers whether she should place her scarf on it as a way to claim the spot. The way a schoolgirl would save a seat for her crush. Her attention turns to the crackling embers performing in the fire, dancing and waving before rising into the blackness of the night.

Jake makes his way back with two drinks in hand. Mariah's eyes follow the movement of his steps as he approaches her.

"Are you here with someone?" he asks, handing her the drink.

She lets the question linger as she reaches up to grab the cocktail, noticing it is in a proper margarita glass with a spice rim and all.

"I am not," she replies, knowing her voice sounds hesitant.

"What about brunch in the city tomorrow?" he asks.

Mariah considers his question for a moment. There is a drift of presumption in the way he asked, yet she is willing to play along. She finds Jake's directness rather intriguing and refreshing. She much prefers this to the annoying requests she often gets from single guys to go out on a date with all the melodrama involved.

"I'm not sure. I think I might have stuff going on," she replies, hoping for a convincing comeback.

"Come on, it's just brunch. I'm flying back to New York in the late afternoon," he pleads, holding her gaze.

"Alright. But I get to pick the place." She smiles, breathing the seductive air around him.

She stares at him in wonder. What's behind the charming smile, Jake? She chooses to ignore the small voice flashing a Casanova alert.

WHEN MARIAH ENTERED KINDERGARTEN, she was quickly diagnosed as a selective mute. When her parents picked her up at the end of the day, the teachers told them Mariah hadn't spoken a single word. This silence continued for several weeks. It was confounding to the teachers, as well as Mariah's parents, that she refused to speak while the students were in the classroom. Once the students had left for the day, however, and just grown-ups were in the room, Mariah chatted away nonstop, her voice hoarse from lack of use.

Her parents were called into the school to meet with the special education team, where they were introduced to the world of selective mutism.

"It is a childhood anxiety disorder and will very likely remedy itself with minimum support," the special education team assured them. The team went on to describe a plan of action involving special education services as well as direct instruction by the classroom teacher.

Mariah's parents sat there, surrounded by strangers, unsure how to react. Her mother reached for the tissue box to dab away her tears, unable to ask any of the questions rushing through her head. It was her father who took control of the situation, asking the simplest of questions: "How do we help her?"

"She can start meeting twice a week with the behavioral therapist at the school," one special education teacher offered. "We will increase the sessions to three times a week once the paperwork goes through."

The special education team also recommended medication to address her anxiety.

"Let's put the medication on hold," her father said. "Let's give therapy a chance first." In the end, her parents had walked out of the meeting armed with a folder packed with articles and resources to help their daughter overcome the disorder.

The school intervention continued into second grade, where Mariah gradually began to show improvements. By the time she completed third grade, Mariah had blossomed into a confident student. She had mastered her phobia. Her ease around people of all ages began to impact her life outside of the classroom as well. One day, on their walk home, she asked her parents to sign her up for the town youth basketball league. Her parents stared at each other in disbelief. "Who is this kid and what has she done with our daughter?" her mother mouthed with delight.

Mariah had heard kids in her grade talk about their teams at recess. They brought basketball and soccer balls to school and organized their own pickup games. One day she happened to be standing by, watching them play, when a tall boy with bright red hair called out, "We'll take that kid," and pointed at her with a swift move of his chin.

She found herself in the midst of a basketball game. She was unaware of any rules and was clumsy at dribbling the ball, but her ability to jump and forcefully grab rebounds earned her a spot on future teams.

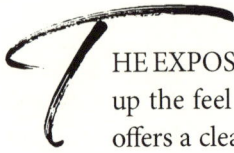

*T*HE EXPOSED BRICK interior of the restaurant conjures up the feel of a rustic old cottage in Sicily. Their table offers a clear view of Bostonians and adventurous tourists navigating their way down the always vibrant Salem Street.

Two glasses of half-consumed Bloody Marys grace the now empty plates of tiramisu French toast and frittata.

Mariah breathes in the aromatic kitchen smells as her eyes trace the row of large jars of olives adorning a corner of the bar.

She reaches over and grabs the bud vase with the single wildflower and takes a whiff. Her eyes follow the intricate patterns decorating the thin petals, while her ears welcome the cheery thrums of the mandolin and guitar that bounce happily in the background.

"If I were to pick my own name it would be Rose, although it would break my mother's heart if she knew of that secret desire."

The conversation had morphed from the typical icebreakers of the weather and the restaurant's friendly atmosphere to more personal topics.

"Why the name Rose?"

"I once came upon one of those baby-naming books. I must have been twelve or thirteen years old. I remember feeling like it somehow described me," Mariah says, her hands fidgeting a green linen napkin into a disastrous origami shape.

Her eyes survey her gnawed nails and she lowers the napkin to her lap, where she continues the folding game. She thinks about her name, the cause of a family feud, a small square on the fabric of her family identity quilt. Her grandmother, a black southerner who grew up under Jim Crow laws, had felt strongly about the name Maya, a tribute to the poet, but at the time of her birth, the name Mariah prevailed, and even the mention of Maya Angelou would forever bring a sense of discomfort to the adults in her life.

Jake stares at Mariah expectantly. Mariah hadn't thought about the name Rose and its meaning in a long time, so she had to pause and search her memory. She gives her eyeglasses a gentle lift to readjust them to the bridge of her nose. She only realized she was wearing them this morning on her way to the train to meet him. Mariah had been up early organizing her files for an upcoming settlement meeting on her current civil action case.

I should turn around to put in my contact lenses, Mariah thought, but felt silly at the idea of going to such trouble. *Who am I trying to impress?* Jake had noticed the frames as soon as she walked into the restaurant. "Nice," he commented, pointing at his own eyes. She wasn't sure if she felt relieved or regretful.

"Well, the name is supposed to mean tolerant, methodical, and someone who believes in law and order. People who know me will attest to that." She is, after all, an attorney for a small law firm charged with constitutional rights cases. "It also means a person whose biggest challenge is uncertainty; trust me, that's me. Of course, it also means all these other sweet things like generous, sympathetic, and compassionate. Well, those are qualities I aspire to. But honestly, it wasn't the meaning so much that drew me to the name, as it was its history."

He sits with his arms on the table, clearly interested in hearing her personal revelations, so she continues.

"Most people are familiar with the rose as the flower of choice to signify love. But its meaning goes beyond love; it also signifies politics, conflict, and war."

She takes the napkin from her lap and folds it, little layers in different directions, thinking maybe she can make a rose. But she can't. She places the napkin on the table, softly patting it to stop her fidgeting.

"Roses are one of the oldest specimens of flowers. They go back about forty million years. Then you add the symbolism of the red rose and the white rose in the fighting between York and Lancaster to control England. They called it …"

"The *War of the Roses*," Jake completes her thought.

"That's right. That last piece sealed the deal for me."

"So much beauty and controversy wrapped up together," Jake says. He pauses a moment, stroking his cocktail glass, then asks: "Are the thorns to symbolize how tough you are? Like, 'don't be fooled by my beauty' kind of thing?"

Mariah laughs. "Maybe there are some of those self-defense presumptions there too. Or maybe the thorns are just a reminder that we are not perfect. Or that there is beauty and pain in the world and they can coexist and that is OK." She suddenly realizes how much she has talked and shifts the focus away from her. "Anyway, what about you? Is Jake short for Jacob?"

"No, just Jake," he says, clearly hoping to end his explanation. Mariah sips of her drink and puts the glass down, nudging him along. "And?"

"My mom came from a Jewish family, but they weren't very observant, so Mom and her siblings didn't grow up with the Jewish religion or traditions. My mom named me Jake. Perhaps that was the closest she came to acknowledging her Jewish roots. So, yeah, just Jake."

Mariah senses the discomfort in his voice so she reels in the conversation. "I find it fascinating how people choose names for their kids. And how culture plays a big role for many families. I had a friend in high school named Osmar. His name was generated through a combination of the first syllables of his father's and his mother's names, Oscar plus Mariela. It's a tradition in many Hispanic cultures."

Mariah eyes Jake curiously. She can easily read the grin on his face, so she knows he's interested. But there is something distracting about his gaze, like he isn't completely in the moment with her. Or maybe he's just trying to get his head around all of this, just as she is.

"Are you in love with someone else?"

Mariah rubs her face, surprised by Jake's directness.

"Are you always this forward with the ladies?" she asks, aware of how the deep tone of his voice massages her ear canal.

"I don't meet ladies very often," he says, unapologetically smirking.

Definitely a charmer, Mariah thinks. Yet, there is something in the way he is looking at her, the intensity of his stare, that makes her feel exposed—or is it wanted? And then there is that feverish chemistry from the night before that still lingers. There is no mistaking the physical attraction. But there also is something else brewing.

She clears her throat, a habit of hers whenever something very personal is about to emerge.

"I was engaged to my best friend. We went to college together. We had an eight-year engagement that ended last year. He is a molecular geneticist who leads a research team at the University of Wageningen University in the Netherlands." She looks at her glass and swills the last bit of tasty liquid, all that remains of her Bloody Mary.

Before she is aware of it, Mariah shares her life story. She is surprised at how natural it feels to talk with Jake about Rafael. She shares how she had loved and still cares deeply for him. But she values being her own person, pursuing her passions and interests without having to ever justify or explain her choices. It is true that she missed being in a relationship at times, but it is also true that she didn't regret her choice to be on her own.

"It turns out that long-distance romance was not for me," Mariah finishes by way of an explanation.

Mariah watches Jake hang on to every word, as if missing the least little piece of information could prevent the earth from spinning. But she is also distracted by his piercing blue eyes, which make her skin sizzle. She isn't used to this level of physical attraction. She attempts to redirect the conversation with the hope of giving her body time to cool down. A waiter stops by to refill their water glasses, and Mariah welcomes the distraction and quickly recovers.

"Left or right wing in politics?"

"What! I am offended." Jake raises his bristly eyebrows. "Is this question a test?"

"Well, it could be." Mariah shoots him a devious smile. She is enjoying Jake's playfulness. *Beware of long-distance relationships,* warns her brain, but her body isn't listening.

"Are you interested in gauging my political and social ideology, or discovering which political party I tend to vote for?" His grin clearly shows how much he enjoys the taunting.

Mariah tilts her head gently, silently inviting him to continue.

"I believe women have the right to decide for themselves anything pertaining to their own bodies. I believe people should have the freedom to marry the person they love. I believe it is the role of the government to protect civil liberties and human rights. I believe in equal opportunities for all. I believe weapons should only be in the hands of the military. Should I go on about welfare, immigration, and euthanasia?"

Her pleased smile tells him he has, indeed, passed the test.

After a four-hour conversation and a delicious brunch, Mariah stands. She feels a pang of regret sinking in as she stretches out her hand and says, "Well, Just Jake, it's been really nice to meet you."

Jake springs up in one quick jump, completes the handshake, and adds, "Wait, the day is not over yet."

As he turns around, he takes in the empty room, devoid of the large crowd of diners that had been there when they first arrived. He looks perplexed when he realizes brunch is over. He doesn't seem ready to say goodbye to Mariah.

"It's such a beautiful afternoon," he says. "What about a walk over to that famous place for some fresh cannolis?"

Mariah's sweet tooth does a happy cheer at the thought of the delicious treat, then resolves to listen to the continuous warning signals her brain is sending.

"Sorry," Mariah says. "Look. This has been so very pleasant. I have really enjoyed your company, but you live in New York City and I live in Boston." She gives him an apologetic look.

Despite the fact the waiter is hovering, hoping to clear the room, Jake takes his chair and turns it around and straddles it. He is so close Mariah can smell his aftershave. Instead of being overpowering, it is a clean, masculine, mate-attracting musky scent that her olfactory receptors find seductive.

Jake peers into her eyes and Mariah realizes how young he seems. Panic strikes her as her brain reprimands her with an accusatory finger: *You are at least five years his senior! What are you thinking?*

His eyes hold her gaze as if he is trying to decipher her internal conflict. With a sudden move, Jake pushes away from the table.

"Wait here." He touches both her shoulders and a volt of electricity roots her to the spot.

Jake pulls his phone from a vest pocket and disappears out of the restaurant. Mariah rolls her eyes and smiles. It has been a long time since she has felt like a schoolgirl. Men no longer awaken in her this type of excitement, the sensation that love lurks around the corner, and that before you know it, the chase is over and done with and love has you all wrapped up. It is true she'd found love with Rafael. But it was a love SHE had chased. Being chased by love is a totally new sensation.

Jake makes his way back to the table, a boyish grin on his face.

"What? Did you change your flight to tomorrow?"

"No. I just gave my boss my two-week notice."

She shoots him a quizzical look.

"Lady Rose, it appears you will not have an excuse to deny me a second date since I will soon be a resident of the wonderful city of Boston." A triumphant smile spreads across his face.

REEDOM, she whispers, reading the label on the bottom of the tube. She applies a generous rub of the new lipstick across her bottom lip. A loud smack escapes from her pout as she stares at her face in the full body mirror. Eleanor directs an approving smile at her reflection and blows herself a kiss. Her dancing feet direct her to the large walk-in closet in the bedroom.

"Stand tall, Eleanor," she says. "You are a true bundle of joy!" She pats her buttocks playfully and dismisses the flashing memory of a teenager unhappy with the growing rhythm of her legs. *Giraffe legs*, some kids had teased her. Even now, a grown woman, she has to fight the urge to hunch her shoulders as a way to shorten her height.

Her *Allium schoenoprasum* tattoo peeks through the strap of her low-cut dress. When she first got her tattoo, Andrew teased her that the flower looked more like the glans of a circumcised penis than the intended exuberant chive blossom.

Eleanor is meeting with prospective clients this morning. But her excitement has little to do with that particular meeting. It has more to do with her friend Mariah. She picks up her phone and sends another text message. She'd sent several this morning already and is anxiously awaiting a response.

Her mind shifts back to the meeting ahead. This new client is interested in providing in-store weekly complimentary cooking classes for regular customers. With the added idea of partnering with local farms and fisheries to bring her customers fresh organic produce.

Eleanor is the genius behind Bring on the Spice, which had

begun years ago as a meal club company. Coming from a family of chefs, understanding meal textures and flavors, her specialty is recipe creation. She can transform a cumbersome recipe into a basic three-step meal. Her motto is *KEEP IT AT FIVE*, as none of her recipes exceed five steps. Her goal is to make real-food cooking accessible to anyone. But her biggest draw comes from the intricacy of combined spices and balanced flavors. Her dishes spring to life with a drop of sweetness and a pinch of heat. Spices previously considered rare and exotic—galangal and anar seeds among them—are becoming a staple in most kitchens as flavoring agents.

Lots of similar companies were popping up now, but Eleanor had seen the opportunity early on, and today Bring on the Spice is the brand name that pops up on your browser and showcases those funny commercials of kids lecturing their parents about eating balanced meals with fresh produce. Her successful ads had inspired a whole new generation of young, aspiring chefs.

It was a hard-won reputation. Some of her competitors had online resources that helped personalize their clients' experience. But Eleanor had gone beyond that. Her people intuition coupled with a business background led her to see opportunities hidden to others.

Eleanor breathes in, recognizing the familiar dance-in-the-guts feeling she is accustomed to when making a new deal. "You got this, girl" she tells herself, reflecting on her latest achievement. Last year, she hired a team of experts to offer face-to-face consultations.

"People want personal attention and human interaction," she explained when hiring a local nutritionist who focused on all aspects of nutrition and healthy living.

"My clients want pampering and quality. I will package it all up into a holistic bowl of pear soup!" she had joked to the nutritionist.

The versatility of her business contributes to her great success. Bring on the Spice allows her clients to order ingredients for delicious and healthy recipes online. The company also has set up several boutique markets throughout the city where clients can go to pick up their own recipe packages with preselected portions and talk to a food expert.

"We are drawn to your new spice idea." The potential clients had said as a way of presenting their proposal. They had learned how Bring on the Spice had recently launched its own line of spices, including grains of paradise, the so-called silent spice. This new idea had caught not just the prospective clients' attention but that of food magazines and cooking shows. Her food jargon is becoming mainstream.

"There are spices whose primary job is to bring out the flavor of other spices. They are the agents of harmonious taste," she explained in a recent interview as she crushed open a tamarind pod and invited the reporters to try the sticky pulpy seeds. "Get ready for a burst of flavor," she warned the willing tasters as they popped the sweet, tart, and aromatic seeds into their mouths.

"You go girl," Eleanor says, giving her lipstick-painted lips an admiring glance.

Just then the phone rings and Eleanor skips back to the bedroom to answer it.

ARIAH WAKES WITH A JOYFUL, self-satisfying smirk. She is wrapped up in soft blankets against the chill of the October morning, thinking about the previous day. It feels surreal. Her stomach flips with glee. She checks her phone, notices the long list of messages from Jake, and smiles. She scrolls down to Eleanor's texts, which are just as many as Jake's, urging her to call *"ASAP."*

She reads Jake's texts, stopping to savor each message. Their date had ended with a glass of wine after dinner. They never made it out of the North End, going from brunch to cannoli to an afternoon coffee to dinner.

"I am moving to Boston for the sole reason of dating you," he had whispered to her as a way of saying goodbye. *What kind of guy does that? And what kind of girl falls for it?* She ignored the internal voice of caution. It occurred to her that she should have checked in with Eleanor at the party before agreeing to see Jake the next morning. Perhaps the urgency of her messages had something to do with it. Mariah considers delaying the call, uncertain whether she wants to hear Eleanor's opinion about Jake in case it doesn't match her own.

Mariah checks the time. The digits showed 7:09 in the morning, too early to call Eleanor. She will wait a couple of hours. They have plans to meet up later today to go gift shopping for the wedding of an old college friend.

She reads Jake's flirtatious texts over and over. She stares at his last text: *"About to fall asleep. I'll be dreaming of you tonight."*

Mariah thinks about the end of their evening. Jake had called a taxi to take her home before taking him to the airport. He opened the car door to let her in. Mariah's stomach flips as she remembers how he offered his hand as a means of support, but kept holding onto hers the entire ride home. She stayed perfectly still, afraid any slight movement would break the magic.

"I'll see you in a few days," he whispered, planting a floating kiss on her lips.

She crinkles her lips, sniffing for any traces of him. As she contemplates a number of responses from Jake, a new text pops up on her screen. *"I know you are awake,"* with a selfie of Eleanor wagging an accusatory index finger. A phone icon follows the message.

Mariah calls her.

"You have some explaining to do, young lady!" Eleanor's excited voice resonates on the line.

"Wait! How in the world did you find out?"

"Never mind how I know. Start talking."

"I don't know where to start. Actually, you know when it started. You were there by the firepit, although you were probably too stoned to notice." Mariah remembers how Eleanor's attempts to imitate Cher had sounded more like Big Bird.

"Oh, no question about that. And yes, I did see you two. We all saw the sparks coming out of every orifice of both your bodies. I think the whole universe felt the fucking fireworks."

"Oh, stop it! All of that seeing fireworks came from you being high." The friends laugh in complicity.

Mariah recounts the previous day's adventure, stopping at every turn to answer her friend's questions. Eleanor is clearly delighted about this possible relationship. She had tried to set up Mariah with acquaintances of hers and Andrew's, but Mariah had refused to be subjected to a matchmaking experiment.

"We didn't consider the possibility of a Mariah-Jake affair. Well, I guess it never occurred to us that he would be willing to leave Gotham City because you, I am certain, would never leave the City on a Hill. Plus, I had assumed all this time that your hesitation to date was because you had resolved to someday get back together with Rafael."

"Eleanor, it's only you and my mother who believe that I need to have a partner in my life. She's still pushing me to go on a date with some guy from church. Anyway, how did you find out?"

"Jake called Andrew at two in the morning to ask him—no, wait—to *beg* him to put in a good word for him. He kept Andrew on the phone till about five this morning talking and asking about you. The more Andrew said, the more obsessed he became."

"Oh no! I'm sorry. And poor Andrew," Mariah says sheepishly.

"What about you? Aren't you going to ask me all the dirt about him?"

"I've figured by now that he must be pretty clean since you didn't start this conversation with something like there is no way in hell you are dating that douchebag."

Eleanor erupts in joyful laughter. "You are right about that," she says. "The truth is that Jake is a nice person. At least the Jake I knew. Who knows, people do change. We haven't seen much of him for over ten years, but I can tell he is still the same Jake, just a little older, wealthier, and sexier. He contacted Andrew a couple of weeks ago, out of the blue, so Andrew invited him to my party. Jake adored Andrew when they were kids. He followed Andrew around like a little puppy. It's nice to see them reconnect. Wait, did Jake tell you he used to date Andrew's sister?"

"No. He didn't. Was it serious?" Mariah asks, not sure if she wants to know the answer.

"I'm not sure how much I should tell you, since Jake always was reserved about his personal life. But, OK, they started dating when they were in eighth grade and then through most of high school. She dumped him for another friend of theirs who she's still married to. One of those 'it was meant to be' things."

"What about Jake? Don't tell me he has been nursing a broken heart all these years?"

"Are you kidding me? No way. That guy has had his share of romances. No broken hearts for you to fix there. By the way, he did tell you about his job, right?"

Mariah lets the question linger. She thinks about Jake's forward and bold personality. Is that what makes him so attractive to her? She had known plenty of sensible girls in relationships with troubled guys who were committed to saving them, misguided by the illusion that they could change them. Mariah has no interest in falling into the *I can fix him* syndrome, yet somehow, she could now almost understand the thrill. She takes a deep breath and savors the image of Jake sitting across from her at the restaurant, staring at her as if she were the only thing worth looking at in the entirety of the room.

"He did," Mariah answers, remembering the small twinge of thrill she had felt at the thought of dating a hedge-fund trader.

WHEN LUCAS CLIMBED INTO HIS 1967 PICKUP TRUCK, HE FOUND a big, cutout heart taped to the dashboard. Smiling at the message written on it, he pulled off the tape and caressed the heart before folding it and putting it in his pocket. He turned on the ignition, and when the engine rumbled to life, he cranked the heater fan up a few notches and then sat back in the cacophony of sounds to wait for Meg. She had the timing down to a science. She will wait for him to enjoy this moment, the paper heart, her message of love, and a new promise.

The truck was a wedding gift from his parents almost half a century ago. Its beautiful original fire-engine red had weathered and settled into a matte pink. But when it was new, Lucas drove his new bride in his new wheels to a cabin in the highlands of the Berkshires, where they spent two weeks under the spell of an all-inclusive mountain resort.

Paris had been his first choice. He always had dreamed of a Paris honeymoon. He envisioned walking with Meg through the grandiose Jardin du Luxembourg, sipping coffee and snacking on pastries while watching Parisians stride by, or walking into a *fromagerie* to order a portion of their creamiest Camembert cheese.

Meg had never visited France before, but Lucas was a frequent tourist there, and had been since he was young. His parents made two and sometimes three trips a year to various parts of France, since their restaurants featured southern cuisine with a French flair. They'd opened the restaurants after leaving their native Tennessee, and their ice-cream business, to venture into the culinary world of the north.

Lucas loved those trips because of the adventures they brought. When he and his sister started middle school, he still looked forward to those trips as a way to avoid going to school, but his sister felt differently. She was a few years older than Lucas and less of an adventurer. She also happened to love school; missing school was more of a punishment than a treat for her. Pulling her out of school became so detrimental to her that Lucas's parents resolved to leave her under the supervision of her grandparents while they embarked on their travel escapades with a happy Lucas on their heels.

One of the earliest trips to France took them to the village of Giverny, home of the grand master of Impressionism. Lucas had learned about Claude Monet in art class, and then they created still-life paintings of flowers, imitating Monet's use of colors and shadows.

Lucas remembered the teacher reading a picture book illustrating the luminous water lilies and climbing roses. But nothing prepared him for the joy of seeing it all come to life. The reflection of the light casting glimmering movement on the water's surface was mesmerizing, even for a young lad of fourteen.

Lucas's parents loved the clear turquoise waters of the French Riviera and the endless purple fields of Provence. They were captivated by the Mediterranean magic of the South of France. But no matter where their adventures took them, they always ended their trip back in Paris, even if just for a few nights.

During one of those Paris trips, his father presented his mother with a heavily ornate padlock. His parents' initials carved in antique lettering decorated the lock.

The back of the lock showed a winding line that curved into two intertwined hearts. It was easy to miss it if you hadn't grown up with a father who left love notes around the house for his wife to find. The intertwined hearts were his signature. Lucas hoped that one day he would be as loving a father and as attentive a husband.

Lucas had been admiring the padlock when his father reached out and handed him a black leather pouch. Lucas pulled at the drawstring to find a skeleton key snuggled inside.

The following morning, after a delicious café au lait or hot chocolate, and buttery croissants, the trio walked the short distance to the Pont de l'Archevêché. Lucas's eyes lit up at the sight of thousands of locks clinging securely to the fence of the bridge.

"This is the Love Lock Bridge," his dad explained. "Lovers from all over the world come to this very spot. They affix their love locks to the bridge with a promise of eternal love."

Lucas smiled at the memory from all those years ago, and then thought about the cutout heart in his pocket. He was still grinning when Meg made her way into the warm truck. He reached over for a kiss, a lover's thank you for her new promise to restart the weekly visits to see a psychologist. Lucas felt the hope settling in.

"Wouldn't it be nice to go to Paris someday and find the lock my parents left at that bridge? I still have the key," Lucas said.

"Yeah, that would be nice," Meg replied, trying her best to sound sincere. Her once vibrant green eyes were faded now, sunken deep into her head as if the enchantment of the world had been jinxed away.

ARIAH STANDS IN THE FOYER, her back to the large Moroccan mirror with the carved wooden frame. Jake is coming over for dinner, and her small apartment flickers with candlelight. A couple of weeks have passed since that first brunch, and the idea of dating a Wall Streeter is slowly sinking in.

She only knows he works on Wall Street because she had asked him on their first date. He kept checking his phone throughout the day. By dinner she asked him directly, and he had explained some pieces of his job. She knew he was only offering generalities, as if he was worried that giving her too many details might dissuade her from her decision to see him.

If Mariah were completely honest with herself, she would recognize that Eleanor's surprise at her interest in Jake had some validity. She is well aware of Wall Street men's reputation of living in perpetual frat house mode, which is definitely not her type. She knows they can be addicted to a constant adrenaline rush, and of being infatuated with drinking, drugs, and strip clubs. Mariah imagines that all this would make them prone to boredom, which makes monogamy a challenge—again, not her type. It's not that she hadn't thought about all this before she agreed to go on a second date.

"I am letting my emotions dictate my choice this time," she had argued with her logical mind, determined to see things through with Jake.

Mariah and Jake have talked on the phone every day since they met. She has come to know Jake's assistant quite well— maybe a little too well, she reckons. As it turns out, Jake is not as readily available as he professed to be. Their phone conversations are constantly interrupted. Jake was apologetic at first, and Mariah assured him that she was absolutely fine with the disruptions, and she was; because they only happened during the day and she also was engrossed in her own work world. But each night, Mariah climbs into bed and expectantly awaits his call. Jake calls her from his landline phone or the Blackberry tucked away in his briefcase and, for those few hours, there are no interruptions; it is just the two of them.

Mariah has felt airborne all week. Now she understands the Cloud Nine imagery; she feels like she really is walking on air. She takes another quick look at herself in the mirror, cups her hands around her cheeks, and pulls back the excess flabby skin beneath her chin. "Stupid roll of shame," she mutters to her image.

She gives her head a quick side-to-side shake in an effort to loosen her hair. She scorns a streak of spiral curls for refusing to bounce up, and narrows her eyes in annoyance, fighting with her hair for revolting against her.

"Really? You are going to play this game today?" *¡Pelo malo!*

She adds one more playful insult to her rampage, remembering how Rafael used to tease her rambunctious curls back in college. She smiles, remembering his enthusiasm to teach her Spanish. She had taken Spanish as a second language in high school, but it was not proficient enough to allow her to formulate cohesive sentences. Thanks to Rafael's persistent nature, in just three months of a daily dose of Spanish she was fluent enough to carry on a basic conversation.

She looks around the room, pleased. The whole apartment resembles a glowing cave taken from one of those winter wonderland scenes. She straightens the large painting, the only art adorning the living room. The action is not so much an attempt to set the frame straight, but rather a checking-in gesture. Two silhouetted young children run through a field of purple baby's breath, giving the ground the illusion of a magic carpet about to take flight. The E. L. Love signature at the bottom could easily be mistaken as part of the purple ground cover.

Not now, Mariah whispers to the familiar yearning. The hollow left behind from the feeling of abandonment. The image of a mother and daughter snuggling peacefully, reading a bedtime story that she so desperately clings to, although she knows deep inside they do not belong to her, that they were borrowed from someone else's universe—a picture on a magazine or the memory a friend had shared.

Once in the kitchen, she takes one more look at the vegetarian lasagna settling in the oven. She is happy with how that new recipe turned out.

"A new recipe. That's a bold move," Eleanor commented when Mariah had stopped by the store to pick up the boxed meal containing all the needed ingredients. But Eleanor knew that it is not out of character for Mariah to embrace these types of risks.

Mariah opens a chilled bottle of sweet rosé and sets it on the counter, gently placing the cork back in the neck. The rosé would pair great with the roasted beet, goat cheese, and pistachio salad, Eleanor assured her. She had struggled with the dessert idea, remembering the embarrassment she felt when Jake offered her his napkin to clean up the cannoli cream dripping heavily on her blouse. She pours herself the last glass of Chardonnay from a bottle on the counter and adds the empty bottle to the collection of items in the recycling bin. She walks to the snug living room to wait.

Mariah reaches for the cheese plate at the center of the antique cocktail table and grasps a couple of wheat crackers, but then remembers all the reading she's been doing on gluten-free diets, so she picks up a clump of green grapes instead. She is fascinated by the world of gluten free, which is surprising, since she isn't the type to fall for new trends.

A friend from work had been following a strict gluten-free diet after her youngest daughter was diagnosed with celiac disease. Mariah's curiosity piqued when her friend described how much more energetic she felt since she implemented this new lifestyle diet. Plus, there was the added bonus of shedding some unwanted pounds. Listening to her was like listening to one of those religious fanatics. Her friend was convinced that this was the answer, the nirvana of all diets.

"Isn't it hard to find gluten-free alternatives?" Mariah wanted to know, imagining a little section of the supermarket with a lower shelf labeled "gluten-free products" the way you would find a kosher selection around the Jewish Passover holiday.

"No, really. There are so many options out there. In fact, the choices can actually be a bit overwhelming. Just like a secular diet, some foods are healthier than others. And just as many are packed with sugar. You have to constantly read the labels. People think gluten free means healthy. That's a total misconception. The fact is that a lot of the gluten-free products are actually highly processed, offering very little nutritional value."

She went on to tell Mariah the story of how she had taken her daughter on a vacation to a little New England town.

"We stayed at this cute B&B in the middle of nowhere and were shocked to see different gluten-free breakfast options each day."

She was happy to report that they had the best gluten-free waffles she had ever had. Mariah had stifled a laugh as she questioned in her mind the authenticity of those gluten-free waffles.

Mariah knows plenty of people who had tried all the trendy diets from paleo to primal to Mediterranean.

Even Eleanor had been following a strict VB6 diet for several years.

"Girl! Jump on the wagon. Vegan Before Six is where it's at," she tells Mariah much too often.

"Food is not just fuel, my friend," Mariah pushes back each time. "It's an experience to be enjoyed." Her body, now heavier than in her college years, could be considered slightly overweight. On most days, Mariah describes herself as a vegetarian. Though not a strict one, as she could never resist a juicy homemade burger with extra pickles.

"I should go back to a clean diet, no preservatives and no chemicals," she thinks now, remembering the term used by her mother. Growing up, her parents had been cautious about the food they brought into their home. Canned foods and sugary cereals were choices inaccessible to her as a child.

The ding-dong of the doorbell alerts her to Jake's arrival. As she walks to the door, the floor seems to have disappeared and she is walking in space. Jake stands on the door's other side, holding a small bouquet of flowers. Just one look at Mariah and his face lights up with the radiant intensity of Sirius, the glowing star.

"Nice irises," she comments, motioning him inside.

"Is that what they're called?" he says. "They are the same kind you got me when we walked by that flower shop the other day."

"Yes, they are." Mariah is glad Jake had taken notice of that small detail.

ANDREW MARRIED ELEANOR, his high school sweetheart. He had not paid much attention to her when she was a freshman and he a junior, but in the fall of his senior year, she managed to capture his interest. It was an innocent romance. However, they agreed to part ways after he graduated from high school. "You should experience college life without feeling held back," Eleanor told him that summer before he went off to college.

Andrew applied early decision to Stanford University on the West Coast. He wanted a school that offered the opportunity to engage in deep research starting in freshman year; math and science were his preferred subjects. Andrew was also certain that he wanted to go to a school in California. He'd fallen under the spell of the San Francisco Bay Area on a summer family trip that included a bike ride across the Golden Gate Bridge and a day spent strolling through the enchanting redwoods of Muir Woods.

While it was true that his impeccable grades opened the door for him at the various Ivy League schools, his extracurricular endeavors made the biggest impression on the admission offices.

Andrew had asked his high school counselor about opportunities to volunteer abroad during the summer of his eighth-grade year. They researched several possibilities together. Andrew considered a "Teenage for a Change" program inspired by the Peace Corps, but during his search, he came upon a small nonprofit youth foundation run by a group of Haitian professionals living in the USA. Andrew ultimately chose this option because he liked the idea of working with local kids and helping the community address issues related to clean water and reforestation. He completed the required paperwork and submitted his application. His parents were thrilled and supportive; it wasn't unlike Andrew to venture into this type of experience.

Andrew traveled to Haiti every summer through high school and college. The program matched him with a local family who became his host family for years to come. Andrew studied French as a second language in school, and although conjugation of verbs worked differently in Haitian Creole, it was close enough that he could understand the necessary expressions to get by. He tutored his Haitian siblings in math, and that facilitated his acquisition of the local dialect.

Andrew enjoyed participating in the household's daily affairs. He helped with the chores by carrying water from the town well back to the house, feeding the chickens, collecting fresh eggs from the coop, and shelling beans for the midday meals. Andrew was not bothered by the lack of electricity or the vicious mosquitoes that feasted on his American blood each night. He genuinely cared about people and learning about different cultures; he considered material comforts inconsequential. He still felt that way. Andrew experienced a true immersion while living with his host family, and with that came the formation of a friendship that would last a lifetime.

This was the virtue that he brought into his romantic relationships, not that he had that many. He dated a girl briefly while in college, and that was it until years later, when he fell for a fellow practitioner during his residency.

It quickly turned into a serious relationship. They planned to get married after a few months of living together. All seemed fine until, one day, Andrew came home to an empty apartment. All was gone, except for a single pile of his own clothes heaped in the center of the living room. His attempts to contact her were of no use. The scars of her betrayal, vanishing from his life without warning, were things he thought impossible to overcome.

It came as no surprise to anyone that Andrew blamed himself for the failure of the relationship. He tortured himself thinking about how unhappy she must have felt to make such an abrupt exit. He racked his brain searching for any unspoken signs of disillusionment. Had he been that self-absorbed that he hadn't seen the signs of a failing relationship?

"You know, Andrew, it takes two to tango," his frustrated sister pointed out matter-of-factly. "You can blame yourself all you want, drown yourself in self-pity, but at the end of the day, it takes a terrible person to do what she did. No matter how unhappy she was, she should have had the decency to face you instead of breaking your heart, stealing your things, and escaping in the middle of the night like a cowardly thief."

His friends tried to distract him with "there are more fish in the sea" idioms, but Andrew was not ready to go back to the singles club. There was a big part of him that felt hopeful, so for a long time, he walked into the quiet apartment expecting to see her sitting there, a mug of coffee in hand and a book blocking her face, as if her leaving had been only a bad joke, a "just to see if you would miss me" kind of lover's test. And so, he was drowning in self-pity, and he wanted to stay there. He felt that's where he deserved to be, a junkyard for damaged merchandise. Maybe women didn't consider him a worthwhile investment. Maybe he wasn't marriage material.

Many of the same friends who tried to comfort him with what they thought were words of wisdom, were married or in serious relationships themselves, and Andrew envied them. He wanted that. Still, some of those same friends told him how lucky he was to be single.

"The grass is always greener on the other side," his friends said, well meaning, no doubt.

"The grass is always greener where you water and tend it the most, and I failed to do that," Andrew told himself.

It took years and the reappearance of Eleanor in his life for Andrew's heart to heal from the deception. It was easy for Eleanor to fall back into the comfort of an old love. It wasn't that simple for Andrew. Yet she waited.

"HOW DID IT GO?" Andrew asks Eleanor as she drops two large paper bags on the kitchen island next to his empty beer bottle. Once again, he sends a mental thank you to the universe for this woman who had danced her way back into his music-less life and put an emotional Band-Aid over his bruised heart.

"The shopping would have been more enjoyable if we had actually had the option of buying what we wanted to buy. But oh no, God forbid you buy someone something not on their wish list. Look at this." Eleanor searches through her designer bag and pulls out a package of eight folded papers of registry printouts.

"That is for the wedding registry," she says. "And these are for the baby shower." She lays out the multitude of folios on top of the counter. The manager at one of her stores was pregnant and the staff had organized a surprise baby shower for her.

"This is such a foolish and selfish idea," she vents. "If people choose to have a baby, they should make sure they can afford the additional expense. They shouldn't expect their friends to dig into their own pockets to pay for the cost of their newborn."

Eleanor had not been too keen on the idea of having children as a young adult. She had done some occasional babysitting while in high school, but even the easy cash was not enough incentive to lure her into becoming a permanent babysitter. When her parents tried to convince her to work as a camp counselor during the summers, she had refused adamantly. Instead, she chose to bag groceries at the local supermarket even if it meant less money and weekend hours.

I don't get kids and they don't get me. She had found this phrase useful when explaining her lack of desire to be around children.

Her parents had teased Andrew back then, when Eleanor and Andrew's parenting possibility seemed an eternity away. "I hope you like cats and dogs, Andrew." But the truth is that Andrew had been okay with Eleanor's decision. Even now, after all these years, he didn't feel the need to be a father. He liked children, but not the responsibility and eternal worrying that comes with them.

"I don't think it's about the gifts. I suppose prospective parents want their families and friends to come together and celebrate," Andrew says tentatively.

"It just bothers me," she continues. "It seems people are always finding ways to get others to give them free things. Maybe it's because I just hate the whole registry idea. For God's sake, if you want to give someone a gift, you should just do it, and people should receive it with gratitude. Did you see what they put on their registry?"

She points to a highlighted item indicating it had been purchased. "Look at this," she says. "That's a baby stroller for one thousand two hundred and thirty-nine dollars. You would think for that money the damn thing transformed into a car when your teenager became old enough to drive."

"Is that the cheapest item on the list?" Andrew asks in genuine shock. Eleanor had succeeded in catching his attention.

"No, here. The cheapest item is the crib mobile for five hundred dollars."

"Seriously? What kind of mobile is it?"

"I don't know. It must be some very fancy shit."

"It's probably some artsy piece," Andrew says.

"For that price, you'd think it's an original Flensted or Calder mobile."

Eleanor tips over one of the large bags and pulls out a small box, pushing it toward Andrew. She waits expectantly. Andrew holds the box with one hand and stares at the picture.

"It's my gift for the baby shower. And no, it was not one of the most expensive items. Can you guess what it is?"

"Some kind of camera?" Confusion spreads across Andrew's face.

"It's a gadget. A cloth bracelet comes with it, and you wrap it around the baby's ankle. There is an app that parents download to their phones to monitor their child's heart rate and sleeping pattern. It also checks the baby's temperature and sends parents an alarm text if the child has a high temperature."

"Now, that is a useful thing to have. Do they make them for grown-ups? You should have gotten another one of those for the wedding gift and be done with it." Andrew is engrossed in reading the small print on the back of the box describing the ingenious high-tech gadget and its promise to make parents' lives easier by giving them peace of mind.

"Here is what we got for the bride and groom. Mariah, the boys, and I decided to go in on it together, and we bought them this."

Eleanor pulls out the box and opens it to showcase a beige set of table runners. She carefully frees one from under the pile of tissue paper and spreads it along the kitchen table.

"You went in it together and got them two tablecloths?"

"Well, not just that. We got them this to go with it." She clicks her phone to life and scrolls through her photos. Finding one, she flips her phone over to show Andrew the modern marble slab top dining table with its sleek steel pedestal base.

"Whew!" Andrew whistles in astonishment. "That's a beautiful table."

"Yeah, right? Those guys have good taste. All the stuff on their registry was beautiful, totally high end, nothing tacky on that list."

"Gus will *have* to go to the wedding now, after all that money you made him spend on the gift," Andrew teases.

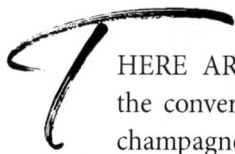

*T*HERE ARE JUST A FEW PEOPLE remaining in the conversation, Mariah observes as she swirls the champagne in her flute. Her eyes follow some of the participants retreating; perhaps the arguments had gotten too personal, she reasons. *Good, it's a party, after all.* She stares at the sparkling bubbles furiously beading up in her glass as if possessed by the energy of an erupting volcano.

She thinks back on the tense, three-hour drive to Vermont for the wedding. Although it is early November, the picturesque drive held true to New England foliage in the fall. The colors were beautiful. But that seemed irrelevant to the conversation inside the car. Eleanor had been excitedly asking Mariah about Jake, her favorite subject these days.

"So, things are getting kind of serious, eh?" Eleanor asked, and Mariah responded with a throaty *ah-huh*. Her way of indicating that perhaps this was not the best topic of conversation given that only two of the people present had a positive view on the matter.

Mariah quickly glanced at Max out of the corner of her eye and noticed his sudden interest in the passing trees.

"Maxwell, I know you're not super thrilled about Jake, and I really get why." Mariah addressed Max by his formal name, a practice she reserved for times when she needed to let him know how much she could use his affirmation and support.

"Jake does come across as a pompous and controlling kind of guy," she said, "and I will be the first to admit that, but he really is a gentle, kind, and decent person. I just need you to trust me a bit and try to look past his bold Wall Street persona. Deep down, that's not who he really is."

"I just don't trust the guy," he replied. "He is so self-serving. I have met plenty of his type. They are like packs of ravenous wolves. They think they rule the universe, and everything and anything should be at their disposal. To them, everything is a means to something, including people. I mean, look at him. He moved his office here on the spur of the moment just to get you to date him. That's pretty screwy. Besides, it's not just me, Mariah." Max had avoided her gaze, a hint of apology in his voice.

"I know. Gus can't even deal with hearing Jake's name. His nostrils flare up like a dragon ready to blow," Mariah said, smoothing the flouncy ruffle across the V-neckline of her black, bodycon dress.

Eleanor burst out laughing at the wheel. "That's totally messed up. Jake is the only fucking topic that you and Gus can agree on. It took Jake to come into Mariah's life for you and Gus to finally connect. I fucking love the beautiful irony."

The two friends joined in with Eleanor's amusement, welcoming the opportunity to conclude the conversation.

"I'm glad I brought the two of you together even if it is just to conspire against my happiness." Mariah stretched out her left arm toward the back seat and Max greeted it with a gentle squeeze.

Mariah hands the empty champagne flute to a passing server and makes her way to the drink station to order a glass of red wine. She nurses her buttery Cabernet while trying to shake off the unpleasantness of the interaction. Although she feels disappointed about Gus and Max's lack of enthusiasm toward Jake, she loves them for looking out for her. She also understands their concerns; it was the same concern her parents expressed when they met him.

"The guy can't be trusted," her father had said, adding, "Those guys prey on women. They are gifted with a cutthroat, calculating, evil, greedy soul."

"I just don't trust a man of such pretense," her dad had muttered. Her mom evaded her eyes, implying that she agreed with her husband's assessment of Jake.

Mariah does not deny that Jake's personality is his biggest asset, but recognizes that it is also his curse. He is the guy you want to manage your money, but not to marry your daughter or best friend.

A happy wave from across the room gets her attention, and she returns the motion. Gus had made the trip by himself, skipping the church ceremony altogether. *Such a Gus thing to do*, Mariah thinks as she makes her way to the small group standing by the buffet table. His charming wink pulls her in.

"It's not that he is just an egomaniac. The guy has zero brains and no scruples. He cheated his employees out of their own money. And he has never paid taxes in his life!" Mariah listens to the young woman who clearly has had a bit too much to drink. She continues on with her spiel while throwing in fact after fact about why Patrick Barrett would not be a good president.

"Look, I don't necessarily love to pay taxes either. I understand; it's burdensome, but I do it. Paying taxes is an obligation." Mariah nods her head in agreement.

The elections are two years away, yet the polls show a narrow gap. People continue to raise questions about Patrick Barrett, voicing their concerns not only about his character and his temperament, but also his racist views.

Mariah decides to join the conversation. "I agree," she says. "I think he is out of his league. He doesn't have the experience or the right vision for this country. His name-calling tactics are sickening. Calling his opponent a faggot and a wetback is just disgraceful."

The young woman interjects with a playful laugh. "He's handsome, I give him that. I think he should forget about running for president and become a movie star instead."

Gus speaks up. "Barrett is not a politician, so he hasn't sold his soul to big corporations and lobbyists. He speaks his mind, and that's very refreshing." He pauses, keeping his eyes on Mariah, a devious smile planted across his face. The action is so direct that those who don't know them would think it is a personal attack.

But Mariah knows Gus's preferred topic of discussion is politics, and he is well versed in the subject. He enjoys taking the opposing side for the sake of argument. Even after all these years, Mariah isn't sure where Gus's true political beliefs stand.

"And besides," Gus adds, looking directly at Mariah, "it's not like Mr. Héctor García is the model of morality. Having an affair with his personal assistant and then lying about it are telling of what type of person he is and the kind of president he would be."

Mariah decides she's had enough politics for one night. Yes, it is true García had a romantic relationship with his secretary and then tried desperately to cover it up, but there is nothing wrong with two consenting adults having a sexual relationship, especially if they are both single. The problem is not the affair, Mariah thinks sadly. The problem is they are two men, and many people are still more comfortable with men shooting bullets at each other than loving each other. Shooting Gus a smile of appreciation for the lively debate, she sips the remainder of her wine and walks over to Eleanor, who is chatting away with the beautiful bride.

THE FIREPIT raged with twirling orange and red flames. Meg stared at the blinding blaze as if in a trance. Lucas sat quietly next to her sipping his whiskey and humming a melody known only to him. Their dog Maddy sniffed curiously at his feet.

Meg remembered their yard many years back when the patio was not there. Instead, there had been an intricate playscape. The previous owners were both engineers from Australia, and they had designed a state-of-the-art play structure. The clubhouse at the top gave the appearance of a distorted house, something taken out of the magic of *Alice in Wonderland*. It was large enough to accommodate a family of four if they chose to camp up there.

The pulley system allowed the children to bring necessities up and down. Meg loved the climbing wall best of all. She had been an active child growing up, not afraid to climb the trees along their farmhouse's property lines. She remembered the anticipation of welcoming her baby girl and how much she had hoped for a chance to relive her wondrous childhood experiences.

The crackling of the fire brought Meg back to her immediate reality, just in time to see Lucas give her one of his winks. Meg smiled and quickly retreated back to her memories. Where was she? Oh yes, the swing set. She touched her flat belly almost by impulse and remembered.

Back then, her belly was the size of a basketball. People often complimented her, saying how beautifully she carried: "It's all belly! You are so lucky. You will lose that extra weight in no time." The truth was it didn't matter one bit to Meg what she looked like. She was pregnant. They were having a baby.

After six years of marriage and three miscarriages, Meg and Lucas had come to terms with the possibility that parenthood was not in store for them. They had convinced themselves that it was not meant to be. The doctors had done their tests and the specialists had tried their methods; all had been unfruitful. Until one day it happened. Watching the fire, Meg wiped the tears that cascaded down her cheeks with a swat of her hand. She had gotten efficient at inconspicuously wiping away tears before anyone had a chance to notice them.

The memory came and Meg grabbed on, unable to let it sail by. She grimaced at the vile taste that rose to the tip of her tongue. Sadness behaves like that sometimes, bringing along its own poignant taste. She remembered how, as she walked around the play structure, she had felt the kicks and stretches taking place within her protruding belly. The baby had been more active than usual. She attributed that to her and Lucas's own excitement as they embarked on their hunt for a home—a home with a yard.

The baby news had arrived by chance. Meg was experiencing shortness of breath, fatigue, and joint aches for weeks. She had gone to see her doctor, convinced that he would send her home with a mono diagnosis. The doctor had been concerned about the fast heart rate reading and sent Meg to the lab with a clipboard packed with lab slips to test her thyroid hormones. Results from the blood tests showed that her thyroid hormones were level and antibodies were fine. Something entirely different was causing the symptoms.

The news of her pregnancy struck Meg so violently that she began to quiver. She ran to the nearest lavatory where she threw up uncontrollably. Lucas walked in to find her sitting on the cold floor sobbing streams of happy tears.

Part Two

a field of apologies
growing
spreading
a promise of devotion
make way for the cornflower

*O*N THEIR THIRD MONTH OF courtship, Jake surprises Mariah with a long weekend getaway to Block Island, one of the small islands off the Rhode Island coast. The late fall is his favorite time of year to visit the island. Although it is a bit cold, the island is free of summer tourists, making the hikes quieter and thus more peaceful.

Jake is eager to show Mariah around the island, an unknown territory to her. He vacationed there as a child and then worked there during summers in college as one of only two taxi drivers. An old lady named Martha owned the company. She drove the second taxi.

She looks beautiful even when she sleeps, he muses. Her easy breathing and expression create a peaceful radiance that seems to warm up not only the bones in his body, but every tangible object in the room.

The soft down comforter wraps around her body, revealing only the crown of her head. His drilling eyes travel down the length of her body and rest on her blue toenails. Her right foot sneaks out of the warm blanket cocoon like an exhaust pipe releasing burnt up heat from her body.

Jake smiles at Mariah's continual fuss about being cold. *How can a creature that is always cold impart such warmth to everyone around her?* he whispers in her ear. The clear warning of his subconscious interrupts: "Don't fuck this up, Jake."

He glances at the light fighting to get through the wooden blinds. That large window offers the best view of the ocean when unobstructed by blinds and silky curtains.

Jake grins, savoring the evening memory of making love to the sound of the raging winds. He feels his naked body instantly reacting to the carnal evocation.

He inches closer to Mariah, and the sudden movement awakes her.

"Morning, Sleeping Beauty," he announces, tugging at a curl. "Are you ready for a bike ride through paradise?"

Mariah's eyes sparkle as her hand reaches up to touch his face.

"I love the color of your eyes in the morning light," she whispers, her outstretched index finger sensually tracing the outline of Jake's cheekbones. His bright blue irises shaming both the sea and sky holding hands outside their window.

Her finger travels down to his chin. Their lips connect, leading the way to a new dance of the senses, their bodies mimicking the rippling movements of the crashing waves.

The day they arrived they walked around town and visited the Island Historical Museum. Today Jake is taking her up the island's northern tip to a historic lighthouse. He pedals ahead of her, knowing she's following close behind as she takes it all in: the old stone walls overflowing with miniature rugosa roses, the serious bikers wearing designer biking gear and clip-in pedals, the dazzling blue water with foamy waves.

"I love this side of the island best," Jake says as they slow down for another scenic stop. "This whole area is an undeveloped beauty. It's a resting stop for many species of birds. We might be able to see falcons and red-tailed hawks this time of year."

"I had no idea hawks and falcons were migratory birds," Mariah says. "I'd love to spot a raptor."

They park their bikes at the edge of the road and venture onto the path leading down to a ravine. Jake takes Mariah's hand to help her navigate across the slippery boulders. He is overtaken for a brief moment by her easy way of trusting others, of trusting him.

An image from a couple of days ago flashes furiously in his mind like a possessed traffic light. He had come home to find a

FLOWERS ON THE WALL

brown envelope. He stared at the label behind the large plastic window and with a swift pull ripped the envelope apart. His expert eyes scanned over the words, searching. He lingered on the crucial sentences and let out a sigh of relief. Four months ago, he had been hand delivered a similar envelope, and inside that one he'd found a copy of the sexual harassment complaint letter from one of the paralegals at his office. Jake had chuckled and dismissed the claim at the time. His lawyers wouldn't see the humor, but they'd certainly handle his indiscretion, alleging it to be an *unfortunate misunderstanding.*

"I'm looking forward to the live music and cocktails outside our hotel tonight," Jake says, pushing away the memory and grabbing onto her hand a little tighter.

"Definitely. And what's on the agenda for tomorrow, my sexy tour guide?" she teases.

"Funny you should ask. Let's see." Jake pauses, thinking about all the things he wants to do to Mariah, the many ways he would like to make love to her. Yet, he decides to filter that thought and declares instead: "I want to take you on a hike to the basin near the shore. Those hollows have the best walking trails. We'll stop on the way to see the Community Rock. You're going to LOVE that!"

"Wait, is that the Settlers' Rock?" Mariah had read something about the Settlers' Rock on their visit to the museum the day before.

"No, this rock is more like a community bulletin board for the locals. One day you might find it decorated with wildflowers and cutout hearts to announce the wedding of someone. Another day it might have a crate filled with jars of homemade honey." He had seen all of these in the past.

"For people to take?" Mariah stares at him incredulously.

"No, they leave an empty can to collect the money. You

know, one of those honor systems. But I've also seen it decorated with dozens of lit candles honoring the memory of a deceased loved one."

"Do people leave messages for each other like love notes?" Mariah asks.

"I don't remember seeing that, but I have seen inspirational quotes painted right onto the rock," Jake says.

When Mariah and Jake arrive at the rock, they do not find celebratory notes or homegrown produce. It is rather a junkyard of empty beer cans and debris that decorates the rock. Mariah begins to collect the trash and stuffs it into her small backpack. Jake's quiet curses match the hard lines around his eyes. A discarded cardboard sign that reads "*someone sucked my dick on this rock*" leans behind the rock. Mariah quickly folds the sign and adds it to the collection in her backpack.

The twenty-minute flight back to Boston is uneventful, unlike the violently nauseating turbulence they had experienced on the way there.

"I'm sorry about the rock," Mariah whispers softly to Jake as they wait for their taxi to arrive.

"Leave it to tourists to fuck up everything," he comments with disgust. "They took a beautiful local tradition and wiped their arses with it." He can't hide his disappointment.

*M*UAH! EXPLODES FROM HER LIPS as Eleanor kisses Andrew on her way out the door.

"Stay out of trouble!" he shouts after her.

"Better tell freaking trouble to stay out of *my* way!" she shouts back with a laugh. Eleanor has an early meeting with the staff at one of her stores. There was an incident early last week involving a customer who had become verbally aggressive toward the store manager. The customer accused the business of purposely misinforming their buyers by advertising that their products were locally sourced. "*You are selling shrimp from Asia,*" the outraged customer stated.

The manager had apologized and explained that most of their shrimp were sustainably farmed freshwater varieties, but the store did buy them frozen for longevity purposes. The customer had demanded to see the owner of the store. Eleanor had driven to the store with copies of purchase orders indicating that their shrimp comes from the cold waters off the Atlantic Coast, from Virginia down to South Carolina.

Eleanor had called today's meeting to reassure her staff and to thank them for the manner in which they had dealt with a difficult customer. She breathes a big sigh of relief. There had been many times over the years when she had been forced to buy Asian shrimp due to an unforeseen shortage of Gulf shrimp. "That's why our business clause clearly states that *most* of the ingredients are locally sourced," she explained to the store manager after the customer had gone on her way, less upset after receiving a complimentary box containing three meals and a twenty-five-dollar gift card.

Andrew flips over his calendar and gives today's agenda one final check before heading off to work. Two eye surgeries. He had resisted the urge to start his own practice early on, and now, working under the umbrella of a large medical institution, he can come home at the end of a busy day and not have to worry about being on call. He works with an efficient staff who manages the administrative work, his least favorite part of the job.

Plus, for two months each summer, Andrew travels to Haiti to work at the local clinic. He had partnered up with one of the main hospitals in Port-au-Prince to identify patients with the greatest need for eye surgery. The majority need glaucoma operations. Andrew either flies down by himself, or is accompanied by a curious fellow surgeon who wants to help for a few days. Indeed, he had gone from a teen camp counselor to running his own clinic. Sure, he isn't Dr. Paul Farmer, but no one could dispute the impact he is making on the people of Haiti.

The practice works in partnership with a private ophthalmology school outside the capital city. The students spend most of their days at the clinic. His director had approached him on numerous occasions with propositions to lead the intern program, but Andrew declined each time. Being director of the program also means teaching one class per semester, plus numerous meetings with professors and administrators. He is not interested in any of that.

"It's only a three-year commitment, and it comes with a generous bonus," his supervisor had tried to persuade him once more during their last phone conversation.

Andrew hesitated a moment to collect his thoughts. "I just don't have the time, Scott," he finally said. "And you know how I feel about the college's exclusive enrollment. It doesn't sit well with me." Andrew held the phone a bit tighter and shook his head. He moved his phone to the other ear as he paced about the kitchen.

He could hear the rustling of papers coming from the other end, and he imagined Scott swiftly signing letters and waving his secretary away.

"But you are already part of it," his supervisor finally said. "Our success is directly tied to THAT institution. And look, you have already been taking in mentees for over five years."

"And that's as far as I will go. Plus, it's different. I get to choose my mentees." Andrew heard his own voice racing and picking up speed.

"I hear you, Andrew. I really do. It's an admirable thing you do choosing to mentor those black kids. I get that, but imagine how much more of an impact you could make if you were supervising an even larger group of interns. You can even have your own group of colored folks for all I care." Andrew heard the loud sound of a door shutting. He wondered if Scott thought better of it. *It is so like you to hide behind closed doors to let out your serpent tongue*, thought Andrew.

"I'll tell you what. If you can convince the college to allocate ten full scholarships a year for my colored folks—as you call them—I will take the director job." Andrew was pleased to have thought of a decent compromise.

"Well, now Andrew, you know they won't do that. I might be able to persuade them to give out one scholarship or maybe one and a half, but I don't even think they get that many black applicants," he said, a clear chuckle traveling quickly into Andrew's ears.

Andrew rubbed his clenched jaws. "Scott," he paused, carefully selecting his words. "I challenge you to consider this. If—and that is a big if—it is true that the college doesn't have that many applicants of color, doesn't that indicate there is a problem?" *Come on, prick, be a decent human being.*

"Look," Scott cleared his throat, "if you change your mind,

you know you are our top choice. We would love you to be in charge of that whole thing."

Scott's dismissive response indicated the conversation was over.

"Sure," Andrew sighed shaking his head, but what he really wanted to say was, *GO TO HELL, SCOTT!*

"Don't give Scott the satisfaction of even listening to him," Eleanor commented later that evening. She poured a fresh splash of gin into his glass, added a few tonic water ice cubes, and handed the cocktail over to Andrew.

"Scott and his cronies are a big bag of stinky white turds," she added. "They live in their own privileged white man bubble."

"I just really don't get it. You should see the dorm facility and the food in the cafeteria. It's as if the students live in a five-star, all-inclusive spa hotel. It's so sumptuously lavish." He downed his second gin and tonic before adding, "All that wasted money could go into promoting a more responsible and equitable endowment to benefit not just students of color, but any low-income students as well."

She finished making her own cocktail, then wiped down the counter. This was a circular conversation that they'd had before, and they both knew where it was going to end.

"But Andrew, benefiting those people is exactly what *they* don't want," she said. "They have a very profitable business formula selling a product they designed for a very specific audience. Parents pay a lot of money to have their children go to a place like that where their children will be interacting with other people that look and sound just like them."

She continued. "Remember years back the whole racist scandal surrounding Tommy Hilfiger designs not being meant for people of color? Whether he said it or not is beside the point. The consequence of that rumor led his business to double its earnings."

"Yes, I know, dear." He had no further response. He had brushed aside her warm smile full of pride and love. She was just trying to help, he knew that. But he becomes frustrated when he can't do the work he sees needs to be done. That's why he loves the work he does now, on his own schedule, his own terms he can help improve the quality of life for so many people. Giving someone the ability to see their physical world is as much a gift to him as it is to his patients.

Andrew grabs his workbag, a combination of a backpack and brief case. He drops his phone in a jacket pocket and picks up the empty coffee mug sitting on the counter. He'd wait until after the surgeries to sip his cup of coffee.

MARIAH MOVES HER FACE THIS WAY and that, settling it into the headrest cushion. She was pleased with this last-minute decision to pamper herself. *Ahhh...* she exhales, practicing the mantra of letting go as her cheeks press comfortably against the memory foam pad of the cushion.

Mariah forces herself to engage her senses and take in the energy of the room, to acknowledge her surroundings. *Be present*, she recites silently, trying to comply with the newest health guru recommendations.

She begins with the largest organ of her body, her bare skin sizzling under the heat of the warm blanket. *Soft*, her brain informs her.

The gentle knock on the door interrupts the fluidity of the instrumental music, the type with the beautiful subtle rhythm that creates the peaceful setting.

"Come in," Mariah responds to the awaiting master of the senses behind the door.

Mariah had been halfway home when she decided to pull over for a late afternoon snack, her mind replaying the details of the case settlement meeting. She scrolled through her phone while waiting for her order, hoping to find a message from Jake—*Nothing*, she whispered, trying to push aside his one text from this morning. It had been brief and impersonal. She had wondered if he had changed his mind about the move. *Has he realized that I am not worth the trouble?*

She instantly flung away the question.

She scanned through the list of marketing emails. Her eyes followed the flickering ad for the new spa facility downtown, just a few blocks from her building. *A well-deserved recompense for a pain in the ass resolution,* she thought, and tapped the CALL NOW icon. A cheery voice greeted her. Mariah asked about the Grand Opening special advertised in the ad. The receptionist cheerily informed her that they had a few open spots for this very evening, and if she came by tonight, she would get the two-for-one deal. Why not? She booked the appointment, requesting a female therapist. She had resolved to stay away from male masseuses after the incident a few months ago when she could have sworn she felt a live member rubbing gingerly against her hand. She was tense during the rest of that massage, fearing her clinician was enjoying the experience a tad too much. Whether intentional or not, it didn't matter. *I am sticking with the girls on this front.*

The masseuse introduces herself, but Mariah's ears are grabbed back and thrown into the melodic veil encircling the room. And so, the name was lost to the waves of sound.

"Do you have any pain or discomfort I should be aware of?" she asks.

"No," murmurs Mariah, beginning to feel discouraged. *Are you kidding me? I answered that question on the New Patient Form. Don't they share that information with the clinicians?*

The masseuse steps around and touches Mariah's shoulders. She slides her hands back and forth as if trying to decide how much work Mariah is worth.

"Are there any areas you would like me to focus on today?" she asks softly.

"Shoulders and feet, please," Mariah says, preparing herself for what seems to be turning into a tête-à-tête, not of her choosing. She'd already decided at this rate she probably wasn't going to come back for the second massage, the free one.

"One more question. And I promise it will be my last," says

the masseuse as if able to read Mariah's thoughts. "Gentle, or a combination with deep pressure?"

"Deep pressure, please," answers Mariah, hopeful that this *would* be the last question.

And with that, her brain lifts up the curtains, releases her senses, and allows her to sink totally into the experience. *Ooh,* Mariah breathes out as the warm towel slowly unrolls down her neck and onto her lower back. A minute later the warmth lifts and the expert's hands begin to move in a circular motion across the length of her shoulders. A rhythmic dance begins between the quick tapping of the fingers pressing down into her skin and the dragging motion of elbows traveling deep down and across the muscles of her back.

The movements of the masseuse quickly morph into that of a wild gazelle migrating from one region of the map of her body to the next. Her gentle hands guide Mariah to turn over, only her hands doing the talking this time.

The gazelle leaps to the base of the table. Mariah feels the gradual tugging of her toes, grateful that she has ten digits and therefore will experience this delicious sensation ten times over.

The gazelle's closed fist opens and closes with urgency inside the arch of Mariah's foot. She separates each toe, pulling and bending with care, the way a child would check the readiness of a loose tooth.

The touching ceases and Mariah waits expectantly. The cold gel coated over her feet surprises her, and just as her body is adjusting to the new temperature, the gazelle quickly wraps a hot cloth around each foot like a precious gift.

Her brain picks up the eucalyptus scent, and she feels the delicious sensation of something soft and warm twisting its way behind her neck. The eucalyptus fragrance is stronger now, with the small pillow nestled under the base of her neck.

Another quiet *ahhh* escapes her throat.

The gazelle's hands travel back to Mariah's shoulders, her expert fingers kneading with the extreme focus of a pastry chef. Mariah feels her hair being set free, her long, coiled locks cascading down her face. She follows the sensation created by the trenches that each finger makes as it travels up her scalp, up, down, and yet up again. The gazelle takes hold of Mariah's head and gives it a slight pull. Her head goes straight back and from side to side between the gazelle's hands. She feels her neck elongate with each pull.

The dance begins to slow down with a gentle squeeze of the shoulders. Mariah recognizes the touch, the culmination, the finale.

"I will be outside the door with some water. Take your time and come out when you are ready," instructs the magical beast.

Mariah breathes a soft dragon breath, forcing her mind to return to her body. She will schedule another appointment for next week. *Make sure you request the gazelle!* shouts her brain.

*I*T HAD BEEN SNOWING all day. Although it is the first of December, Christmas lights had heavily adorned the city for weeks leading into Thanksgiving. The spirit of the holidays perfumes the air. The magic of Christmas, the season of giving; the one time a year when people open doors for each other and smile at strangers on the subway. It is this spirit that forces Max to play nice with Gus as they sit at the restaurant waiting for the girls to arrive.

Max's mind wanders off briefly to that warm spring morning back in college. He had liked that girl a great deal and she had liked him back. Everyone knew it, including Gus, who did not hesitate to make a move on her one day.

The girl had been sunbathing on the dock by the edge of the lake. That's where Max found Gus smooth-talking her, the way he still does when facing a breathing female. Max confronted him that night and accused him of caressing the girl's arm. Gus had given him a drunken laugh and denied anything intimate had happened. "I was merely spreading sunblock along her upper arm," he shrugged. But Max lost interest in the girl and the seed of distrust in Gus set in.

Max ponders those fifteen years since college and how they seem to have melted away in no time. He thinks about how much had happened since the four friends went off to live their own lives in pursuit of their own goals.

For Max, it meant enrolling at NYU Law School immediately after completing his undergrad studies. He landed a job at a lucrative firm right in the city, where he worked for several years, until one day he awoke to the realization that he'd had enough. Every morning he dragged himself to work resenting the noise, the fellow passersby, and the monotonous pavement. It was as if he was trying to break away from it and the city refused to listen, to let him go. He felt entangled, as if he was being slowly swallowed by the hot belly of the city. Its quick pace had tired him out.

One morning he marched into his boss's office and handed in his letter of resignation. The following week he rented a moving van, packed his belongings, and drove away toward Boston, not giving the Capital of the World the satisfaction of one last glance in the rearview mirror. That was over a year ago now. He thinks about his small rental apartment in Somerville. How is it that such a small space had helped restore a sense of peace and balance for him?

Max studies Gus now, wondering if he remembers the incident with the sunbathing girl. Probably not, as he never acknowledges any wrongdoing in the first place. He feels a pang of regret, a mourning of some sort for a friendship that still hangs suspended on that warm spring day.

"Are you still living in the Back Bay?" Max asks, feigning interest.

"Yeah, the same place above the Italian restaurant," Gus responds, taking a big gulp of dark ale.

"And all that craziness, the noise and smell of good food doesn't get to you? I feel like I would be hungry all the time."

"Not really. You get used to the noise quickly. It comes with the urban territory. Plus the bedroom is toward the back of the building. I don't mind the smell. I guess you just get used to that, too, like anything else."

"What about those big commercial garbage trucks at four in the morning?"

"What happens at four in the morning?" the girls ask joyfully on cue, taking off their snow-covered hats and discarding their gloves, setting free their newly manicured fingers.

At thirty-four, Gus was partying as hard as he was back then. Going out for beers after work on a Tuesday night was no different from going at it on a Saturday night. People at work were impressed with his ability to handle alcohol and sleepless nights. Gus could pull off an all-nighter and still function at full capacity the next day.

"I am a creature of the night," was his usual response.

"He is childish and annoying, but he's our Gus," Mariah and Eleanor were accustomed to saying by way of offering an explanation. They cared for him deeply. They saw him as the crazy uncle; every family had one of those. And then there was his romantic life. Gus had been navigating his way in and out of relationships for as long as they had known him, never staying with the same person longer than a handful of months.

There was only one time he had broken that dating pattern many years ago. The friends had thought Gus would finally settle down with that girl from Trinidad. They had met at a train station on a Sunday morning, both waiting to board the commuter train outbound, escaping the city heat for the luxurious ocean breeze.

She was as smart as she was strikingly beautiful. The fact that she was so physically attractive was not surprising to any of his friends. Gus had a reputation for choosing incredibly beautiful mates.

They all thought Gus had found his match. But after eight months of an invigorating romance, the flames died out and Gus resumed his place in the single male club.

"Gus was just describing the glamour of living above a restaurant," Max says, getting up to help by taking the girls' jackets and hanging them on the row of doorknobs serving as pegs behind their booth.

The friends hadn't seen each other since the wedding. Their plans to meet up the day after Thanksgiving did not materialize. Mariah had ended up going to the Big Apple to spend Thanksgiving with Jake, who was stuck there trying to finalize a business deal.

"So, I took this girl out the other night," Gus says. Everyone listens expectantly for what would surely be an interesting tale.

"She chased me for half a mile down Boylston Street until I realized she was actually following me. She had been honking nonstop, but I assumed she was annoyed at me for maybe cutting in front of her or something."

"Wait, but why was she chasing you in the first place?" Max wants to know.

Gus pauses for effect, swallowing his beer. "Apparently I bumped her car at the light before entering the rotary. Honestly, I did feel a slight contact, but a bump? That was an exaggeration, I told her."

"So what happened?" Mariah asks.

"I listened to her patiently, as she recounted the event," he replies. "She walks to the back of her car and points to the bumper where she felt the impact. I kept staring at the spot unable to see any dent, but I didn't want to sound like a dick, so I kept apologizing. She took a couple of pictures. Again, of what, I can't tell you. She wrote down my insurance information, and I had her write down her own on the back of an old supermarket receipt."

Max pauses again, scanning the table for reaction.

"And so?" Mariah asks.

"After we were done with all the unpleasantness of the incident, I offered to take her out for coffee."

"Of course you did," Mariah teases.

"She gave me a funny look, but I told her it was the least I could do to restore her faith in humanity," he grins.

"Did she agree to go out?" Mariah asks.

Gus smiles mischievously and gives her a wink. "Picture this. A woman following a man down a side street into the center of town. There was no annoying honking this time, just one curious woman following a charming guy to a coffee date."

"So are you taking her out again?" Eleanor asks. Gus shrugs nonchalantly. "You are such a nightmare," she says. "And speaking of nightmares, you guys. Last night I couldn't sleep so I got up and turned on the TV. I was just flipping through the channels and started watching this movie. At first there wasn't much to it and I was even getting sleepy, which was the point of it. But then a creepy part started and, of course, I couldn't stop watching because I just needed to know what would happen at the end. Brrr, it's making my hair stand on end just remembering."

The three friends sneer.

"You know you don't have a tolerance for horror," Mariah says.

"Don't you dare laugh at me. There weren't any freakish creatures of darkness in this one, but I swear it was ten times worse. I swear it would give *YOU* the heebie-jeebies too."

Eleanor goes on to describe the horrific scenes of the clumps of bloodworms and parasites squirming around feasting on blood they had sucked from the woman's ears.

"Wait. How did worms get there in the first place?" Mariah wants to know.

"Well, the fucking feathers. That's how. It was Quiroga's story of *The Feather Pillow* all over again, but worse. Yes! Ten times worse." Eleanor ends her story by announcing she was replacing all her feather pillows for good old polyester ones.

Max feels Mariah staring at him.

"You have been staring at your drink for a while," she says when he looks up. "What is it saying to you?"

"I'm thinking about asking Luna to move in with me," Max says, his eyes still focusing on the amber liquid.

"Oh my God! That's great!" Mariah says warmly.

"When are you going to ask her?" Eleanor asks.

"Will you stay in your place?" Mariah asks.

"You know she'll make you throw out your furniture and replace it all with hers," Gus says.

Max shrugs. "I don't know any of that yet," he says.

"Well, I say let's toast to love and friendship and whatever other good stuff comes along." Eleanor lifts her wine glass and her three friends join in the toast.

"To love and friendship," they shout in unison.

MARIAH WATCHES THE TALL, SLENDER MAN from afar.

He faces the large corridor leading to the arrival gate. "Terminal 1" is printed on the large yellow sign above the double doors. He smooths his golden tie and gives his suit jacket a gentle tug on the bottom hem and then glances around nervously—or maybe in excitement. With the back of his hand he wipes at the thin layer of sweat on his brow. His high cheekbones and narrow forehead perfectly balance his oval face. A small mole sits on his right cheek directly below the eye, marking the outline of the eye socket. His dark, thick hair is brushed back neatly and secured in place by layers of hair gel. Semi-rimmed black frame glasses like the kind Kevin Costner wore in the film *JFK* partially conceal his wide eyes.

Mariah considers his facial hair, the scruffy looking stubble showcasing a few days of shaving freedom or perhaps the intention of growing a beard. She wonders for a brief second how it would feel to kiss a man with a beard. She had never been attracted to the rugged look. It seems so barbaric. The Spanish word for "beard" jumps into her head; *"barba,"* she whispers, wondering if there is some connection to its root meaning. She thinks of the power and significance of the beard in the olden days, far back into the Middle Ages, when touching another man's beard resulted in a call to duel. She steals one more look at the stranger's whiskers, deciding they suit him well.

She imagines Jake's face. What would he say if she asked him to grow a beard? She touches her own face, reacting instantly to the possibility. Would it tickle her face? Would it scratch her cheeks annoyingly? Or would it add a hint of sensuality and playfulness to a sexual encounter?

The tall man unbuttons his jacket and gives the corners another tug. He looks so out of place. Is it the beige linen suit in the midst of the New England winter? Or the bouquet of red roses covered with silver specks of glitter? In any case, the tall man looks not much different from the tropical bird perched upon a walker's shoulder she saw that time during one of her runs around Jamaica Pond. The walker had stared ahead as if walking an exotic feathered friend in the middle of a crowded city was the most natural thing. The bird had moved its vivid head left and right, perhaps also finding the experience natural, or maybe just resolved to its fate.

Mariah feels the vibration of her phone buried deep inside her winter jacket and pulls it out expectantly.

"Just landed. Can't wait to see you," reads the text, followed by a smiley face. She sends back an excited face.

Mariah walks a few steps closer to the arrivals door where the small crowd stands waiting for the travelers to exit. She positions herself right behind a lady with an orange fleece sweeter and a cozy brown hat with furry earflaps. Jake would be one of the first passengers to exit the plane; it was the way he traveled, first one in, first to walk out. The orange fleece would serve as a bright traffic cone to alert him to look in her direction.

Jake had been in Los Angeles for business all week and was scheduled to fly back to Boston early this morning. They planned to meet for lunch near her office building, but Jake had called last night to tell her he had decided to fly down to Florida for a quick detour to see his mother for the day instead.

"You are such a mama's boy," Mariah commented when she heard his last-minute decision. It was meant to sound playful and endearing, but it had the opposite effect. She felt the dead silence on the other end of the line, just the heavy breathing to indicate he was still there. Mariah tried to rectify the situation,

"Hey, it was meant as a joke. A cute joke," she said.

"It's fine," Jake responded, but Mariah had felt the automatic pullback. She regretted her comment. Jake had been talking jauntily about his family, a topic he rarely spoke of. He shared memories of his father, describing him as a workaholic who tried hard to compensate for his absence by taking the family on grandiose trips. Jake told her how L.A. always reminded him of his dad.

"He took my sister and me on one of those city tours to see the Walk of Fame," he said. "That was the one thing my sister was adamant about seeing, being a teenager and all."

He went on to describe how he had decided that the Walk of Fame was not that interesting, so while his father was busy taking pictures of his sister—a demanding teenager—he had gone off on his own to explore the collection of souvenirs inside a nearby store. He came out of the store some time later to find that his dad and sister were gone.

"You would think a seven-year-old kid would be scared. Not me. I was thrilled by the idea of being on my own, excited to go and explore," he said.

Mariah was relieved to hear that young Jake's adventure of navigating the city on his own didn't come to full fruition, as his father found him just a couple of blocks away playing with a postcard carousel. "He was scared, and my sister was pissed that they had to interrupt the tour because I went MIA."

"Why do I have the feeling you were one of those kids who was always in trouble?" Mariah laughed into the phone, delighted to hear Jake's childhood tale. They talked excitedly about their New Year's plans, which included a visit to meet his mother. "Maybe my sister will make an appearance and you could meet her, too," he said, full of hope. But everything was shattered by her playful comment.

"I think Jake and I just had our first fight," she texted to Max after Jake hung up the phone with the pretext of having to check in on a client. She knew he was upset by her "mama's boy" comment. She just couldn't understand why it bothered him so much.

The muscles tightened in Mariah's chest. She asked Max if she should call back Jake to apologize, but he had advised her to let it be. *"Clearly he is uncomfortable talking about family stuff. Let the guy be. If you don't make it into an issue, then he won't either."* Mariah decided to follow Max's advice and busied herself making a large casserole of American chop suey for dinner. She would welcome Jake back with his favorite dinner. After all she, too, fell prisoner to her own family secrets.

Mariah thought of the crystal vase holding the small bundle of deep blue cornflowers, an unspoken apology to Jake. They were waiting on the night table next to the side of the bed he used, the one closest to the door.

The tall man with the glimmering bouquet shifts uneasily on his feet. It occurs to Mariah that perhaps he, too, is apologizing to his someone.

The double doors open and Mariah spots Jake, his skin kissed by the radiant sun of the City of Angels. His eyes dart about for a few seconds, taking in the collection of greeters. His eyes rest a little longer on the orange flannel. Mariah offers him a hesitant wave, unsure if he had spotted her. But then he walks toward her with determination, his warm smile a confirmation that Max was right.

"IT ISN'T IMMATURITY THAT gets you into trouble," Gus's friends often teased him. "It's your good heart that gets you tangled up in all sorts of shit."

And perhaps they were right. There was that time a stray dog ran right into his moving car. He had called 911 to request aid because the dog was alive, but covered in scrapes. Gus put his arms around the dog who was making soft whimpering sounds and moved him to the sidewalk.

Common sense told him to be careful, as a scared dog might lash out at him, but he wasn't worried about his own personal safety. In the absence of a blanket, he'd stripped off his jacket and wrapped up the dog. Less than ten minutes later the paramedics arrived on the scene and were able to locate the owner using the information on the dog's collar. Gus followed the ambulance to the nearest animal hospital and stayed in the waiting room until the owner arrived.

The woman was grateful to Gus for calling the paramedics and apologized for the damage to his car. Gus reassured her it was fine and gave her his personal information, offering to pay for the medical bills. He never heard back from the dog's owner until a few months later when the notice arrived.

Gus was met outside his building by a young county officer who presented him with a legal summons. He opened the envelope to learn that he was being sued by the dog's owner for medical expenses and personal emotional stress caused to both dog and owner on the basis that dogs were considered personal property. Gus was facing criminal charges.

In the end, Gus agreed to pay the twelve-thousand-dollar penalty even though he knew the court would not hold him liable. The dog had been running free, in which case the owner would be considered responsible for the costs associated with the accident, including the damage to his car. At least that's what the lawyer he consulted said.

Gus thought about the time in college when the four friends had decided to drive to New York City for a long weekend. Gus was driving Eleanor's car and Mariah was sitting in the passenger seat. They all had decided she made the ideal copilot and was taxed with quizzing Gus on his homework as he drove.

They were on I-89 in Montpelier. Eleanor was sleeping and Max was in the back seat reading when Gus made the decision to pull over and give a hitchhiker a lift. The stranger was at the car ready to open the back door before Mariah realized Gus's Good Samaritan intentions.

"Thanks, man," the stranger addressed Gus. "How y'all doing?" he had asked the crew. Max and Eleanor moved closer together to make room for the newcomer.

"Where are you headed?" Gus interjected, eying his visitor through the rear-view mirror.

"I'm hoping to make it to a friend's house in Boston. What about you?" The sudden quietness surprised the three friends. Mariah shot a quick look back to meet Eleanor's wide, fearful eyes. Eleanor had a way of sensing looming danger. Mariah tried to keep her composure and not let Eleanor's panic frighten her.

"We're visiting friends in Brattleboro," Mariah cut in, relieved that she could recall the name of a convincing town.

"You gonna pay that dude, Rick Abath, a visit?" the stranger asked. The reference to the watchman of the night of the Gardner Museum heist did not register to the vexatious listeners, but he ignored their quiet nods as he shared his opinion, which came across more as a declaration: "Abath was totally in cahoots with the robbers. That's obvious since they didn't blow his brains out.

A total of $500 million worth of art. That's what they took. Poof! All gone. No one got caught. What about that?"

He gestured wildly with his hands as he launched into a rant of conspiracy theories about various government plans and murder plots. It was as if he had been concocting all those schemes in his head while walking solo and now that he had found an audience, his words flew out with vengeance. He started by describing a series of events and then told stories that accused the American government of orchestrating the attack on the Twin Towers on 9/11.

"A total inside job carried out successfully by installing explosives throughout the building in advance," the stranger declared. Eleanor, Gus knew, was holding her tongue.

The friends tolerated the stranger's monologue until he ventured into some anti-Semitic propaganda about Jews plotting to take over the world and their effectiveness in fabricating the story of the Holocaust.

"How the fuck can there still be any doubt that the Holocaust happened?" Eleanor blurted out, unable to hold back any longer.

"Hold it, Buttercup; don't shoot the messenger," the hitchhiker responded, giving Eleanor an encouraging grin.

"I'm getting off at White River Junction to fill the tank," Gus quickly interjected. His eyes glanced back at his guest as he pulled off at the exit.

Eleanor, Max, and Mariah rushed out of the car as soon as the engine died. Gus stepped out to pump the gas and the stranger remained in the car. Gus made his gas selection and removed the gas cap, all the while assessing the situation. He inserted a credit card into the machine and turned around to look at the stranger. Gus lifted the pump nozzle and slipped it into the gas tank. He clicked the metal tab to lock the trigger in place to allow for auto-fueling, walked around to the passenger side, and opened the door. He tried to engage his guest in trivial conversation about traffic, but was taken aback by the hitchhiker's dismissal.

"Hey dude, do you have a condom on you?"

"No. Why would I? Why do you need one?" Gus asked, surprised at the obvious answer, but startled by the stranger's question.

"Well, I was thinking, it's kind of getting late. I'll just stay the night in Brattleboro since you are headed there anyway. You wouldn't mind if I crashed with you guys for the night, would you? I think Buttercup and I hit it off great. I just want to make sure I protect my guards, if you get my meaning."

It took Gus a few seconds to match Eleanor's name to Buttercup, and the three friends approached the car before Gus could think of a response.

They merged into traffic, and the next thing they knew, they were being pulled over by the State Police. Gus had stepped on the accelerator with gusto after leaving the gas station, but the friends didn't question his driving. Gus was unreliable in many things, but safe driving was not one of them. The flashing lights startled everyone. Gus pulled over and stared at Mariah.

"What now?" he muttered, pretending to be irritated.

The officer approached the car and asked the required questions about whether Gus understood why he was pulled over and did he know how fast he was going.

"Yes, sir," Gus responded.

The officer asked Gus for his identification and Mariah noticed Gus writing a quick note on the back of the registration she handed him from the glove compartment.

The officer instructed the driver and passengers to step out of the car and proceeded to inform them that the vehicle was being towed for safekeeping due to an expired license plate.

The four friends climbed obediently into the tow truck as

they waved goodbye to the hitchhiker who had refused the offer of being dropped off at the nearest rest stop.

No one knew the complete story of Gus writing a note to the cop asking for help. It wasn't until a few years later that he revealed the truth after the news broke that new evidence had been found related to the case of the Isabella Stewart Gardner Museum robbery.

EG FOLDED COMFORTABLY into the insomnia with the familiarity of a dear friend's embrace. She felt the memories filtering in. The deep hollows of her ears recalled the sound of her husband's whispers, now muffled by the passing of time. Her chest warmed up as she thought about how he had lured her into love by reciting long passages of romantic poetry back when they were young. Back then, the world seemed simpler, less frightening. She mouthed the words of the opening stanza of Lord Byron, "She walks in beauty." She thought of Lucas's whispers and reassuring kisses, a failed attempt at consoling her for the terrible loss.

She touched her eyes now, expecting to feel the ache. The way they had felt raw and swollen from heavy grieving tears. She had ordered her eyes to stay shut and would have kept them sealed for an eternity, just so she wouldn't have to face the nightmare that awaited. Warm tears pushed through her closed eyes as she remembered how she had reached out from under the blankets only to feel the emptiness. Her tentative fingers following the fresh stitches across the length of her lower belly like a drunken centipede. The magnificent belly was absent. Gone were the kicks and turns of her baby girl.

She heard tentative steps coming into the room. Lucas must have heard them too, for he stopped his poetic whispers to listen to the medical staff. The attentive nurse had wanted to know if he could bring Lucas some extra blankets or pillows.

"You should try and get some sleep," he had suggested gently in the knowing way nurses have. Meg sent a quiet thanks to the devoted nurse. If they couldn't bring emotional consolation to the grieving family members, they certainly tried to compensate by bringing some physical comfort.

"You should also try to eat something," the kind nurse had added in a gentle voice.

Meg tried to remember Lucas's response to the concerned nurse, but the soft breathing filling the space brought her back now. She opened her eyes and watched Lucas. The sun rays kiss his face. She traced the silver patch below his lower lip and his eyes blinked open. She tried to control her empty swallows and pounding heart so as not to alarm him.

"Morning love," he whispered in a soft, sleepy voice, as if he could smell her melancholic perspiration.

Meg cuddled closer and he wrapped his arms around her like a protective shawl. His soothing hush muffled her sobs.

"I'm here. I got you," Lucas repeated as he held her tighter.

MARIAH WRAPS THE HEAVY WOOLEN SCARF AROUND HER NECK and hunches up her shoulders to keep the angry wind from lashing her cheeks. She is walking the short distance to her apartment after spending the night with Jake at his hotel. For several months now, he'd been talking about renting a place and had looked at several options outside the city, all with easy access to the highway, as he frequently traveled back and forth to New York City. Mariah secretly hopes he will take his time as she enjoys the adventure of spending nights with him in his hotel room. These four months with him have felt like a secret love affair.

They celebrated Valentine's Day by ordering a room service dinner of baked lobster ravioli and indulged on truffles and chocolate mousse cheesecake for dessert. How she had savored that first spoonful of delicious chocolate heaven. They ended the night by watching Mariah's all-time favorite movie, *Dirty Dancing*.

Mariah stops on the sidewalk to retrieve her phone from her jacket pocket and takes off her mitten to bring the screen to life. Eleanor is sending another message inviting Mariah to a yoga class that afternoon.

"*I won't Yoga with you, Eleanor, but I will take you out to dinner after you are done. We will give free reign to post Valentine's Day chocolate desserts.*" Mariah can already feel her taste buds' immediate jubilation at the thought of sweets. "*Let's meet at the bar across the street from the yoga studio.*"

"*Fine,*" flashes the quick response, "*but you are coming with me next week,*" Eleanor adds.

"*All I want to know is, what happened to that elite athlete I used to know? What have you done with her?"* Eleanor's final text reads, accompanied by several question marks. That comment takes Mariah back to memories of college where she had, indeed, been a good athlete.

Mariah felt exuberant about going to college. She had worked very hard all through high school to ensure her grades were top-notch. Her standardized test scores reflected that hard work. Her involvement in theatre production as well as her spot as captain of the varsity soccer team had made her a sought-after candidate for many Ivy League schools. While college meant freedom to many of her peers, for Mariah it meant finding a place to belong, to be noticed. At times she felt resentful of how much freedom she was given while growing up.

The offers began to pour in during the fall of her sophomore year. By the time she started her senior year, she had received over a dozen offers from recruiters around the country. Her hard work had earned her the option of free tuition to a vast number of prestigious institutions. In the end, to everyone's amazement, Mariah turned them all down.

She chose a liberal arts college nuzzled deep in the mountains of Vermont. It was a Division III school, which allowed her to pursue her passion for sports. Although she was interested in the rigorous academic experience it offered, the opportunity to spend a semester studying abroad ultimately helped cement her decision. She wanted to be in a place where she could explore options and not be confined by expectations.

Mariah walks into the restaurant and quickly spots Eleanor's slender figure talking amicably to a young couple sitting at the bar, the two martinis by her side indicating she had already ordered her a drink.

"How was yoga?" Mariah asks, planting a loud kiss on her friend's welcoming cheek.

"Perfect," Eleanor says, handing Mariah her cocktail garnished with a double olive. "Here, a dirty martini for a dirty girl."

"To all dirty girls!" She clinks Eleanor's glass and asks, "Why isn't your face puffy and sweaty? Did you shower at the studio?"

"I did gentle yoga. It's more like a stretch. Hot yoga is the crazy bitchy one that leaves you looking like crap, but feeling like you took part in an all-night orgy." Eleanor smooths her printed T-shirt over Lululemon yoga pants, adding, "I am telling you, you need to try it. You'll thank me later. OR, maybe Jake will thank me." She pauses to take a sip of her drink, then casts a mischievous eye. "And how is that lucky duck doing?"

"He's good, but I think he's getting tired of living out of a suitcase. Did he tell you? He's been looking at renting a place, possibly a house in the suburbs. You better watch it, you might end up having Jake for a neighbor. He keeps asking for my opinion, but I honestly don't have one. I don't want to say something that will influence his decision."

"And why don't you suggest he move in with you?" Eleanor asks, knowingly.

"I don't think so. I'm not sure how I feel about that right now. It's feeling too fast and too soon. You know me, I'm so used to being on my own, having my own personal space. I'm not sure I'm ready to give that up. Things are good the way they are. Why tamper with … Oh my God!" Her gaze falls on the door, then quickly away. "Don't look now, but the woman who just walked in looks like Professor Honda. Do you remember her?"

"Not really," Eleanor says, moving her drink to the side to make space for the chips and salsa being delivered by the barkeep.

"She wore those hideous vintage glasses straight out of the 50's."

"Wait, I know who you're talking about. I remember her. Did she lead the term abroad trips to Spain?"

"Yeah. And she also taught some of the political science classes. She had a funny way of waving her hand like a flamenco dancer when greeting people." She mimics the gesture and giggles. "The woman who just walked in did the same thing. She could be her younger twin."

She takes a sip of her drink and remains quiet for a moment, reflecting on the past. "Sometimes I wonder what became of our professors," she finally says. "You know, like what they might be doing right now?"

Eleanor pops a crispy chip in her mouth. "Well, many of them are probably retired or taking an eternal nap six feet deep underground."

"I should look her up, Professor Honda. I should drop her a note."

"Let's hope she is in the retired group," Eleanor jokes.

"God, you are such a morbid individual, aren't you?"

"You know who I remember?" Eleanor gives Mariah a sinister glance.

Mariah rolls her eyes. "Professor Fong Siu?"

"You ladies ordering dinner tonight?" the barkeep interrupts, his hands working a drying rag. He doesn't write down anything as the two rattle off an order of squash carbonara, pork tenderloin, radicchio salad, and a double chocolate lava cake.

"Got it!" he says, walking away.

"I had the biggest crush on Fong, for like forever." Eleanor reminisces. "That guy was hot. It was like staring at your favorite dessert while you were on a diet. You could only salivate, and were happy doing it, because you knew you couldn't have a taste."

Mariah thinks back to her professors, and it is the face of Professor Honda that lights up in her mind's eye. Professor

Honda had made a big impact on her career choice. Mariah was certain she wanted to be a lawyer, but hadn't made up her mind about what branch of law she would pursue. For a while she thought she would work with policy or perhaps run for political office, which meant majoring in political science or government. In her junior year, she became fascinated by civil rights and constitutional law. Professor Honda was her legal history teacher. Soon after having class with her, Mariah decided to direct her studies toward history and political science.

"Sometimes I wish I were back in college," Mariah says nostalgically.

"Yeah, those were some fun years," Eleanor agrees. "I sometimes think about how incredibly lucky we are to have survived it all. We did a lot of crazy shit, all of that drinking and night skiing after eating mushrooms. God, we were reckless. Well, we were, not you. You were always the voice of reason. Thank God for the Mariahs of the world."

It wasn't like she hadn't had her own share of fun, Mariah thinks to herself. She'd enjoyed going out with her friends, and going to parties around campus just as much as anyone, but she was measured with the drinking. She had grown up in a family where drinking was part of a celebration, whether they were welcoming the weekend with a glass of wine over dinner or having a social gathering with friends. Drinking did not present a badge of freedom or rebellion to her the way it did for many of her peers.

"My parents taught me to drink responsibly," she would often declare to her high school friends while enjoying an inebriated buzz. But that wasn't the full story. It was her parents' absence that created the opportunities for her.

"Remember that time we decided to bring a bunch of friends down to stay at your parents' for the holidays?" Eleanor says. "I think it was the time we planned to rent that ski house, but there was hardly any snow. We were like, fuck skiing! Let's just go and binge drink for two weeks."

"Yeah my parents were easy targets," Mariah forces a laugh. "They were never around. I don't think they ever knew of our shenanigans." She feels the familiar resentment begin dripping down inside her like a leaking pipe. "We drank ourselves shitless down in our basement. It was pizza, booze, and movies for two weeks."

She remembers how even in high school when her friends came over to spend the night in the basement, there was never a fear of an adult walking in on their teenager rascality. "You are so lucky," her friends had marveled with envy, her "I know, right?" response plastering over the rejection she felt at the lack of parental oversight. Both her parents had been occupied with their own preoccupations. Mariah had listened to her friends complain about their own parents. "They are such a bore. They are always nagging me." She didn't think that sounded so bad.

"We all thought your parents were the coolest," Eleanor says.

"I don't know about cool," Mariah shakes her head. "They just didn't bother with all those rules and crazy restrictions." She remembers her dad once cleaning up puddles of rancid teenager puke.

*J*AKE AND MARIAH WALK TO BRUNCH down a shaded side street. The small bakery owners, an elderly Jewish couple, open only on Sundays. Their menu— breakfast all day—makes it popular among locals.

"How did you and Rafael meet?" Jake asks out of the blue.

"It was during our senior year in college. Eleanor called it 'brain at first sight.'" Her eyes sparkle at the memory. "And of course she was right."

Rafael was the president of the International Student Club when Mariah joined, hoping for an opportunity to practice her Spanish with some of the Spanish-speaking members. A warm feeling gushes over her as she remembers Rafael's deep laugh. The young, Afro-Caribbean man from the Bronx had indeed captured her attention. No, it wasn't because of the colorful personality and sun-kissed skin characteristic of people from the Dominican Republic, the land infused by the magic of indigenous-European-African sparks, but rather, by the imaginative way he spoke. His intelligence and eloquence grabbed her on the spot.

"Sometimes we talked straight through the night and late into the morning. I ran on coffee and he on powdered doughnuts. Rafa is the type of person whose passion sifts through his body. People always want to be around him. He has this way of making you feel potent, capable of solving the world's most taxing problems."

"Well, I'm sure glad he is leagues across the ocean now," Jake says, giving a mock wipe of his brow.

"You have nothing to worry about. Rafa and I had something very special, but it was more of a partnership of mutual respect and loyalty."

Mariah and Rafael cared a great deal for each other, but not in the traditional flaming love that overtakes young lovers. They quickly became accustomed to each other and were willing to maintain their partnership, believing it would eventually transition into marriage.

"Rafa is one of the lead researchers on molecular mutation, and that is exactly how he would introduce himself if you ever met him." They break hands to let a woman pass walking her poodle. "Cute doggie," she says, turning back to Jake. "His team has made all sorts of groundbreaking discoveries in antibiotic compounds. His original study of the proliferation of drug-resistant bacteria landed him the opportunity to lead his own team of researchers. It was an opportunity of a lifetime for him. Plus, he was able to bring his bug research team with him. Critters research was something he'd been doing just for fun, but now he had a chance to have someone else pay for his side indulgence."

"He studies bugs? For fun?" Jake asks.

"Well, it's not what pays the bills, but it's where his passion is. Rafa loved bugs even as a young child. His big sister likes to tell stories about how he spent hours digging for ants in the yard and begged her to go outside in the rain to collect worms for him. He loved watching the worms, but was afraid to touch their wiggly bodies. I think he is still afraid of them.

She knows she's talking about Rafael too much, but he asked. And it's perfectly safe, because she's 100 percent over her former boyfriend. She keeps glancing at Jake out of the corner of her eye for any reaction, but he keeps his gaze straight ahead.

"Anyway," she continues, "even as an adult, we took hikes deep into the woods and flipped over large rocks and chunks of tree bark to look for colonies of termites. He always carried this little notebook with him in his back pocket. It's funny; he still does that, you know, carry a mini notebook in his pocket.

It was fascinating, really. He was able to look at a single termite and determine which caste system it belonged to. They are very social insects; they follow rules much like bee colonies do with workers and queens. That's the part that had always amazed me. The way those bugs interacted, not just with their habitat, but with each other."

"You say I have nothing to worry about, right?" Jake finally says, pulling her closer while attempting to make his question sound more like a joke, but Mariah could sense the hint of uncertainty lingering. That's what she had been looking for. Even after five months of courtship, Jake, with all his master-of-the-universe aura about him, is in constant need of validation when it comes to his relationship with her. Mariah's parents call it unhealthy jealousy. Mariah knows it is a lost cause to try to convince them otherwise. They would just have to learn to see past that side of Jake and get to know the one she knew and loved. Mariah is resolute that they just have to acknowledge and adapt, the way a middle-aged woman adapts when she discovers the lapping of her soft buttock cheeks resting on the back of her upper thigh. Flap, flap, flap, sings the blubber with every step.

She grabs Jake's arm a bit tighter and, as the March wind urges them forward, changes the conversation to eggs benedict and freshly baked blueberry muffins.

*M*ARIAH EASES HER WAY DOWN INTO the overstuffed chair at the coffee bar as the chorus of *Walking in Memphis* picks up. She pulls out her work computer and sets it on the small round table by her side, humming through the partially memorized song as if she, too, were walking in the land of the *Delta Blues.*

She glances around the room—just a sprinkle of customers, all focused adults. A room freed of the young afterschool crowd (each week seemingly younger) armed with extra-large beverages saturated with exorbitant amounts of whipped cream, their books and binders spread on the table like items for sale at a flea market, their phones just a fingertip away.

The harsh throaty consonants and repetitive *sh* traveling from a couple across the room send Mariah on a visual inspection. She sees the couple a few tables over and allows her ears to venture into their conversation. *Russian*, she guesses at the language being spoken. The man stares attentively at the much older woman sitting across from him as her intonation fills with passion. Mariah wonders at the content of the discussion: Coquetry? The bearer of bad news? Job interview? Or perhaps a mother and son just talking about the weather.

"Double espresso macchiato for Logan!" calls out the barista, his inky wool hat matching the pigment of his radiant, ebony skin. Mariah considers the ear flaps, fastened securely around his face, two rainbow pom-poms dangling beneath his chin. How could he stand the heat? Then she notices the two sets of eyebrow rings screaming *I am my own person; the New England weather bows down to me,* and she smiles.

Mariah grabs the brown accordion folder sticking out of her

bag and sets it on her lap. She had left the office mid-morning after the team meeting, needing a different space to work, to think. She sifts through the folders, reading the names of possible clients on the color-coded tabs. Her phone beeps and she stares at the caller's text for a brief second.

"*Dinner after work tonight?*" A winking smiley face follows Jake's question.

Mariah considers for a moment and then replies, "*I'll order takeout.*"

"*Can't wait!*" flashes his quick response.

Mariah sets down her phone hesitantly. She thinks back to the conversation she had last night with Eleanor. She'd asked Eleanor about Jake's childhood since he was still a tad reserved about his upbringing.

"He hardly ever speaks about his family," she told Eleanor, pleading with her to share details of his younger years.

Mariah noticed how Jake dropped general comments here and there, but when she asked him questions that required more elaboration, he offered a quick response and then changed the topic. The obvious stress of his body language alerted her to the fact that he was retreating. Mariah had learned not to ask probing questions. She just took in the brief stories as they came, like a crucial piece of a puzzle. And so it was that most of what Mariah knew about Jake's past came not from Jake, but from Eleanor.

"I'm not surprised that he is shying away from sharing certain things about his family life with you," Eleanor had said. "It's not that he is embarrassed about it; at least I don't think he is. My guess is it's just easier to try and block out things about the past that were painful or confusing. I think that for a young boy, those experiences were hard to handle, and unlike most of us girls, guys in general don't think that talking about it does any good. They see it as a weakness to dig into emotionally unpleasant memories."

After a little convincing, Eleanor went on to tell the whole story as she knew it. "His father died of a heart attack when Jake was in middle school. His mother was forced to get a job after learning that the family business was in financial turmoil since Jake's father had taken a second mortgage on their home to invest in his already failing business.

"Oh my," Mariah said under her breath. "I didn't know."

"That's not all," Eleanor continued. "Jake had listened from the entryway as the lawyer explained to his mother that earnings from the sale of the business would be enough to pay back the bank loan, but he didn't see how she would be able to keep the house since there were no savings to speak of." She went on to describe how Jake's mother had been shocked at the realization that her husband had concealed their financial situation and maintained the pretense that they were financially sound.

"Oh my," Mariah repeated.

"I'm telling you. It was weird. He kept taking the family on their usual lavish trips and vacations to Europe and on winter trips to Aspen like everything was fine. Jake's parents drove luxury cars; a Ferrari and a Mercedes-Benz. His sister received a Porsche as a high school graduation gift. There were no visual indications or signs of financial stress, and if there had been, his mother chose to ignore them. After his father's passing it quickly became clear to the young Jake that their lives were going to morph drastically overnight.

"Oh, poor Jake," Mariah said.

"And that's not all!" Eleanor continued. "His mother followed the advice of the lawyer and within a couple of months, Jake and his mother moved into a small government-subsidized apartment in the middle of downtown. His sister, eight years older than he and a senior in college, refused to come back home. She blamed their mother, accusing her of not caring enough to be involved in the business, as if she would have been able to prevent the sudden downturn in their standard of living. The blame transformed into rejection, as if it was easier to grieve her father by rejecting her mother. She got married right after graduation and moved to Arizona with her husband, never to return to her hometown."

"He never mentioned he had a sister," Mariah said.

"Jake's mother's behavior had been just as drastic. She retreated into herself, cutting ties with anyone that reminded her of her past, including her own son. She found a job working at a local travel agency during the day and at night worked at a supermarket, so he saw very little of her. Her muffled cries in the middle of the night were the only indication that she was still around. Jake was never sure whether she grieved for his father, or for the life she no longer had. He didn't blame her; how could he? He, too, felt like a static image captured in the sfumato of a Da Vinci masterpiece, his own colors blurring and evaporating."

"So then what happened?" Mariah couldn't imagine that things could get worse, but guessed they probably did.

"When Jake went off to college, his mother informed him on the drive down that she had been seeing someone and had decided to marry him. Jake knew who the suitor was. He was the owner of the local travel agency where his mother worked. Get this, Mariah. Even worse, Jake knew that he was married. When he asked his other point blank about it, she just said they had been separated for a while and were getting a divorce."

"Tell me that's the worst of it."

"I'm not done yet. Mr. Cooper, the boss, had two sons, one of whom was close to Jake's age. She had visions of celebrating holidays as one happy family. He just couldn't do it."

"He never went?"

"That first Thanksgiving, Jake did what his sister had done years back and found excuses to stay away. He didn't return to his old neighborhood until years later, to attend a high school reunion at the insistence of a childhood friend. But, by then, his mother and her new husband had moved to Florida."

"That's where we visited her." She had been surprised when Jake invited her down to meet his mother over New Year's, but she had taken it as a hopeful sign as well.

"I'm not sure what led up to the reconciliation, but she contracted Alzheimer's a few years ago," Eleanor continued. "He's been devoted to her since then, even hiring a nursing service to help care for her."

Mariah and Jake had celebrated New Year's Eve at an elegant waterfront restaurant near where his mother lived. Although Jake had mentioned his mother's condition beforehand, nothing could have prepared Mariah for the sadness she witnessed seeing his mother in a state of perpetual confusion. She read the pained expression on Jake's face and found it to be a swirl of pity and regret. It broke her heart every time Jake's mom stared at him, perplexed, and asked if he was one of her caretakers.

Mariah thought of little Jake and of her grown, adult Jake. How easy it was for people to judge her big Jake for adopting that bad boy image, not knowing that it had helped him survive. It had given him an identity, a way to claim respect and acceptance among his peers. She could now begin to understand why calling him a *mama's boy* had provoked such a strong reaction.

Jolted out of her reverie as someone brushes by her chair, Mariah sips her coffee, the rich aroma delivering its promises. Her brain registers the caffeine and her body welcomes the pleasant feeling of hyper awareness. She opens the brown accordion folder and gets to work.

"HAVE YOU TOLD RAFAEL about Jake?" Eleanor wants to know. She has Mariah on speaker phone so she can talk and cook at the same time. She had been working arduously on creating a new repertoire of holiday desserts with an international flair, even though Christmas is still eight long months way. Tonight, she is trying out *buñuelos,* the traditional Mexican dessert credited for inspiring the creation of churros, doughnuts, and funnel cake.

Eleanor walks around her luxurious kitchen, designed with two islands surfaced in black walnut butcher block. The larger of the islands acts as a prep workspace. It is equipped with a deep sink, a dishwasher, and a drawer-style microwave that fit seamlessly under the counter next to the built-in wine cooler. The additional island is set a tad higher. Its rich chocolate color makes a striking statement to guests, luring them in, inviting them to gather around, sit, and stay awhile.

"You know that multitasking is a hoax, right?" Mariah teases.

"I am not multitasking. I am talking on the phone with my best friend who is inspiring me to create." Eleanor delicately spreads the homemade flour tortillas on the cooling rack.

"Oh, am I your muse now?" Mariah asks.

"So, have you?" Eleanor repeats, ignoring Mariah's attempt to change the subject. The response doesn't come, but Eleanor gives it more time. She measures out a generous teaspoon of chili powder and adds it to the Ethiopian tea spice to make the dipping syrup. The tea spice is her personal twist to the traditional cinnamon coating the recipe calls for.

"I did," Mariah finally answers.

"Well? Did he flip out?" Eleanor stops and wipes her hands

on the fold of her apron. She taps her phone to private mode and brings it to her ears, afraid of missing anything coming from the other end of the line.

"No. He sounded genuinely thrilled. I don't know. I mean, it's been almost two years."

"What are you doing?"

"Talking to you."

"No, Mariah, I can picture you sitting there doing something."

"I'm just doodling. Giving a model on the cover of a Laura Ashely catalogue a mustache and wolf-like eyebrows that make quite the statement with her elegant maxi dress."

Eleanor giggles. "That's pent up energy, if I ever saw it. Spill it. What are you really thinking? You're not regretting breaking up with him?"

Mariah hesitates. "You know the story. It would never have worked out. He knows I never would have lived abroad. His project was for four years. And then it was extended for more."

"You know the story better than anyone. Part of me wanted to move across the ocean to be with him. But we both knew it wasn't going to happen. My life was here."

And Eleanor knows Rafael never would have put Mariah in a position where she would feel like she had to choose. So, they did what they both considered the sensible thing: They broke off the engagement.

"I am such a bad person," Mariah continues before Eleanor has a chance to disagree. "I tried calling him last week, but he didn't pick up and his mailbox was full. I ended up writing him this long email about Jake. It was like a love letter except it was about a different guy."

"And what did he say? I bet he told you what a terrible person you are," Eleanor teases, glad that Mariah had mustered the courage to talk to Rafael about Jake.

"He wrote me a beautiful letter back. You know Rafa; even his words feel like a backrub. It's fine. I just wish I had told him over the phone." Mariah's lament lingers in the air for a few moments, a sign that she is ready for the conversation to move on.

Eleanor does not miss her cue. Her voice perks up and she turns her phone back to speaker mode, "And how are his bugs doing?"

Mariah lets out a childish laugh. "You should not be making fun of him. Our Rafa is going to save the world someday," she says with pride. "He wrote about some mosquito fiasco. Apparently one of the lab interns replaced some light bulb in the laboratory specimen tanks and used the wrong one. It freaked out the female mosquitoes and screwed up their reproductive cycles."

"I imagine it's not that hard to find replacements," Eleanor says.

"Yeah. I don't think Rafa is worried about that."

"How long can those little suckers live given they don't meet their fate with an angry slap?"

"It depends on the species."

Rafael had taught Mariah a lot of random things that gave her good cocktail fodder. Eleanor loves watching her perform among a group, rattling off facts. Even though she didn't find it all that interesting, she lets her continue now.

"There are thousands of species of mosquitoes," Mariah says, her voice speeding up in excitement. "Some live for a few days and others can live for several months. One of the things Rafael's team is experimenting with is manipulating the environment to see what conditions will expand the mosquito's lifespan. You know what's crazy? He told me once that mosquitoes have killed more people than all the wars in all of human history combined. They are like little ticking time bombs."

"My God, Mariah," Eleanor stops her. "You are totally turned on by all of this, aren't you?" She imagines her friend's blushing face. "Some of us are turned on by naughty-dirty talk, and some of us by mosquitoes' guts … Oh my God!"

"What?" Mariah cries in concern.

"Oh no!" Eleanor adds in distress, banging on a large pot for a special sound effect.

"What? Do I need to call 9-1-1? Wait a second. I'll be right over."

"No, not necessary." Eleanor grips her phone, trying to suppress her snickering. "There's just a drunk mosquito masturbating in my wine."

Mariah burst out laughing. "Clearly, you have no shame."

MARIAH GRABS HER PURSE AND STEPS OUT of her office, shutting the door silently behind her. She had tried to ease her anxiety with deep breathing exercises, but failed. Going out for a smoke seems justifiable.

"Norma-Jean, I need some fresh air," she whispers to the secretary who has a phone cradled expertly between her right ear and shoulder. She responds with a bright red lipstick-smile and a quick nod followed by a rapid hand gesture indicating *go*. Mariah smirks at the middle-aged woman's approval, relieved that she had been on the phone and therefore unable to offer her daily dose of unsolicited motherly advice in her thick New Bedford accent: *Take a sweater with you. You work too much. Too much coffee is not good for you.* "The nagging witch," she had dubbed the office secretary. Mariah had arrived before six this morning to tie up some paperwork, but her attention was kidnapped by thoughts of Jake.

She walks out of the building into the street and spots an empty bench. Mariah claims it, allowing herself to be entertained by the busy moving crowd while images of Jake pirouette hazily in her mind. Her eyes take a quick sweep behind her before she reaches for a cigarette and lights it with expert hands. The loud drag surprises her. She chuckles, thinking of what Norma-Jean would say of this secret habit.

Mariah stares at her phone and it stares back at her in silence. She is eager to call Jake, but she learned early on that you don't call or text your Wall Streeter boyfriend at 8:29 a.m. the first Friday of the month. "Girl, that's the biggest economic release of the month. Those souls are holding on tight for dear life hoping to make—or at least not lose—tons of money," Eleanor informed Mariah when she complained about Jake ignoring her calls that one Friday morning. She hadn't mentioned her new discovery to Jake; instead, she made a note on her calendar for future reminders, the same way she marks the arrival of her next menstrual cycle.

Eleanor also educated her about other blackout times: The opening and closing of the market are the busiest times of day. She warned Mariah to stay out of Jake's way during those hours, and Mariah had been grateful for the advice.

"Call Mom," Mariah commands her phone. She needs a distraction. Their conversations these days are either about Jake or politics. Today it is about politics. Her mom had sent her an article from the *New Yorker* describing people's concerns about García.

"I am so tired of the media." Mariah could feel her mom's rage through the sound waves. "They have zero dirt on him, so they write about people's made-up concerns, which are clearly nonsense."

Mariah's family is a big supporter of Héctor García's candidacy. They had followed his political career as a young senator from New Mexico. "Mom, people are not ready for a Mexican-American president."

That statement unleashes several strong remarks from her mother, and Mariah decides to listen. To take in her mother's voice, even when she is upset, is magically soothing. The morning sun hides behind the city high-rises, and the trapped spring wind kisses her cheeks. Mariah reaches inside her purse, glad to be greeted by the large infinity scarf. She hears Norma-Jean's voice in her ear: *Keep a scarf in your bag.*

*J*AKE IS DISTRACTED FROM his trash-sorting task in the parking lot of Mariah's apartment building. The town had recently adopted a new way of bagging recyclable material. A job that he had helped Mariah do many times, and which would generally take him ten minutes to complete, preoccupied him for an entire hour today. His mind is traveling away from his body only to come back again to discover that his sorting needs rearranging.

Although it is just the end of May, the weather feels more like summer. Jake is spending the day at Mariah's place while he arranges for the movers. He had hoped for a formal invitation to move in with Mariah, but it had not materialized, so he was forced to find a place of his own.

He ended up renting a house outside the city—a beautiful old farmhouse with easy access to a lake and some hiking trails. He had been uncertain about what type of permanent housing situation to pursue. In the end, he reasoned that a house in the suburbs would give him and Mariah the option of escaping the city when in need of some peace and quiet. Not that he would admit to this if questioned by anyone, but Jake's motive also is linked to his desire to lure Mariah into moving in with him even though she'd given no indication she wanted to do so. If she is not certain about him moving in with her, perhaps she would be more receptive to the idea of moving in with him. He remains hopeful.

Mariah's place is in a central location overlooking the Common. The doorman, Mr. Hobbs, had been suspicious of Jake at first.

"I see you have finally charmed Mr. Hobbs," Mariah said one day.

"I just followed your brilliant idea and asked him about his grandchildren."

Jake no longer is stopped for questioning or looked upon with scrutiny by Mr. Hobbs before being allowed to enter the building, and today he whisks right past.

When he returns to Mariah's apartment with the empty recycling container in hand, the radio station is playing the latest pop hits and she is baking her Nana's blueberry muffin recipe. Her hips move effortlessly to the music; she is a graceful dancer, Jake observes. He loves to watch her move, especially when he catches her unaware. Her body teases and savors the beat, as if she is swimming in the magic of sound waves at the point of convergence where brain and body meet. His face radiates pure contentment.

Mariah notices his playful stares. Her index finger beckons him to join her.

"*Come here, lover boy.*"

"*And if he doesn't answer?*" Jake responds, knowing she is referencing a scene from her favorite movie.

"*Oh lover boy,*" she sings back teasingly.

"*And if he still doesn't answer?*"

"*I simply say.*"

Jake sways his clumsy body, arms stretched toward her. He showcases his signature move, the pretend maracas, from side to side. Mariah's joyful laugh surpasses the volume emanating from the speakers.

Jake pulls Mariah gently into a cuddly embrace. He caresses her cheeks with his. Her eager lips reach up searching greedily for his. The tender butterfly kisses linger for a bit and then gradually succumb to a rapid exchange of playful nibbles and savory licks.

Maria's flowery apron slides carelessly onto the floor. Her dress meets the same fate. Jake's expert fingers trace the rim of her lacy black brassiere. His thumb rubs diligently against the side of her swollen bosom. Mariah holds Jake's waist tighter, fighting for a full breath to fill her lungs.

Jake caresses the base of her neck with his moist lips; she trembles at the sensation. Her quick fingers unfasten her bra, giving her chest the freedom it desires. He decorates the base of her neck with tender bites, his body craving release. The final undergarment swiftly disengages, leaving her body exposed, ready to be possessed.

"THE OWNER OF THE RESTAURANT just got back from spending the whole month of July in Italy," the eager bartender explains as he skillfully fills Mariah's wine glass. "They found this amazing winery in a little village called Montefalco in the hills of Umbria. The dry clay and sandy soil produce really thick-skinned grapes that create strong, explosive flavors as the wine ages."

He holds up the bottle and points to the label. "It's the Capricho. It's a darker red with tremendous tannins and acids. The name Capricho means *whim* in Spanish, but it's also a lively type of music in Italy."

"The Spanish translation also describes someone who is a spoiled brat," Mariah can't resist commenting once the young lad is well out of earshot.

Her Spanish, although a little rusty, remains deeply embedded in her subconscious, thanks largely to Rafael. The semesters of Spanish classes topped with a full immersion experience living in Spain had paid off. But it all would have faded away without Rafael's determination to speak only Spanish with her.

Mariah and Jake love to dine at this restaurant. Tonight, they sit at the bar. John, their usual bartender, has the night off.

Mariah shoots Jake a conspiratorial smile and he nods in agreement. This must be the new bartender in training John told them about last week when they stopped by for late night spirits.

The location of the restaurant couldn't be worse: The second floor of an old factory building in an old industrial section of town. Because it is situated on a busy street, taxi drivers refuse to drop off or pick up passengers outside the restaurant.

Diners familiar with the area know to drive past the restaurant for two blocks, and then make a right turn by the local high school, a large brick Gothic-style building that had somehow escaped the wrath of a modern wrecking ball. This one-way street leads the driver to a series of narrow side streets, some of which are labeled with a bright orange DEAD-END sign. But, as any local knows, some of those streets are actually not so DEAD after all.

Although Mariah and Jake are not local to this part of town, through trial and error they have discovered the best streets to park, just a five-minute walk from the restaurant.

"I swear this is a social experiment," Jake had laughed while looking for parking, launching into a theory that the owner had chosen that locale to weed out the crazies from the sane.

A choir of hearty laughs erupts from one of the tables, and Mariah turns to survey the diners, their faces attentive to the item inside a small box that is being passed around. Her eyes travel around the room as if checking to see if anybody else is in on the secret box of the laughing table. But everyone else seems drawn to their own affairs. The hushed and bubbly conversation dances from table to table except for the large table set for a party of eight. Mariah eyes the big RESERVED sign acting as the centerpiece suspiciously.

"I thought they didn't take reservations," she motions to Jake, but he shrugs, his attention fully grasped by the silent NASCAR race on the glowing television screen behind the bar. Mariah's fingers tap gently on the pounded copper bar top to the beat of the classic rock playlist, and her bobbing head follows. She stares at the high ceilings with the exposed pipes and ducts, a reminder of the building's history. The original brick walls are decorated with vintage posters advertising wine and spirits.

Jake gives her thigh a gentle squeeze. "I'll be right back," he says.

Jake heads toward the stairs in the direction of the bathroom. The faint bergamot trail left behind by the passing blonde catches his attention and draws his eyes to her seductive saunter, a movement that demands to be noticed. His breath quickens at the sight of her strapless beige blouse and tight jeans clinging to womanly curves. He follows her up the stairs, his eyes affixed to her backside while his ears delight in the click of her high heels echoing off the old wooden stairs. Jake shakes his head at the landing, as if acknowledging some internal reproach, and brings his hands together, interlacing his fingers. He gives his outstretched arms a quick shake as he pushes the door open with a casual shove of his right shoulder.

The young bartender stops in front of Mariah, pouring the empty water glasses. "So, what do you think of the Capricho?"

"I love the sweet aroma and the earthy taste. It is absolutely delicious," Mariah confesses. She is truly enjoying the subtle flavors of the forest emanating from the earthy wine.

When Jake returns, they listen to the eager lad share additional information about the wine selections while Jake studies the menu. He leans over. "Should we go for the usual?"

Mariah nods affirmatively, her eyes on the almost empty bottle of Capricho.

"We'll share the five-course, prix-fixe meal," Jake says. Mariah can already taste the restaurant's playful amuse-bouche, always an intricate and surprising burst of flavor.

"The golden beets and goat cheese salad is the perfect preamble to the steak and ratatouille," suggests the eager bartender. "You will not be disappointed."

They order their individual flights of wine, which come carefully paired to enhance each dish.

"Raspberry chocolate tart or lemon ricotta cake for dessert?" asks Jake, though he's not looking at her.

Mariah's upper body jumps, a reflex from the muscular hand firmly massaging her inner thigh.

"Chocolate tart," she whispers, afraid to follow his desire-filled gaze toward a passing flash of beige, to find it leads to another woman as it so often did.

MEG STARED AT THE DRY MINT LEAVES unfolding in the hot water, her hands hugging the body of the mug. It did not require much effort for her to conjure the prolonged sound of the sirens as the ambulance approached their house, their new home, so long ago. She saw this memory emerge, gently fusing with the steam of her tea. Even her olfactory nerves remembered the smell of new carpet emanating from the renovated playroom that lingered in the air.

She had woken up with a start in the middle of the night. What felt like a baby kick at first had turned into a painful pinching sensation just below the belly, so she had walked downstairs and poured herself a cup of warm water with a slice of fresh ginger root.

She considered waking Lucas up, but decided to walk around the kitchen some more. Maybe if the baby settled into a comfortable position, the pain would go away and she would be able to resume sleeping. The thought of sleep made her smile. She hadn't been able to enjoy a deep sleep once she reached the second trimester since she'd always been a toss-and-turn sleeper who started the night face down on her belly. She missed that feeling.

Meg grimaced as she remembered the pain. The intensity had made her shriek out loud. She doubled over and dropped onto the kitchen floor.

Lucas heard her cry and ran down the stairs and into the kitchen to find Meg sobbing, holding her womb. He embraced her shaking body and immediately noticed the pool of blood surrounding her.

Meg didn't remember much about that moment on the kitchen

floor. But she did remember the insistent sound of the ambulance as it approached their home. She remembered thinking all she had to do was keep her baby safe.

She remembered rubbing her belly and whispering to her baby girl how much she loved her. *You don't have to rush out just yet*, she said. *Your parents have waited a long time for your arrival and could wait a bit longer. Don't rush yet, baby girl,* she begged.

Meg came back to her reality. Her tea had gotten cold. Memory is a treacherous gift. In this moment, how she wished she could summon the happiest of memories with her baby girl. Those seemed to dissolve quickly, leaving behind a bundle of gripping, repugnant memories. She picked up the six white pills lined up in perfect formation on the counter, her daily allowance. After so many years, Lucas still kept her medicine locked away. She popped them into her mouth one by one and swallowed them dry in a big gulp of shame.

"THAT'S RIDICULOUS! THERE were just flirtatious looks," Jake shouts and argues, but then becomes silent as he sees the additional envelopes resting in the outstretched hand of his lawyer, who wears a worried look on his face. There are four new allegations, each woman describing similar sexually charged advances. Jake had agreed to a settlement, determined to conceal this information from Mariah.

"I'll get us a drink," Jake announces as soon as they step into the bar. Mariah nods in agreement as he edges his way, leopard-like, through the crowded bar, a smell of sophistication swirling around him. Several stares follow Jake, a blend of the sexes. Mariah smiles. She is used to heads turning when Jake walks by, the vision of an ideal utopian crush.

She thinks how his hawkish nose complements his distinctive cheekbones, flawlessly aided by his derring-do smile showcasing a perpetual state of triumph. Even the dark-red scars left behind by the storm of teenage years decorating in balanced symmetry his set of cheeks seem to harmonize the rhythmic movements of his Titan shoulders. Mariah's eyes follow Jake. His straight blades not only speak of his physical strength, but also highlight Jake's ambitious personality.

"Want to sit?" mouths the heavy-set guy at the other end of the bar, maneuvering his way off the stool. Mariah offers a grateful nod, hoping she hasn't misunderstood his offer. She readjusts her skirt with a gentle pull and reaches for the half-empty bowl of peanut mix. *Why do bars offer patrons free peanuts, yet charge them for a small bottled water?* Mariah pops a salty nut into her mouth. A handful later her brain begins to register a sensation of thirst. *Aha*, Mariah reasons, *it's all part of the master plan to keep us drinking.* She smiles at the simplicity of it.

The two busy bartenders move with agility behind the bar, taking and delivering orders, all the while smiling as if nothing pleased them more than to get people drunk. Mariah studies the assortment of bottles beautifully displayed on the bar's back wall, staring at the row of clear jelly jars outlining the bottom shelf, their tea candles flickering and shining brightly. Directly behind the candles, as if part of a religious ceremony, stands a mis-matched offering of liquors, some with a metal pour spout at the ready.

Mariah's eyes travel to the top shelf, the place of high honor where the delicate and exclusive spirits dwell. She thinks of Jake and Rafael. *Where would you place them on this rack?* Her eyes dart down to the shelf below that displays the collection of unpredictable intoxicants, each calling out to be picked. That's Jake's place, she reasons, and then claims the top shelf with the smooth predictable liquor for Rafael. Jake is the type of drink that would make your head spin at the first sip, but then dissolve into a massive hangover the next morning. You'd rejoice in it, though, reliving the memories of the night before.

Are you the one for me, Jake? Mariah wonders as she pops another salty nut. She can see Jake at the far end of the bar still waiting for an opportunity to place his order. She wonders what he will order for her. And then she ponders, *Am I a top rack kind of girl to him?*

She turns her body around slightly to better eavesdrop on the conversation behind her while she awaits his return. The discussion seems to be about healthcare. Mariah's ears perk up. Her firm had recently filed a lawsuit on behalf of a man who was forced out of work after being diagnosed with a chronic disease.

As a result, her client had lost his health benefits.

"We're trying so hard to connect with our daughter, but we are exhausted," the man says to his companion. "We can't afford to both take time off from work, so we ran the numbers and decided that it made more sense for me to stay home because at least I got two weeks of paid leave."

Mariah had met this couple before. They were regular attendees at the annual fundraising event organized by Gus's mother. The taller of the two is Pete, a good friend of Gus.

She pulls out a mental file and tries to remember what she knows about Pete, what is his job and what is his family background. It is a social strategy she practices. The answers come to her without much effort. Pete is a physician at a small hospital outside Boston. Her brain continues to add onto the information as if reciting a list of grocery items. He grew up in El Paso, Texas, the oldest of four children. His Chicano father taught Spanish Literature at the University of Texas. His mother, an Anglo-Saxon from Maine, had been an elementary school teacher. Pete had gone to college in Maine, where he lived with his grandparents to save on room and board expenses.

Mariah studies Pete for a moment. He appears to be a few years older than his partner Sean, a truck driver; or *driver of trucks*, as he had introduced himself when Mariah first met him. Her brain jumps to Sean's file and the memory of a personal interaction resurfaces. She smiles, remembering she liked Sean.

Mariah recalls talking with him about his interest in organizing a trucker's union last year. She hopes for the opportunity tonight to check in with him and ask for an update.

"It's so frustrating," he had shared with Mariah then. "Truckers can choose to join the Motor Transport Workers Union. The union does help improve working conditions to some extent, but the issues affecting truck drivers are so specific that I feel we need our own union to represent our particular concerns."

"And are your concerns centered on pay?" Mariah had asked.

"Yeah. A big part of it is wages. Like right now I make an average of forty-three cents a mile with no benefits, and I'm home three days a month. I try to put in lots of overtime, but it's not even worth it."

Mariah had asked him why he became a trucker in the first place. She was curious about his choice. She had a mental image of what a trucker looked like; no doubt, a very Hollywood stereotype version at best, since she had never met a truck driver in person. Sean did not fit the movie profile.

"I just love road trips," he said. "I have this crazy obsession with maps. I've been collecting them since I was young. I must have over a thousand maps tucked away in the bottom of my dresser. It's crazy, I know, but I like to keep them near." He had clearly been proud of his collection.

"When I was a kid," he continued, "my room was filled with all kinds of toy vehicles. I had posters and pictures of old trains and engines all over my walls. I guess in a way the maps are compensating for that; the grownup version of it, I suppose."

"And now that you have a baby, I bet her room is decorated in a transportation theme with posters of trains all over the walls," Mariah guessed.

"No way!" he said gleefully. "Cece's room is Vineyard all the way. And I'm fine with that because once she's old enough, it's going to be train city everywhere! I figured I'd let Pete have his way for now."

Mariah smiled an accomplice's smile, remembering her friend whose son shared the same train obsession. His playroom was full of train tracks, train set tables, and a vast collection of Thomas the Train Engine accessories, which popped up around the house without warning. Mariah told Sean about her friend's son.

"Yeah, that was my childhood," he chuckled. "I am proud to say that at the age of six, I could name a great number of loco-motives. My parents indulged me in my obsession by taking me on train trips, not only across the states, but also to Europe," he added. "I always thought I would end up being an engineer of some sort, but right after college, I read about a trucking com-pany that was offering free training and guaranteed you a job after completion, so I thought, why not? And went for it."

"Wow, so it was a spur of the moment thing?" Mariah asked.

Sean had wrapped up that conversation with, "Yeah, it started out as a short-term adventure, but as it turned out, I really enjoyed it, so I stayed. It was a fine job for a single guy, but now that I'm a married man with a baby, I can see how I might need to reevaluate my job situation."

Now, here in this bar a year later, Mariah glances over at Sean sitting next to Pete. Sean seems less vibrant and optimistic tonight. He appears quiet and distant.

The conversation seems to have morphed into sports as com-ments about possible Red Sox trades are now being discussed; a topic that brought just as much stress to just as many people as did health care.

Jake makes his way back, balancing a beer in one hand and a cloudy-looking cocktail in the other. She recognizes the deli-cious chemical compound.

"Have you thought much about being a dad?" Mariah asks as she reaches over for her agave infused Mezcal. She beams, pleased at his choice.

"Well, it's not something I think about all the time, but yeah, I can definitely see myself being a dad and chasing a few little kiddoes around if it is in the cards. What about you?"

In truth, Mariah had not thought much about being a mother. She grew up as an only child and assumed that someday she would also have a child of her own. There was not much talk about babies in her family. Not the way many parents would hint to their single adult children about finding a mate to marry and procreate.

"Yeah, maybe someday. If it's in the cards," she says, taking a slow sip, envisioning Jake chasing after a herd of children.

EG'S EYES SCANNED THEIR ROOM of guests while Lucas listened attentively to the monologue transpiring between two of them. His face did not hide his astonishment at how people could do that, carry on a conversation with no regard to the listener and his desire to contribute to the conversation.

"Let's go girl. Bathroom break!" he called out, excusing himself as he grabbed Maddy by the collar and walked out the door.

Meg, meanwhile, stood by the kitchen counter staring at the small glass jar, lost in its content. These memories enveloped her in a tight embrace even as her hands arranged and rearranged sweet treats on the dessert tray. The sea glass, feather, marble, and dried-up daisy trapped inside each hid an unspoken story. The back door opened and Lucas walked in with Maddy not far behind. Meg felt a guilty flash as she realized she hadn't noticed Lucas depart moments earlier.

"Nice walk?" she asked, unable to meet his eyes.

Lucas reached for her slender hand, knowingly, and walked her toward the living room to rejoin their visitors, the dessert plate balanced on his free hand. Meg felt his concern flowing through his hand and the familiar voice whispered inside her, "He will leave you again." Meg squeezed his hand tightly.

Lucas read her quiet plea while unspoken memories rushed in with an ease that suggested they were often invited. It had been so easy, so comforting to surrender his body to a total stranger to be cared for, and to experience forgotten carnal pleasure, if just for that one night. He caressed his wedding band with a flicker of guilt. He had walked into a bar and taken his ring off and, just like Frodo Baggins, the realization of an adventure had materialized.

He returned the hand squeeze.

Meg sat on the rug opposite David and Martha Patricks, the couple from across the street, as Lucas placed the dessert plate on the table. She watched him invite their guests to help themselves, then join her on the rug. He raised his glass, inviting her to raise her own half-empty glass of wine. No matter what Lucas did, he was her heart and soul. She knew that she would forgive him. She already had.

"Here it is, to great news," he said.

"To the adoption being finalized!" the couple answered in unison as David brought his phone to life and showed Meg a blurry picture of a baby girl, his proud grandfather smile plastered all over his radiant face.

"Our daughter Joyce just got the call earlier this week. They are flying into Moscow tomorrow to meet with their contact person from the agency, and the following day they'll fly to the orphanage in Vladivostok," he said.

"She is a cutie," Meg commented at the frozen image on the screen. "What's her name?"

"Well, it's kind of complicated," his wife said eagerly. "These kids are given names at birth, so their names become part of who they are, even though some adoptive parents want to mark the transition by renaming the child. You know—new home, new family, new name, well, a new life. A fresh start so to speak. Plus, a lot of those names are ridiculously difficult for Americans to pronounce, so it makes sense for many families to give the child a new American name."

The wife stopped for a moment to look at her husband who had made a throaty sound that could be interpreted as *too much information, dear*. Or perhaps he wanted to add something else. But since he remained silent, the wife saw it as a green light to continue. She went on.

"They haven't decided about the name yet. They want to meet the baby first. Joyce was telling me about her friend's daughter who had to write a school report about where her name came from. She was adopted from Cambodia. Her name was Claire. The poor little creature wrote this whole story about how her parents had a naming ceremony for her when they adopted her and how they had chosen the name Claire because her mother had a best friend named Claire growing up, but her friend had moved away. She missed her so badly that she thought, 'Someday when I have a baby girl, I will name her Claire.' Well, now this little Cambodian girl is writing this report and goes on to say how much she hated the name Claire because it was not her real name."

Meg shifted her legs, wondering when the story was going to end. Why doesn't her husband stop her?

"She wanted her real name back, Bopha or whatever it was," the woman continued. "The name had some special meaning in her language. She told her mother she was going to change her name back when she grew up. I mean, can you imagine? Oh, that poor mother! How ungrateful and selfish is that kid?" She raised her hands and looked to the ceiling in exasperation.

Meg's jaw dropped. It was a common response when listening to her neighbor talk. The only thing the two couples shared was their love of dogs. The Patricks had a friendly Labrador retriever. Her phone buzzed in her back pocket. She pulled it out to check, although she was already certain of the source.

She had two missed calls. She swiped through her texts and smiled to see the sender, her daughter, a beautiful young woman

FLOWERS ON THE WALL

content with living a single life. She had planned to stop by tonight and join them for drinks and desserts with the neighbors, but it looked like she wasn't going to make it. Meg felt the familiar guilt wash over her as she thought about her dutiful daughter who felt the need to call her several times a day. Her pretext, *I am just checking in,* as if to imply she was the one in need of supervision, yet her motive was crystal clear to Meg. *She wants me to be present, still trying to save me from myself.* How hard a reality it had been for Meg to grasp onto the notion that facing the sorrow of two miscarriages and yearning for a deceased daughter did not mean the forsaking of the one still living.

She set the phone back down on the round coffee table, deciding to return Mia's call after the guests have left. Meg braced herself, knowing she would continue to get calls and messages until a contact of some sort was made. She reached back for her phone and texted, "*All is good here,*" then muted the sound.

Meg adored Mia and wanted more than anything to have her undivided attention and endless company. But she knew that was about the most selfish thing a parent could do to an offspring. She tilted her head to look at the large painting over the fireplace and a wave of sadness downturns her mouth at the image of the young girl chasing a colony of seagulls. The excitement on her face matched the strokes of red, orange, and yellow that silenced the blue sky.

Tonight's party was Lucas's idea. He was the socialite of the family. He would find any excuse to have people over. While Meg did not fit the socialite bill, she did possess a candid and easygoing personality. She had a gentle disposition that made people trust her. Perhaps it was her aura of unconsciously gravitating to the suffering of others. Nowadays, though, she much preferred the company of animals if given the choice.

Finally, Meg and Lucas said goodbye to their last guest, Mrs. Connor. It had been another successful gathering, they both agreed.

"Remind me not to invite the Patricks over next time," Lucas joked.

"Don't kid yourself. We both know they will be the first on your list next time, and the one after, and the one after," Meg teased back.

"What about Mrs. Connor?" They both dissolved into laughter.

Mrs. Connor, the widow from one street over, had decided to get a tattoo with the word *Pógmé* along her middle finger.

"She stuck that finger up proudly any chance she got," Lucas chuckled at the Irish translation of "kiss me."

Lucas pulled Meg down on his lap. He wrapped his arms around her and whispered, "How is it that a guy like me ends up with a girl like you?"

Meg stayed there, feeling the warmth of his breath, his strong chest a safe haven. She offered a warm embrace, knowing he carried guilt for having walked away that one time, knowing he had felt suffocated and craved some release. She stood up hesitantly. *I can't tell him about quitting therapy*, she thought as she made her way to the kitchen. She busied herself by putting away all the perishables and washing the large glass platters.

The sounds of Lucas's steps and Maddy's bark interrupted her mental meanderings. He embraced her from behind and buried his face in the nape of her neck. She loved it when he did that. He had a way of finding her and bringing her back home. He inhaled her essence with the urgency of a running vacuum cleaner. They stayed still for a bit, their breaths rhythmically communicating. Meg turned around to face him. He had aged, *we have both aged*, she reflected.

"I'm taking Maddy out for one last walk." He planted a kiss on

Meg's soft lips and grabbed the dog leash by the side door.

"Make sure you take the flashlight or I'm telling on you!" Meg called after him. Lucas grunted playfully. He had promised his daughter that he would take a flashlight on his nightly walks with the dog.

"Come on, Maddy girl!" Lucas called out, clicking the flashlight on and off in Meg's direction. The dog ran out in front of Lucas and the door shut softly behind them.

Meg didn't mind having a quiet moment to herself. At the kitchen sink, the running of the water lured her into the past. It wasn't as frightening to go there anymore. But it was still too painful to bring someone else there with her. The thirty-five years old scars remained just as raw and tender. No shrinks or close friends were ever invited, not even Lucas could navigate those dark alleys buried deep in her memories. She knew that Lucas's quiet evening walks with Maddy gave him a similar solace, a peaceful trip to the most painful of memories.

"WHAT IS WITH HER?" Gus asks Mariah, his head signaling out Eleanor who had dropped her bag on the table abruptly and headed straight to the bar.

"She's in a *don't fuck with me mood* today," Mariah replies. "She yelled at me for picking her up five minutes late and just about chewed out a poor woman in the bathroom who was trying to apologize to her for almost shutting the door in our faces when she didn't realize we were right behind her trying to come in, too."

"And Eleanor was upset that she didn't apologize?" Gus's voice amplifies to match the vibrancy in the room.

"No, quite the opposite. She was upset that the woman felt that she owed us an apology," Mariah says as she reads over the "*I'm running late* message" from Max. She turns her phone off after a quick "*OK*" reply and places it in her bag following the no-phone-at-the-table rule the four friends had agreed upon.

"I'm confused. Was that not a nice thing to say? I'll take a sorry any day," Gus says.

"Well, that was kind of Eleanor's point. She thinks women apologize way too much. She thinks women would be more respected if we stopped over-apologizing. She actually told the woman that she didn't have to apologize, which scared the heck out of her."

"So what was she supposed to say instead of saying sorry? Obviously she didn't want to be a jackass by smashing the door in your face," Gus says.

Mariah waves her pointer finger for emphasis, in beat with her words. "She told the woman, 'Don't apologize! Next time just say: Here! Let me get that for you. I meant to keep it open.' I mean, she schooled the poor woman as if she were a first grader."

"I get it," Gus says. "Leave out the sorry part. Only say sorry when you've done something wrong, kind of thing. I'll have to remember that."

"Gus, this is meant for women. Your gender should be working on doing *more* apologizing, not less." She mock-dismisses him with the back of her hand.

"Well, it looks like she's going to be fine." Gus points over at Eleanor chatting with the bar owner, a middle-aged charismatic hippie-type who from time to time pops into the bar to chat with the patrons, his upbeat personality infused by the spirit of alcohol or drugs—or both.

Mariah follows Gus's gaze, her neck stretched out to see through the crowd, a combination of first timers and tight-knit regulars much like themselves. Mariah lets out a satisfying smile as she takes in the scene around her, welcoming the loud laughs that accompany the constant clatter of dishes. It isn't just the stellar bartenders who draw them to this dark and high spirited three-section bar time and time again. It is rather the charm of the rustic feel that Mariah, particularly, enjoys. They rarely ever venture onto the top floor where the live music and dance floor were, or to the small game room in the back where the college flock battle through a game on the dart board and pool table.

"Yeah, this place has that magic power of erasing your blues." Mariah says.

Eleanor remains at the bar. The chirpy owner has hopped along and the attention is now replaced by the familiar barkeep.

"Try this," he says, handing Eleanor a colorful late summer cocktail.

Eleanor wedges herself closer to the counter and takes a hasty sip of the drink. Her second swallow erupts in her head, lighting up her senses. She lifts the glass and takes in the pulpy syrup slowly dancing its way down to the bottom. She feels her skin sizzle then delights at how quickly it ceases, leaving instead a refreshing coolness.

"The secret is in the smooth peach puree and rhubarb bitters," the barkeep says, adding a playful wink.

"God dammit Tommy, you never disappoint me."

She takes one more gulp before maneuvering back to the table.

"Move over," she orders Gus, pushing her body onto the bench.

"What is it with you today?" Mariah asks as Eleanor squeezes in next to her.

"Are you mad at me for yelling at that woman?" Eleanor asks, her head resting on Mariah's shoulder. "Because you know, I am not going to apologize for it, right? I was just expressing my frustration, and women should be allowed to do that without feeling judged. It doesn't make me a bitch, you know!"

"No, it just makes you an ass," Gus says.

"Honestly, I am just tired of playing games in this chauvinistic world. No matter what, we women always get shortchanged."

"So, what happened?" Mariah asks.

"You know how I have been working to launch a new series of recipes for my gluten-free clients?"

"Yeah, you're working with that grain. Not quinoa, the one that looks like a poppy seed," Mariah says.

"That's right. It's called teff. Quinoa is becoming a thing of the past even though it's an incredible superfood. But people like to move on to new trends, so teff is the flavor of the month."

"What makes it special? Is it just that it's gluten free? Or is it packed with anti-wrinkle pixie dust?" Gus asks with thinly veiled sarcasm.

"The grain is great. It definitely holds its ground compared to quinoa," Mariah says. "It is high in minerals, protein, and fiber. We've used it in some of our baking recipes in the past because it adds a nice fluffiness to breads, but my goal is to create easy, everyday dinner meals with it. And while it doesn't have anti-aging properties, some consider it a great weight management food. A lot of people like it because of its nutty taste, which is ideal for savory dishes."

Eleanor pauses to take a long sip of Mariah's water. "I have been working with this teff supply company out of California," she continues. "The Ethiopian government has a very tight grip on the grain and is restricting exportation; there's a lot of fake teff on the market. So, this multimillion-dollar company is run by two brothers: the shithead twins. Their business carries the top-quality stuff, but they have no scruples. You place an order only to find out that your shipment has been sold to someone else. We have been ready all week waiting for the order. We had the photographer, the chefs, and the beautiful fresh ingredients all lined up. We also had over two thousand cute little promotional boxes waiting for their sample-size teff pancake mix." Eleanor feels the tension clawing her muscles, her clenching fists giving an unconscious pound on the table as she remembers the conversation she had with the supplier.

"The turds wouldn't return my calls for days so I called them up again this morning, totally enraged. It wasn't until I told one of the supply managers that I had been in touch with my lawyer and was ready to sue their asses off that one of the jerks got on the phone.

"They tried to feed me some pathetic bullshit about the weather in Ethiopia and how it had affected the crop. To which I said 'Fine, then shorten everyone's order and let everyone walk away with some.' But no, they wouldn't do that for most of their clients. They couldn't cut down their orders, he said. So I said, 'Then why the fuck did you cut me out?' And do you know what this asshole's response was? He said, 'That's the nature of the business and why don't you man up, get over it, and stop being a bitchy cunt.'" Eleanor lowers her eyes and takes a sip of her drink.

"And there you have it. Not only do they cheat me out of my pallet of teff; they send me off with a title of a pussy bitch." Her voice shakes as she speaks.

"To hell with those caca face losers," Gus says.

"Yeah. I know. It's just that it stinks to be treated like that. I am sure their male clients don't get the bully-special they gave me. Those misogynistic assholes."

"Here," Mariah hands Eleanor her cocktail. "A toast to businesswomen around the world for putting up with men with really small penises who try to compensate by being jackass pigs. May you continue to have the courage to piss on them any chance you get."

As they put down their glasses, she goes around the table with her eyes, pausing at each friend for suspense. "Anyone interested in hearing about where Jake is swooping me off to next weekend?"

"Oh, this better be fucking good!" Eleanor feels her shoulders relax.

"Hi Mia!"

"Hi Momma!" Meg's daughter picked up on the second ring. "How was the party?"

"It was fun. Great! We had a really good time."

"And how is Daddy doing? Did you let him get away with building his own chocolate fountain out of recycled milk jugs?" They both laughed at the mention of the chocolate fountain.

"I promised him he could do it for the holiday party this year. Let's hope he forgets." Her comment made her daughter laugh.

Lucas was a tinkerer, had been all his life, finding any excuse to build things under the pretense of crafting useful things for his girls.

"What about the car?" her daughter wanted to know. Meg's initial silence revealed more than she wanted to declare.

"We are getting there," Meg finally said.

"I'm just glad that he has finally agreed to let go of the old pickup truck."

Lucas had agreed to get a new car, not because he thought that the old truck was unsafe, but because it would bring his daughter some peace of mind.

"He's been reading about new car models," Meg said. "You know your father. He does not trust the new automatic engines with all their digital bells and whistles, but he's trying to be open-minded. He's studying all about the engines. My only request is that it's simple."

"I really think you and Dad should at least go for a test drive." She had been making the case for an eco-friendly car. "I really don't understand what the hesitation is, Mom. They really are not as complicated as you make them out to be."

Her parents' apprehension about getting a smart car or even a hybrid was due to her mother's lack of confidence with technology. She trusted things that she understood, or that, if broken, her husband could fix. She was in awe of the advancements in the auto industry, but only from afar: Cars that turn on by a quick press of a button while the driver sits at the kitchen table sipping her morning coffee; cars all warmed up inside by the time the driver grips the steering wheel. She was a bit more incredulous about the self-driving models. Now *that* was something she never imagined she would see in her lifetime. Technology was a moving train going at a blistering speed, and she was happy not to be on board.

It's not that Meg was a technology grouch. Her daughter knew she had embraced many aspects of it, especially her smart phone, a Mother's Day gift from Lucas several years back. She had gone into the store for the complimentary class and learned the basic functionality.

She even let Lucas convince her to use the navigation app. Meg tried it once, but considered it a big distraction, so she stuck to her old GPS navigation device.

"I'll come by this week and we can do some research together." Meg gave a faint confirmation, but her daughter knew she saw through her ruse to purchase a smart car.

Just before her mother hung up, she asked, "Is Dad out with Maddy?" The dogs were always "the girls," at least that was how Lucas referred to them. But if the girls were asked, they would utter a very different opinion. In as much as "the girls" loved the dogs, Maddy now and Topper before her, when the girls were younger, the dogs belonged to Lucas. They knew it, and the dogs' loyalty to him validated that truth.

MARIAH HAD LIVED ON HER OWN since graduating from college, but her apartments had always been within close proximity to her parents. She never felt that she could venture too far away. Her parents tried to convince her to live abroad, but their efforts were in vain. Her sense of duty kept her near. Her mother was forever accusing her of being an Old Soul, and Mariah had resented the title, knowing that she was never given a choice.

She walks into her tidy kitchen, unpacks the containers of Mexican takeout, and sets them noisily on the countertop. Jake is planning to come over, but not until later tonight. He has been dealing with renovations in the old farmhouse he rented before he moved the rest of his furniture in. The house required much needed updates. The owner had tried to sell it without success, so he'd gladly taken Jake's offer to restore the house in exchange for the rental fee.

The contractors had finished painting the walls the week before. They were now working on installing light fixtures and carpeting. Jake couldn't stop talking about the view from the large kitchen windows into the woods. The rush of October colors emanating from the thicket made it difficult to look away. Mariah could only imagine how beautiful it would be with the trees heavily topped with New England snow.

When Jake mentioned his decision to rent a house outside the city, Andrew quickly offered their in-law apartment. It was a small, but comfortable suite separate from the main house and adjacent to the resort-style pool. Jake had declined the offer. He was not fully comfortable with the idea of being a long-term guest and imposing on his friends.

Mariah clicks on her phone to find out the reason for the beeping sounds alerting her of a missed call. She reads Max's name on the voicemail screen.

"Can I call you now?" she texts.

"On my way home. Will call you in a few," he responds.

Mariah takes out a veggie burrito and sets it on a plate. The tip of a sugary churro sticks out of the brown bag and she gives it two small nibbles. She twists the opening of the bag, leaving the remainder of the fried dough inside and hides the evidence behind the boxes of organic granola cereals where it joins her secret stash of sweets. She has been conscious about her sugar intake ever since the other night when she noticed Jake staring at the large woman eating a generous helping of Oreo cheesecake. Was that disgust she'd read on his face? She had been enjoying her own slice of heaven, but quickly lost interest and pushed it aside after he said, *"You and that woman are having the same dessert."* She grabs the pile of napkins from the takeout bag.

"Seriously?"

It annoys her to no end the number of napkins takeout restaurants wasted.

Mariah bites into the large burrito and squirts of *crema* drip down the corner of her mouth. She grabs a clump of napkins from the restaurant's pile, deciding she would exempt Mexican restaurants from the list of napkin-wasting establishments.

Her phone rings. "What's cooking, good looking?" Max asks. He reserves that playful greeting for her and Eleanor.

Mariah starts talking about Jake. They had just celebrated their one-year anniversary, and sparks continue to burn like red embers in the belly of a dormant volcano. Her attraction to Jake goes beyond physical. "He is like a cryptic box, a lovable bundle waiting to be deciphered," she had joked earlier with Eleanor.

"And how are your people?" Max asks after a few minutes.

Mariah recognizes his courteous attempt to shift away from Mariah's love story monologue. Mariah knows that Jake is still not on Max's list of favorite people. That although he had gotten used to the idea that Jake had become a perpetual element in Mariah's life, he is not going to do a happy dance every time she blows in Jake's name.

Mariah understands the subtle hint and forces herself to focus on her folks, the subjects of Max's inquiry. It is no secret how Mariah's parents feel about Max. She knows they secretly hoped she and Max would end up together. They had always favored him even over Rafael whom they adored. She feels a pang of guilt at the soulmate she had presented to her parents. It had taken many interactions with Jake for them to even start to arrive at a place of trust. Mariah notices they had ceased bringing up their constant Wall Street horror stories, her first indication of hope.

Mariah had used her skills to formulate and introduce convincing arguments at key moments to shine a much-needed light on their acceptance of Jake. Her parents originally mistrusted the New Yorker for the same reasons Mr. Hobbs, her building doorman, had. But just like Mr. Hobbs, Mariah had guided Jake in how to earn her parents' trust.

"My folks are fine," she responds. "I swear, though, the older they get, the more childish they become. They go on and on like those babushka dolls, except in reverse," she says, shaking her head with a smile.

"And growing younger is a bad thing because…?" Max teases.

"You try reasoning with them next time my dad needs to be convinced that it's not a good idea to ride his bike to the store in the middle of winter. It was a losing battle last winter. Mom told me he just ordered new tires to winterize his bike."

She walks to the living room and perches on the sofa, knowing the chat will last awhile.

"I went by today to drop off some dinner only to find my Mom perched on a ladder cleaning the gutters and my Dad working on his bike," she says. "This is after they'd spent all afternoon raking leaves. There were about ten bags of leaves lined up on the curb when I got there. I didn't bother picking a fight about that. They just would have lied about paying the neighborhood kids to help with the raking. They are impossible. They think they are still teenagers."

"Look at it this way, at least they are not moping around the house in their pajamas all day."

"True," she laughs.

There is a small pause and for a sliver of a moment Mariah is transported back to the time when her mother had lived with her for a brief period after Mariah's father moved out. Mariah had been too afraid to ask why, yet she often noticed the suspicious ways her mother stared at women when her father was around. Even so, her parents patched things up and moved on with their marriage as if whatever happened had been just an unpleasant hiccup.

"What about our lovely Luna?" Mariah asks before her own doubts and jealousy set in.

"She's good, but always so busy," Max responds casually, though Mariah could translate the hidden message in his deflated voice.

Mariah knows Luna is a sensitive subject for Max these days. It is clear he had fallen head over heels for her, but Luna has other priorities. She is working on finishing up her dissertation while holding down two part-time jobs to make ends meet. Max had offered multiple times to help her financially, but she refuses to accept any money from him.

Mariah's heart aches for Max. She offered to speak to Luna on his behalf to explain to her that money had very little meaning for Max, that his offer did not come with strings attached. She wanted to tell Luna how in love he was with her and how it broke his heart to see her working so hard when he could easily cover the cost of her apartment and school tuition just to make life a bit easier for her.

"I am still happy to talk to her, Max," Mariah offers.

"That's OK. I don't want her to think we are ganging up on her. She gets upset at me every time I bring up the subject. I don't want her getting upset at you, too."

Mariah loves how natural and easy it feels to talk to Max. They had been the closest of the four college friends. Max had been her confidant, the first person she called for a word of comfort or vote of approval.

"And how are *your* people?" Mariah asks.

"You know, same old, same old. My sisters are running around as busy as always. They have been putting a lot of time and money into creating business opportunities facilitated through the free trade market government program. I helped them a little bit with the legal part of it, but you know me. I can only take that drink in small doses. I swear, it's like taking a laxative. But the company generated massive growth. It was a very profitable decision as far as revenues are concerned."

His voice becomes quieter. "I've got to tell you, though, I'm grateful that they married partners who love and support them. I think those guys keep them grounded."

"It's too bad they have to live overseas," Mariah says, knowing how much it would mean for Max to have his family closer.

"I guess that's the trade-off you make. They have to be able to manage and monitor the business closely. But my youngest sister is actually moving back to Houston. It sounds like she plans to stay in Texas and commute to Mumbai for business.

"I know they're happy with the lives they've chosen. I guess

I am just bemused at how well they seem to be able to manage their professional and personal lives. I wish I were a little bit more like them sometimes. They seem to thrive in that environment, while it would choke me to death.

"That's great news about her moving back though. When is that happening?" Mariah briefly imagines Max's childhood long ago. She remembers his stories about his younger sister following him around, her Disney princess dress getting in her way and tripping her. No doubt he felt a special connection to his younger sister.

"Soon. Before Thanksgiving anyway."

"Oh great! Will everyone just meet in Houston for Thanksgiving then?" Mariah asks.

"Yeah."

"And are you planning on going down to see them?" Mariah asks, her tone encouraging.

"I haven't decided yet. I know I should. I just can't deal with their constant questioning about my future plans. At times it feels like they resent that I don't want to join the family business. I don't think they quite understand how much I don't like doing that work."

"Maybe they're not so much resentful as they're hopeful."

"Yeah. Maybe."

"You should definitely go, though. You always come back happy and glad you did. Plus, think about your nieces. They love their Uncle Max. It would be great for them to see you." Mariah knows Max had a soft spot when it came to his nieces.

"What do you think about me bringing Luna down to meet them?" Max asks hesitantly.

Mariah knows he had already told one of his sisters about Luna, and she had burst into cheers and encouraged him to bring her down for Thanksgiving.

"Are you worried about your sisters, Luna, or yourself?" she asks. She remembers how Max had shared with her Luna's reaction when he had asked her to move in with him. "I think I freaked her out with the moving in together idea," he had told her.

"Me? There is nothing I would like more than to introduce Luna to my family. You know those people that laugh easily? Well, my sisters are not like that. Plus, I worry that Luna might feel I am pressuring her. She keeps saying how she wants to take this relationship slowly. And I worry about Luna's reaction to the lavish ways my sisters live. I haven't seen the house in Houston, but I can promise you it is some extravagant mansion. I just don't want to screw things up, you know?"

"I think your sisters are going to love Luna to pieces. I hope she decides to go down with you. They will be relieved to see how kind and wonderful Luna is and Luna will see how crazy your sisters are about you. They'd probably be relieved that they won't be stuck taking care of their old maid of a brother forever," Mariah teases.

"Damn, who can blame them? I wouldn't want to be stuck with myself either. I would make a very cranky, lonely old man," he chuckles.

Part Three

oh, delicate friend
visitor from the south
you tell the story of long ago
majestic magnolia
waltzing with love and lust

OVING HIS BUSINESS TO a new state had proven a much more cumbersome task than Jake had anticipated. He sometimes finds himself doubting his decision and wondering if he should have stayed at his old job to face the allegations head on. Should he have listened to his lawyer when he tried to persuade him to stay, reassuring him that *his misunderstood comments* were a common thing in this alpha business and would not end his career, "just stop meeting with women behind closed doors."

But as soon as those doubts visit, a faint voice inside his head perks up just in time to remind him of his limited options.

"You fucked up," says the inward timbre.

Jake follows his instincts, yet the resentment he feels for his old boss is raw and bitter. He hears the voice of the president of the company ring in his memory: "One of the women is suing for monetary compensation, but the others want some sort of public apology and I don't think you want that, none of us do. I think a resignation might be prudent."

Jake understood the unspoken choices: Stay and have his employer quietly settle the claims, but keep a close watch over his affairs, or leave the company and start somewhere new and answer to no one.

Jake had been busy meeting with clients all morning, many of whom had decided to stay on even though Jake was moving his operation to Boston. Jake was relieved. His lawyer said, "It has nothing to do with being loyal, and everything to do with the fact that you keep adding a substantial number of digits to their bank accounts each year. Jake, you're a money-making machine. They don't care who you fuck. They know they'd be fools not to stick with you."

Jake signed the final papers of the sale of his NYC penthouse and the movers are meeting him there now. At 212 West 18th Street, he walks around with a pang of nostalgia as he says a final goodbye to his home for almost six years.

"What's her name?" the realtor asks, collecting the paper-work of the sale into a neat little pile.

"Nah, no girl. Just a job. But I guess that's about the same thing, isn't it?" he answers, dangling a hint of flirt.

"Well, I hope your…" she pauses to create dramatic fingers quotes, "…jooob appreciates what you are leaving behind," she adds with a conspiring smile. She folds the newspaper ad into the pile with an air of contentment.

Jake knows she's happy with the sale. They don't come easier than this. The luxurious, jaw-dropping floor-to-ceiling windows with 360° panoramic views of the most amazing city landscape in the world and the beautiful rooftop garden with its gorgeous view of the Hudson River had gotten over a dozen offers on the spot. The lucky buyer offered one million over the asking price as a result of the bidding war and, as the realtor had told him, had handed her an additional check for ten thousand dollars, "for all your troubles," he said.

"Would you like to grab a drink to celebrate the sale? It's on me, of course," asks the hopeful realtor.

His, "Thanks, but I kind of have to run," response comes out so spontaneously that even Jake is surprised. "I'm trying to avoid rush hour," he quickly adds.

He stares at the mail neatly stacked on the kitchen counter and then sorts through the pile, the last crumbs of connection to his apartment. A shiny official envelope catches his eye. He tears off the top of the envelope and flicks through the personal-ized thank-you letter inside. He stares at the words: *We are most grateful for your generous donation and we thank you for your continued support, Team Barrett.* The signature at the bottom of the letter feels like a dagger making its unhurried way to his core.

Jake's phone vibrates in his jacket pocket, helping him release the nagging feeling of confession. How could he explain to Mariah that this move to Boston has nothing to do with being a prince charming, as she sometimes called him, and more to do with being a selfish coward, as he often calls himself. How many times had he been on the verge of telling her the truth or at least some version of it, only to change his mind at the very last minute. His speech rehearsed in front of the mirror memorized to perfection: *I got in a bit of trouble at the office—some big misunderstanding and my boss gave me the choice of resigning and leaving quietly, taking some of my clients with me, or face the sexual harassment allegations.* He had envisioned so many scenarios and guessed each time at what Mariah's response would have been at the mention of sexual harassment. But he had a response prepared for that as well: *Of course it's all a big fat lie, but it was all becoming too much of a nuisance to deal with, so I left.* The image of a disappointed Mariah walking away from his life had been the safeguard for his unlawful behavior.

Jake places the *Team Barrett* letter back inside the envelope and tosses it into the trashcan under the sink. He reassures himself that his monetary contributions to the Barrett campaign were just a business investment, an insurance of sorts. *How could Mariah fault me for that?*

He drops the handful of mail into the side pocket of his rugged saddleback leather briefcase, waves goodbye to the realtor who is scribbling something illegible on a yellow notepad, and then makes his way to the underground garage to retrieve his BMW.

His eyes quickly adjust to the commotion, the imperfect cohesive tapestry of the street, an anthology of sounds, fumes, flashes, and pirouetting flags. At the approaching intersection he reels in the impulse to speed through the yellow light, and taps the green phone icon on the dashboard.

"Hi, Love," Mariah's melodic voice resonates through the speakers, and the *Team Barrett* dagger tunnels in deeper.

"I'm leaving the city just now. I'm sorry. It's much later than I had planned," Jake says apologetically. "I was hoping to drive right to your place tonight, if that is OK."

"I hoped you would, as a matter of fact," she says flirtatiously. "I'm watching a show about bizarre animal practices. They're talking about porcupine mating."

"Gee, that's a scary thought. I feel sorry for those poor fellas," Jake jokes.

"It's the females you should feel pity for. Those poor girls only have an eight- to twelve-hour fertility window a year. Listen to this: They attract their mates by urinating from high up in a tree. Fine, it's not very romantic. But then they go around rubbing their genitals all over the tree to lure the male with the strong scent."

"Kinky. I like it."

"It gets better." Mariah explains how the female porcupine takes advantage of her arousal and will have sex with many partners of her choosing until the male porcupines become so sexually exhausted they almost pass out.

She continues to enlighten Jake with animal mating rituals, giggling with delight at the beauty of the animal world. She explains, with awe in her voice, about the exploding and snapping of bee drones' genitals after mating, the two penises of the garter snakes, and the dolphin penis's ability to swivel and explore objects much the same as a hand.

Jake listens, feeling the animal galloping of his own heartbeat. He smiles and presses down on the gas pedal just a bit harder.

I T WAS A CRISP DECEMBER morning. The weather forecast predicted snow showers over the weekend, but not a single flake materialized. Meg grabbed the crossword puzzle from the dining room table and made her way to the kitchen. She placed it on the counter next to a pencil and set to work. A rustling sound from outside stopped her after she had filled in several clues. Meg stood up and wiped her hands rhythmically on the side of her pants, dusting away an invisible legion of dust as she walked to the window.

Outside, the trees along the fence stood erect and alert, silently touching the edge where the clouds came down to meet them. Though fall was long gone, some clusters of bright orange maple leaves hung stubbornly on the lower branches. *I don't blame you,* she whispered, and let her eyes follow the path leading to the old shed. She shook away the urge to walk into the old shed and lock the door behind her, to be swallowed by the darkness. *The night of the ambulance* snuck in and wrapped her memory tight. That's how the quiet voice inside her head had come to call that night, too painful to be given any other name.

The paramedics rushed her in the stretcher, the florescent ceiling lights burning her pupils. The tangled mound of thin tubing and IV lines was piled up on top of Meg like a ravenous anaconda. A hallucinatory sensation replaced the pain. It must have been the painkillers. She was annoyed at Lucas for not telling the paramedics that she didn't like drugs in her body.

Meg remembered reaching for her middle to find her round belly and how relieved she had felt. A buzzing sound kept her alert. There were voices, loud voices, at first. Then more voices, concerned voices. The voices became muffled sounds that fought to stay on top, but the medications were strong, the sounds eventually drowning, until even the voices were gone.

The light blue nightgown she had worn that night had been one of the earliest Valentine's gifts from Lucas, so long ago. It is curious how something so trivial can stick in your memory like a vicious, hungry parasite. She wondered what had become of it. Did someone at the hospital try to wash away the evidence? Or did someone (there is always a someone) know that by choosing the fate of the gown for her that night, it would save her the agony of a decision someday? She was grateful to that someone.

The sound of the creaking side door startled her. Lucas walked into the living room holding a small paper bag. He looked at Meg, a showdown of concern on his face. She conjured a reassuring smile at the comforting set of eyes, those deep forest brown eyes she adored. Their constant reminder of how wrong her parents had been. They had warned her about her choice when she brought Lucas home to meet her family that first time. She assumed her progressive New England parents would be fine with the tall brown scholar at the door. It wasn't until days later when her mother questioned her about the seriousness of the relationship, saying, "Your grandparents will not approve of him," that she realized their own racial intolerance.

"I brought us some ice cream for an afternoon snack," he declared, hoping to distract her.

"Good thinking. Maybe that will help bring the snow!" She pretended to be surprised at his ice-cream indulgence.

Lucas enjoyed ice cream with childhood fervor. They lived just a short walk from the town's main shopping center where an ice cream parlor featured a vast variety of homemade flavors. When they bought their house, Meg knew this was one of the selling points for Lucas. The idea of walking down the street for ice cream was something that brought him a great amount of contentment.

She also knew that for Lucas, it wasn't just about the ice cream. It was the memories it conjured up. His father had been in the ice-cream business. He had learned to make ice cream and then gone off to Nashville to start his own ice-cream store before venturing further into the food industry by opening his first restaurant. He had partnered up with an old high school friend to start the ice-cream store and, together, they began the adventure of a lifetime.

The enterprise had ended years before Lucas was born when his father sold the stores to his partner. But his father continued to make homemade ice cream every Sunday. While many of his friends were at church, Lucas was at home happily churning ice cream by hand.

Meg reached for the bag and took out the vanilla ice cream. She smiled at the predictability of the moment. Vanilla for her, chocolate for him, nice and simple. Meg nodded with pleasure.

The crossword puzzle made its way to the top of the catalog pile. Meg will go back to it before bed tonight, while Lucas reads. She pulled out a set of small bowls from the cupboard, her daughters' old ice-cream bowls, a Christmas gift from Lucas's parents an eternity ago. She scooped out a regular serving of the ice cream in each bowl and handed Lucas his helping.

*T*HE SMOOTH MOTION of the silk scarf feels soothing. It distracts Mariah momentarily from the phone conversation with Rafael. She rubs it between her index finger and thumb, delighting in its glistening sheen.

For a quick moment her mind jumps to last night. Jake had noticed the open box on the bed. "From your secret admirer?" he had asked with an edge to his voice while pointing at Rafael's card. She let his question linger, but his searching eyes waited for a response.

"It's just a Christmas gift, Jake," she had said, trying to keep her voice level. She felt the familiar tug of war between her heart and brain. While her heart pumped excitedly and justified his jealous actions, her mind sent flashing cautionary signals. *He follows the scent of every beaver's butt that walks by, ready to pounce. How many of them has he fucked behind your back?*

Mariah folds the obedient fabric and snuggles it gently in the bottom drawer of her lingerie chest. She adjusts the phone against her ear and climbs into bed, returning to her conversation with Rafael. They had been discussing the new hype over manuka honey.

"I ran into two women at the supermarket," she says. "They were talking about how manuka has tons of natural antibiotics. They're using it to treat diabetes and even for curing cancer. You don't actually believe that, do you?"

"What can I say, girl? I believe what I see."

"No, you don't. Rafa, you spend your days hanging out with things you can't see," Mariah teases, pulling absentmindedly at a curl behind her neck.

"You are unequivocally right, and that's exactly what I love the most about my job. I know those bacteria are there even if we can't see them."

"Oh cute, just like *The Little Prince* and his rose."

"Most definitely," Rafael laughs. "Although I tell you, whenever we reach any major breakthrough, it's not the Little Prince I relate to. I have this crazy moment of total euphoria. It must have been how God felt during creation."

"I see. We believe in God now. Wait, no! We think we *are* God." She imagines Rafael sitting on his throne and giggles at the thought.

"I'm just saying," he continues, his tone completely serious. "It's not so much that we are playing at being God, it's the fact that we are being God. I mean, I can make those bacteria do things even if I can't see them." He pauses for effect. "I can make them fart. Chica, I can make them poop!"

"Now that's too much information. I don't want to think about my yogurt being a cup of bacteria farts and poop." She quickly wipes away the image forming in her mind.

"Don't worry. Those are nice, polite, well-behaved, and good bacteria. Your guts will thank you for consuming them."

"Hold on, back to the honey, though. Was that woman right?"

"I don't know much about it, but it makes sense, given the bioactive properties of the manuka flower's nectar." Rafael goes on to talk about bees in general, emphasizing the job of the worker bees and how they pass on the nectar through an intricate tongue-to-tongue maneuver.

"Great, you're telling me that honey is nothing more than sticky regurgitated sweet syrup," Mariah humors him.

"I know, right? It's deliciously repulsive," he laughs. "Speaking of which, we flew in this group of high schoolers from London. They published a fascinating paper on mosquito saliva."

"Mosquito spit?" Mariah asks, not wanting to miss any key information.

"Well, no. But they do produce saliva and they inject some of it while blood-feeding which, by the way, only the females do. Male mosquitoes don't feast on blood; they feed on nectar and water. Anyway, for most people the reaction is a minor itch, but for others it elicits a bigger allergic reaction. These kids have been able to map out the proteins and chemicals in the mosquito saliva. It's not an original work by any means, but it was quite nice to see their excitement in presenting their work. By the way, you would appreciate this part! There were eight girls and three boys on the team."

"Nice! *Mujeres al poder*! Right? Women power! Does your mom still say that?"

"That's right. Funny that you remember that." He seems pleased.

"How is she?" Mariah asks, visualizing the five-foot-tall woman with the thunderous laugh.

"She is good. Keeps nagging me to fly down for a visit. It's been several years since I visited Mosquito Land."

"Those vicious Dominican mosquitoes will be happy to see you too," Mariah laughs.

"No kidding! I tell you, those little suckers managed to trespass the screen fortress no matter how tightly my grandma tucked the net between the mattresses. I would wake up in the morning to find half a dozen little vampires lounging around belly up, too heavy with my blood to make an escape."

"And then you took revenge?" She imagines little mosquitoes wearing miniature capes and bloodstained tuxedos.

"Nah, I'd lift the net open and shuck them off. You know, they were just doing their thing—trying to survive like anyone else."

Mariah ends the call and stares at her phone, her mind back to the scarf incident.

Rafael also holds onto his phone, then slowly sets it down on his desk. A sad smile flashes across his face. He had wanted to ask Mariah about Jake, but decided to hold back. He had known about his existence since that long email he got from her over a year ago, and had been keeping a close eye on Jake's affairs since then. Rafael had been waiting to hear about the level of commitment of the relationship from Mariah.

He is concerned about many of the things he had discovered about Jake and is hoping to be wrong. Rafael learned Jake had managed currency hedge funds for many years, including some real estate hedge funds in Singapore. He had scrolled through dozens of pictures of Jake surrounded by beautiful, young Singaporean women. He interpreted that as a sign that Jake liked attention from the ladies. But then he had learned that Jake had some connections and dealings with high-ranking officials there. He hoped, for Mariah's sake, that those were legal dealings.

Rafael learned that Jake had some questionable business practices closer to home as well. He had started out working for a large hedge fund company that bought out fledgling companies and then turned them around to be sold for handsome profits. There seemed to have been some scandal of laundered money surrounding one of those companies at the time of his departure, but Rafael couldn't find out the extent of Jake's involvement. With a shake of his head, he resolves to let go of his concerns. *Mariah is not going to put up with any nonsense,* he reassures himself.

Mariah sets her phone on her night table. She gives the pillow a gentle fluff and turns off the light switch. *Rafa dear, I am in a serious relationship with Jake,* she whispers.

"Mariah, you are such a wimp," she scolds herself. She had the intention of telling Rafael about the seriousness of her commitment to Jake, but had lacked the courage once again. She reaches for her phone in the dark and types a quick message to Rafael, but stops to ponder whether she should send it. Her finger taps the send button before she can change her mind.

WHILE MANY OF THE GIRLS her age were dealing with body image issues, Meg remembered how her daughter had seemed confident in her own body. When one of her closest friends was dealing with bulimia, her daughter had come to Meg for suggestions on how to support her friend.

There were also rumors about girls in her grade who were cutting their own arms. Meg was terrified. She overheard a parent comment after a PTO meeting about how many teenagers and even preteens engage in this self-destructive practice as a way to self-regulate their emotions.

She went into her daughter's room in tears that night and sat on her bed. Her daughter was working on a social studies project. Meg took her daughter's hands in hers, tears cascading like a broken faucet.

"Is everything OK at school?" she asked.

"Mom, why are you crying?" her daughter's face was full of anguish.

"There is all this talk about kids in your grade hurting themselves. I just wanted to make sure that you know if there is anything happening in your life right now that is worrying you, you can tell Dad and me. I know you also have lots of teachers at school that you love and trust. Honey please, promise me that you would never do anything to hurt yourself, please."

Meg's sobbing erupted in anguish. She knew better than to show this much emotional vulnerability to her daughter. She worried that it made her look unstable and weak. But her daughter embraced her gently.

"Momma, please don't cry. I promise, I'm fine." She was

unable to meet her mother's eyes since her own tears began as a pang of guilt settled deep in her core.

"Please don't cry," she said, cautiously pulling her arms away, afraid the faint lines decorating the inside of her thin arms would betray her.

*A*T SIX O'CLOCK on a crisp-cold Thursday morning, Jake waits, espresso in hand, at a West Village café. He reads carefully over his notes and a satisfying smile emerges. *Show time,* he whispers to himself, ready to charm a new client who is considering a significant real estate investment in Singapore.

Jake had been in New York City all week. Although it had been over a year since he moved his business to Boston, he continued to travel back and forth to meet up with clients. He is flying back to Boston tonight and then continuing on to Singapore in the morning.

There were several clients whom he had helped secure property investments in Singapore back in the '90s, and they had just about tripled their investments. That success had brought in several new clients.

Jake thinks about the first time he ventured into this business in Singapore. It had happened by chance, an opportunity of sorts. He had been sitting at a bar conversing with a client who was looking for counsel on what to do with a huge sum of money that needed to be *moved pronto,* the client had explained, a little flustered, not from the amount of ale he had ingested, but from the realization of the serious ramifications of what he was asking. Jake heard the urgency in the man's voice and quickly saw an opportunity.

"We could set up an offshore account using a shell company." Jake had suggested tentatively.

His client listened with great interest, Jake's confidence masking his lack of experience and vast ignorance on the matter. With the fierce ambition of a young stockbroker propelled by the possibility of a quick and handsome financial gain to support his online gambling, Jake dove into the project head-on.

Through some other investment dealings, Jake had built business connections in Singapore and used some of those contacts to navigate the government regulations.

Jake put the necessary paperwork in motion, and two months later, he received government approval and was ready to proceed with the trip to finalize the deal. That first trip had required Jake to remain in Singapore for over a month. Although foreigners were required to undergo a detailed application process, Jake had convinced his client that the fastest way to receive approval was for him to invest in a small local business.

"This will be a write-off business with no major financial gains for you as it mainly benefits the locals," Jake had explained to his client. "But the contribution to the government officials will speed along the process."

"You are a bribing guru," the client had joked, and although Jake felt proud of the title, he shook his head and answered, "It's the power of persuasion and greed. We all want something or someone that we cannot have. So, it's as simple as knowing what people want and presenting the offer on a silver platter."

"A deal that leaves everyone feeling happy is a pretty darn good deal in my book!" his client had joked, unaware of the money flowing directly into Jake's personal account instead of the fictitious local businesses.

Jake felt a pang of satisfaction remembering how in no time he had found a way to funnel not only his client's cash flow into a legitimate bank account back in the USA, but also his own. Now, ten years later, he was proud of the efficient network he had put in place. Jake underlined the *Helping Hands* heading on his notes. It was the name of the private charity company he was setting up for this new client. Jake smiled at his good fortune of attracting eager investors, his mind's eye projecting his generous profit from this shell company.

The *tsch, tsch, tsch* of the milk frother machine calls his attention. He eyes the wall clock with the words "Coffee Time" steaming out of a coffee mug and sips the last bit of his espresso as he thinks about Mariah's last-minute decision not to accompany him on this trip tomorrow. He tries to ignore his sense of relief.

"WHAT IF I BOOK US a room at the hotel right by the airport? I will even insist they find us a room on the thirteenth floor," Mariah had offered last night when she called Jake to explain her reason for not accompanying him on the trip to Singapore. They often had laughed about the absurdity of hotels that refused to label a thirteenth floor. Asking for a room on the thirteenth floor had become a private joke.

"I can meet you at the hotel. We can spend the night together before your morning flight," she had said.

"My consolation prize? Nothing I could do to change your mind? It's not too late."

"I'm sorry. I just have lots to prepare for this upcoming case," she had lamented with a touch of guilt. She had wanted to make their second Valentine's Day a big deal, but was representing a new client. The woman, or "her protester," as Jake had come to call her, had been holding a mostly solo protest for over two weeks outside a department store claiming that the store charged higher prices than other stores of the same chain in wealthier neighborhoods. A metal sheet had fallen on her while she stood outside the store. According to the defense, construction workers fixing a sign had dropped a large metal frame by accident at the same time the woman was walking by.

She sustained a significant gash from the corner of her eye to the base of her nose on her right cheek. The horrified woman wisely took photographs of her face and videos of the construction workers on the storefront smiling and making rude remarks. She called an ambulance and sat on the sidewalk and waited. Some passerby offered to help her clean her bloody face, but she was too terrified to move her hand away.

"No worries," Jake had said, ready to end the conversation. "The Lion City is not going anywhere. There will be other opportunities. How is the case going?"

"It's so challenging getting reliable witnesses to come forward," she had said. "We have our own client's testimony and the evidence she brought with her, but even her evidence is insufficient without the right witness to corroborate her story."

Mariah had been working on this case for over five months now. At the beginning it felt like a sure win, but now it was heading down a path of uncertainty, and it was taking Mariah a lot of time and work to reel it back in.

"We'll celebrate before you go and then again when you get back," she had promised him.

Mariah arrives at the hotel a couple of hours early. She checks in and drops off her overnight bag in their room and sprinkles the rose petals she brought on top of the bed. "Desire," she whispers to the soft descending orange flakes. On the small table by the window she sets champagne on ice, then descends to the lobby to meet Jake.

In the less crowded section of the lobby, the incandescent light of the gumdrop glass chandeliers catches her eye. These are the only design features she would consider salvaging in the event of a fire, she decides.

The leather chesterfield sofa welcomes Mariah with a small sigh. She glances at the travel magazines piled up on the nearby coffee table and picks one out indiscriminately. The magazine is inconsequential, just a charade for her goal of people watching.

A parade of rolling suitcases moves obediently in and out of the revolving doors. Some people are leaving the hotel; others just arriving to perhaps turn around and leave again in a few hours. Mariah's gaze follows a group of adults making their way through. They are dressed in lime green T-shirts adorned with a large cross logo on the front, each member carrying an identical drawstring tote that matches their bright attire. *A church missionary group*, she guesses.

The single, lingering ring of the reception bell startles her. A tall, bearded man with a receding hairline smiles at the baby on his arm; the sound of the bell had captured the attention of the baby. The baby bounces happily and reaches for the bell, his newly found source of entertainment. Mariah catches herself wondering about the mother of the infant.

Her eyes dance around the room in search of a woman that fits her mental image of the mother, but her brain stops her, alerting her of a possible erroneous assumption. *Perhaps this is the complete family, Mariah,* her brain whispers. She directs her gaze toward the door just in time to see a familiar face.

She spots Jake right away as he enters through the side door. He is not a big fan of revolving doors. Mariah waves him over.

"How was your flight?" she asks.

Jake drops his carry-on garment bag on a nearby chair and pulls her close to him, as if any words would be just a waste of time. His wet, persistent kisses send urgent warnings to her body of what is to come.

Jake picks up his bag and takes Mariah's hand. They walk without speaking up the two flights of stairs to their room. Mariah sweeps the key over the keypad and pushes the door handle down. She steps in with Jake following close behind, his breathing communicating urgency. A mischievous giggle escapes her lips as she watches Jake grab the *Do Not Disturb* sign and place it outside the door.

Mariah holds his hand and leads him to the petal-adorned bed.

"HOW DID IT GO at the prison? Did any pervert try to seduce you today?" Eleanor's voice rumbles through the phone into Mariah's ear. She is a big opponent of Mariah's work with inmates at the city penitentiary.

"That was a one-time thing and he was not trying to seduce me." Mariah exhales with frustration. "The guy was reaching out, asking for help."

"Yeah, by wanting to be your pen pal. No thank you!" Eleanor says in reproach.

"You should come with me some time. You'll see firsthand the despair. As a matter of fact, you should come and teach a cooking class."

Eleanor cuts in before Mariah is able to elaborate on her scheme. "You know there is no way in hell you will convince me to drag my ass in there, right?"

Mariah is certain of that, so she stops trying.

Over a year ago, Mariah had been approached by a colleague and asked if she was interested in being part of the Family Justice Initiative the firm was trying to organize at the city penitentiary. Her colleague managed to enlist a handful of volunteers with the firm promising a bonus as an incentive. A few lawyers had been part of the initiative in the beginning, but once the fund for the bonus ran out, so did the volunteers.

"You will find it so rewarding" a fellow lawyer had promised hopefully.

Mariah had agreed to do it more out of pity for the fellow coworker than anything else. She thought she'd help for a couple of months, yet here she was now, a year later. She felt totally committed to the program.

Through the Family Justice Initiative, Mariah works closely with a program counselor to provide family-centered services to incarcerated parents. The program is designed to strengthen family relations, to maintain family ties.

"Why can't you go and hang out with the villain ladies instead?" Eleanor's question is intended more as a suggestion.

"Oh my God, there is no winning this argument with you. Female inmates can be just as dangerous as male inmates, you know? Besides, I did ask them when I first started, but they had enough volunteers working with incarcerated mothers. It's harder to recruit volunteers to work with fathers."

"No shit, that's because women don't go around killing for the thrill of it."

"OK, Sherlock Holmes. Hold your horses. No one is coming after me. I promise."

That seemed to appease Eleanor. "Fine. What did you teach those criminals today?"

Mariah's team had been designing workshops to help inmate fathers build parental skills.

"We have several skill groups going. There's one cohort up for parole at the end of the month, that has been working on skills needed for reunification as they transition back into their children's lives. They have been working very hard at forming and maintaining strong bonds with their kids."

Mariah's team designed activities to train parents by teaching them the language of school so they could have conversations with their children about their school experiences.

"Today we had a couple of teacher volunteers who came in to teach the fathers how to help their children with homework. They also learned how to play board games and practice reading picture books."

"Maybe you should bring Jake in with you next time, you

know? Just in case any of your crazies are getting any shitty ideas," Eleanor suggests.

"I will ask Jake. And then you promise you'll get off my back?" Mariah says while a dust of wonder crosses her mind: *Was Eleanor's suggestion Jake's idea?*

"You have my word," Eleanor declares with relief. "Oh, before I forget, are you following that case about the couple down on the Cape?"

"Yes, I actually know the lawyer representing them. It's crazy, right?"

The story had been circulating all over the news for the past few hours. The couple had been running a prostitution business catering to sadistic clients. The FBI task force broke into their house and found the couple hiding in their attic where they also found a makeshift office with files containing information about juveniles. The agents also found several boxes containing graphic, salacious photographs. The FBI released raw video footage of some of the victims, their images and voices altered to protect their identity.

"The girls had been beaten and forced to do drugs and left for days with nothing to eat except bags of chips and stale crackers," Eleanor says.

"I heard they were chained to the frame of the beds with just enough length to reach the bathroom. Monstrous," Mariah adds.

"The whole thing feels surreal. It's so freaky. These people were like your typical couple living in a nice family neighborhood and even running church groups," Eleanor says.

Mariah shakes her head. "You just never know, do you? They showed pictures of the white van they used on Sundays to help transport rented chairs and tables to Bible study classes, and at night, they used it to get their hostages to various motel rooms along Route 6. They kept the girls tied up and moved them around from motel to motel so they never spent more than a few nights together."

"I hope they get their dues in prison," Eleanor says. "Can you imagine? They have been doing this for over ten years and no one suspected a thing."

Mariah places her phone down after saying goodbye to her friend. More and more these days, she has the feeling she is living in a Marvel world of one-dimensional villains. She tries to shake it off and releases the couple's story from her mind by thinking back to the fathers who would soon be released. She needs something positive and hopeful to hold on to.

Mariah wonders about the work the prisoners had done, and the promises they made to themselves, their loved ones, and to society. *Parole*, a French word meaning "spoken word." These prisoners had given their word that they would do better. She hoped for everyone's sake they were able to keep it.

Eleanor's concerns for her safety warms her heart. She is grateful for the people who love her and saddened by the notion that the pursuit of happiness is not a fair game for everyone. She thinks again about the inmates. Mariah remembers the first time she visited the prison. She drove over right after work and navigated the preliminary security with no problem. A guard then escorted her to a different wing of the facility.

Mariah entered through a set of guarded doors and stepped into yet another checkpoint, where she was told she didn't have clearance to enter because she was wearing a skirt. Mariah questioned the rule and was told the usual.

"Ma'am, we are just following safety procedures here. It is for your own good."

Mariah left the building and drove to a shopping center in town where she purchased a pair of jeans. She returned to the prison, a little less brave this time.

Mariah thought about the incident, glad she had decided not to share that story with Eleanor. She only told her about the personal note she got from an inmate thanking her for the talk she gave and asking if it was OK for him to continue to write to her. He was hoping for a friendship. Mariah realizes now she should have kept that story to herself as well.

The phone rings and Mariah knows it is Eleanor, perhaps with one last warning.

"Sorry," Eleanor says, "I meant to ask about your case. How is it coming along?" She had taken a particular interest in Mariah's latest case. Perhaps she had sensed how personally invested Mariah was. She had recognized the level of preoccupation and stress.

"It's going well. Things are finally beginning to look good for her." *Good in a bad sense*, Mariah thinks to herself. The doctors had been able to save the woman's eye, but the cut had run deep, damaging a nerve. Her client lost 90 percent of her peripheral vision in her right eye.

"Yeah, Andrew told me that by the looks of the report the woman was going to lose part of her sight. That sucks," Eleanor laments.

Andrew had looked over Mariah's client's medical record. Mariah wanted to hear his medical opinion and had asked him to explain the injury and all the complications attached to it. She wanted to ensure she understood fully the medical aspect of the case.

"He didn't tell me much, but he was excited that you asked him to testify."

"Yeah, I might need him as a backup to explain things to the jury because the doctor who did the surgery is terrified of public speaking. We have been prepping him, but he gets so nervous that his voice shakes down to a whisper. I might need to cut him short and have Andrew step in," Mariah says.

"You should have him do it either way. Andrew will charm the heck out of the jury," Eleanor replies, and Mariah laughs, knowing she is right. Andrew possesses the type of handsomeness that forces you to forget your thoughts because your brain is too distracted by the pleasing images your eyes are so busy capturing. And in case your eyes fail you, your ears step in to absorb the hypnotic enchantment of his voice.

*I*T IS A BEAUTIFUL SPRING EVENING. The cold rain showers had ceased for a few days, allowing enough time for new grass and early spring buds to emerge. Mariah nestles close to Jake, the chilly air making her shiver despite the several layers of clothing she wears. The movie theatre is only a short walk from her apartment. Mariah enjoys living in this part of town; she loves being surrounded by so much history. She has been spending some time at the house in the suburbs with Jake, but it is clear that her preference remains the city. If Jake noticed her lack of interest in the suburban life, he has disguised it well. Mariah is glad he is willing to spend time in the city and stay at her place on occasion. She is pleased with that arrangement.

"I think you have been faking a New England persona this whole time," Jake says, kissing her cold nose.

"Well, why do you think I keep you around? My warm teddy bear."

Mariah and Jake had taken this walk so many times. The first time Mariah walked hand in hand with Jake across this city green he had commented on the beauty of the city at night. He had loved the character and culture of the city as a tourist and was excited to experience it now as a local. Mariah had been eagerly awaiting her favorite season to claim its place in the cycle. In just a couple of weeks, the radiant blooming would overtake a long stretch of the park.

"I can't wait!" she had said to Jake. "It's like living inside a rainbow."

She loves that about living in New England. Not long ago, the region was covered with mounds of soft, sparkly snow. The feathery crystals lured skiers from all over the world to its mountains. Sure, it wasn't like the deep sea-effect snowfall of the Hokkaido Island during its winter monsoon peaks, but New England's double black diamond runs hold quite the appeal for many adrenaline-seeking skiers.

Mariah points across the park to the quiet street with her favorite coffee shop.

"Can you believe it? It's evening, and the place is buzzing with the same gusto as when it opened this morning."

"Well, they understand the business. If you treat your customers well, they remain loyal because they are happy."

"I know. It seems so obvious, right? I don't understand how some places just don't get it. Remember that restaurant near my parents' house? The host is always in such a bad mood. It annoys me to no end."

"You don't have to go there, you know," he teases.

"I know, but the food is so darn good. You're right, though, maybe I should just get takeout," she says, thinking that was a reasonable compromise.

"You just shouldn't support a business that doesn't treat you well. Whether it's food or goods, businesses should cater to the buyers, to their customers, not the other way around."

"Yeah, this coffee place has it all figured out. Maybe we should stop by for a nice cup of chai latte after the movie," Mariah suggests, remembering the last time she was there. She had dropped her latte, spilling it all over herself and the table. One of the baristas came over to clean up the spill even when Mariah offered to do it herself. They had also made her a fresh latte free of charge in spite of her insistence on paying for it.

She had taken Jake to this coffeehouse during one of the early days of their courtship. They sat at one of the small tables the store had strategically arranged on the sidewalk and Mariah ordered her usual latte concoction that the barista had designed for her. It was one of the advantages of frequenting the same coffeehouse: The baristas get to know you by name and could make your preferred drink as soon as you walk through the doors, so that by the time you get to the counter, your drink is ready to be quaffed.

"What's in that ugly building across the street?" Jake had asked, looking up at the old brick edifice.

"I am embarrassed to say that I actually don't know what that building is. I mean, it does give off the impression of an old colonial structure, doesn't it?" Mariah said. "Wouldn't it be awesome if that was one of the many hidden places where women of that time period met to free their bosoms from evil corsets, drink a pint of ale, and smoke a good cigar?"

They had had a good chuckle at that although they both agreed that such places must have existed.

"Let's skip coffee tonight. There is something I want to show you after the movie," Jake suggests.

Mariah doesn't miss the mischievousness of his request.

"OH MY GOD! That expression on your face is priceless," Jake declares, showing Mariah a sequence of pictures he had taken of her at the moment of her realization that, not only had he given up the house in the suburbs to set up residence in the city, but he had found something in such a prime location.

Her laughter balances between a joyful laugh and a cackle. Mariah's cheeks feel sore as her mouth hangs in disbelief upon learning the location of Jake's new apartment.

Jake had signed the closing documents just that morning. Eleanor had accompanied him for the final walk-through the night before. He had just told her about the offer a couple of days before and sworn her to secrecy. He wanted to surprise Mariah. Although Jake liked living in the house out in the suburbs, it didn't feel like home because Mariah was so seldom there. He had given up on the illusion of coaxing her to move in with him, so he decided to find a permanent living arrangement in the heart of the city. At least that way he would be closer to Mariah. He waited patiently for the right apartment to come along, and his patience eventually paid off.

"Why didn't you tell me you were looking to buy in the city? Did you really have no idea that the apartment was in this building? In the Ugly Building?"

"I wanted to surprise you. And, I had no idea the apartment was here. I cross my heart," Jake responds with the proudest grin.

"How is that possible? What address did the realtor give you?"

"She told me to meet her by the entrance of the garage across from the movie theatre. We just started walking down the same side street I just took you on to get here. Everything looks so different from the back of the building. It just didn't occur to me to ask her for an address. She knew I wanted something in this area, which was tricky, because so few places go on the market here."

"Or maybe she was afraid that you would probably refuse to go in if she brought you to see it from the front of the building," Mariah adds.

"She totally admitted to doing that right after she told me that the place didn't actually have an address," Jake chuckles.

"Are you serious? What does that even mean?"

"Well, it does have an address in theory. The address is actually the name of the building, Treize, followed by the city, and then the zip code."

"Treize, thirteen, I love it!"

"I knew you would." Jake pulls her close for a tight embrace. He had suspected she would be excited about the coincidence.

"Can we go back in for a second tour?" Mariah asks, delighted.

"Do you want to go through the dungeon in the back or through the front?"

"Dungeon, please!"

The back entrance of the building features a manicured garden with three separate paths leading to separate entrances of the building. There are six floors and each floor is its own unit. The building is designed to expand horizontally as opposed to bolting upright. Jake kisses Mariah and holds her close as they ride in the private internal elevator to the top floor, his heart full of hope.

"I love the space. It looks like a gigantic playroom for grownups. Look at these floors." Mariah walks around, dazzled by the elegance of the space. "Does each apartment look like this?" she asks.

"I asked the realtor the same question. She told me that they remodeled the whole place eight years ago. The contracting company that bought the building designed each apartment in its very own unique way. She said the floor right below is very traditional, featuring some original nineteenth-century flair like double wing doors and original chandeliers."

"I would love to know about the first floor. Do you think the dungeon is the preamble to the theme of the apartment?" Mariah asks excitedly.

"Here, let me show you something." Jake takes Mariah's hand and walks her to the rooftop terrace. Mariah's eyes pop in disbelief. In front of her is a magnificent garden complete with large potted plants and green ground cover. She walks over to touch the rows of evergreen, and then steps onto the grass-like material and touches the ground cover, expecting it to be some form of artificial turf.

"What is this? Is it real?" Mariah asks, fascinated by what appears to be a bed of miniature three-leaf clovers.

"It's the real deal," Jake offers with a wink.

"This is incredible! A real backyard on your roof." Mariah walks around marveling at the budding plants. In her mind she can already picture the beautiful bloom not far ahead.

Jake leads her to the wicker lounge chairs. Mariah can't help but smile at the rows of dwarf weeping cherry trees sitting comfortably inside large planters that create a sense of privacy. She doubts Jake realizes the enchanting beauty that would materialize in no time. These beautiful clusters of flowers announce the beginning of spring and are eagerly awaited by the cherry blossom enthusiasts as they only lasted a couple of weeks. Mariah pictures the delicate flowers, addressing them in her mind. *You speak of fragility, a reminder that life is beautiful, yet tragically short.*

Jake pulls out a bar of dark chocolate and a bottle of red wine from a basket. He uncorks the bottle and takes a generous sip, passing the bottle to Mariah.

"May this be the first of many happy occasions at the Ugly Building," he says with a flourish.

Mariah takes a sip. Now that it's all happening, she tries to push back the warnings of her friends and her parents. She hands back the bottle, ignoring the sudden cloud of doubts settling in.

"SO, WHAT HAPPENED?" Jake asks over the phone. He had been antsy all morning, waiting to hear the verdict.

"We won the trial. We got her a nice award," Mariah declares.

Although Mariah had secured her firm a substantial sum of money, she had to go back to her boss several times to ask for additional funds to pay for more disbursements. She was ready to be done with the case; it had dragged on way too long. She cared about her client, but resented all the time it had taken away from her personal life.

"The jurors cried, watching the videos. She sat on the sidewalk for over an hour waiting for help. She kept repeating, 'I think I am going to lose my eye.'"

"Did the store manager come out to try and help?" Now that the case is over, Jake wants to know more of the details.

"Nope. But you could see them inside the store watching. It was infuriating to witness that type of coldness."

"So, what happened?" Jake leans in, hanging on every word.

"We found out that the manager tried to stop the woman's protest after a few days. I guess they hoped she would get tired and stop coming, but she kept at it. They tried to talk her out of it, to reason with her, but she didn't budge."

Mariah goes on to explain how on some days other neighborhood women joined her and the store manager would call security to intimidate them and force them to move across the street. But her client came back day after day.

"They even hired a company to come power wash the sidewalk in front of the store. They were given instructions to wash away ANYTHING that stood in their way, implying the woman and her followers. Can you believe that? As if they were a piece of trash, I told the jury."

"And they got away with that?" He sounded incredulous.

"Well yeah. And it worked because it stopped all the other women from coming back."

"And you think the accident was not really an accident?"

"I don't think it was intended to harm the woman to the degree it did, so in that sense it was. But they were trying to scare her, for sure."

"Did Andrew have a chance to testify?" Jake asks.

"No, we will need to take him out to console him. He really wanted to be put on the stand, but our surgeon did a fine job. He was able to pull himself together and present a thorough and intelligible account. It was just what I needed him to do, you know, paint the picture, and he did. His nervousness worked in our favor, showing that he cared about the patient."

Mariah gives Jake some lines from her closing argument, enough to placate his interest, and then hangs up, her body still charged with adrenaline. She has a strong understanding not only of the wording, but also of the many possible interpretations of the federal and state Constitution as well as its amendments. She has a gifted capacity to think critically and analytically about legal code. However, Mariah struggles a great deal with projecting confidence when arguing a case. She'd received a lot of coaching over the years and still participated in mock court sessions before a major case.

She is glad she had spent the time preparing well for the case. She got a nice settlement for her *protester* and the store owner had agreed to make adjustments to their prices so as not to discriminate based on location.

Mariah picks up her phone again and calls Eleanor. Although she is certain that Andrew had given her a full account of the trial, she wants Eleanor to hear it from her.

"We did it!" she announces cheerfully.

EG WOKE UP EARLY overwhelmed by the anxiety of seeing Dr. Moll, her new therapist. She went through the list of psychotherapists she had seen over the years, too many to remember by name. What she was able to conjure with ease were the diagnostics they have attached to her heartache. The labels, a collection of words as frightening as the ailment itself: post-postpartum depression, emotional detachment disorder, manic-depressive, mood disorder, emotional disturbance, post-traumatic stress disorder, then back to depression. She wondered if Dr. Moll would just grab one of these titles or bestow a new one upon the evil shadow that followed her.

"She is a healer, Mom," her daughter had said as a way to coax her into trying therapy once again.

"We follow a holistic approach to therapy," explained the chatty healer with the large Harvard University diploma expensively framed above the electric fireplace. Dr. Moll had listened encouragingly to Meg's cautious telling as she described the feeling of being in a perpetual stage of mourning. After their first meeting, Dr. Moll had sent her a package containing a leather-bound journal in which she had scribbled a dedication. It had been the kindness and compassion she felt in that note that had convinced her to make a second appointment.

Meg reached over and opened the journal. She flipped through the pages now filled with her own writing. She was startled by the distant sound of sirens and the memory began to play in her mind as if on autopilot.

She remembered tiptoeing into the nursery to find her daughter sound asleep. Nothing is more peaceful than *your* child cuddled up with sweet dreams. That had been a good week for her daughter. There were so few of them. There was usually a good day here and there, but a full week was quite extraordinary. It brought new rays of hope. The medications were helping her build stamina; she was spending more of her waking hours playing and being a happy baby.

Meg was scheduled for a long run that day, her Saturday run. She remembered rubbing her knees and hesitating for a brief moment, but then popped a couple of anti-inflammatory pills and swallowed them dry. Meg was not a big fan of ingesting drugs of any kind, but her knees were bothering her again from the strain of excessive running. She knew the drill by now. She would have to go and see the doctor who would suggest she give her knees a rest, and then go ahead and prescribe anti-inflammatory pills anyway. On the next visit he would refer her to a physical therapist. The PT would see her for eight sessions— the maximum covered by her insurance—and would suggest that she continue with his suggested exercise and stretching routine at home.

"It's all about realigning your body. A proper alignment for your body will recalibrate your joints and help get rid of the knee pain," the physical therapist would declare in a memorized credo.

Against her best judgment, Meg decided to skip all that for the time being. In her defense, she had been taking over-the-counter anti-inflammatory meds and doing the alignment exercises religiously at home. She was just skipping the middleman's suggestion to stop running, as that was the one thing she would not do without. Meg needed to run the way a nicotine addict needed a cigarette to soothe nerves or escape for just a moment.

Meg had also been icing her knees and taking natural supplements of ginger root and dandelion leaves to help her tired, swollen joints.

With a satisfied smile, she completed her stretches and hopped up from the floor. *Stretch accomplished. Check!* She made her way to the kitchen for a quick breakfast of microwaved oatmeal with a handful of almonds. The timer stopped, flashing an "enjoy" wish on the small screen. Meg pulled out the gooey mess, which had spilled over the edge of the bowl. She chuckled at her inability to get the timing right, time and time again. She added a squirt of honey and half of an overripe banana left in the metal fruit bowl.

Meg remembered the loud steps and clanging sound emanating from the basement. She had stopped to listen, trying to guess the sound. It was a game she played, trying to guess which machine her husband was dissecting. Meg heard the throbbing of the washing machine, furiously swirling its victims around. No machine necropsy today, she guessed. Lucas was only doing the laundry.

Laundry was part of Lucas's weekend routine. He brought the clean laundry upstairs and Meg did the folding. It was the best of all arrangements. He loved doing the laundry not so much because of the prospect of ending up with clean garments, but because he enjoyed the opportunity to interact with the appliances. Lucas loved contraptions, the larger, the better.

On countless occasions, Meg had ventured down to the laundry room to find Lucas deeply absorbed in an assortment of machinery guts spread out in front of him. It would take him a few minutes to become aware of her presence, and then he would offer her a sheepish excuse. "I thought I heard a rattling sound coming from the motor. I figured I should have a look at it, just to be sure."

Meg knew there had been no rattling, creaking, or crinkling sounds. But she gave him the smile of a co-conspirator just the same.

"So glad you can take care of these crazy machines before they take over the world." She had planted a soft kiss on his lips that day and then turned the baby monitor on before leaving him free to reenter his sanctuary.

Meg grimaced at the next part of the memory. She had come home from her run to find a note on the counter. It read, "We are at the hospital." That Saturday had been the end of all good days to come.

She blinked to release the tears trapped behind her eyelids. Her eyes closed again, and before she had time to stop her brain, her memories traveled to an earlier time, the day her daughter was born.

Meg woke up to a feeling of emptiness she couldn't place. But then she remembered where she was. The hospital. She remembered what had happened. By the time the paramedics rushed her in, she had already lost so much blood that both her life and the baby's was at risk. Nurses began typing her for a transfusion, but her blood pressure dropped so drastically it sent the baby into cardiac arrest. Suddenly she found the hospital staff running beside her hospital bed as they rushed her to surgery for an emergency C-section. During the preparations, they set up the blood transfusion. Nurses prepared the instrument tray and the doctor and anesthesiologist explained the critical next few minutes. When they finally extracted her little baby, she was rushed to ICU. All these years later Meg still felt the emptiness. It was five days before she could hold her little girl.

Meg wanted to breastfeed her baby, but her attempts were fruitless as the baby was unable to latch on. The original symptoms of lack of sucking and swallowing reflexes suggested the presence of some form of brain damage, possibly cerebral palsy. The baby had been kept in the neonatal unit in intensive care, fed through a feeding tube while the specialized team determined a diagnosis.

Tests results showed no signs of internal brain bleeding, and the possibility of cerebral palsy was ruled out. Instead, the tests detected the presence of a mass near the coccyx bone.

Her daughter had been born with a tumor, a terminal tumor.

MARIAH ADORNS THE LENGTH OF THE TUB'S ARMREST with small tea candles and sinks up to her neck in hot water and bubbles, a glass of red wine nestled on the side of the tub in between two of the candles. Her gaze follows the bright glow cascading from the skylight that runs the length of the ceiling as she soaks and sips her wine, remembering what she'd said to Jake about this tub.

"I love this beautiful tub," she declared. "It feels like bathing inside a masterpiece."

This feature had been one of the selling points of the apartment for Jake, and she totally understands why. She remembers his mischievous smile as he told her how he had spent months secretly looking for an apartment to buy in the city. She loved the twinkle in his eye while giving her a complete tour, reciting word for word the realtor's spiel.

"Bamboo is a pretty hard wood, plus it's water resistant. They polish and oil it to give it this beautiful natural look," Jake explained, using his best realtor voice, unable to accurately re-create the moment of his erupting "WOW" at the sight of the deep bathtub. Nor could he verbalize his awe as he walked around the free-standing tub, feeling its smooth texture and how it reminded him of one of those traditional Japanese soaking tubs. He savored the realization that the tub was the perfect size for two adults to sit together and soak comfortably.

Mariah smiles, remembering how Jake had continued the tour with his enthusiastic descriptions. "I know. It's quite eye-catching. The whole flat is designed with an open space feeling. They did such an exquisite job bringing in natural light. Wait until you see the master bedroom," Jake, the realtor, had commented with obvious flirtation. Mariah couldn't help wondering if the actual realtor had acted with the same level of coquetry.

"You might be wondering about the natural lighting and whether it's practical during the hot summers and brutal New England winters," Jake said, pointing out the magnificent view of the sky above.

He went on eagerly without waiting for a response. "Well, they just remodeled this building about eight years ago. They gutted the whole place. Only the outside retained its original façade. Everything is state of the art. I honestly don't know much about skylights in general except that these have great insulation. We have all that information somewhere." He opened his hands to flip through an imaginary folder and then went back to explaining.

"The company is known for high-quality skylights. They use tempered, double-paned, and gas-filled glass. There is also something…," he paused to search for the words to explain the double-paned glass, "well, something super cool about how they use mirror particles to reflect the solar heat back out. You see, a lot of home owners are installing these around here. It's part of a new green initiative. Maybe you've heard of it."

He looked at her the way the real realtor must have looked at him. Mariah noted that no, she had not heard of it, assuming that must have been the response Jake had given the realtor, when in fact she did know all about the green initiative. But she followed along, enjoying the roleplaying and Jake's excitement.

"People can actually get a tax break for replacing old windows with these," he explained, before directing her to the next room.

The water temperature in the tub had dropped to tepid, so Mariah steps out, absently watching the remaining bubbles twirl their way down the drain. She dries off and puts on fresh underwear followed by a clean pair of tights and a cotton t-shirt, her mind and body noticing the familiar pang of apprehension settling in. Jake had loved the house outside of the city. She had tried, really tried to share his enthusiasm, but her heart was in the city. Jake had given up the city he loved and the house in the suburbs. *What else could I ask of him*? asked her heart. *Why the uncertainty?* her brain questioned.

She twists her damp hair into a tight topknot. These days she much prefers to let her hair dry naturally into loose, spirally curls. Her hair is a combination of coarse and fine strands that blend together to create the sort of curls that entice a curl seeker to run to a beauty shop for a curling iron.

When she was a teenager, her curl patterns were a bit different, *The nightmare on Frizzle Street,* she called them. She'd wash her hair each night and coat it with a generous pump of leave-in conditioner before putting it into four long braids. In the morning, she undid the braids to reveal a cascade of soft and bouncy locks. A high school friend had tutored Mariah in the physics of curly hair, saying, "Stop fighting your curls and embrace the mane the almighty gave you!" She reproached Mariah for her attempts to tame her long coils by submitting them to a daily dose of flat ironing.

Several ringlets spring free and Mariah tucks them gracefully behind her ears. She picks up her dirty camisole and underwear and drops them into the hamper. The cleaning lady had been kind enough to offer to wash whatever pieces of laundry she left behind since she was already doing Jake's laundry, so Mariah had gotten into the habit of leaving a few essential pieces of clothing at Jake's place.

Mariah loves Jake's apartment and the convenience it brings with it. He had hinted for her to move in with him time and time again, but Mariah still feels reluctant to make that move permanent and give up her own apartment.

"It's not a question of commitment," she said to Eleanor. They are approaching two years together and Mariah is content sharing her life with Jake. "It's not a question of love, either," she had felt the need to explain. She still felt a strong pull to her old apartment, even if just for one night a week. She found the decision of a permanent arrangement suffocating, like a wool blanket that was both heavy and itchy.

Her eyes travel the length of the inside of her bare arms. She traces the heavy scars, a collection of underground tunnels, each concealing its own story. A chilling thrill travels up her spine as memories of those teenage years behind closed doors emerge, when she'd discovered a dark pleasure. What began as a tentative picking at an old scab had escalated into a routine of self-harm. Her heart sinks as she resurrects the memory of that old friend. She feels the dormant thrill brewing deep, ready to erupt. A metallic taste fills her mouth as the thought of the small blade hidden deep inside her toiletry bag taunts her.

Mariah reaches for the oversized cable-knit sweater. She walks back to the bedroom and packs her small duffle bag. Sensing Jake's figure behind her, she turns around and meets his warm eyes. He holds her gaze.

"There's no need to explain, my Lady Rose." He doesn't understand her hesitation, but he respects her needs. He pulls her closer and nuzzles the base of her neck, holding her there until he begins to feel her body slowly disengaging.

"I'll see you tomorrow after work," he says, brushing his lips across her forehead and planting a soft kiss on each of her eyelids.

Jake had awakened in her a new appetite for adventures, an old familiar thrill that had lain dormant for quite a while. But is Jake taking from her more than she should give? Had her silence at his indiscretions given him an unspoken approval? "Watch out for his wandering eye," her mother had cautioned her.

Would that be her life, a continuous loop of proving to others that she was enough?

Mariah leaves the question lingering in her mind as she walks into the elevator. She knows it displeased him to see her go on Sundays. She feels the heavy emptiness settle in between them like a rancid piece of meat.

*T*HE MORNING SUN made its way through the bedroom windows with vicious determination. At the insistent sound of blue jays in the tree outside the window, Maddy perked up her ears alertly and responded. At that, Meg turned over and lowered the setting of the air-conditioner. The month of May had brought in an unusual heat wave.

Meg had never been an early riser. Those years of early morning awakening to feed the baby were pure torture. She had no problem staying up late into the night. She was like a nocturnal creature that felt more in her element as night deepened.

She thanked her lucky stars that Lucas's sleep patterns allowed him to do the morning shifts when it came to caring for the kids. Usually, by the time Meg rolled out of bed and made her way downstairs, the family had already been fed a delicious homemade breakfast. She would walk into their playroom and gaze at the block city or art gallery that had bloomed while she had her final morning dream.

Meg would watch from afar, not wanting to interrupt the magic occurring before her eyes. She'd grab a plate and sample one of Lucas's morning surprises. She had stopped trying to guess the ingredients a long time ago.

Lucas's sense of adventure carried over to his culinary prowess. He was clever with flavors and texture. His daughters would devour a pile of delicious fluffy pancakes without ever noticing that he had replaced the plain processed white flour with quinoa, coconut, or buckwheat flour. Nor could they guess that the fluffy and delicious scrambled eggs were packed with cauliflower puree and that yellow squash was cleverly hidden in the yummy blueberry muffins.

Today, Mia was coming over. Ha! Speaking of an early riser, that girl was just like her father who was up by five every morning of the year. Meg considered the popular saying, "the acorn definitely doesn't fall far from the tree," when it came to her daughter.

Meg heard a sizzling sound. The sweet smell of onions caramelizing tantalized her nostrils. Lucas was making Nana's egg recipe, which he always paired with her favorite, hoecakes with homemade apple butter.

"Good move," she praised Lucas quietly, peering at him from the dining room.

Nana's scrambled eggs were legendary in the family. Meg smiled, thinking of how she herself had failed at re-creating her own mother's recipe. She took great pleasure in boasting how it required an extraordinarily patient cook like Lucas to come close enough to executing Nana's egg recipe with some level of success. After generating the elaborate mixture of eggs with various cheeses and spices, the brave cook had to commit to twenty minutes of monotonous, continual stirring to allow the mixture time to congeal into a delicious mush.

When Mia was young, breakfast was simple. She was easily impressed with her dad's goofy creations. Now it took more planning. It was harder to trick a young woman into eating a kale muffin. Her daughter's idea of breakfast these days was a banana and a coffee, which she consumed on her walk to work.

As the kids got older, Lucas's cooking skills became more creative. Meg remembered the picky eater years.

"Why can't we just let them eat bread and butter if that's what they want to eat?" Meg had pleaded in exasperation one day. But Lucas would not succumb to that. He saw the challenge as an opportunity. He studied recipes old and new and quickly mastered a new repertoire of delicious options.

"Need a hand?" she asked, stepping into the kitchen. Lucas wiped his hands on his cotton twill apron, the one his girls had decorated with fabric markers for a Father's Day over two dozen years earlier. The pictures and letters had faded, yet both Meg and Lucas could read the pictures and scribbled writings as clear as when they were first written. It was sketched in their memories like a love letter.

"You can work on the coffee," he offered, pointing at the percolator waiting by the sink. Meg noticed the frother and sweet spices on the small plate.

"We are going all in," she said, picking up the coffee percolator and smiling excitedly. Lucas had bought a batch of freshly ground coffee to brew and would grate a whole hazelnut kernel and add a generous pinch of nutmeg to the steamed almond milk, then a dust of ground cinnamon atop the froth.

"She sounded so happy over the phone when I talked to her last night." Meg turned around to await his confirmation.

"She sure did. She's a happy kid, Meg," he said, caressing her cheeks. The sound of the timer interrupted the moment. Lucas walked over to check on the bourbon-baked French toast, the bubbling brown sugar indicating its readiness. Meg left the kitchen for a minute to inspect the dining room table. They had set it up last night, a habit she learned from her own mother.

Meg readjusted the assortment of tulips in the large clear vase. *A perfect love*, she whispered to the flowers, thinking of their hidden message. She snapped a bloom and tucked it carefully into her ponytail as she made her way back into the kitchen.

$\mathcal{S}$HE PULLS THE DOOR SHUT behind her and stares down at her sneakers, the neon green ones with purple stripes. *The Wind Chasers*, a name given by the shoe designer, had transitioned right out of the box and onto her feet. Breaking in new shoes was never her favorite thing to do, but that sentiment did not apply to sneakers.

Mariah is, in fact, a big fan of sneakers. It is her preferred footwear when not restrained by the expected heels at the office. The sneakers are often paired with a comfortable, sporty outfit. She feels a special affinity to women at the supermarket who parade the aisles dressed in designer workout outfits. Mariah can't help but stare at them whenever they walk by, each time wondering in which category to place them. Most of them placed in the sedentary group, individuals who are in it just for the look, showcasing the latest workout fashions, yet refusing to break a sweat. This would be her preferred group if given the choice. Mariah drops her keys behind the large planter in the hallway and runs down the four flights of stairs. Not so much of a hiding spot, Jake had teased her.

Mr. Hobbs is behind his desk in the lobby. She re-adjusts her baseball cap and blows him a kiss in response to his concerned warning, "Slow down, young lady." She smiles, recognizing his *tsk-tsk* sounds much like a parent would do right before asking the heavens, *"What am I going to do with this kid?"*

She steps onto the sidewalk and yields to an older woman pushing a baby carriage. Her companion, a petite brunette closer to Mariah's own age, carries a shopping bag. Mariah notices the French baguette peeping out of the bag teasingly. She recognizes the crusty loaf, a trademark of the neighborhood's bakery two blocks over; "a delicious hole in a wall" is how the locals described it.

Stop thinking about food or this run is going to suck, Mariah tells herself. She picks up her pace, leaving the carriage, the women, and the ever-so-delicious-looking French baguette behind. She stops at the crosswalk and makes her way to the other side of the street, glancing at the majestic "Angel of the Waters" fountain, her favorite among the extensive collection of statues and structures displayed around the park, America's first public garden. She grins; this is her city, her home.

Her ears tune in to the heavy traffic, but quickly pick up the radio blasting out a Michael Jackson hit. The four windows of the car are rolled down as the blond driver puffs clouds of smoke. A cigarette is trapped between her thumb and index finger as if ready to conduct a symphony. *Yup, this is my city,* Mariah chuckles, and strides ahead.

She checks in with her body, which had begun to settle into its own running rhythm. Her feet send up a happy message, their approval of the new sneakers. Mariah's eyes feast on a beautiful approaching sight, the exuberant magnolia trees. She runs under their canopy of strong branches that spread out like open arms. The imposing fragrance penetrates her nostrils like a swarm of bees searching for pollen.

A collage of decaying flowers and violet petals decorate the sidewalk. Mariah allows herself to be led by the trail of brown pulpy mush while she ponders the way of nature, the way of life. These mystical flowers with their ever-so-sweet smell cling to your memory for an eternity, the discarded wilted petals a reminder that nothing lasts forever. The magnolia flowers speak of perseverance, yet they, too, come to an end.

Mariah inhales a deep drag of the scent. She forces her lungs to hold the smell, hoping to fill her organs with the magnolias' beauty, and with their message of perseverance.

She runs across the park and onto the breezy path that snakes along the river. Her lungs flush out the scent of the flowers and welcome the river air with greedy gulps. Her panting breath gets shorter with each passing stride.

These days, running feels more like a chore for her. She finds herself making excuses for not being able to run more frequently.

"What happened to the girl who ran all those marathons?" Eleanor often jokes.

It is true. Mariah had been a runner. Not just someone who liked to run, but a committed runner. She had run several local and destination marathons while in college.

Deep down, Mariah knows that it had little to do with availability and more to do with lack of desire. The truth is that running no longer brings the satisfying after-run high she had once felt.

The adrenaline rush and opioid release produced by practicing law seems to have replaced the need to exercise.

But she jokes back to Eleanor, "More blubber than my knees can handle is what happened."

Mariah picks up her pace and crosses the bridge. The other side of the bridge is the two-mile mark, so she heads back the same way. She reaches her destination and stops to stretch her hamstrings and get several sets of jumping jacks and walking lunges in before heading back home. She thinks about the conversation she heard Jake having on the phone last night.

"It's just not going to happen. Let's go for a total sell out. The sooner I am done with this bullshit, the better," she had overheard him declare.

"*The Singapore accounts,*" she thought to herself.

Jake had mentioned to her his plans to terminate his business dealings in Singapore when she had asked him about the pile of forms and the unopened letters from the Internal Revenue Service she saw on his desk.

"I'm getting a lot of pushback from several clients who have vast investments there," he had explained. "I'm working on putting together an exit plan to reassure my clients that their portfolios will be taken care of under the new broker I am recommending. My lawyers are trying to convince me to stay on with the accounts."

"They must know you well enough to know that if you decide on a business action, there is nothing that can deter you from it," she said with a reassuring kiss.

Mariah delights in the familiar flash of happiness brought forth by the thought of Jake. She picks up her pace as she remembered she still needed to wrap his birthday gift. The big red envelope is sitting on her kitchen counter and Jake is due to come by any minute.

Time and time again Jake has shown her that he was ready for her, that he had waited for her. Mariah thinks about the contents of the envelope, her own way of showing him that she, too, is ready for him. She smiles with anticipation.

*M*EG STARED AT THE baby picture of Mia wrapped in the yellow polka dot receiving blanket, her puffy eyes showing the newborn trademark. That last pregnancy had also come as a shock—baby number five, she had called it. She had cursed her body for the unjust way it chose to permit her the status of motherhood.

She remembered dealing with the stress and uncertainty of caring for a terminally ill child while harvesting a new growing life inside of her. How can a person reconcile that reality, she'd asked herself over and over.

Even now, all these years later, Meg still felt racked by guilt for not jumping with joy at the discovery of her pregnancy. She had focused on staying strong for her older daughter and worried that she wouldn't be able to tend to her fully if she were preoccupied with the creature growing inside her, who would then turn into a demanding newborn. She also worried about the health of this new baby, *baby five*. Would it survive long enough to be born, or become yet another ghostly angel? Meg remembered each one of those babies even if her womb had discarded them before their organs had a chance to form. *Or would you survive only to live on borrowed time like your beautiful sister?* Meg paused to think about her younger daughter now, marveling at the amazing young woman she had grown into. Lucas was right. Her daughter was happy.

She traveled back in her memories, remembering being pregnant with *baby five* while driving her sick toddler to the hospital in the early hours of the morning. Her chemo was scheduled for seven o'clock on most mornings. Sometimes Lucas was able to join them, or at least could drop them off on his way to work and then pick them up at the end of the day, but most of the time it was just the two of them, she and her daughter facing darkness. Yet, there was also *baby five*, curled up, growing, unaware of the nightmare happening outside the womb.

She remembered Nurse Helen, who was at the front desk on most days. Her bright smile and sing-song voice had been an unconscious attempt to paint rainbows over the gloomy air of the cancer treatment center. The ocean blue walls were heavily decorated with pictures of popular characters from children's books in an attempt to hide the breathing machines behind the doors.

Meg remembers the platters of freshly baked cookies and pastries donated by local bakeries, well-intentioned people wanting to do good by presenting their delicious offerings. But even their savory aroma of sweetness had failed to erase the smell of the poignant sorrow that lingered and clung to all living and nonliving organisms within close proximity.

"Let me take a closer look at that fancy crown you have on today," Nurse Helen had said to her daughter one day, leaning over to examine the tiara on the thinning bed of soft curls and then exaggerating her appreciation at the jeweled sight.

"And look at those pretty shoes!" the kind nurse said, bending over to admire her daughter's sparkly Cinderella shoes. Those were the only shoes her daughter would wear in or out of the house. Nurse Helen would look up at Meg warmly and then inform her of the morning plans.

"Dr. Grabel is making her rounds. We can get started." She would point toward the familiar hallway. Nurse Helen didn't administer the chemo. She got the paperwork ready and directed the patients to the nurse who took it from there.

Meg knew that wing of the hospital like she knew her own home. If the lights went out, she was sure to find her way to that chemo room without incidental bumps. She still saw that room even now during her waking hours and walked it in her sleep as she navigated in and out of the occasional nightmares.

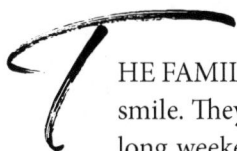

*T*HE FAMILIAR SMELL OF their apartment makes her smile. They had taken a road trip to Quebec City for a long weekend to escape the August city heat. Mariah drops her travel bag in the entryway. Jake trails behind, still on the phone with his lawyers. Mariah kicks off her designer ballet flats to the side and considers abandoning them by the tote bag. She reconsiders and picks up the bright red leather shoes with the signature medallion symbol and heads straight up the stairs to her and Jake's master bedroom.

Mariah thinks of what fun it has been to sample new and delicious Quebecois cuisine in the small bistros along the narrow streets of the old part of the city. She remembers how excited Jake had been to try the cheese curd fries saturated in thick gravy; *poutine*, the locals call it. But for Mariah, the best treat had been the assortment of maple-based toffee candies. She enjoyed them to such a degree that she left the restaurant with a small takeout box stuffed to the rim with the syrupy candy to bring back to Eleanor. She hoped Eleanor would be able to re-create the delicious treats back in her own kitchen.

The evenings spent in this majestic metropolis brought their own thrill of intimate dinners at trendy spots around the city. Mariah's favorite outing was the late-night drinks at the 360-degree, rotating, glass-walled restaurant with its breathtaking views 180 meters up in the starry sky. Mariah had not missed how Jake's eyes had feasted on a different view, the tall waitress with the dark, silky skin. That was plain to see. What was privy to her was the intentional way Jake twisted the amber lager bottle as if resolved that his hand must be satisfied in this way rather than give in to his desire to reach out and touch the bare shoulders of the stranger serving their meals. Mariah ignored his distraction, but the smell of his sanguine seduction settled heavily in the pit of her stomach.

This morning, Jake had wakened early. The sound of heavy clicking from his laptop keyboard punctuated by quietly voiced "*fucks*" startled her.

"It's fine. I'll need a few hours to make some calls," he said when she asked if everything was OK.

Mariah had showered, changed into comfortable clothes, and left the hotel. She tried to silence her worries by indulging in a morning of shopping in luxurious boutiques, but her attempt failed, and she soon found herself immersed in a recent incident.

It was less than a month ago when Mariah had walked inadvertently into his office. She had caught a flash of horror on his face as he gaped at the screen as if he had seen a ghost. It was then that her own eyes had swept over the image of two naked bodies. His quick reaction to shut down the lid of his laptop offered her an opportunity, but she chose to pretend not to notice. Yet, even today, as she paced around the stores, she could clearly visualize the dark-haired man with the petite female's head buried deeply into his groin. The thought of questioning him then had nauseated her. Confront or ignore; she had chosen to do the latter.

Isn't this what one is supposed to do? Choose a person and stick to one's choice? she had reasoned with herself.

Mariah glances over approvingly at the red ballet flats sitting by the foot of the bed. She reaches for her handbag and pulls out a small sack, an impish smile tugging at her lips as she places the pouch under Jake's pillow. She anticipates his mischievous grin at the discovery of the black silky underwear briefs concealed inside.

This weekend Jake had surprised her as he had on so many other occasions. Mariah loved these *escape surprises*, as he liked to call them. The previous trip had also been to Canada. It was just an overnight trip. They took a private jet to watch a match between the Boston Breakers and the Vancouver Whitecaps. Although she no longer followed the sport of soccer closely save for, naturally, the World Cup, she loved that Jake had thought to take her to see a professional women's soccer match, knowing he was not particularly enthusiastic about the sport.

Mariah sits on the edge of the bed and takes out the bright orange index card. On it, Jake had written *Grand French House of the North*, her clue to his solve-the-destination game. Leaving words on an index card was the frisky way he presented her with each new *escape surprise*. Eleanor teased her when Mariah first told her about Jake's little game, but Mariah secretly adored his playfulness.

She returns to the entryway to retrieve her bag. Mariah can hear Jake's voice seeping through the partially closed door of the office.

"Yes, I'm pretty sure about it. No, we don't have to see how it's going to play out. I am telling you how it's going to play out. It's over. You come after me again and I'll send the cops after you." Jake's angry delivery lashes a chilling warning. The slamming of the door tells her he had noticed her presence.

Jake's words stay trapped behind the door. He concludes the call leaving the caller midsentence. The small phone makes a crashing sound when it hits the floor. Jake's strong foot completes the job, sending the phone's guts flying out in all directions. He stares at the scattered pieces, uncertain of their future. He disposes of the small, flat battery and random broken pieces by dumping them into the trash. He holds the circuit board close to his eyes for a moment, considering the information trapped inside the small microprocessors. The small drawer beneath the heavy mahogany desk opens obediently with the turn of the key, and Jake hides the phone brain between a stack of notepads. A sigh of relief escapes him as he locks the drawer. The fifty-thousand-dollar payment had included the acquisition of that phone with the memory chip hosting the compromising photographs.

Mariah tiptoes upstairs and sets the orange tote bag on the divan by the side of the bed. She begins to unpack while her mind savors the memories of the adventurous experiences Jake had arranged for them to share in the past, from simple yet unexpected places to exotic and hidden treasures.

There was that beautiful candlelit ride on a horse-drawn wagon in Montana; it was as if they had traveled back in time. Mariah had felt mystified by the magic of the glorious sky. She had cozied up next to Jake, happy to be experiencing the vast beauty with him.

They had stayed at a working cattle ranch that had been transformed into a pristine, luxurious resort that gave its guests the opportunity to relax and partake in daily ranching experiences. Jake had chosen to go on the cattle drive. "You just want an excuse to wear your cowboy boots and hat," Mariah had teased him. She attempted fly-fishing, but returned empty-handed.

Another time they traveled a bit off the beaten path to wine country. They'd met up with some of Jake's college friends in Napa for a day, but then continued on their own adventure to explore the more secluded wineries in the heart of Calistoga. Not only had they indulged in delicious wine, but Mariah allowed herself to be convinced to climb on board a hot-air balloon ride. "But," she insisted, "only if you agree to join me in a mud bath before dinner."

Then there was the orange index card whose clue had read, "Alonso, watch out for alligators!" That trip was to the sophisticated city of Naples on the Gulf of Mexico, which captivated them upon arrival.

Mariah and Jake had walked along the lengthy stretch of pure white sand at sunrise, the impactful sound of the turquoise waters forcing them to push work out of their minds and focus completely on one another. They held hands and planned out their day while stepping over the discarded seaweed the ocean spat up the night before. Their bare feet sank into the powdery sand creating a soft sifting sound. Mariah kept her hunting eyes on the sand, stopping now and again to pick up a shiny shell.

Yet, sometimes the clues came in more tangible forms, as when he invited her on a trip to Omaha, Nebraska, for the sole purpose of viewing an exclusive Chihuly glass garden exhibit. Mariah had received a small parcel delivery at work with no note attached. The sender only revealed the picture of a flower sketched on the orange index card and a delicate bouquet of hand-blown flowers securely padded with fine threads of tissue paper.

She was entranced throughout the exhibit, her perception of each glass piece varying according to the natural light permitted to filter in as the day dwindled into night. She could still remember the vibrancy of the color palette: reds, oranges, yellows, and ambers dancing together, their tones transcending in and out of their natural pigments. "It's like being inside an explosion of colors," she gasped as she followed the organic movement of shapes and forms, much like an enchanted garden with its bioluminescent flora.

The clue "Santo before Monday" on the orange index card took them to the old city of Santo Domingo. She remembered their evening strolls on the cobblestone streets of the beautiful city in the heart of the Caribbean, the oldest in the New World, historians claim. Their toes rejoiced in the freedom afforded by the trendy Brazilian flip-flops slapping merrily on Calle de las Damas, the Street of the Ladies, where noblewomen promenaded in their finery many centuries ago. Now, the colonial ruins whispered songs from century-old pirates and Spanish merchant ghosts.

The scent of sea salt mixed with the aroma of old cigars followed them around like loyal companions. And then there were the flowers. Mariah wasn't prepared for the experience of the astonishingly splashes of hibiscus. She paused at the thought of the tropical beauty. She wondered about this flamboyant, trumpet-like flower flashing brightly in all colors of the rainbow: *What do you speak of?* Mariah imagined their curling petals attempting to conceal a secret, a shameful truth. *OR perhaps, you are just proud to show your deep self, your feminine prowess with your exaggerated long pistil.*

This tropical adventure of fresh passion fruit juice and strong black coffee was filed away in Mariah's memory. The old city vibrating with Latin rhythms had lured her into falling in love not so much with its magical surroundings, but with the tall, sun-kissed man wearing a happy grin who walked by her side.

"AHA! HERE WE ARE BACK AT THE SCENE of the crime. Just think: This is where it all started," Jake says, making a sweeping gesture over the firepit. He pulls Mariah into one of the empty chairs and sits down across from her, sipping his warm bourbon. The night is quieter than it had been two years ago when they had first met. Tonight's sky is dark and starless, but the blaze of the firepit is a reminder of the night in question. This time Eleanor had only invited her three friends and their companions to celebrate her birthday.

"You tried so hard to get rid of me, remember?" he smiles at Mariah expectantly.

She replies coldly, still upset at what she had discovered earlier that day. "I don't think that is entirely true," she says tersely. "But maybe I should have."

"And this is where I introduced Jake and Mariah," Eleanor announces to Luna as they approach the fire with beers in hand. She takes full credit for Jake and Mariah's affair, her tale of their meeting growing more elaborate over time.

"Yup! And we will be forever grateful to you, our dear Eleanor." Jake raises his drink to Eleanor, who grins with immeasurable pleasure because, indeed, it was Eleanor who indirectly had brought them together. He ignores Mariah's warning look, hoping no one else caught it.

"By the way, what's up with the new attraction on your front lawn?" Jake had asked Andrew earlier, but was told to ask Eleanor for an entertaining response.

"Are you freaking kidding me? The Director of Human Resources at the clinic decided this would be a great community building exercise," she continues on her rant.

"People are supposed to surprise other people by sending a flock of pink, plastic flamingos to their front yard in the dark of night. This is so irritating. I feel like we are back in high school fighting a popularity contest." There is no stopping her now.

"Did you see the gigantic sign?" She pauses and waits a second. Jake, Luna, and Gus shake their heads in unison.

Mariah jumps up to join Max by the pool. Jake's eyes follow them, his neck muscles tensing. That morning Mariah had found pieces of broken phone at the bottom of the trash in his office.

"What's this about?" she had asked, holding the discarded pieces in her hand. He felt the anger of her discovery swell up and began to wrap himself into the urge to unleash his sharp accusations for her lack of trust and invasion of his privacy. But Mariah's eyes had lingered on his face as if offering him the opportunity to explain, and the lies to cover up materialized on his lips with such ease that it surprised even himself.

"I got myself in a bit of a shamble with the Singapore accounts. I sort of knew some of the stuff was borderline illegal, but I didn't realize how much of a problem it is."

Jake had reacted to the panic and fear on Mariah's face and stopped. "It's all fine now. It's dealt with."

"I am not interested in being with a fraudster, Jake." came her calm warning.

Eleanor bursts into a playful laugh. "It says, 'You have been flocked!' But, it's more like 'you've been fucked,' in my opinion."

She explains the hassle of trying to figure out who hadn't been flocked and then following up with the company to come and collect the flamingos.

"Who has time for all that nonsense? Andrew thinks it's a cute idea, that his HR guy should get credit for trying, but is he planning to deal with the freaking flamingos? Of course not! I'm going to have to deal with it," she huffs in exaggerated exasperation.

"Or you could just leave them there with a 'help yourself to a bird' sign," Gus offers.

Jake looks across the yard. *Would she leave me if she discovers the bulk of my fuckup?* His eyes rest on Mariah, but he can only see her profile. He watches as her lips move gracefully in animated dialogue. He can't hear her words, yet he can sense the power of her delivery. Mariah radiates a kind of calm confidence, the type that draws people in to spill out their secrets in the hope that some of that confidence will rub off on them by the mere act of being near her, an absurd type of osmosis.

Jake's chest feels warm, not from the heat of the bourbon, but the familiar triumphant feeling, the one that says, *I am a lucky bastard.* He is very aware of the degree of contentment he feels waking up every day next to her, his Lady Rose. And even though she isn't happy with him right now, he knows she'll forgive him. He was sure of that. Now that they live together, Jake finds himself fantasizing about life as a married man. He had played mental scenarios of marriage proposals, uncertain of Mariah's response. He looks at her now and his mind mutters the words, "Don't leave me, Mariah," wishing for telepathic prowess.

*M*EG STARED AT THE lit candle burning brightly on the mantel.

"Happy Birthday, sweetheart," she whispered to the photograph in the picture frame. One small set of large brown eyes stared back at her. She traced over the glass gently, as if afraid that her fingers might erase the image. She thought about the day the photograph was taken. She was meandering around busily, hanging up birthday decorations in the hallway and in the playroom while her toddler tagged along excitedly. Meg picked up the white frame, staring at the image of a younger self, captured in a hand clapping motion. She could see the strain of keeping up with a toddler while caring for an ill child reflected on her face.

That was the day her oldest daughter turned eight. Both sets of grandparents were there to celebrate just like they had been in years past. The birthday girl was outside tying balloons to the black aluminum fence. Lucas had set up a large table with chairs early that morning for the decorate-your-own chef hat craft activity. They had invited a few girls her daughter knew from school to celebrate her birthday.

"Can we have a cooking party? We can make lots of treats with Papa," her daughter had requested. It came as no surprise, since cooking was her favorite thing to do, especially with her enthusiastic chef of a father.

Meg knew a baking activity in the late afternoon would be too strenuous for her daughter, so she coaxed her into a more manageable task.

"Sweetheart, wouldn't it be great fun if everyone got to decorate their own cupcake?" Meg asked tenderly. Her daughter's eyes lit up and Meg knew she was on board.

Lucas was thrilled with this arrangement. He baked the cupcakes with assistance from his daughters early that morning, when his older daughter's stamina was at its highest. They made strawberry frosting and set up the rainbow and chocolate sprinkles on separate dishes for decorating, and the girls smeared frosting all over their father's face. The kitchen had been enchanted with their jubilant laughs.

As the voices rang with the birthday melody, Meg kept a tight hold on her daughter, not knowing this was the last birthday her daughter would live to see.

MARIAH SITS COMFORTABLY on the living room couch. She feels the subtle heat of the smartphone cuddled snuggly between her ear and shoulder blade. She inspects her stubbed nails with shame. Her teeth had managed to eat through a perfect two-day-old manicure in just a few minutes.

"So, older and wiser, huh?" Mariah asks Rafael bouncily. She had called across the Atlantic Ocean to wish him a happy birthday.

"Definitely older. Wiser is, well, debatable," Rafael replies, clearly pleased to hear her voice at the other end.

"Did you do anything special? Wait, did the staff surprise you with a cake?"

"No, to the first question and yes to the second," Rafael replies with a laugh. "I have a slice in front of me now, with my favorite buttercream frosting and a half-burnt candle."

She pictures him spending his birthday the way he had for almost a dozen years: tending his lab. Every year, his colleagues "surprise" him with a rousing round of "Happy Birthday" in different languages represented by the multilingual team."

"Did I ever tell you that mosquitoes can smell human breath?" he says cheerfully.

Mariah settles in, very much enjoying hearing about Rafael's bug friends. She knows he's redirecting the conversation to avoid her annual lecture about leaving work early to treat himself to a dinner out.

"They have this cool mechanism that allows them to follow the trails of carbon dioxide we leave behind when we exhale," he says, pausing for her reply.

"Does that mean people with bad breath get bitten more often than their conscientious teeth brushing counterparts?" Mariah asks, laughing.

"Girl! That would make a good argument for brushing one's teeth, wouldn't it?" Rafael chuckles.

"How is it going in the world of DNA anyway?" Mariah inquires, her fascination showing in her voice.

"We're looking at mutation characteristics. It has been hard because of the mosquitoes' short life span, but now that we can manipulate their environment, they are thriving beautifully. It's incredible how we have been able to extend the lifespan to several months for a dozen species that originally only lived a couple of days."

"Tell me more," Mariah says.

"You're the only one who's interested in my work," Rafael says. "Okay, you asked! We are close to finding a way to completely manipulate mosquitoes' genome sequences. Imagine when we are finally able to go beyond genome editing to engineering nuclei. My hope is to create a new breed of mosquito and equip them with the good stuff; they are naturally built to be carriers. Our goal now is to rewrite their DNA so they can carry the antidote to many diseases."

"Yes?" Mariah says, prodding him on.

"You see, we already know that mosquitoes are attracted to certain human chemical odors like smelling people's breath, right? Well, what we now know for certain is that they are also able to pick up bodily scents undetectable by humans. I have a team already working on replicating human body scents into perfume and body spray that will attract certain mosquitoes while repelling others. In essence, people will potentially attract particular mosquitoes that are carriers of whatever medicine they need. We won't need pharmacies because most medicine will be flying around, inserted in mosquitoes' abdomens. Think about it, we wouldn't even need to inoculate children from terrible childhood diseases. Just spray your kid with the right type of scent, take him out for a hike, and *buzzzzz,* bite! He is vaccinated!"

"Rafa, you love those bugs so much you would spend a lifetime figuring out a way to change their DNA to restore their bad reputation," Mariah says.

The conversation shifts back to Rafael's birthday and Mariah bestows him one last happy wish before hanging up.

What if, she asks herself, imagining for a swift moment what her life would be like had she decided to follow Rafael. Her index finger searches her phone for pictures of him, of them. Her lips stretch into a broad smile at the innocence of the younger faces.

"You okay?"

Mariah turns her head in surprise, wondering how long Jake had been standing there.

She stands. "Are you spying on me?"

"Maybe I should be, given you're sneaking down here in the middle of the night to talk to your ex."

The distrust on his face quickly switches to shock as her phone flies from her hand to land with a quiet thump on his chest.

"You have the nerve to accuse me of sneaking around? I have seen the pictures of you whoring."

Panic gives way to shame. Jake's mouth opens, but the sounds stay trapped.

"That's what you wanted, to push me. You didn't have the decency to tell me yourself."

Jake 's eyes flicker like a set of defective light bulbs. He bites his lip and rubs his face. His shoulders move in unison to his heavy breathing, but his lips stay sealed.

Mariah steps right in his face. "You fucking coward!" she yells, her pitchy voice matching the hard jabbing of her index finger on his chest. Her stomach churns as she remembers the files she found in his office. The sexual harassment letters contained attachments of photocopies of the adult toys he had given his secretary.

"Is this what this is about? Are there more women coming after you?" Her fierce eyes deliver a warning.

Their eyes lock for a dozen heartbeats. Mariah feels the hot tears build up as if propelled by the heavy flow coming down Jake's face. She reads his despair and has to fight hard the desire to comfort him. She hears the clamor of her own internal voice pleading, *You are not a fucking paragon of virtue yourself. He comes with real issues and fucked up baggage just like everyone else.* But her unleashed anger lingers, swirling around them like suffocating puffs of smoke.

"Get away from me!" she yells at his attempt to reach for her, the defiance and fire flashing in her eyes.

"I can forgive, Jake. My whole fucking life has been about forgiving those who are supposed to love me, but I won't let you turn your fuck up around and make it about my fuck up. This is not my mess to fix. So, fix it and fix it good, Jake."

A long sigh escapes his mouth followed by a stuttering, "I am sorry." Mariah ignores his plea and flips off the lights as she exits the room.

The abrupt bang of the bedroom door startles him. Jake feels the weakening of his knees and collapses into the couch. He closes his eyes, holding his throbbing head in his hands.

$\mathcal{L}$UCAS KNOCKED GENTLY ON THE DOOR. "What about some lunch?" he asked Meg. She had been locked in her studio all morning working on a new painting after her daughter had sent her a small bouquet of white and purple baby's breath flowers. The attached note read:

'Everlasting love'

Lucas had surprised Meg by setting up a small art studio for her, hoping she would find solace in her old love of painting. He worked busily behind closed doors in what they called *the pink room* … what had been their older daughter's bedroom. Meg hadn't been in that space since the day of the funeral when she'd packed up the toys and clothes in boxes and carried them to the attic.

"It's just about done," Lucas announced one night as he made his way under the warm covers.

"You know how I feel about *that* room," Meg warned him with weary, heavy eyes.

"I know," Lucas whispered and caressed the loose strand of hair dancing on her face.

"It's just an idea. If it doesn't feel right then we will move on to a different idea," Lucas reassured her. He had tried once before to reclaim the space by turning *the pink room* into a playroom for their younger daughter. She yelled at him and had refused to enter the room altogether.

Lucas felt his insides tighten as he remembered how he had packed a small duffel bag and moved out for a few days after that argument. When he returned, Meg had welcomed him back without questions.

Meg had taken his hands in hers and held them tight. She traced the palms of his hands with her lips mouthing quietly, *I am sorry.*

Lucas snuggled tentatively a bit closer. His fingers caressed hers playfully. "I love your hands," she had whispered. "I wish I had the gift of reading people's palms."

"What would you see if you were reading mine?" Lucas propped his back against the headboard and pulled Meg a bit closer to his chest.

Meg had traced the long line closest to the thumb. "I think they call this the lifeline. I would tell you that you will live to be 108. That's a lucky number, you know. I would also tell you that the small lines connecting in and out of the lifeline are the people you love. Your family and closest friends; they will go in and out of your life, but never venture far."

She followed the line running down the middle of his palm. "I think this is called the headline. If you cup your hand just a little, that middle line will connect to the third line, the one closest to the pinky. That's the love line. You see?" She had paused and looked at him expectantly.

"They all connect together to create an outline of the letter M. Well as you know, M is for Meg. So I would tell you that you are going to be stuck with me for a very long time." And with that declaration, she had offered Lucas her biggest apologetic smile and he had pulled her closer to face him. When he turned off the lights, he had found her lips waiting for his.

Lucas snapped out of that memory and gave the door a third knock. This time, it yielded a response from inside the room.

"Come in," Meg's voice sounded through the door.

Lucas walked in, his eyes readjusting to the dark room lit only by the small metal desk lamp, its flexible hose neck projecting directly onto the wall casting shadows that felt as real as a live audience. She had once used an old Kodak projector. That's how she had created this collection.

Lucas set a plate of grilled cheese with extra tomatoes on the small table near the window and then sat on the floor in silence, just as the drawings of the flowers that surrounded him remained silent testimony to the years. They traveled as if following a hidden pattern from the baseboard of the floor up to the edge, where the wall kissed the ceiling. Some were abstracts, others so detailed with keen accuracy as if perceived through the eyes of a botanical artist.

Large bouquets of empty stems rested neatly by discarded piles of broken daisy petals on various parts of the walls. The botanical landscape of large-scale flowers, overpopulated by buttercups and daisies, stood in mural-like formation. Some overlapping so that it was hard to decipher whether they were real or an imagined hybrid summoned by Meg.

Lucas's eyes followed the colorless stretches forgotten or abandoned that seemed to stare back from their assigned spots. He felt the sadness and the pain that each line sketched.

He turned around to face the window in search of the lonesome vine of the morning glory. He found it and felt his body react. It twitched its way in and out, traveling the whole length around the room and finally wrapping its way hopelessly on the large heads of the burgundy red sunflowers trapped in the far corner of the room. Meg had worked on that particular drawing for a week straight, only stopping for a few hours of sleep.

The original beige color that he had used to paint the room, thinking it would make it seem much larger, now appeared to peer resentfully at the visitors from behind the cluster of flowers.

Lucas remembered the damp smell that once lived in the

room. It clung to you and tricked you into thinking of a rain forest until your eyes adjusted to the graveyard that swallowed the space.

Meg had refused any type of lighting in the room.

"It flares up my headaches," she had said, but Lucas understood her attraction to the darkness. It, too, was a familiar friend for him.

And so, the only light in the room had come from the soft glow emerging from the old Kodak slide projector. The faint humming racing into the room like bees and butterflies looking to make their homes among the brambles of branches that, over time, seemed to force their way out, looking to escape the scene. During the winter months, the clanking and hissing of the old hot water radiator added a sense of urgency to the lifeless flowers on the wall.

Meg's eyes moved from the small bouquet of flowers to the vivid sketch that was materializing as if the flowers were disappearing from their vase only to reappear on the wall.

Lucas smiled a sad smile. The bouquet of flowers, a silent acknowledgement his daughter sent her mother each year, a reminder that she, too, felt the sadness of a lost sister. He breathed in the loss, but stared at the vision in front of him.

"WILL YOU MARRY ME?" Jake's words fly out. When his ears decipher the words he is speaking, his brain alerts him to his unconscious act and his heart begins to pound at the absence of a response from Mariah. He immediately regrets being so impulsive.

Mariah rolls over on the bed gently, her body still euphoric from a Christmas morning of lovemaking. For days Jake had tried to make amends. When she ignored the parade of flowers, and the storm of posted notes with the single word, *sorry*, he had placed around the apartment, he had pleaded with Eleanor to advocate on his behalf.

"She knew of your Casanova complex and chose to ignore it for two years. She will either dump you or give you a chance. Ignoring people's transgressions and shortfalls is something she does well, and that makes you a lucky bastard. But let me be clear, if she chooses to give you a chance and you screw up again, I swear you'll be leaving Boston a castrated Casanova, by my own doing. Trust me, I know my way with knives."

Jake nuzzles a bit closer to Mariah and takes her hands in his. He kisses her fingers meticulously, one by one. She mimics his kisses, migrating to his muscular torso and eventually lands on his lips. Her tongue traces the outline of his lips and sensually penetrates his welcoming mouth. Her body moves with ease and familiarity

"Ohh," Jake grunts in delight.

Mariah slithers her way back to reclaim her place on top. She pulls her face back and peers into Jake's eyes. He smiles with relief, the twinkle in her eyes delivering the response to his earlier request. Jake caresses her face, their bodies surrendering to desire.

"*O*H, THE SMELL OF A NEW car!" Lucas commented, expecting one of Meg's playful comebacks. They were driving their new hybrid to Lenox for a Valentine's Day weekend of folk music, fine wine, and exquisite dining. Lucas was at the wheel chattering away about how much different it felt from driving a conventional vehicle.

"Our daughter was right. It's so much smoother and quieter," he remarked, and then went on excitedly to explain the regenerative braking mechanism of the engine. Meg nodded and pretended to listen, but her thoughts were elsewhere, riding waves of memories.

She was thinking about her youngest daughter who had been so unlike many other children. Not the sort, for instance, who would pack up a bag and threaten to run away as a way of drawing some parental love reaffirmation. Nor had she dragged her small mattress into the yard in protest that her parents had not given in to an egocentric childhood desire. Her daughter, at a young age, had learned to separate herself emotionally from the turmoil of her household by escaping into her own imaginary world.

There was a period in which she spent hours digging small trenches and covering them with rows of small twigs. They asked about her game and she said, "The little people underground need a home. They have rainbow skin and long noses like elephants." She had created a perfect world where families were happy and whole. Where perhaps there was a mother whose eyes did not resemble a lifeless zombie because she couldn't bring herself to deal with the painful reality of her own world on most days. She was a mother who welcomed invisibility and chose to blend seamlessly into a pale wall overshadowed by life. Her heartbreak from the loss of one child prevented her from being fully available to her other living child.

Meg released the memory, ready to break away from her past, but a newer, happier memory jumped in. Her daughter was in the yard again, but this time Lucas was at her side, their hands protected by flowery garden gloves. They sang as they loosened the soil in the vegetable beds, Lucas using a regular trowel and she a child's version. It was a beautiful spring day, still too cold for most vegetables, but just safe enough for lettuce and snow peas. They had started the seeding indoors weeks before, and now the new plants were mature enough to be transplanted outside.

Meg had watched and listened from the kitchen window at her daughter's excited shouts. She dug out a small rock only to surprise a sleeping frog underneath. She scooped up the small frog in her hand with the excitement and glee reserved for a child her age and brought it inside for her mother to see, her small hand outstretched in offering.

Meg smiled and breathed deeply, looking out at the passing countryside, ready to be present. She glanced at Lucas whose eyes were dancing between the rearview mirror and the road ahead. He slowed down to allow an impatient driver to pass him. Lucas and Meg didn't miss the collection of hula doll dancers shaking their hips violently on the rear dashboard as the car sped past them. There was a bumper sticker with the words *Eat More Kale* staring back at them judgingly.

Lucas commented, "Perhaps that driver should eat less kale and more dill, or take a pill." He smiled at his own joke.

"Music or news?" Meg asked, already knowing his response. She tapped the screen on the dashboard and a list of stations flashed to life. Meg scrolled up and down with her index finger settling on 90.9 FM, Boston National Public Radio.

"*All Things Considered*, it is then," she announced, turning the volume up a tad. The distinctive voice of Robert Siegel resonated, forcing both Meg and Lucas to pay attention. Meg listened, trying to follow the thread of the interview, but felt distracted by the sound of the voice of the young woman who was answering Robert Siegel's questions. The sound made her feel the way she did when scrunching her nose, listening to the likes of Katey Sagal singing a melody.

Meg moved her finger back to the small touch screen and tapped on Magic 106.7.

"Just until the interview is over," she said, pointing playfully at her nose.

"*Today's Hits, Yesterday's Favorites*," Lucas replied, attempting David Allan Boucher's hushed voice. Meg smiled. She loved the "Mystery Man" disc jockey whose sexy voice had lulled Bostonians to sleep for decades.

"Remember that time we were getting ice cream downtown and we heard him order a milkshake?" Meg asked, remembering how they had turned around in unison at the sound of the voice belonging to the host of Bedtime Magic, expecting to hear the "Welcoming you with open arms" slogan.

"Yeah, that was nice, but weird," Lucas answered. "I wonder what he would have answered had we asked him if he was in fact *the* David Allan Boucher?"

"He would have probably denied it, don't you think? He kept the mystery so long. I tell you, though, the face did not match the image I had attached to the voice. It's not that I was disappointed by any means. It's just that I was way off," she trailed off, remembering the stranger with Alan Boucher's voice.

"Of course, it could have also been an impersonator," Lucas said. "He probably gets a chuckle seeing people's reactions."

They listened quietly as the cohost of the show now shared

2

bits and pieces of current news and events, embedding jokes about her personal life as a single mother. Then the voice of Billy Joel took over, followed by George Michael and a young voice belonging to a more contemporary singer.

"Any idea who that is?" Lucas gestured toward the screen and raised a questioning eyebrow. Meg shrugged and looked out the window as if the name of the artist might appear on one of the passing billboards.

The *Text Stop Ahead* sign on the side of the road caught Meg's attention. She wondered how many vehicles she would see at the stop when they drove by it.

"Did you see that sign about texting we just passed?" Meg asked.

"I missed it. What did it say? No texting and driving?"

"No, it actually informs drivers that there is a text stop ahead."

"Wow. Now, that is something," Lucas replied.

"Remember when we were teenagers? Our parents were so freaked out about us being safe drivers."

"Yeah. They worried about us driving under the influence of alcohol and drugs."

"Today we have to add technology distractions to our worries."

"This generation has evolved into social media junkies unable to disconnect from their online personas," Meg lamented.

"I wonder at the number of accidents that must have occurred to bring about this Text Stop movement," Meg commented with a heavy heart.

"*HAVE YOU ASKED HER YET?*" reads the text from Andrew. There'd been several of those inquiries in the past few days. Jake regrets having told him. *At least I didn't tell him about the failed attempt.*

Jake is not a fan of unsolicited advice. He had been thinking and calculating his next move ever since Mariah's silent agreement to marry him. Her recent decision to move in with him had felt like a great triumph.

"*I am a man with a plan.*" He replies to Andrew, hoping it is enough information to satisfy his curiosity.

Jake pulls out the filing cabinet drawer to the sound of a metallic shriek, then hastily withdraws a folder. He can almost hear the content mocking him. *You will be back for more.*

"I am done," he responds to the taunting.

Jake opens the folder and extracts the contents one paper at a time. He inspects each piece before feeding it into the shredder that whirs hungrily as if receiving a much anticipated meal.

The quietness feels almost ritualistic to Jake. He hunches over and unclasps the cover of the mulcher as if to ensure the machine has done its job. He stares at the fragments of the letters and photographs of women now blending together in a colorful heap of shred. His shoulders relax as if an internal weighted vest is slipping away.

The loud clanking of the elevator as it stops alerts Jake to Mariah's arrival. The jittery thumping of his heart joins the concert of the butterfly wings flapping in the depths of his core.

"Your face looks radiant," Jake says, inspecting Mariah's shiny face, the result of her organic oil facial.

"You have learned quickly," Mariah teases with a kiss.

"How was it?" Jake asks expectantly. His nervousness is making him overplay his enthusiasm.

"Great. We decided to add a deep tissue massage and were glad that *the gazelle* could squeeze us both in. Mom usually goes for the Swedish massage because it's gentler, but she let me convince her to try the deep tissue massage this time. I think it was the hot stones that convinced her." Mariah continues to recount the spa day adventure with her mother, their March tradition of welcoming Spring together.

"You like it?" Mariah holds out her hands so Jake can have a complete view of her fingernails. The acrylic impostors smiling brightly, a happy conspirator that conceal its owner's compulsive habit.

"It's called *In the Name of Hibiscus*. You see? It goes from a darker pink at the base to a lighter shade toward the tips." Mariah lifts her foot up in front of her and Jake catches it midair. She leans back and falls into the couch, her arms outstretched to welcome Jake into a happy embrace.

"I got a little something for you," he declares.

Mariah smiles seductively.

"Get your mind out of the gutter, at least for now," Jake teases back.

"Here." Jake hands her a delicately wrapped gift box. Mariah looks up at him with curiosity. The box opens to reveal a pair of long lace gloves. Jake is a master in the art of gifting. He has found a nice balance when choosing gifts for Mariah that zigzag between extravagance, simplicity, and thoughtfulness.

"They are gorgeous," Mariah comments, her fingers gliding through the delicate garments.

"There is something inside …" Mariah stops mid-sentence to retrieve an emerald-cut diamond set in an elegant band.

"My Lady Rose, would you whisk away my despair and

complete my otherwise lonely existence by becoming my wife?"

"But Jake, I have already said yes. I thought you understood my answer the first time you asked." Mariah smiles with a small hint of embarrassment.

"Oh, I know. I just wanted to do it properly this time," he says with a boyish expression on his face.

"Jake?" Mariah hesitates just for a second. Jake looks up expectantly.

"I would love to be your wife. And Jake? Will you be OK with a shortish engagement?"

"Of course. Jeez, I almost thought that you were going to change your mind. Short is good. What about a two-hour engagement? That might give us just enough time to call a few people over and make it official. Or, maybe I will just stop talking and you can tell me what you would like."

"Wait!" Mariah says. "No, I still want my fancy dress and beautiful wedding reception. Maybe we could call the manager of that hotel we stayed at on Block Island. This will be a good chance to go back and reclaim the community rock. I am sure my mom would love to be in charge of that. So, I am thinking somewhere along the lines of two months." She moves closer for a tight snuggle.

"A May wedding on Block Island. Perfect." Jake kisses her forehead triumphantly. After two years and six months of dating, two months is not a long time to wait.

"DID YOU CALL THE VET?" Meg was sitting on the couch patting Maddy on the chest and then moved her hand up to rub behind her floppy ears. Maddy snuggled closer and Meg could sense the pleasure in her breathing.

"Yes, she wants us to bring Maddy in this morning during walk-in hours. We need to collect a stool sample to bring in."

"I'm sure there's nothing to worry about," added Lucas confidently.

"Maybe we should start feeding her regular store-bought food instead of the homemade recipes you have been concocting all these years," Meg said only half joking.

"It has nothing to do with my culinary practices, I assure you," Lucas laughed and pulled her closer.

Lucas knew how to calm her down, how to make her feel safe.

Maddy, their young mutt, had recently developed a taste for dirt. It hadn't worried Meg and Lucas much until they noticed that the dog was also losing weight.

"She has definitely lost a few pounds, but nothing alarming," declared the vet. "Eating dirt is a good indication of mineral deficiency. My sense is that she might not be getting enough minerals in her diet," she added.

Meg shot Lucas an accusatory glare.

"But I'm going to order some blood work just to be sure. We want to see that all is well with her guts and her thyroid." The vet scribbled a few words on a slip of paper and directed Meg and Lucas down the hall to a small office.

Meg took out the small plastic bag containing Maddy's stool sample. The fecal testing would help identify the presence of intestinal parasites, the vet assistant explained. She injected Maddy with a small amount of thyroid stimulating hormone and instructed them to return four hours later to have Maddy's blood sample drawn. It would be just enough time for the hormone to get into her bloodstream.

"How long will it take for the tests to come back?" Meg asked impatiently.

"It usually takes two to three days. I would say more like three days. This sample won't be picked up by the lab until tomorrow morning," she said.

"Let's go, Maddy girl," Lucas said, rubbing Maddy's ears tenderly. "And let's stop at the pet store to get you some food," he added, certain of Meg's smile behind him.

Part Four

alstroemeria of the Incas
turning and twisting
when all fall around
you wait
you stay
mending broken promises

*T*HE FOUR FRIENDS are celebrating Mariah's engagement. She had called them all one by one after she and Jake had concluded their own celebration. They had chosen a date together, and Mariah wanted to make sure her friends had it so they could save the date, even though she knew she was not giving them much advance notice.

"Are you pregnant?" Eleanor asked in response to Mariah's news. Gus sent a *"Congrats!"* message. Max's response carried a different tone: *"I hope he has the good sense to treasure the gift that you are."*

Eleanor had chosen a Mediterranean restaurant on the outskirts of the city. In her opinion, it offers the best spanakopita and baked sweet potatoes, and Mariah is a big fan of sweet potatoes, in any form.

The friends are just settling down at a high table by the window when they hear the high-pitched cacophony of three waiters singing a Happy Birthday song to an elderly woman a table over.

"I wonder why restaurants don't just sing the regular birthday song? Some of these restaurants' hybrid compositions are just ridiculous," Eleanor comments while arranging her bag at the foot of the table. "If you are going to use the tune, why not just help yourself to the lyrics?"

"Well, simply because they can't," Mariah explains. "They are not legally allowed to. Haven't you noticed that even in movies and on television shows they tend to avoid singing the birthday song? They do everything with the cake and all, but avoid singing the song, unless they have paid the fee."

"Are you serious? *Happy Birthday To You* is copyrighted?" Gus asks in disbelief.

"Yeah, a bunch of artists have been challenging the publishing company who vehemently claims they purchased the legal rights from the original publishers. The artists argue that the song should belong in the public domain. Meanwhile, restaurants avoid paying licensing fees by writing their own in-house variations."

"Wow!" Gus reacts in surprise. "Only in America."

"*HAPPY ENGAGEMENT TO YOU, HAPPY ENGAGEMNT TO YOU,*" sings Eleanor to the tune of "Happy Birthday to You," and the friends follow along.

"A toast to Mariah for finally allowing herself to get hitched," Eleanor proclaims with great joy. "Two down, two to go!" she adds with determination while pointing her finger at Max and Gus.

Mariah turns her gaze from her exuberant friend to Gus. "You ditcher. Why weren't you at the fundraising event last week?" she asks, hoping to redirect Eleanor's current matrimonial focus.

Gus had introduced Mariah to the nonprofit foundation Make Ways for Women, back when they were in college. Gus's mother was Executive Director at the time. The foundation's mission is to train inner-city women for the work force. Many of those women are young mothers who have completed their GEDs or are transitioning back from a drug rehabilitation program.

"Oh, sorry. I thought I told you that I wasn't going to be able to make it this year. Too much shit at work. Was Pete there?"

"No," she says, turning toward her friend. "I didn't see Pete and Sean there. I actually was hoping to get a chance to talk to Sean. When I saw him last year, he and Pete were talking about health insurance costs. I talked a little bit with Sean. He seemed tired and distracted. It sounded like they were having a hard time caring for the baby. So I didn't get a chance to look for them. Jake and I got stuck hanging out with some of the people who run the foundation. They're trying to recruit new board members."

"And you said no, right? N-O," Eleanor jumps in with an air of judgment.

"Well, not exactly." Mariah bites her lower lip in embarrassment.

"Mariah! Really? When will you learn? People are going to squeeze the life out of you if you let them. The more you give of yourself, the more they grab. It's not that freaking hard," she adds in exasperation.

"Watch me." Eleanor holds out her hand in a high-five motion and declares in a role-playing voice. "I am honored to be asked, but let me get back to you." She exaggerates the intonation of the last sentence.

"Cut her a break, would you?" Max jumps in to block the attack.

"Anyway …" Mariah gives Max a little "let her be" look and continues her conversation with Gus. "How are things going with the baby?"

"Actually, not so well, as of a couple of weeks ago," Gus says.

"Oh no, what happened? Is the baby OK?"

"Yeah, the baby is fine. She is doing all that stuff that babies are supposed to do. The problem is Sean."

The three friends stop to listen as Gus describes how Sean has checked out on Pete and the baby.

"He felt that it was too much for him to deal with. Too much to handle, I guess."

"WOW! That is totally fucked up," Eleanor responds.

"Pete said Sean had been drinking a lot. Apparently one day Pete came home from work before dinner to find Sean passed out on the couch and the baby crying bloody murder in her crib."

Mariah covers her mouth to the horror she is hearing, "That's terrible. Poor Pete," she says.

"Yeah. It's pretty messy. It seems Sean had a bit of a situation with the police. Apparently, the highway patrol knocked on his truck while he was sleeping at a weigh station. Sean opened the door for them to do their random search." The friends listen, captivated as Gus goes on to describe how the officers found illegal drugs inside the cargo bin.

"Why did he open the door for them? Did they have a warrant? Did he not know it's against the law for officers to wake an off-duty truck driver?" Mariah does not wait for a reply, but goes on to retell a case she followed years ago involving a trucker who filed a civil rights lawsuit against the highway troopers for emotional damages and for permanent injunction with the hope of dissuading rogue cops from carrying on with this illegal practice.

"This trucker was awakened from his sleeper berth," she says. "The cops demanded his ID. They had no probable cause or even a warrant, so the guy refused to show them his ID just on principal. He was forced out of his truck, handcuffed, and arrested."

"On what grounds?" Eleanor asks, shaking her head.

"Criminal offense," Mariah replies, then utters in air quotes, "obstruction of justice."

"Why anyone would choose to be a truck driver is beyond my comprehension. It's like people don't give a shit about those poor souls. The work they do forms the pillar of America. They spend all this time away from their families to haul goods across the country," Eleanor says with genuine concern.

"Well, Sean was cooked, so I don't think he was capable of making reasonable decisions, plus they found the narcotics. Pete had to go and bail him out." Gus explains how Pete had called him in the middle of the night and asked him to come and stay the night with Cece so that he could drive to New Jersey to pay the fine.

"He was so angry. And I don't blame him. Imagine if he hadn't found someone to stay with the baby. To take your child into a police station to bail out her father? That ought to be a recipe for a psychological case down the road," Gus declares.

"It must be hard. The parenting thing, I mean," Mariah says, thinking about how Pete was forced to become a single parent who must also bear the responsibility of watching after the other parent.

"Well, it definitely complicates things," Gus says, looking at Eleanor. "I'm with you on that front. No kids for me. Thank you very much."

"What about you?" Mariah elbows Max, encouraging him. They both knew what his response will be.

"Yes, Luna and I both want a few." He smiles unapologetically, the spark in his eyes speaking louder of his desire to be not just a father, but a father to Luna's future children.

"What about you, bride to be?" Eleanor taunts. "You sure you don't already have a little muffin baking in that oven?"

"Yes, I am sure," Mariah replies, "and stop sounding so witchy. You're freaking me out. I don't have to worry about you kidnapping my baby in the middle of the night and running into the woods to eat him, do I?" Mariah jokes as Eleanor rubs her flat stomach, calling out, "I'm coming to eat you!"

Mariah smiles a sad smile. No, she is not pregnant . Jake had asked her months ago to have a baby with him. She had felt a brief thrill at the idea and considered flushing her contraceptive pills down the toilet, but the thought was short lived. What a shameful secret, she thinks.

She allows the image to float in her head for a few seconds and wonders at her motherhood prowess. Would she become the type of mother she wished she had had growing up? Mariah ignores the echo of her inner voice, *What if you are gifted a cursed womb?*

EG ROLLED OUT OF bed reciting the mantra given to her by Dr. Moll: "Today is here for me." She made her way downstairs holding onto those words like a promise. She considered how she had not felt the crippling exhaustion in several days, but did not dwell on it for long. She knew better than to be too hopeful.

Meg had kept her weekly visits with Dr. Moll. The good humouredness of the therapist had drawn out Meg's words with ease. She found herself looking forward to their sessions which, during nice weather, were conducted outside by taking a stroll down bustling Beacon Street.

She turned the electric kettle on and waited a few minutes for the steam to appear, then poured herself a cup of hot water and dipped in a bag of jasmine green tea. Meg inspected the cast iron skillet sitting on the burner, still warm. She grabbed the empty cereal bowl by the sink and helped herself to some of the thick steel-cut oatmeal from the pan, added some agave and a handful of almonds to the paste, and sat by the window to consume her breakfast.

There was no sign of Lucas or Maddy anywhere. The house was completely silent except for the crunching sound of the almonds in her mouth.

Meg thought about poor Maddy. The vet had called to explain the test results.

"It's a case of hypothyroidism." The vet had gone on to explain how the thyroid glands were being attacked by the immune system and how this is a common disease in dogs.

Meg had almost laughed with disbelief when the vet informed her of the diagnosis. Many years back, her own doctor had been certain that *she* was having thyroid problems, only to find out she was expecting. She thought of that possibility. What were the chances?

"Treating hypothyroidism in dogs is much easier than treating it in humans," the vet explained.

"I'll prescribe thyroid hormone supplements, but there are also some natural herbal treatments available. I'm happy to talk to you about that. I know how you and Lucas feel about traditional medicine," she said.

Meg unplugged her phone from the charging station and opened the running application. She swiped to find her recent playlist, always amused at her ability to set this up. She thought about the technology that allowed her to track her weekly runs and to run with such a variety of music. She could even listen to talk shows about politics, the economy, or the occasional comedy episodes to make her run go by quickly.

Meg remembered running with a Walkman and then a Discman back in her youth. She thought about the story of how the company cofounder had challenged the executives to create a simple and easy-to-carry device that would allow him to listen to classical music on his long flights. The engineers had presented him with a prototype of the Walkman, which became an instant sensation among his own grandchildren. The company quickly realized the potential. Instead of marketing the tool to companies and businesses, they targeted the youth market.

She reflected on how parents at the time were concerned about the negative impact those gadgets had on their children's interaction with each other and the world around them. Her own parents had accused her and her siblings of being too self-absorbed and enveloped in their own worlds. Meg chuckled at the realization that the parents of her generation had similar worries about all these technologies this generation had to navigate.

All this distraction and social media pressure, the need to carry a smart phone at all times with the sole purpose of sharing pictures, was something that concerned her. What will become of this next generation? Even dating was now done online.

Would people eventually have to relearn how to talk to each other face to face? Meg felt a pang of nostalgia. She missed the time when people would write "Dear John" letters when they lacked the courage to terminate a relationship face to face. Now a quick text did all the work; it made it too easy for people to give up on relationships.

It was no secret that Meg liked having a smartphone, especially for running. She wouldn't deny that the experience of running with a smart device these days was a far more pleasurable experience than jogging with a *Walkman* tightly clasped in her hand.

Her thoughts were silenced as loud barking announced Lucas and Maddy's return. The back door opened and a cheerful "Morning, Love!" greeted her.

Lucas sprinkled a clump of lilac florets next to the empty oatmeal bowl, and Meg reached over just in time to catch one of the delicate flowers in her outstretched hand. She brought the single bloom to her nose and inhaled the sweet aroma, smiling at a memory of her mother planting a set of three burgundy-purple bushes when they had first moved in, "to drive away the evil eye," her mother had said.

"How was the walk?" Meg asked, her eyes fixed on the vibrant flowers that seemed to whisper jovially in the language of youthful innocence.

"It's quite pleasant. Good running weather, I suspect. It's pretty, too, if you run by the lake. Lots of great tulips blooming. Just be prepared for the strong smell of mulch. Oh, I bumped into the Patricks there. They're watching over their granddaughter for the week. It sounds like Claire and her husband are going back to adopt another baby. An older child this time, maybe five or six years old. Apparently it's getting harder to adopt newborns."

"Good for them!" Meg wondered briefly what it would be like to be a grandmother.

"Lucas," Meg said, remembering the Walkman. "I was thinking about those little stereo cassette players."

"What about them? I think we might still have a couple of those up in the attic somewhere."

"I was just thinking that I always hated how they all had the word 'man' in them. First there was the Discman, and then the Walkman."

"Do you think it's a direct translation from its original name in Japanese?" Lucas said.

"Definitely not. It's totally a chauvinistic American thing. I think in Sweden they called them the Freestyle and in the UK they called it the Stowaway. Only the USA focuses on all this gender nonsense."

"Were you thinking about them because you were wondering whether they will make a comeback?"

"No. I was actually drowned in nostalgia. It strikes me as a perfect metaphor for how simpler life was then. You pop a tape or disc in the device, press a button, and off you go. I miss that sense of simplicity."

*I*T HAS BEEN OVER TWO MONTHS since Mariah moved in with Jake, yet the feeling of being an impostor swaddles her each time she steps out of the elevator and is greeted by the grandiose entryway. How she wishes she could breathe and sniff in all the luxury like a quick hit of cocaine.

She walks into the apartment and immediately sees the large cat lying comfortably at the foot of the sectional couch in the family room. "What the fuck!" she yelps, looking around for an explanation as her brain throws in possibilities. Has she walked into their neighbor's apartment? *No.* Then what? Maybe the cat belongs to their neighbor. But how did it get here? Had Jake offered to cat sit? She would certainly have remembered if he had mentioned it.

"Jake!" Mariah's hesitant voice calls out into the quiet house, her eyes wide open, staring at the orange cat with a tabby stripe-patterned coat. There comes a response not from Jake, but from the cat. The self-assured feline has no problem introducing itself. It purrs and walks past her in the direction of the kitchen, its flirty tail wrapping gingerly around Mariah's ankle, a sign of territorial belonging.

Mariah's eyes follow the fur ball that had clearly lost interest in the human and instead found a sunny spot by the window to lie down.

"Jake?" Mariah calls out again, her voice indicating understanding as she takes in the water and food dishes by the side of the refrigerator. A small contraption with the appearance of a spherical robot straight out of a *Star Wars* movie sits at the other end of the kitchen, a couple of feet from the guest bathroom. Mariah assumes it must be the cat's litter box. Mariah spots the note left on the counter and reads it aloud, knowing that it will explain the appearance of the sleepy mouser.

He has been following me home all week. He had no tag on. I asked the neighbors downstairs and they said they see him around all day and have been leaving food out for him. I drove him to the Animal Rescue Center this morning and they said we could keep him. They had him all immunized and checked. He needs a name. P.S. Can we keep him?

Mariah sets the note down and imagines Jake waiting in the cat room while the vet tended to the stray cat in some small office across the hallway. She wonders about his reaction to the crowded and gloomy space being profoundly repugnant. Was he coaxed by the feline cries or did the biographies hanging on the cages convince him? Mariah remembers the cleverness of the bios written from the point of view of the cats.

Mariah imagines Jake's childish grin when told by the vet that he could keep the cat. She had known he was a cat lover; dogs, too, as a matter of fact. He had been talking about getting a dog for quite some time, but dropped the idea after Mariah reminded him that with all his traveling, she would be the one stuck taking care of the dog, and she had no interest in doing that. She knows how much work dogs required. Now here she is facing this beautiful animal, unsure if beautiful is the right way to describe Jake's new four-legged friend. Mariah kneels down, offering her hand for the cat to inspect. Her fingers receive a wet sniff and a gentle lick, which she interprets as the cat's permission to be petted.

Mariah strokes the soft cat hesitantly on its side, her fingers sinking into the heavy fur. The cat eyes her suspiciously, but remains beside her. Mariah had grown up around dogs, so feels a bit out of her comfort zone now. She has not spent much time around cats, but she is certain of one thing: Cats behave very differently from dogs. *Your type likes to do things on their own terms. I respect that,* she whispers to the motionless animal.

Mariah reaches into her purse and pulls out her phone. She snaps a picture of the cat and texts it to Jake: "*I just met the new member of our family.*"

His response is immediate: "*Does that mean we are keeping him?*"

"*As long as you know what to do with him. That includes litter box and all,*" Mariah responds, her message followed by an alarmed emoji.

"*Cats are easygoing and great companions, I hear. AND the vet said that Winston Churchill had one that looked just like him.*" Mariah loves that Jake plays up her devotion to the willful prime minister.

"*If you are going through hell, keep going,*" she texts one of her favorite Churchill quotes back, smiling as she remembers the recording he sent her the morning after their engagement in which Churchill declared, "My most brilliant achievement was my ability to be able to persuade my wife to marry me." Mariah had loved Jake's goofy note about taking love advice from her *old pal.* He had written the note to introduce the link to the recording, showing a static black-and-white photograph of a smiling Churchill. An iconic image with cigar in hand and his signature Homburg hat perched upon his head.

"Hi, handsome; I am Mariah," she introduces herself to the cat with one hand still burrowed deep into the cat's fur. "How do you feel about Copperknob for a name?" The orange ball of fur stands up and bumps its head on Mariah's knees. Mariah sits on the floor and welcomes the cat into her lap.

"I will take that as a yes." She smiles at the purring cat that had just been informally baptized with Winston Churchill's childhood nickname, a name attributed to his head of shaggy red hair.

EG STARED AT THE PICTURE of a younger self posing next to a teenager balancing a soccer ball on her head. Her daughter's skin baked a shade darker by the summer sun seemed to repel the paleness of her own skin, whose idea of tan came closer to that of a ripe strawberry. Meg picked up the frame and daggers of guilt shot deeply into her insides, remembering that day so vividly.

"Where is the camping chair? And where is that soft blue blanket?" Meg had rushed around the house trying to gather the things she often brought to the games.

"It's where you left them last time," Lucas joked. And, indeed, she found them in the coat closet in the sunroom where all sports-related paraphernalia lived. Meg walked around the kitchen table and gave the purple irises a gentle pat, their drooping petals a reminder of what she had lost. It was Mother's Day that weekend. Her own mother had sent her purple irises for many years. It was Lucas who continued this ritual now that her mother was gone. *Courage,* she muttered to herself.

Their daughter had made the varsity team. They were all ecstatic. She had trained so hard all summer. The tryouts were excruciating to watch, and to think that even though she was selected to play on the team this fall, she would still need to go through the same selection process again the following year.

"There are some bleachers at the field," Lucas said, calling to her from the driveway.

Meg was new to this world of elite soccer. She had been bothered by the shift of playing the game for fun to now playing the game to win. She stayed away from the politics behind the decisions about playing time. She heard the girls complaining about some players getting more playing time than others, and that made her question the integrity of the game. It appeared that the coaches had their own secret rules about playing time that had less to do with fairness and more to do with ability and who could make the right play to win the game.

Then there were the parents. It had taken some getting used to their constant shouting of: "Be aggressive! Go after her, full force!" Or the "Oh crap!" shouts when the opponent team scored a goal. Or their continuous yelling of instructions at their daughters from the sideline as if they needed the additional pressure from their parents to be motivated.

Meg hadn't played organized sports growing up, but she had attended sports camps in the summer. She was familiar with the thrill and excitement of competitive sports. She was a big baseball fanatic, after all. She knew the ins and outs of that game, but soccer was totally foreign territory.

"Mom, please remember they are called goals, not points," her daughter had counseled. Meg chuckled at that and followed her daughter out the door. She still referred to referees as umpires, even after all those years of watching her daughter play the game.

Their younger daughter was a natural athlete. She played softball when she was in third grade. Meg had been recruited as coach of that team. Then her daughter discovered soccer and she was hooked. She spent hours dribbling the ball out in their backyard. It was Lucas who had to step up as assistant coach. He played soccer in his younger years, so he was thrilled about his daughter's interest in the game. While Meg saw the game as dangerous and filled with conflicts, Lucas saw it as exciting and strategic.

He taught her how to practice ball control by dribbling the ball using the outside, inside, and the soles of her feet. Even when she watched TV, her soccer ball would roll like a pendulum back and forth between her feet.

When her daughter got to high school, Meg was concerned about the degree of commitment expected from these young athletes: three games and three practices a week, including a Sunday evening game. But her daughter was so happy and had balanced her schoolwork and sports expectations so seamlessly that Meg had to put her concerns aside.

"Have we played that team before?" Meg asked from the backseat of the car.

Meg always allowed her daughter to ride in the passenger seat next to Lucas, to and from the games. She knew what a big treat it was for her daughter to go to her games siting in the front. Meg was so proud of her daughter; this was one way of showing her that.

"Yeah. They're pretty good. We played them early in the season. It was a close game but we lost 4-2. I had two assists, right Dad?" Her daughter stopped searching for a hair elastic in her sports bag to look at her father.

"Yeah. I think that's right. Amanda was the goalie. I only remember that because they got a penalty kick because the ref called a handball on her. We were all shocked. They are usually more lenient with the goalkeeper." Lucas went on, "You guys marked well in that game."

Meg listened, pretending to understand the soccer jargon.

She watched as a player kicked the ball toward her daughter. She ran at great speed and trapped the ball in the air, her two long French braids flipping all around like an extra pair of arms. She scanned the field, dribbled the ball to open space, and gave a nice through pass to the striker for a clean finish.

Meg watched proudly as her daughter ran up to her teammates to pick them up or high five them when they scored a goal.

Her encouraging cries resonated throughout the game.

"We got this!"

Other parents often commented, "That kid of yours is just a sweetheart. She is not only a heck of a midfielder; she truly is the spirit of the team."

Meg was glad that others saw what she and Lucas saw in their daughter. They marveled at their daughter on and off the field. Her kind disposition earned her many beautiful friendships, some of which she maintained to this day.

Meg set the frame back down and caressed the happy teenager. *May nothing ever extinguish your light*, she muttered, pushing away the memory of herself swallowing handfuls of white pills that very same night the picture was taken.

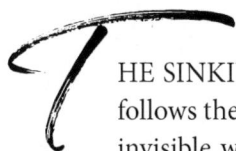

THE SINKING FEELING OVERTAKES HER. Mariah follows the young girl, her shoulders drooping with an invisible weight. She recognizes the weight, the pressure to always be *more than.* The relentless attempt to make up for the pain of her parents. Her desire to fix what life itself had broken. Then she sees the hand reaching out for the girl. The girl holds onto the hand and her mother smiles.

The sound of the budding branches tapping at her window awakens her, and the young girl stays trapped in her dream. Mariah's eyes adjust to the morning light as she realizes she is back in her childhood room in the metal-framed bed high off the ground.

"Can I have a bed that I can climb up to?" she had asked her parents. They were hesitant to get her bunk beds, so they had found a happy compromise. Her father took Mariah to a thrift store to choose a bed frame, and she quickly spotted the white wrought-iron antique frame with an intricate canopy.

Her father had built a platform a few feet off the ground, and Mariah helped him build the wooden steps. She had also wanted wraparound curtains. The heavy burgundy velvet fabric transformed the bed into a hideaway.

Jake was in Singapore this week tying down the loose ends of his business dealings there. Mariah had asked if he wanted her to go along, but he had assured her that it was something he needed to do alone. When they were discussing the trip, he had brought Mariah closer for a prolonged kiss. "I am done with Singapore. And I am done with working sixteen-hour shifts. I am done with that part of my life or anything that threatens this, us." She was taken aback by the relief she read on his face.

Mariah is glad she decided to come home last night. She brought takeout from the local Thai restaurant her parents liked, the one with the rude hosts Mariah often complained about. Even so, she found herself returning there time and again like an obedient pigeon. She did keep to her promise of just doing takeout, though. She and her parents watched some of the campaign highlights while forking their way through generous helpings of pad Thai, green curry, and chicken satay.

"That man has no shame. No integrity. How can someone like that be taken seriously?" Her mother shouted at the television screen while serving delicious banana pancakes for dessert.

"He makes me sick to my stomach. I wish someone would just slap that sardonic grin off his face," she added in disgust at the image of an animated Barrett flashing on the television screen. One glass of wine turned into several, and Mariah thought it wise to stay for the night.

Mariah comes from a family of activists who follow politics closely. She had grown up with the understanding that people had the responsibility of civic engagement by participating in the political process. Her father had done a lot of work for organizations that promoted social and economic justice.

Activism plays a major role in her life. Even as a young child, Mariah had accompanied her father on door-to-door canvassing efforts, assisted with voter registration, and driven the elderly to voting booths. In her office, she proudly displays a large framed newspaper headline depicting her father and some of his friends at the Million Man March in Washington. The collage of brown faces smiles at the camera with pride and resolution. The large sign, "I am my brothers' keeper," towers behind their heads as a confirmation of their commitment.

It had been a long time since Mariah had spent the night with her parents. She inspects the walls of her old room, following the collection of magazine cutouts. There is a picture of Prince posing seductively on a motorcycle, the "Purple Rain" written on the poster matching his glamorous purple trench coat, next to the lopsided smiley face of Kirk Cameron surrounded by his *Growing Pains* family. Her eyes rest on the poster of Mia Hamm. The poster is yellowing and its corners are curling in. The player is captured in a midair kick, the intensity of her determination painted all over her face. She remembers her historic hat trick, the last goal coming from behind the midfield line during the Women's World Cup final so many years back. It was an achievement never before accomplished, not even by the great Pele. She had loved this particular player so much that her mother gave her that nickname.

Her eyes travel to the youth-size jersey above her bed. Her father had framed it with pieces of reclaimed wood from an old birdcage they had found at a yard sale. Mariah had helped sand and polish the frame. She smiles at her name printed in large red capital letters. She remembers convincing her teammates and then her coach to showcase the players' first names instead of their last. She stared at her name. "Wished for child," her mother had once said was its meaning. She smiles at the warm feeling in her chest.

It wasn't easy growing up with a mother who went from looking at her with adoration to avoiding her company for days on end. The countless times her mother would look at her, her eyes unblinking as if she was uncertain of who Mariah was. Then came the images of Mariah waiting for her father to leave the house so that she could rush upstairs to knock on her parents' bedroom, knowing her mother was inside. The sadness that kept her locked away for days was something that Mariah resented.

Yet, the feelings that have endured etched to her memory came from the times when her mother seemed afraid to hug her for fear she might hold on so tight that she'd squeeze the life out of her. Mariah remembers her mother checking on her time and time again during the night or sleeping by the side of her bed.

"I thought I heard you cough during the night," she'd say.

Mariah knew her mother was playing out some horrific scenario in which her daughter had stopped breathing in her sleep and she was not there to save her.

Mariah walks around the room. She fingers her way through the bookshelf layered with dust. She spots an old shoebox. The outside has retained its original appearance, but Mariah had transformed the interior. She used cotton balls to create a padded lining with a soft piece of chenille. She used recycled egg carton cups to create individual compartments to display the jewelry she fashioned.

Mariah picks out a ring with a large aquamarine stone. For the band, she decided to twist the wires into a wavy pattern. It is a beautiful design, although probably not the most comfortable piece of jewelry. She slides it onto her own pinky finger next to her engagement ring and holds her hand out to admire it.

She walks over to her desk—an old teacher's desk salvaged from their church yard sale. She stares at the carvings on the surface of the desk. Some are old markings of long ago and other, newer sketches of initials inscribed by Mariah and some of her closest friends. She opens the bottom drawer and peeks inside. A guilty smile emerges at the sight of the small collection of brown and black dolls tucked away underneath a pile of *Teen* magazines. She pulls out the dark-skinned Cabbage Patch doll and rubs its soft yarn hair. She shakes her head regretfully, for not even the "adoption papers" that had come with the doll had been enough to grab her interest. In spite of her mother's efforts, the young Mariah found creative ways to bring home the unrealistically proportioned pale skin dolls from her friends' house, "a doll play date" she called it.

Mariah makes her way to the bathroom in the hallway, but sees the light in her mother's art studio. It surprises her.

"Momma?" she calls out softly. Even as an adult, this room whispers sadness.

She remembers her mother spending long hours locked in this room. She is certain that at times she heard her mother's muffled sobs. *The room of sorrows*, Mariah had called it. As a child, she assumed every home had one of those. Just like a house needed a bathroom or a kitchen, it also required a room where its grown-ups could drown themselves in sadness behind closed doors.

Sometimes her mother would open the door and invite her in. Mariah would take tentative ceremonial steps and sit on the floor, her eyes mesmerized by the beautiful flowers drawn directly onto the walls. Her mother would set up her old projector and look at the family slides. The images depicted landscapes, trees, and flowers. They were places Mariah remembered visiting with her parents, but it was her dad who carried the old compact camera and took the pictures.

"Dad captured the images and mom set them free," she whispers, remembering. She feels the presence of the memory and the way the flowers seem to whisper to the tune of a forgotten lullaby.

Her mom would click image after image and then set on a particular one. Sometimes she asked Mariah to help her choose.

"Pick the one that speaks to you," she would say encouragingly.

It had unnerved Mariah to be given the honorary task. She didn't want to make the wrong choice. She wanted nothing more than to please her mother. But no matter what choices she made, her mother always smiled with genuine pleasure.

"Good choice. That image has a lot to say, Mia, doesn't it?"

she would add with an accomplice's wink.

Her mother would project the photo right onto the wall and capture the shadowy image of the slide.

"What colors do we need, love?" she would ask, and Mariah would open the colored pencil box and pick out colors that matched the pigments she saw in the image.

"The room of sorrows," Mariah whispers, imagining a place wanting, waiting for life to reappear. The memory of a swarm of deformed shadows cast by the sliver of lights that pierced through the partially closed window curtains comes to her. She remembers the patches of light forming on the walls around the room like hopeful smiles.

At first glance the room of sorrows draws you in, inviting, a visual illusion of sorts. The flowers appear soft, almost real, with a captivating friendliness about them as if with their leaves they allure you to join them and climb into the wall. They seem to rejoice in their isolation. But as you get closer, the flowers droop and the leaves look wilted, decaying and frayed as if they have given up trying to absolve a speck of sunlight to bring them life.

Mariah opens the door tentatively now and steps into the room of sorrows. She is surprised by the brightness of the room. Her eyes follow the ceiling lights. She doesn't remember the large skylight ever being there. Another one of her dad's attempts to breathe life back into her mother, she reasons. Mariah steps farther into the room. She feels the desolation left behind by the passing years, yet she feels a gratitude to the room. "Thank you for taking care of her," she whispers.

She sees the old stepping stool folded neatly behind the door and next to it sits the now-ancient Kodak slide projector. It had once shined its internal light onto the specialized photographs arranged neatly in its interior carousel, the lenses and mirrors on the inside working harmoniously with the light to project, as if spitting out with urgency, the large images of flowers trapped inside. She remembers the depth of the images and the *click-clack* of the slides as they fought their way for the spotlight.

Mariah notices the pencil box sitting on the small table, the same box with a happy Felix the Cat on the cover. The once bright orange background has long since been rubbed off by the passing of time. And right next to the small stool her mother used for sitting, sits the clear Mason jar filled with feathers and other items discarded by nature. Mariah's mother never spoke of it and Mariah had never thought to ask, but the clear jar accompanied her mother the way a security blanket accompanied an anxious child.

She thinks of Dr. Moll, her mother's therapist. Mariah had attended some of the visits with her mother. She had found the family sessions very helpful. At their last meeting she had explained, "For you it is about learning to face a past that has been packed away tightly for so long. But for your mother, it means letting go of a past that she has chosen to relive day after day."

Mariah surveys the walls and feels the flowers observing her as if their spirits were trying to decide their fate. Were they asking to be rescued, or had they resigned themselves to their fate by retreating farther into the wall? Mariah walks closer to the wall, next to the window, and traces the unfinished drawing of the bouquet of baby's breath. It feels warm to her touch. Her hand travels along in search of other clusters, sensing each time a whisper of serenity.

"Hello, old friends," she says as if the flowers had been there all along, waiting for her.

The card "*Ever Lasting Love*" is there, resting next to the colored pencils. Her flat hands trace over the wall, like she had done as a child, yet the mystery has vanished. Roots of guilt tangle around her throat as she remembers the time she found a can of paint in the basement and carried it to this room. One little hand had moved over the drawings and then she had poured the can of paint all over the wall. She breathes in the memory and exhales the sadness of a younger self desperate for her mother's attention.

*M*EG STARED AT THE BRIDAL magazine in the alcove. Her daughter was trying on a bridal gown. She had tried on several already and seemed so elegant in each one. *She is going to be such a beautiful bride.* Meg was certain of that. She reflected on the hesitation she and Lucas had about welcoming their daughter's suitor into their lives. They rationalized their prejudices much like her parents had.

"I need to know your true opinion about each dress. Trust me, you're not going to hurt my feelings. If I suggest something you don't like, just tell me," the young dress consultant said.

Meg was impressed by her. She must be used to helping anxious and overwhelmed brides, but she didn't know her daughter. Her daughter offered the sales lady a polite smile and said, "I have a budget of fifteen hundred dollars. I would like to stay in that range. I'm confident you'll help me find the dress of my dreams." Meg was certain that her daughter would walk out of the store today with a decision made.

"Momma, would you come with me to look at dresses?" her daughter had asked a month ago when she came over to share the great news.

"Sure thing," Meg responded, delighted. "But wouldn't you rather have Eleanor or one of your other friends go with you? I'm an old woman with an old woman's tastes."

"Well, that's why I kind of want you there," Mariah had teased.

"It's just that I already know what I want. I don't want them to dissuade me with their strong opinions. And I really do want to have this be just us," she smiled warmly at her mother.

Meg was thrilled that her daughter was excited about bringing her along. Mariah had involved Meg in every detail of the wedding. Meg was amazed at how beautifully she navigated all the elements of planning a wedding, although it didn't surprise her in the least. Her daughter was one of the most organized and efficient people she knew.

"And how is the mother of the bride holding up?" the dress consultant said, walking in to check on Meg.

"It's hard for a mother, but hard in a beautiful way." She smiled. "Motherhood is an incredible journey."

"I bet. I mean, I don't have any kids yet, but my mother always says that you don't fully appreciate your mother until you become one yourself." The young saleswoman added, "I think sometimes she says it to express frustration, but other times I hear the message loud and clear."

"Yeah, it all boils down to the fact that none of us really understands how much our mothers loved us until we experience that same love toward our own children," Meg explained.

"Once you are a parent, you never stop being one," Meg added, but the young lady had left the room.

If the saleswoman had still been listening, Meg would have told her that when your children are newborns they are so vulnerable; they need you every minute, day in and day out. As they grow older and become more independent, their needs change and your parenting also evolves. She would tell her how the role as a parent seems to transform over time from provider to advisor, as they become adults themselves.

Meg discovered that worrying is one of the things that remains consistent throughout the parenting journey. That piercing worry set root in the pit of your stomach that first night you bring your newborn home, and it is still there as your child prepares to get married and sets out on a possible parenting journey of her own. You still wake up in the middle of the night because you feel a bit too cold or hot and you worry about your child's body temperature. You walk to her crib to check on her or lift a silent prayer as if she were but a gentle spirit above in the heavens. Or perhaps she is a grown woman about to get married in less than a month.

MARIAH PICKS UP THE PHONE to call Rafael. His text messages and emails have come and gone unanswered. She knows he just wants to check in; she just hasn't had the courage to talk to him until now. She had resolved to inform him of her engagement by way of an email. Again, her courage had betrayed her. Rafael picks up after a few rings.

"Sorry, can you talk now?" Mariah asks. She imagines him in his lab or in the middle of a meeting. That is pretty much his life.

"Of course! Wait! Hold on! Give me a sec." Rafael gets off the phone for a few minutes. Mariah hears rattling sounds in the background. The scraping of metal chairs on a cement floor and the quick murmuring of voices make her think she had just interrupted a meeting. It gives her a guilty pleasure that she should be the cause of such commotion.

She is grateful for what she had with Rafael. She hopes he knows she feels equally committed to what they had, the love and respect they shared. How many times has he reassured her that, "Nothing or no one could ever change what we have."

Rafael's distant voice comes back to her.

"God, it's so good to hear your voice, Chica girl," Rafael declares excitedly. Mariah's stomach flips around warmly.

"Was that a meeting I just screwed up for you?" she teases apologetically.

"Don't sweat it. You just saved two morons from being fired," Rafael declares.

"Oh no! What happened? Are they the same ones that screwed up the lights that other time?" Mariah asks, referring to the fiasco that messed up hundreds of female insects' reproductive cycles.

"No, another complete set of morons," he says. "These two guys contaminated several vials by failing to follow proper cleaning procedures. To ignore something as simple and commonsensical as changing your gloves between trays is unforgivable. It's a case of cross contamination 101. Now we have over ten thousand dead wigglers to deal with."

She snickered at the thought of a pile of dead bugs.

"But enough about the exciting world of my flying little gnats. How are things going in your world? Congratulations on the engagement, by the way. I hope that Jake dude knows how lucky he is."

"Max said the same thing. But Rafa, Jake is a good guy. You would approve of him."

"Well, I kind of looked him up a while back," he admits. "According to Google, he graduated from Columbia University with a degree in Economics. He runs his own private management firm. There is a picture of him on a sailboat somewhere in the Caribbean, surrounded by a flock of perfectly proportioned women. I guess when you are a hedge fund dude, you can operate from anywhere. Well, and the beautiful companionship is a plus." His chuckle comes out as a cough.

"Oh, Rafa, stop it. I'm sure you figured out those are old photos," Mariah says.

"You are correct," Rafael laughs softly. "In all honesty, Eleanor told me about the engagement. She gave him the seal of approval. But I gather Max and Gus are still holding back."

"Yeah. It's been a rocky relationship between those three, but I think Max and Gus are finally coming around." Mariah smiles into the receiver, relieved that she could actually make that statement. Max and Gus are indeed warming up to Jake, or perhaps they have just gotten used to the idea that she had chosen Jake and that he is in it for the long haul.

"Anyway, I'm sorry you had to hear about it from someone else. I really wanted to tell you over the phone." Mariah's voice is gentle, apologetic.

"That's OK. I sensed that was the reason you were avoiding me. I hope you know that my biggest happiness is to know there is another man out there that can make you as happy as I would have wanted to if I hadn't been such a self-absorbed prick."

"Stop it. Some people marry people and some people marry bugs. We are all free to marry who or what we love. That doesn't make you a prick. Self-absorbed? Maybe," she teases.

"Well, my *wife* is going to give me the silent treatment after the killing of all these babies," Rafael says. "It's going to take the cleaning crew days to clear out the contaminated bacteria. You miss one step or cut corners and you have a batch of useless samples sitting in your lab petri dishes."

"What are you going to do with the corpses?" Mariah jokes.

"Flush them away. We might be able to use some of the data, but most of it is pretty useless now."

"That sucks," she says. "Did you hear? I am the proud mother of an orange cat."

"Yeah, I heard. How is Mr. Copperknob?" Rafael asks, failing at his attempt to pronounce the name with its rightful English accent.

"He is stubborn and territorial," she says, "but cute and cuddly. Cats are smart, I tell you." Mariah recounts the cat's reaction during a rainstorm just a few days back. She shared how Copperknob had run into their bedroom at the sound of thunder.

"He snuggled tightly next to Jake," she explains. "I mean, it was as if he knew that I, too, was afraid of the thunder and therefore was of no use to him."

"Yeah, I guess that's why people say cats have a sixth sense. It would explain the Egyptians' obsession with cats and the Westerners' belief in their mystical and magical powers. Some people believe cats not only can sense people's feelings, but actually sense the arrival of bad news or even danger. Honestly, they freak me out. I feel like they can look into my soul when they stare at me. Not that I have one, mind you, but if I did," Rafael laughs.

"Oh, come on. I am sure there is one in there somewhere." Mariah says. She pauses, then takes on a casual tone. "Will you be able to come to the wedding?"

Rafael lets out a gentle laugh. "Eleanor told me you might ask. And she also advised me to decline the invitation. Actually, she didn't advise me. She issued a direct order telling me not to go." The line goes quiet for what feels like an extra-long minute and then he adds, "I'll go if you really want me there, but perhaps Eleanor is right. It wouldn't be fair to Jake even if he has given you his approval."

"What if you were in his shoes?" Mariah asks, certain of an honest response.

"I wouldn't like it," he whispers.

*I*T'S A HUMID JULY MORNING and Mariah walks into her office after two months of honeymooning. They had decided to remain on Block Island after the wedding.

She delights in the fresh memory of walking down the sandy aisle outlined by vibrant bundles of alstroemeria. These "lily of the Incas"'s striped petal flowers speak of devotion and friendship, which matched the faces around her. She had walked alone, holding a small bouquet of yellow, long-stemmed irises, her hands covered by delicate lace gloves, her proposal gift. Her parents followed right behind her down the aisle.

The violinist delicately bowed her strings to magically create "A Thousand Years." Mariah felt Jake's eyes pulling her as if following a secret imprinting rule. She walked toward him with bare manicured feet that hardly touched the cool sand, images of their future life together solidifying with each step. "*I have loved you for a thousand years,*" Jake's lips mouthed as she approached the altar, decorated with bright colored irises.

Mariah felt the gentle sway of her gown against her legs. Her grandmother's shawl, a gift from her mother, caressed her shoulders. The bright glow of the orange, red, and yellow background had spattered the sky like an erupting volcano. Later that night, Jake had placed a beautiful floral wreath upon her hair as they climbed into bed. "*My Xochiquetzal goddess,*" he had whispered, completely entranced by wine and euphoric love while invoking the Aztec goddess of love and fertility.

Now, here she is, stepping back into her life, still feeling, as do most wives, the jovial cacophony of butterflies fluttering in her stomach.

Gus had texted her a couple of weeks back asking if she could help Sean land an internship in her firm. She is meeting with Sean this morning, "The Driver Who Drives Trucks," she had written on her calendar.

"He's back in the area trying to make amends, but Pete is not ready to take him back. He left his trucking job and is applying to law school," Gus had written.

"I will definitely see what I can do. Have him call my office and set up a meeting for when I get back," Mariah had offered, adding, "Consider it my thanks for taking care of Copperknob while we're gone."

"Hi," Sean says, rising quickly from the oversize gray leather couch while offering Mariah an outstretched hand. "I just want to say how grateful I am for the opportunity. I'm sure Gus told you about the mess I managed to create for myself," he adds remorsefully.

"Well, it takes courage to clean up one's mess. Let's go and get a bite to eat," Mariah suggests, quietly imploring her fatigued body to muster the energy to walk.

Mariah leads the way to a small sandwich joint not far from her office building and finds an empty table by the front window. She picks up the sign that reads "table for four." The few with "table for two" are occupied. She sits down, but prepares a mental argument just in case the manager feels the need to inquire about her table choice.

Mariah points to the menu high above the bar.

"The ones written in cursive are their signature sandwiches," she explains to Sean.

"What's that box?" Sean asks. "The one with the question mark inside? Is that like the specialty of the day or something?" He points to the far right of the menu.

"Oh, that's the 'I just want something to eat' option. They will make the choice for you. They do ask you whether you are a meat lover, vegetarian, or vegan, so you have to do some thinking after all."

"I will just have whatever you have." Sean leaves his fate in Mariah's hands.

Mariah walks to the counter and places their order. She orders her usual, The Mona Lisa, bacon and all. The crispy waffle-iron-melted Panini comes with gooey gruyère and mozzarella cheese, slices of granny smith apples, tomatoes, and a generous layer of pesto. It is served with a delicious spinach and strawberry salad. She orders two extra-thick strawberry smoothies and walks back to the table, her customer number in hand.

"I ordered us smoothies, too. You're not allergic to strawberries, I hope," she adds, realizing that she should have asked first.

"No, no allergies," Sean confirms.

Mariah considers asking Sean whether he is allergic to eating cochineal bugs, but she isn't sure if he would appreciate the humor in it. Rafael had recently sent her an article about the use of dye carmine as a natural colorant derived from cochineal bugs.

Mariah asked Eleanor who confirmed that, indeed, carmine was being used in the culinary industry as an alternative to artificial food additives.

"Bugs are the clean diet of the future. They are believed to be more nutritious than meat and, of course, are more sustainable," Eleanor said. *That's going to make things complicated for vegetarians and vegans,* Mariah thought. It didn't seem fair that they would now have to think about requesting their fruit smoothies with or without bugs.

Mariah hears her number, and Sean follows her to retrieve their meals and their possibly cochineal-bug-infused strawberry smoothies.

"So, why the decision to go into law? I assumed if you ever

left the trucking business it would be for the magical world of engineering," Mariah asks as they sit back down.

"I kind of hit a very low point after I messed everything up with Pete. I was pretty disgusted with myself for abandoning him and Cece. I checked myself into a center and got all cleaned up. But even with that, Pete still refused to let me see our daughter and I couldn't blame him."

Mariah murmurs an "I'm sorry" as she takes a sip of her smoothie.

"I quit my job and started volunteering at The Center for Human Rights downtown. It's a nonprofit so they take in all the volunteers they can get. One of the shrinks at the rehab suggested I look into it when I mentioned that I spoke some Spanish."

Mariah nods. "That's a great place," she says. "We take some of their cases pro bono. There are a lot of dedicated people running that place. What did they have you do there?"

"I did a lot of technical support and data entry at first," Seans says. "But then they had me more involved with the actual clients as a translator. I learned tons about immigration law and human rights issues related to immigrants. So after a few months of that, I decided I wanted to work on litigation. I applied to law school and, well, here I am, ready to learn from the best."

Mariah tells Sean about a possible new case involving the owner of a gun, a young father. His ten-year-old son had gotten hold of his gun, having found it in the guest room under his uncle's pillow. The uncle, the teenage brother of the father, had been living with the family after being out on probation. The ten-year-old shot his babysitter thinking the gun was a toy.

"No way," responds Sean, who holds his breath while listening to the horrific tale.

"The firm hasn't decided whether to take the case defending

the father; they're awaiting my recommendation."

"So, it's not entirely up to you?"

"No, I make the recommendation, but the senior partners make the final decision. Sometimes I get stuck with a case I don't want. That's the least fun part of this job. "

Mariah had been reviewing the evidence. She would only push a case forward if she were certain she had a good chance of winning.

"Gun-related cases are the hardest for me to defend," she says. "I find it challenging to separate my own personal views of the right to own firearms and defending irresponsible adults who think their rights should be protected even after their child shoots a loved one."

Hearing herself articulate those words out loud, she realizes she had already made her decision. "You know what I fantasize about in my imaginary make-believe world?" she says.

Sean's eyes stay on Mariah. "I can imagine your peaceful world without guns and violence."

"Not quite. I fantasize about the creation of an underground movement, a secret society of sorts, that would take guns out of the hands of criminals and redesign them so when someone pulls the trigger, the mechanism that ignites the gunpowder would create a two-way explosion. One bullet would propel forward and one backward. That way, taking someone else's life would be at the expense of your own," Mariah declares.

"And the members of the secret society would manufacture the guns and release them back on the street?" Sean asks. "I'd like to be part of that society."

"They wouldn't manufacture more guns. They would redesign what's out there and send them back. Once people knew what was at stake, they would either stop buying guns, or they would think carefully before pulling the trigger because they wouldn't know whether there would be two killer bullets released at once." Mariah peers at Sean, who appears lost in thought.

"Did I disappoint you? I know it's not the most noble of fantasies, but it makes sense in my make-believe world," Mariah offers.

"Sorry. No, it's not that. This version of the Russian roulette is brilliant. I was just thinking about how people would probably just learn how to shoot differently."

"Oh darn it! You are probably right. Well. This is the first and last time I share any of my fantasies with you." Mariah gives Sean a teasing smile. She finishes the last of her smoothie and says, "I'm getting a cookie. Would you like one?" as she marches back to the counter to order two oatmeal cookies to go.

EG STARED AT THE alarm clock's blinking red digits announcing it was time to get up. The heat of the August sun forced her eyes open. Meg closed her eyes and ignored the ten and then the eleven mocking her. The sinister veil of mental fog had wrapped its claws around her consciousness. The feeling of emptiness lurked, waiting for its turn to attack. Meg ordered her legs to step out of bed. She pleaded with the abominable boulder weighing her down to release her. She repeated the order over and over in her head, yet her body remained still as a corpse. She thought of Dr. Moll, her cheerful face encouraging her to get up by repeating to herself, *today is here for me.* Meg thought about Mariah, her pleading eyes. She had been so proud of Meg. Yet, her body was unresponsive to command or plead.

Meg thought about Lucas and her heart sank. He showed her his long list of errands last night and said he would be gone most of the day. Meg's panic struck when she realized Maddy would soon need to be fed and taken for a walk. She got out of bed and made her way into the bathroom. Crossing the short distance felt like running a three-mile race through the cold woods in pure darkness. Meg's legs crumpled, her body plummeting to the blue tile floor. Her knees sprung up to meet her chin and her body curled into a tight cocoon.

Mariah had come over last night to share the news of her pregnancy. While most mothers would jump with joy, Meg had stood frozen, her panicked eyes staring at Lucas, begging him to respond, to take control of the situation.

"Urrr," moaned Meg, squeezing her head with her open hands as she tried desperately to shake off the cloying memory of dropping her sick daughter off at school. They had wanted to have her daughter experience some normalcy in her limited life. Meg dropped her off just for a couple of hours each day. That was all the time her daughter's frail body could manage.

Meg sat in the lobby of the school and waited, her eyes never leaving the persistent ticking of the clock up on the wall, its teak wood spikes pointing in all directions. Meg wondered now if that clock was still there. Or how long it had been there. Could it be as old as the school itself? Meg wondered whether anyone would notice if she took it down, smashed it, and tossed it into the large dumpster in back of the building. Would anyone miss that old clock?

The lead teacher, Mrs. Crane, had worked diligently to set up the classroom to accommodate her daughter's needs. She built a peaceful area near the bathroom to allow her daughter a quiet place to go on those days when her medication was likely to make her sick.

She prepared the other students ahead of time on what to say or not to say, and told them what games Meg's daughter liked to play. The teacher gave her the opportunity to be part of a classroom with her classmates in such a dignified way. Her daughter's smooth scalp, absent eyebrows, and pale skin did not scare the other first graders away as Meg had feared. The lovely Mrs. Crane encouraged her to leave her daughter and go for a walk around the school or to get herself some coffee, but Meg had gracefully declined, feeling it impossible to venture far from her sick child.

The sound of the downstairs door opening brought her back to her swaddled body. Meg heard Lucas's hurried steps leading him to the bathroom. *He knows*, she reasons. Her shameful tears fell before she could stop them.

"I am sorry," she whispered. "I tried. I promise, I did try."

Lucas kissed her wet face and turned the water on. He checked to make sure the temperature was the right type of warm, just the way Meg liked it. He helped Meg out of her pajamas and into the soothing bath. He whispered Lord Byron's words: "*She walks in beauty, like the night,*" while soaping her drooping shoulders.

Sadness and disappointment swirled in his mind. He felt his own strength leaving his body like exorcised spirits with every reassuring word he gifted to her. *What happens when there is no more to give?* His quiet inner voice asked.

*I*T STARTED OVER A WEEK AGO WITH SHARP, shooting pains down her lower back. They came without warning. The last one happened the night before as she was putting on her pajamas. It felt as if her back had been jolted with an electric prod. It took some effort not to scream out in pain. Her hands held firmly to the marble top of her dresser, her face grimaced in agony.

"Fuck!" she moaned as she slowly made her way down to the floor and stretched out her legs. She brought her head forward arching her back a bit, just enough to give it a little release.

A soft cry escaped her throat. Mariah took a few deep breaths and straightened her back. She kept her eyes on her toes, relieved that the episode had ceased. Her bright red toenails stared back accusatorially; *painfully red* was the name of the polish. Mariah sneered at the irony.

She rubs her soft stomach thinking about the life slowly developing inside. While the news of her pregnancy after three months of being married was received with great joy by Jake, it wrapped her with apprehension. She still couldn't shake away the nagging feeling that it was too easy, that her mind was just playing a trick and would soon remind her how she didn't want to be a mother in the first place.

Maybe that's it, thinks Mariah, eyeing her middle. *I inherited my mother's cursed womb after all.* Images of Jake fly in, washing away the worries. Jake had felt such excitement at the news. After a missed period, she had resolved to do a home pregnancy test. Her body had always been on a regular schedule, so pregnancy seemed to fit, and she had been right. Mariah smiles, remembering Jake's confusion that quickly turned into a single loud laugh as he read the word Daddy written on his coffee cup. The barista had clapped excitedly and snapped a picture at the wide-eyed-and mouthed Jake.

Mariah is up this morning earlier than usual, having decided to work from home.

"Did you have a good night's sleep, my Lady Rose?" Jake caresses her shoulders with a gentle massage.

"Oh. That feels delicious. Can you skip work today and spend the day rubbing my back instead?" Mariah pleads.

"Trust me. I would rather do that, but I hear babies need lots of diapers, and then there is college tuition and all that jazz in between," Jake teases and then asks, tapping the tip of her nose playfully, "How many times were you up last night? I only counted three."

"I lost track. I can't wait until my bladder is able to handle liquid again. I envy pregnant women before indoor plumbing was invented. They got to use a chamber pot to relieve themselves during the night. That's one artifact that could truly make my life easier."

"Well, nothing is keeping you from reclaiming the ancient practice," Jake suggests. "It is kind of practical, if you ask me."

"You might regret saying that," Mariah shoots back.

"I am so on board with it that you can count on me to be your chambermaid." Jake kisses the crown of her head and leaves with an "I love you" goodbye.

At ten weeks, Mariah's exhaustion is so unbearable that she had to miss Eleonor's birthday party last weekend. Mariah had wrapped a small box with a pair of crocheted baby booties inside; her birthday gift to her friend had to be replaced by the news of her pregnancy over the phone. She had ignored the ceremonial twelve week mark before sharing the news with her parents and closest friends.

Mariah sits on the ivory quilted leather stool at the kitchen counter where the spirited rays of the fall morning sun push impatiently through the tall glass windows. She gingerly picks up the large crystal vase of bright yellow irises and puts them in the center of the countertop so they, too, can be kissed by the warm rays. She eyes the message still nuzzled into the bouquet. *Three years ago, I meet you and in that one instant my life took a turn in the right direction.*

Fresh-cut flowers had become a permanent feature in their home, no matter the time of year. Mariah had bought Jake three stems of blue irises on their first date three years ago. She smiles now, remembering how he replicated the action on their second date without even realizing the significance of the selection. In the language of flowers, deep blue blooms speak of hope. As their whirlwind courtship evolved over the years, so had the color of the irises, transitioning from blue, to pink, to yellow.

Mariah caresses the porous silky yellow petals, spread out like gracious butterfly wings; "passion," she murmurs to herself.

She had taken a class in college, the "botany of love." That's when she fell in love with the notion of flowers having symbolic meanings. She fell in love with the language of flowers.

For her final report, Mariah had to choose a flower to research. She chose the iris. It was a flower that stuck in her memory. She remembered her mother receiving a bouquet of irises from her own mother every year on Mother's Day. At the time it seemed just a mere lovely gesture, but Mariah now wonders if it had hidden significance. Had her grandmother known about the message spoken by the purple irises? Does her mother? She wonders about that for, if she does, she had never mentioned it. But perhaps that's how the language of flowers intends to be spoken: without speaking.

Mariah loved learning about irises, these unique and magnificent flowers that dated back to Ancient Greek times. She was fascinated by their meaning and symbolism that varied with the color of the flower. Mariah determined then that her bridal bouquet was going to be composed of white irises, expressing purity and innocence. But at the time of her choosing, it was yellow irises that adorned her elegant wedding bouquet.

It was Jake who suggested irises for the venue décor. When Mariah asked him why, he winked at her and responded, "Because, my Lady Rose, the goddess Iris paved the path that led me to you."

She thinks about Jake. He never stops amazing her. Although she had never shared her love of irises or her zealousness for the language of flowers, he had picked up on it. He noticed. It is something he was good at doing. It makes him successful in business and in his relationships. After all, he had placed a bountiful bouquet of forget-me-nots, the flower of true love and hope, on the entryway table the day he proposed to her. A coincidence? She was certain it was not. Jake had been speaking the secret language of flowers since their first date.

Mariah places her laptop computer on the shiny granite and reaches for the large mug of hazelnut latte Jake left by the sink. It was part of his morning routine. On most days, he would awake at the crack of dawn and get a head start on emails. He liked having a sense of what might have developed during the night in the business world before he walked into his office. He would wait until seven o'clock, just enough time to walk across the street to Mariah's favorite coffeehouse and pick up her ready to go order, as soon as the manager opened for business.

Jake is not a coffee drinker. He much prefers tea, but Mariah is an unapologetic coffee enthusiast. She loves visiting high-end coffeehouses. She is a big fan of elaborate espresso-based combinations, especially if it includes a head of froth with any form of latte art.

Mariah clicks the key of her laptop, ordering the search engines to do their job. This is how she will spend the best part of her morning: doing medical research online, anything to soothe her anxiety about this abrupt back pain. She had spoken on the phone with her OB/GYN early last week right after that first painful episode, but Dr. Sumers had not felt alarmed.

"Are you feeling any tingling or weakness in the legs?" she wanted to know.

Dr. Sumers had run through a series of symptoms, one of which described the feeling of water dripping down the spine. Mariah felt relieved at her negative answers to the symptoms in question.

"We'll check your weight when you come in next week for your scheduled prenatal visit. Remember that your baby is about to enter the fetal stage, which is the most dramatic phase. There is a lot happening now, not just to the baby, but also to you. And Mariah, have you told Jake about the backpain?"

Mariah had stayed silent a bit too long.

"I don't like to intrude on my patients' personal lives, but at the end of the day, you are on this journey together. Things like this are less stressful when you have someone at home you can share it with." Then she had quickly switched back to the conversation and ended by suggesting some backstretches.

I don't want to alarm him, Mariah reasons now, as she continues her online search, overwhelmed by the endless and mostly useless clump of information. She contemplates the possibilities of her findings. It appears that her symptoms are consistent with that of a pinched nerve. If that is the case, a combination of back-stretches and rest could remedy that. Mariah also finds other, scarier possibilities. But she reminds herself that if Dr. Sumers is not worried, then neither should she be, and with that, she casts aside all frightening possibilities.

Mariah takes a sip of her lukewarm latte and lowers the laptop monitor. She takes out her phone and taps on the application for expectant mothers. She loves this tool; it is the perfect pregnancy guide for new parents. It sends her daily texts with quick descriptions and 3D pictures of a typical developing fetus. She reads the information carefully, trying to memorize the key details so she can share them later with Jake.

She looks through her photos and finds an image from her most recent ultrasound and texts it to her father. "*Good morning, Grampy!*" she writes below the picture. "*Pick up the phone,*" she adds.

"What a nose! That poor dear, between Jake and me there is no hope for a reasonably proportioned schnoz," her father jokes.

"What about that massive forehead?" Mariah asks.

"I think you and Mom should claim that brain. It is a known fact that kids get their smarts from their mothers," her father replies. "Is Jake going to be around tonight? You should hop over for pizza and ice cream."

"Sounds good. I'll let Jake know to meet me there. We could celebrate the baby officially becoming a fetus. Now Jake won't be as freaked out by the images because they will be a bit more distinct from here on out. The baby will look more human."

"I do have to agree with Jake, honey. Those earlier pictures of a five-week-old baby made it look like an angry alien."

MARIAH AND JAKE ARE eagerly awaiting next week's checkup. She had shared the news last night about the backpain incidents, but played them down just enough so as not to alarm him. She had been pain free for a few days now and is feeling energetic and rested.

"This kid is growing up a storm," Mariah announces delightedly, showing Jake the picture on her phone with the caption *your baby is now the size of a lime.* She is enchanted by the new development of their growing baby at twelve weeks.

Jake's hands rub her belly gently.

"Congrats, kiddo! You have graduated from being a fig!" he announces excitedly.

"I think we might get to listen to the heartbeat next week," Mariah comments, reading over the *What To Expect* book.

Jake gives Mariah's belly a gentle kiss. His head rests next to it and his wide eyes stare admiringly at her bare belly, just a small pouch across the lower abdomen.

"This thing just popped up overnight," he smiles happily.

Mariah catches him staring. "What?" she asks, caressing his face.

"Can't a man look at his pregnant wife?"

"I was just thinking about how great it is that my morning sickness is gone."

He had kept a small thermos with fresh squeezed lemonade by her night table and a dish filled with ginger candy by the sink. These had been the only things to calm the unpleasant nauseous sensation that overtook Mariah each morning. While Mariah had experienced a ravenous hunger at the start of her pregnancy, her body is now showing less interest in food altogether. She attributes it to the nausea. Even the smell of Jake's aftershave, a fragrance that she once adored, sends her straight to the toilet bowl.

The frequent urination is burdensome and the fatigue still lingers, but those are insubstantial discomforts. The bloating and constipation are frustrating, but not even all these symptoms combined can come close to washing away Mariah's contentment.

It is true that she had not planned her adult life around the idea of being a mother the way many young woman do. She likes children, but she often finds herself questioning whether she is capable of enduring what it takes to be a mother.

Mariah had grown up feeling she had to compensate for a sister that existed only in her parents' memory, a sister who was never spoken of and whom she only knew from images frozen in the photographs that decorated the mantel above the fireplace. Her own memory is incapable of reaching that far back to her early childhood years when she trotted happily behind her big sister.

Mariah had gotten used to her mother's over-protectiveness as a child. She never found it upsetting that her mother fussed over her at the sign of a minimal cough or scraped knee. Even at an early age, Mariah could read the fear and anguish in her mother's eyes.

Jake takes out the baby journal they are keeping.

"It doesn't matter how many times I open this book. I always go back to glance at the first page. I just can't help it," he smiles warmly.

The first page of the baby book features a picture of Jake grinning from ear to ear as he holds his cup with the word "Daddy" written across it.

"I still can't believe your favorite barista heard the news before I did," Jake fakes a complaint.

He picks up the pen and looks at Mariah expectantly. Mariah dictates and he writes. They had added pictures narrating the progression of her pregnancy week by week with a full account of how Mariah is feeling. The baby journal also features drawings. There is a sketch her father had drawn of the baby nursery and several watercolor drawings from the collection her mother mails her almost every week.

ARIAH IS DOWN ON HER BACK, toes pointing up to the sky, working on her ten-minute daily stretching routine. She adds some knee twists and backbends. She feels the tranquility wrapping up her body, realizing that these poses not only help her with alignment and stretching, but also bring her some much-needed relaxation. She is beginning to regret not giving yoga a second chance back when Eleanor began her yoga frenzy and tried unsuccessfully to drag her into the studio.

Mariah's first yoga experience had been less than enjoyable. She found it stressful and intimidating. She tried to follow the quick instructions, but not knowing the yoga lingo made it virtually impossible to ease her body into any expected pose. The instructor had alerted the practitioners of the upcoming transition from downward dog into a half pigeon, and then went on to guide them through the pose:

"*Fly your right leg up so it extends away from you. It will now travel forward to the back of your right wrist. Don't forget to breathe. Straighten your left leg back behind you. You want to make sure that your back thigh is rotating inward and those toes are pressing down into the mat. Lower your right buttocks to the floor. Hold it there and keep balancing that weight in both hips. Use your hands to push up your chest, inhale and rise up. Breathe deeply to elongate your spine. Exhale and follow your torso, extending over your right leg. Stay here for a few breaths. On your next exhale, send your right leg back up and into Downward Facing Dog.*"

Mariah had tried to listen to the instruction, guessing the pose half the time, while trying to force her body into submission. She reflects on that yoga experience, the stress of trying to follow the instructions. Yet it is the current peaceful state of her body that drives her to the decision.

"Why not?" Mariah asks herself and picks up the phone to text Eleanor.

"*So what about that yoga class you have been shoving down my throat all these years?*"

"*No way! For real?*" Eleanor's text response was decorated with exclamation marks and clapping hands.

"*My lower back has been acting up a little. I have been doing stretches at home, but I thought maybe I should give yoga a try, if you go with me,*" she adds hopefully.

There had been an additional reason for her yoga interest: her constipation. It had gotten a second wind, much like a marathoner in her last leg of a race. She had read that yoga poses were proven to be beneficial to the digestive system. It turns out that twists and turns worked internally, as well, by massaging the digestive organs. Mariah was pleased at that revelation. She was hoping yoga would work its magic and help alleviate her current painful experience. This morning it had taken her close to forty-five minutes to complete the bodily transaction. Not even her collection of celebrity gossip magazines aided the process.

Dr. Sumers had suggested a small dose of milk of magnesia, but Mariah was hesitant to ingest any form of laxative, fearing it might harm the baby. Mariah remembers reading an article years back, describing how many people develop a laxative addiction as a way to get rid of unwanted calories; a delusional way of losing weight, and how they become addicted to the feeling of *emptiness* through the repeated use of laxatives.

The article had also alluded to a small sample of those people who had transitioned from being laxative addicts to becoming addicted to the pain elicited by defecation; to the strain of pushing waste out of their body, which their body had become accustomed to interpreting as an orgasmic experience.

Mariah shakes her head in amazement. She reflects on how much she has taken her own body for granted, with smooth stool release at the top of the list.

The loud vibration of her phone alerts her to an incoming message. Eleanor's text consists of five rows of folded hand images, Namaste, the unified hand symbol used by yogis.

Mariah looks down at her outstretched legs, and then texts back.

"*In need of some workout outfits. Wanna go shopping this weekend?*"

"*Absolutely!*" flashes the response. "*I will ask around for best places for women in your condition.*" A smiley face accompanies Eleanor's response.

"*The condition is called pregnancy. You don't have to be afraid to say it. It's not like Lord Voldemort. Plus, you can't catch it by naming it.*" Mariah adds a few smiley faces with half a dozen exclamation marks at the end.

"*One never knows. There is no harm in being cautious,*" her friend replies with the same number of exclamation points.

Mariah rubs her outstretched belly expectantly. Now that she is in her second trimester, the excitement of feeling her baby move for the first time occupies her mind day and night.

Her eyes travel down to her stretched-out underwear. *This is exciting*, she says to herself. *I need new underwear that can hold my new, extra-large, awesome ass.*

"GONE TO THE DOG PARK," read the note on the counter, the pale orange maple leaf kissed by the December morning frost in place of a signature. Meg held the leaf and breathed in deeply. The colors and smell of the Green Mountain State.

It seemed like just yesterday they were making the drive up north to drop Mariah off for freshman orientation week. The three of them had attended all the parents' meetings and learned about the college application process. The Dean of Students had spoken about how stressful and daunting it could be for both the student and the family. But the stress and inquietude never materialized for their daughter, who approached the college process the way she approached every challenge she faced. Mariah read the catalogues and talked to her counselor. In the end, she put together a narrow list of possibilities and asked her parents to drive her to them. She had chosen schools that were within driving range from home. She listened, but disregarded her parents' encouragement to venture across the country or to take a gap year and travel or work overseas.

Mariah had made up her mind. She set her self-directed path and marched upon it with determination. Much like she had done as a twelve-year-old when Meg had walked into the bathroom to find a smiling Mariah holding a pair of scissors to her hair, while her two long braids lay tangled up like dozing snakes in the bottom of the sink.

"Now I won't have curly hair anymore," she had offered as a solution to her mother's refusal to her constant plea to allow her to straighten her hair. Meg had walked out of the bathroom in search of the phonebook. She fingered through the Yellow

Pages and dialed Sonia's Hair Fashion. A week later she found herself lost in the narrow streets of Jamaica Plain searching for the salon.

"You can park behind the bike shop," the voice with the heavy accent had advised her on the phone when she made the appointment.

The salon was run by a tall, spirited, young Dominican woman named Chantal (her mother Sonia had retired). She brought Mariah's unruly curls to complete submission under the magical spell of the relaxer. Mariah had stared at her reflection incredulously, the full length mirror showing a girl with her facial features wrapped in a curtain of shiny hair as straight as a horse's mane. Mariah did not mind the small burnt patches on her scalp and around the edge of her ears from the vicious power of the chemical.

Yes, Meg reflected, Mariah had always been determined. Now she's been awarded a child of her own. Meg felt her anxiety grow.

*A*T TWENTY WEEKS NOW, Mariah is feeling blissful. "Halfway mark!" she cheers over the phone on a call with her dad.

"She is twirling around like a circus acrobat," Mariah jokes, then pats her stomach gently. "She's showing off for her anxious parents."

Some of Mariah's appetite finally had returned. Her mother keeps dropping by with meals and never fails to remind her to rest: "Sweetheart, you need lots of sleep. You need to take naps. Remember that your body is working very hard to make a placenta." She tries to joke, but her worried eyes dart around, unable to fully relax.

Mariah is in awe of her own body, besotted with the ongoing transformation. The tenderness of her breasts brings with them a beautiful, bountiful set of mounds. Jake had walked in on her standing naked, staring at her own reflection, her voluminous body, her face bright in astonishment.

"Hi, beautiful. Care to share some of that with your husband?" he teased from the doorway.

Mariah pulled him closer. His playful eyes lit up like dancing fireflies. She smiled deviously and handed him the small bottle of coconut oil. She knew he was happy to settle for a rub.

Part Five

a slender silhouette
looking for a suitor
proud gladiolus
a lover
a hero in disguise

MARIAH COMES HOME EARLY from work today. She grabs a green apple and some extra sharp cheddar cheese and walks to the family room followed by the dutiful Copperknob on her heels, his meows a request for some affection. She kicks off her shoes to bring relief to her aching feet and digs her big toes deep into the fur of the sheepskin shag rug. It feels heavenly under her screaming feet. The rug is one of the few remnants inherited from Jake's old life. Well, that, and the Roy Lichtenstein original that now hangs in the office purposely behind the door.

This outstanding masterpiece of crescendo melodrama offered an imposing statement when displayed at Jake's old pad. Yet it feels like a total intruder in their home. Mariah does not hold a dislike for pop art. It is rather this particular piece that unsettles her. She feels that the image of a woman in distress and in a state of hopelessness does not seem like something that should be glorified or showcased. Unlike comedians who make jokes about personal tragedies as a way to reclaim their own experiences, in her view, images of battered women seem to send out the message that women are frail. In her opinion, images like these desensitize people to women's sufferings. Jake explained his reluctance to part with the piece, saying: "The girl is meant to seem hopeless while her words and facial expression tell the viewer that she is in fact courageous and defiant." He had convinced her to keep the piece. But she can't bring herself to display it in a location where she would have to face it with frequency.

She scoops up her orange companion, sets him on her lap, and voices out a command: "TV on." Mariah arranges the snack plate on the couch next to her as the large flat screen comes to life. A request for the news channel follows, and a reporter comes into view. Mariah had heard clips of a report about racial events at a school on her drive home. Students from a local high school were shouting racial slurs at the basketball players from the visiting team, as many of those students were Latinos. Some of the players from the host team had started the shouting from the bench, which instigated many of the spectators to join in.

Mariah's head hangs heavy, her stomach tight with revulsion and disappointment at the recognition of the old Gothic-style building with its imposing cupola. She feels distraught at the notion that not even her own liberal and open-minded city is immune to showcasing their worst selves. Her very own father still bears the visual scar of racism sketched on his skin. It travels from his left temple to the hidden space behind his ear, "a punishment for my darkness," her father called the violent act. Mariah touches her round stomach in response to the movement inside.

The phone buzzes. Mariah picks it up and hears her husband's voice on the other end of the line.

"Hi, Love. I tried calling you at the office, but the secretary said you left early today. What are you up to? Are you okay?"

Mariah waits to finish chewing the last bit of the sharp cheese to answer.

"I left early because I wanted to stop by the mall to pick up a couple of pairs of dress pants and some new underwear. This girl at work swears by these hipster undies that are supposed to flatter you in all the right places. I'm fine with my high-waist Granny panties, but I thought maybe you would appreciate a little more finesse in how your wife presents herself to your feasting eyes these days."

"You should consider going commando," Jake says, half joking, half hopeful.

"I don't think you would suggest that if you saw how my legs no longer close fully when I sit."

"Well in that case, let's keep the commando idea just for home," he teases.

"Jake? Did you hear about the racial incident at that high school today? I just realized that it's the one by that little restaurant we like." Mariah turns the volume up. A young reporter is talking outside the school describing the incident. She is now talking to a group of students who gathered in front of the school in protest. They are demanding that the school follow up with the state Athletic Association to penalize the team for their racist behavior. They ask the school to fire the coaches for failing to stop their players. The protesters are also demanding the suspension of the students who participated by shouting from the bleachers.

"Yeah, people are talking about it here at work. It's crazy," Jake responds. The silence on the other end of the line cues him in. "I'm about done here. I'll head out in a few minutes. Should I stop and pick up some dinner?"

"I would like that," Mariah manages to muffle her sobs before disconnecting.

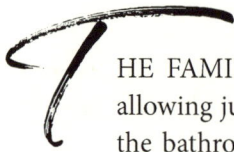

THE FAMILIAR NAUSEA climbs up to her mouth, allowing just enough time for her body to make it to the bathroom. The first two waves of vomit eject all traces of food out of her. Mariah holds weakly to the edge of the toilet seat, steadying herself to stand. The shooting pain sparks like a fierce lighting across her lower back, forcing her to crouch back down.

The pain subsides, making room for the torrent of angry tears that follow. *Useless-Stupid body*, she cries in frustration.

Her eyes fix on her round stomach.

"Why are you doing this to me?" she asks the unresponsive creature inside as if expecting an explanation or apology. She feels the sizzling anger emerge. Her tears pick up speed as she lashes out.

"Do you hate me this much already?" Her hot tears stream down her face pooling into the base of her neck.

"This is all your fault," she sobs, pushing down the soft housing that encases the creature safely inside. The savage need to place the blame of her sickness upon someone, anyone, takes hold of her.

"I shouldn't have kept you," states the raving declaration between her ears, ripping out a loud wail on its way out. She feels her body shake as she fights to grab a full breath between sobs.

"An abortion might be wise," Dr. Sumers had advised her early on. Mariah had kept that information from Jake, afraid that he might have pressured her to follow Dr. Sumers' recommendation. For Mariah, the excitement of becoming a new mother had trumped all concerns about her own health.

She cups her face with her hands and her sobs subside.

"What's wrong with me?" she sighs. She massages her temple in an effort to calm herself down, her eyes feeling heavy and swollen.

The subtle movement of the small being inside her pulls Mariah back as revolting waves of shame and guilt begin to creep in.

"I'm sorry," she whispers and rubs her belly gently. "I am so sorry."

JAKE'S HANDS WRAP AROUND MARIAH'S as they stare impatiently at the monitor. He rubs her knuckles, attempting to ease her shaking tremors. Dr. Sumers had called the day before. After reading over Mariah's latest tests, and mostly everything appeared within the normal range, but she had decided to run some additional tests.

"My concern is not about the baby," she calmly explained over the phone. "It's about your continued weight loss. I want to dig a little bit into it to see if we can decipher its cause. Some women do tend to lose weight during their pregnancies, but mostly during their first trimester.

"I'm just uncomfortable with unexplained weight loss in general. You have almost dropped a full ten percent of your overall body weight. Again, I'm not super worried. I just want to make sure we get to the bottom of it."

The complete blood count Dr. Sumers had ordered revealed abnormal cells. The news felt like the shaking of a passing train. Mariah briefly imagined the heavy cars running over her fallen body, over and over. Mariah's blurry vision tried desperately to find a focal point in the room to comprehend the words jumping out of the receiver. She was engulfed by the revolting feeling of something grotesque gripping her shoulder as if life had decided it was time for her to carry her own sins.

Mariah had convinced herself that she was ready, prepared even, to hear Dr. Sumers' news. What a naïve notion that had been. Your deductive logic does not march in unison with your emotional reasoning, she discovered.

She was transferred to the high-risk clinic, the name as terrifying as its implication. Today she is meeting with Dr. Patel, a specialist in high-risk pregnancies.

Dr. Patel explains the results of the blood work. "We will run some additional tests," she adds while typing into the blurry forms flashing on the screen. "The new tests will check for the presence of tumor markers."

Mariah feels sad on her behalf. It couldn't feel good to be the bearer of bad news day in and day out. She glances over at Jake, his pale face shaken by the new development, his hands had retreated into his pockets. Her eyes go back to Dr. Patel, but this time the sadness and empathy she feels quickly transform into anger. How dare she bring that evil word into their lives?

In a period of two weeks, Mariah's reality had been shaken to its core. The agonizing waiting periods and test results marching in formation one after another. Her existence, once a brilliant sun, is clouded now by a shadowy veil.

Mariah reaches over for Jake's hands. The coldness surprises her. He is the warm-blooded one, her warm teddy bear. She gives his hand a gentle squeeze, and he blinks as if just realizing where he is. He rubs Mariah's hands and offers her a pitiful smile that she knows he had intended to be a reassuring one.

Dr. Patel excuses herself and leaves the room. Mariah and Jake stare at each other and then simultaneously at the computer monitor. Mariah squints her eyes, trying to decipher the writing; perhaps there is a note with somebody else's name. A case of mixed-up identity. It must happen in hospitals from time to time, Mariah thinks.

The door opens and Dr. Patel makes her way back into the room. Mariah is surprised by the loud exhale coming from Jake. Had he been holding his breath the whole time the doctor was out?

"Here we go." She hands Mariah the familiar clipboard with a series of forms to be completed.

"Same lab?" Mariah asks in the absence of other questions. She eyes the monitor one last time, but her name flashes back at her next to the words, "High Risk Pregnancy."

"I will see you in a few days," Dr. Patel says as she opens the door for them.

"WE ARE JUST GATHERING INFORMATION. The more we learn from these tests, the better we can determine our next steps," Dr. Patel declares. She is performing a transvaginal ultrasound to obtain higher quality images.

Mariah is lying down on the padded, yet uncomfortable examination table while Dr. Patel deftly moves the transducer in her vaginal canal.

An image of a blurry baby appears on the large monitor. Mariah smiles as happy tears cascade down her face.

"There she is!" Jake blurts out, unable to conceal his excitement.

"Oh my! That's one strong baby you've got there," Dr. Patel comments at the rhythmic sound of the strong heartbeat emanating from the ultrasound machine.

Mariah appreciates her attempt at neutralizing the mood in the room. She is afraid to look at Jake, afraid that her brave masquerade will fail. It takes great effort to keep herself composed.

"There are no signs of tumors or abnormal growth," Dr. Patel declares after a few minutes of careful examination.

Jake claps his hands and kisses Mariah. He reaches over and thanks Dr. Patel with a strong embrace. She welcomes the gesture with a clear sense of relief. Mariah smiles, thinking of how these special moments must be what bring balance to her job. It is true, doctors have to deliver bad news to their patients, but how magical it must feel to be the bearer of good news.

Dr. Patel completes the examination and retrieves her medical tools. She walks to the sink to discard her gloves and wash her hands. Mariah and Jake stare at each other. He caresses her face and kisses her hands. They had forgotten about Dr. Patel, claiming the moment just for themselves.

Dr. Patel's voice echoes in their ears. "I'll see you next week after your pelvic MRI," she declares, handing Mariah a handful of wipes, and exits the examination room.

$\mathcal{L}$UCAS WALKED OVER AND SAT next to Meg on the couch. He reached for her hand, but she pulled it away defiantly.

Mariah was being seen by a team of specialists working closely with Dr. Patel. Although Dr. Patel had been able to rule out a number of illnesses based on test results, she was still unable to determine the cause of Mariah's weight loss.

Meg had overheard the conversation between Jake and Lucas over the phone. From Lucas's facial expressions and his somber nodding, she could surmise the results from the last tests.

"The endoscopy came out clear. The lining of the stomach is free of any questionable mass. They have only found a small inflammation of the esophagus."

"And the baby?" Meg asked, her blinking eyelashes never leaving his eyes.

Lucas hesitated for just a fraction of a second, but that was enough delay to betray him.

"The baby is fine," he answered, breaking the gaze. Jake had asked him to hold back the details of the minor vaginal bleeding that occurred after the procedure. Dr. Patel had decided to keep Mariah overnight for closer monitoring. "Mom doesn't need to know about this," Mariah whispered to Jake while he was on the phone with her father.

Mariah and Jake had known going in that all these tests were invasive and came with some risks. Dr. Patel had considered the bleeding low risk compared to the information they would generate.

"What else did Jake say? What about the biopsy?" Meg asked, suspecting something was not being said.

"They are waiting for the lab on that. They are keeping her overnight just as a precaution," Lucas said, deciding to share that part of news.

"Is she at least allowed to eat a little something? She hadn't been allowed to eat for twelve straight hours before she went in for the tests this morning." Meg walked over to grab a tissue to wipe her escaping tears. Lucas followed her and attempted to comfort her by giving her back a gentle rub.

"Yeah. She was having some light soup when Jake called."

Mariah's appetite had been almost nonexistent for quite a while now. She had been dealing with nausea and a bloated sensation after ingesting minimal amounts of food. Then symptoms of vomiting and trouble swallowing emerged. There were the additional concerns of aspiration being discussed by the medical team.

"I hope to God she is able to keep that soup down," Meg pleaded between sobs.

Her daughter, the teenager who organized protests aimed at not buying clothes from a number of clothing brands because of their exploitation of starving workers overseas, the adult who started participating in the Walk for Hunger as a sixth grader and continued to walk year after year with the hope of eradicating hunger someday, now inhabited a body that was rebelling against her, driving her to starve.

"How can they not have a diagnosis?" Lucas breathed in gulps of frustration. "It's as if they are just focusing on treating the symptoms as they come." His voice registered his worry.

While some of the treatments did provide relief, the doctors' primary objective continued to be finding the source of her illness. A "failure to diagnose" label was all they had and, contrary to Lucas's perception, this description was something that unnerved many doctors, as it could lead to legal ramifications.

"Should we bring her some personal things from the house?" Meg asked.

"Eleanor is on her way to the hospital. She's bringing Mariah what she needs to stay the night. Jake said we can come by later in the day after she rests a bit."

Meg nodded, searching Lucas's eyes for reassurance.

MARIAH REACHES OVER AND grabs her husband's hand. It is a quiet drive. Their fingers touch, then link, their hands communicating those egregious feelings for which no words existed.

She thinks about the approaching Valentine's Day next week and is surprised by the serene feeling encasing her like a cloak. She thinks about the terminally ill women who write dating profiles for their husbands, sending them back to the world of bachelorhood. The idea had always seemed so morbid to her. Now that very same notion seems as sensible as brushing one's teeth. Mariah squeezes Jake's hand a bit tighter.

Her thoughts travel back to this morning, waking up to the wetness on her cheeks. Her pillow was soaked and she realized she had been sobbing in her sleep again.

At thirty-seven weeks, she is too far along in her pregnancy to fly on a commercial airplane, so they are driving back from New York, where they had met with Rafael and a team of doctors he had contacted.

Rafael had been following and monitoring test results since the beginning of her illness. It was Jake's idea. "You need him and we need him," he had said to Mariah at her hesitation, not just because she didn't want to become a burden, but mostly for her concern about Jake's personal insecurity.

It only required a quick signature to allow Rafael remote access to all her medical records. Even from far away, his love and devotion felt like a tight embrace of care around her. He flew over for a weekend visit to meet face-to-face with some of Mariah's specialists. He checked in with them daily, but it was Jake who answered most days. Mariah was too weary for long conversations.

Rafael arranged for Mariah's blood samples to be shipped directly to his clinic, where he enlisted a group of researchers and specialists to help him study Mariah's case. He was certain the team in Boston was overlooking something. How could they not? Diseases were like a puzzle, in his view. It would take careful and thorough studies, but he was confident they would eventually determine the missing pieces and assemble the puzzle.

His own team had just pieced together the answer to an inexplicable DNA transformation that happened to mosquitoes after they successfully delivered their first bite. They were currently trying to rewrite those mosquitoes' DNA to see if it was possible to prevent or revert the transformation. This data could lead to possible human trials to identify and then prevent many types of cancer. Rafael knew the answers to Mariah's disease were sitting in a lab somewhere. He just needed to keep reaching out and working a bit harder to find them.

"I agree with your dad," Rafael explained. "They have been treating the symptoms. The problem with that is by relieving the symptoms, they may be masking aspects of the condition that could help with the diagnosis," Rafael had argued while trying to convince them to make the trip to New York.

"Well, I think Rafael was right in suggesting this trip," Jake comments, his voice heavy with hope.

"Jake?" Mariah interjects before he can go on.

"Yes, love?"

"I'm tired." Mariah's weak voice is armed with resolution. "I am tired of second opinions, and third opinions, and fiftieth opinions. I am tired of keeping a log to track my symptoms and their triggers. I am tired of trying out new drugs and waiting to see how they interact and play out. And Jake?"

"Yes?"

"I want you to cancel that trip to Cuba next week. I'm tired of hoping for a miracle cure. I have decided to call the National Institute of Health and enroll in the Rare Disease Program. At least something good could come out of all this. I will ask them to collaborate with Rafa so he can still have access to all my records. This is no longer just about me."

"Honey, please. Even Rafael thinks that meeting with the research team in Cuba will be helpful. These are people he knows and trusts. He has collaborated with them for many years. The snake venom research has actually shown some positive results."

"I know it's hard for you. We have all fought this sinister battle, but I am tired, Jake. And I need you to be OK with it."

Jake's hands grip the wheel a little tighter this time, and Mariah's breathing relaxes. She had just done the most difficult part.

"SHE IS ABSOLUTELY PERFECT," Eleanor coos over the baby nuzzled deeply in Mariah's arms. Eleanor's enthusiasm for the new baby has taken everyone by surprise, including herself. She loved looking at the 4D prenatal ultrasound images and shrieked with joy at the vigorous baby kicks against her hand while rubbing coconut oil over Mariah's stretched belly. She had taken the birthing class alongside Jake and held Mariah's hands as she practiced the breathing techniques.

"It really shakes one's view of the pro-choice argument when you are staring at something so incredibly precious. Just look at this magical creature," Eleanor comments, as if thinking aloud. Mariah smiles, amazed that her friend had put into words what she had been feeling since the moment they discovered she was with child.

The feeding nurse claps enthusiastically after another successful session.

"She is tenacious all right!" laughs the nurse. "You know what they say about April babies. Stubborn and bossy. That's right, prepare yourself," she warns playfully, rubbing the baby's nose.

Mariah's breast milk is flowing and the baby had latched on with gusto on the very first try.

They had worried that her body wouldn't be able to produce sufficient nourishment for a newborn, but to her relief, Mariah's body had proven them wrong. Mariah understands the benefits of breastfeeding, not just for the health of the baby, but also for that early bonding experience that is so vital. She needs her daughter to *know* her.

Mariah carried full term. Dr. Sumers had strongly recommended strict bed rest for the last four weeks. Mariah adhered to the constraints, only leaving the house for her weekly checkup.

"Did you see that fancy onesie she is wearing?" Mariah uncovers the baby to showcase the soft violet garment with the word *SNAP!* under a picture of podded peas.

"Our little model," Eleanor claps with glee.

She had worked with a graphic designer to create a series of vegetable and fruit logos and presented the food onesie collection at the baby shower she organized for Mariah.

Mariah had a smooth labor and delivery. Both Jake and Eleanor were in the room with her. As it turned out, all the breathing techniques hadn't been needed.

Although her mother offered to be in the delivery room, Mariah worried about something going awry and wanted to protect her mother from a frightening experience. Mariah's heart aches every time she gazes into her mother's eyes. She could read the sadness, the feeling of impotence weighing down on her. So she had convinced her mother that she should go home and wait for the baby to arrive. That way she would be rested and ready to help take care of her granddaughter.

"God, I am so looking forward to going home," Mariah murmurs, kissing the soft fuzz of baby hair, the little swirl at the top of the crown. The swelling of her face had gone down with only the red spots from the strains of the delivery remaining.

"Are you sure you don't want me to move in for a few days? Just in case Ms. Lil' Boss here decides to invite all her baby friends over for a drinking party?" Eleanor teases.

"I'm sure," Mariah responds. The concern in Eleanor's voice had not been lost on Mariah. "Thanks. I just want Jake and me to figure this out together. Plus, you have already hired us a doula to help with the breastfeeding and to keep us organized. Lil' Boss will be on her best behavior. Won't you sweetheart?"

"Just give me a holler if you need rescuing from too much adoration," Eleanor purrs to the sleepy baby.

"SHE'S A NATURAL," MARIAH WHISPERS to Max, her glance directed at Luna, who is sitting on the floor holding the baby on her outstretched legs. Mariah and Max watch her rub the baby's cheeks with the soft hand puppet of a duckling she'd brought the baby as a gift. Luna was a big gifter, not the last-minute type who ran into the supermarket on her way to a birthday to grab anything that resembled a presentable gift, or defaulted to a gift card. Nor was she the two-day quick delivery Amazon buyer (in fact, she did not even own a Prime membership on principle). Luna was the type of gifter who spent half a day going in and out of shops until she found that perfect "something" which would naturally be accompanied by an equally carefully chosen card for the particular recipient.

For Mariah and Jake's wedding, she gave them a collection of delicate white tea linen napkins which she paired with a set of plain, yet elegant ceramic napkin rings she found at a high-end antique shop. The napkins came from a small artisan business run by a Dutch-Moroccan artist living in Amsterdam. She had read about him, and then contacted him directly since she wanted the design to be a specific pattern and colors that showcased both Jake's and Mariah's love of the city.

"Wow!" Eleanor said, admiring the gift. "This must have cost our boy Max a small fortune," she added, alluding to Luna's expensive taste.

Mariah and Max remain fixed on the Luna-baby interaction. They struggle to suppress a laugh at Luna's awkward imitation of Donald Duck's voice. Goofy or not, the trick is working. Luna manages to keep Lil' Boss engaged and alert for over an hour. The new parents had been trying to keep the baby on a schedule, but so far Lil' Boss offered very little cooperation.

"Can Luna move in with us?" Mariah asks Max loud enough for Luna to hear.

"We're a package deal," she responds. "If you take me in, you will have to take him too." Luna motions to Max with a smile, her *save the Fucking whales* T-shirt two sizes over the maximum required fabric to cover her small frame.

"Never mind," Mariah replies. "I don't need another baby in the house." She throws a cushion at Max who catches it and sends it right back at her.

"Luna," Max interrupts the peekaboo game, "tell Mariah the story about that girl from work."

"It's crazy," Luna declares, taking her eyes away from the baby for just a moment. "She is this young kid, maybe twenty-two. She lives with her parents in either Brighton or Watertown. I am not sure which. Anyway, I think they are Italian, or maybe Greek." Such went Luna's stories, maybe this or maybe that. But Mariah waits patiently for the story to unfold on Luna's own terms. After many long minutes of retelling, Luna is bringing the story to its finale.

"We found out …," she pauses to make sure she still had her listeners' attention, "that she eloped with her uncle. Well, not legally her uncle. Her cousin is married to this woman so that guy is the father of her cousin's wife. His wife died a couple of years ago. Apparently not long after the wife died, he goes out and starts seducing this kid. I swear she is like twenty-two, or twenty-three tops. The guy is over sixty years old. They had kept their little fling secret this whole time. He had come to pick her up at work several times, but we all thought he was her dad."

"Holy cow!" Mariah exclaims, "Do they know where they went?"

"No," responds Luna. "We only found out about the elopement because her sister came into the store to see if we knew anything. She looked more pissed than worried, if you ask me. But people at work think they went down to Florida. Who knows? Maybe Greece."

"Alright Max, your turn." Luna walks over and deposits the happy baby on Max's lap. Max tries to settle Lil' Boss back down in the same fashion Luna had, but the baby begins to fuss and rub her eyes.

"No, no, no young lady," Mariah kisses the baby's feet. "You have one more hour to go before bedtime. Just hang in there."

"Her internal clock is so messed up, it's all reversed," Mariah adds. "She likes to nap during the day and play at night. It's so hard to keep her up during the day." She looks accusingly at Jake who just walked into the room.

"The problem is that she has one of her parents wrapped around her little finger and he would stay up with her just to see her happy." Mariah smiles at Jake as he leans on the edge of the door frame for a good back rub much like Old Baloo the Bear.

$\mathcal{L}$UCAS RAN HIS HANDS ALONG the edge of the top rail of the antique child-size rocking chair, its glazed red paint and rope seat deteriorating from years of intentional abandonment. He inspected the small hand-turned spindle arms, deciding they would be as good a spot as any to start work on the restoration.

He spent the weekend cleaning the wood, meticulously washing away layers of heavy dust and testing for lead paint. Then he spent many hours scraping loose paint with great care so as not to gouge the natural wood.

He smiled at the blissful warm feeling radiating from the small rocking chair. Such an ordinary object, yet so powerfully saturated with memories. Lucas could still picture the small rocking chair in his own bedroom, so many decades ago. It was his sister's originally, and then his own. Their parents purchased it during a trip to the small fishing village of Frigiliana, in southern Spain. It had also come with a matching toy chest. Lucas was uncertain of what had become of the old trunk.

He was up way before morning light ready to delve into the sanding. He placed the dust mask over his face. A sense of déjà vu washed over him. Lucas had sanded and painted the small rocking chair once before. He grabbed onto the memory of his cheerful, pregnant Meg and let his mind savor the vision. She had spent days considering the color for the rocking chair and finally settled on a scarlet red because of its tinge of orange. "It's such a joyful color," she commented while holding the paint swatches before him. His daughter had loved the bright red rocking chair, but then it was put away in the attic along with her crib, her toys, and every piece of her clothing. They had remained there, much like a museum of despondency, not even the arrival of the newborn Mariah would persuade Meg to bring them back down.

Lucas summoned the memory of his oldest daughter, and a warm faceless figure appeared in his subconscious. He could no longer conjure up the defined facial features; time had erased those details. It was the feelings the image transmitted that he recognized. They were his source of strength, his center of gravity, and now more than ever, he needed that courage. Lucas closed his eyes for an instant the way an obedient child waits for a parent's blessing. Now Mariah's face danced in his mind next to her own daughter, *his* granddaughter.

Lucas began the gentle sanding, thinking back about the rocking chair. It had lived in the dark and cold loft, imprisoned by sorrow until just last week. Meg brought it down and suggested he repaint it.

"You should ask Jake to help you," she instructed before walking out the door with two large bags labeled "Big Brothers Big Sisters Clothing Donation." The following morning the Collection Center parked in their driveway to load up the bags of clothes, toys, and baby furniture from the attic. Meg had selected a small box of baby toys to keep at the house for her granddaughter.

Lucas let the scraping sound of sandpaper sing in his ears like a sweet melody. He rubbed the armrest rhythmically back and forth, stopping from time to time to give the area a soft blow followed by a close inspection with his finger. He smiled, satisfied at the smoothness, and gently turned the rocking chair around to begin working on the opposite armrest.

*S*HE WAKES UP WITH a start. The burning feeling in her fingertips is absolute. The dream had been so real that she still feels the suffocating sensation, her body bathed in sweat. Mariah had dreamt of being inside a small chamber, the entrance blocked. She sensed the steam being released by her body was in reaction to a large pile of red-hot stones in the center of the cave, much like a sweat lodge cleansing ceremony performed by many ancient cultures. In her dream, she reached out to pick up one of the fiery stones only to quickly drop it in anguish at the scorching impact.

And on cue, before she can recollect the details of her dream, the soft cries of her three-month-old baby fill the midnight silence. Jake mumbles an offer to get up, but she is already climbing out of bed with an *I'll get her* whisper of reassurance.

Mariah tiptoes out of the bedroom carefully, in an effort not to disturb Jake. The wide hallway is dark, but the glow from the nightlight in the baby's room illuminates her path. She follows the gleam that seems to vibrate with the soft baby whimpering that she knows, if left unattended, will quickly grow into louder cries.

Mariah welcomes the opportunity to get up in the middle of the night and soothe her baby back to sleep. This act is often lost by the effect of the strong medications that force her into deep, groggy sleep. She is momentarily grateful to the sweat lodge dream for waking her up.

Mariah scoops up the baby from the crib in one swift movement and makes her way to the changing table. Mariah knows the routine by heart. It begins with listening; listening to the cry and interpreting what the baby is trying to communicate. Just like the doula instructed, "You have to figure out what your darling baby is asking." Is it the intense sound of hunger? Is it fidgeting colicky, gassy cries? Is it change-my-diaper rhythmic cries? Or a soft "cuddle me" cry that, if left alone, will subside, giving the baby a chance to learn to soothe herself back to sleep.

"Let's get you nice and comfy," Mariah murmurs to the less distressed baby while replacing the wet diaper with a fresh one. "There you go. Is that better now?" she asks the sleepy baby.

She brings her daughter close to her chest and snuggles her there, breathing in that comforting scent of innocence. Mariah reaches over for the baby book sitting atop the small bookcase. *Goodnight Moon*, she reasons, but quickly changes her mind. She knows the story by heart; she could just recite it. Memorizing those stories is a newly found joy, a product of reading and rereading the same lines time and time again. She marvels at the human's ability to show preferences at even this young age. Her daughter had already developed an interest in stories about animals. Her arms and legs move excitedly at the animated way Mariah reads the story, adjusting the sound of her voice to imitate the animal sounds.

There are children's books in every room of the house, courtesy of Jake's sister who traded her presence for books. Jake had made some progress with his attempts to make amends. Her appearance over a year ago to attend the wedding had felt like a positive sign to Mariah, even if she had come alone and stayed through the ceremony only to leave that same evening on the last ferry off the island. She continues to find pretexts for not coming for a visit to meet the baby. Yet every Friday a familiar box appears in the main lobby. Inside there is always a brief message: *happy reading*. Mariah assumes that Jake must have mentioned the baby's interest in animals, for all the books in the last delivery had been about animals, both fictional and nonfictional stories.

But, in spite of the many books around the house, there are just a handful that Mariah gravitates toward: her very own personal favorites. Admittedly, one of them had been in the animal box from Jake's sister. It describes the story of a little rabbit and the parent rabbit playfully describing how much they loved each other. Such a tender story, not what she expected. Her immediate reaction when she glances at the cover of the small board book with the picture of an eager hare on the cover is to link it to the traditional story of the *Tortoise and the Hare*. Even as a child Mariah had been frightened by Aesop's story to such a degree that she was scared of anything bunny-like, including the adult-size Easter Bunny, notwithstanding its soft fur suit and the colorful eggs and candy surrounding its throne at the local mall. *Poor hares*, Mariah thinks. *They must carry the burden of their species because of a storyteller's decision once upon a time.*

She lets the rejoice of the immediate soothing sensation, shared by both mother and daughter, wash over her. The thought of her own mother comes and she grabs it. It offers a different sense of comfort, a ripple between solace and recognition. Her eyes blur and she welcomes the warm tears racing down her cheeks. *Oh Momma, you tried to shield me from your pain, but locking yourself away also meant shutting me out.*

Mariah shuts her eyes and wipes away her tears. She nuzzles her daughter closer and kisses her soft cheeks. She thinks about the book she read to her daughter last night, another animal story. That one was at the top of the chart of her daughter's favorites. It is about several animals saying good night to their youngsters as darkness fell. What a sweet tale of safety and love. She begins to recite the story softly. Her whispers sway in perfect sync to the motions of the rocking chair as she tries to conjure memories of herself cuddled in the protective cocoon of her very own mother.

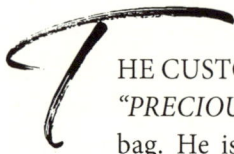

THE CUSTOM PICTURE BOOK WITH THE TITLE, "*PRECIOUS GIRL*" sits by the side of Jake's business bag. He is traveling to Florida to visit his mother for the day, *a quick Thanksgiving visit*, he had reasoned. He is scheduled to take the first flight down with plans to be back home by dinner time.

Mariah stares at the pink polka dot picture book cover with the smiling baby on the cover. She sits on the bed, feeling the impulse to pick it up and flip through the pages to view the pictures. But she holds back, feeling it would betray the specialness of his action. Jake had ordered the personalized photo book online. He had chosen not to tell her about the photo book, a special secret reserved for his mother, she reflects.

A knot of sadness grips her throat as she thinks about Jake's mother. She feels a different type of sadness for her mother-in-law now that she is a mother herself. Mariah thinks back to a time before the wedding when she had tried so hard to convince Jake to fly his mother up even if just for the day, but Jake had objected to the idea, feeling that it was of no use. "She gets disoriented and aggravated very easily," he had offered, a veil of sadness crossing his face.

Her heart aches to see the photo book, thinking of this mother whose mind had retreated into itself for so long that it had lost the ability to recognize her own children. What cruelty, how coldhearted is life to rob a mother of the biggest gift, the memory of her children growing up?

Mariah caresses the cover of the book. Perhaps Jake thinks that seeing the images of a happy baby will bring his mother a moment of clarity, or at least a flicker of awareness, even if she has no notion that the baby in the photographs is her own granddaughter.

She leaves the bedroom to join Eleanor in the family room. She had come over to spend the day with her and the baby, and her parents are coming over later, ready to stay the night, "Just in case Jake's flight is delayed or something," Lucas said. They are always her backup plan, and they love being able to fill that role. It had become part of their routine. They come to stay with her whenever Jake goes on a business trip. She is glad that those trips had lessened significantly. They had dwindled down to one overnight trip every couple of weeks with the occasional day trip to see his mother.

She finds Eleanor right where she left her just minutes ago, staring over the bassinet at the sleeping baby. She had brought several homemade meals for Mariah, hopeful of the new dietary interventions. She had thoroughly researched the benefits of a casein-free diet, and Mariah had asked Dr. Patel about it. "There are some promising findings showing that a gluten-free and casein-free diet can help with gastrointestinal irritation. It can't be viewed as an alternative medicine since we can't determine what this illness is yet, nor do we know whether it's caused by genetic or environmental factors. But we can give the diet a try," Dr. Patel responded, trying to sound hopeful.

Mariah follows Eleanor's gaze over her sleeping baby as memories of last night crawl in. Mariah's eyes had felt heavy with sleep, but she had fought to stay awake. The sound of Jake's voice talking to the baby as he helped her get ready for bed had brought her such joy. Mariah had waited with great anticipation.

"Time for that last feeding of the night. Are you ready for your little hungry monster, Mama?"

Mariah had nodded, stretching out her thin arms to welcome her little treasure into her arms. The baby sucked the soothing nipple of the bottle rhythmically. Jake's eyes never left Mariah's face as he watched this interaction. Mariah had met his eyes and felt certain that he had felt her joy. She had felt the familiar knot settle in her throat.

Mariah takes the scene in front of her and breathes it in, desperate to swallow it whole. She tugs Eleanor's hair gently to grab her friend's attention, the way she had hundreds of times before.

"You will go cross-eyed if you keep staring at her like that," Mariah teases her friend.

"Can't help it. She is so darn cute. I can't believe she's already seven months old!" Eleanor gushes. "Look at that potbelly," she says, rubbing her manicured hands lightly over the baby's protruding stomach.

"What were you just whispering to her?" Mariah asks with a smile.

"I was telling Lil' Boss here how proud I am that she learned to sleep through the night," Eleanor says .

"How are you holding up?" Eleanor asks her friend.

"Fine," she says, trying to sound convincing. She can see Eleanor studying her eyes ringed in dark circles. Her tiredness has become an extension of herself. "I'm meeting some people from work this weekend for a play date and I'm a little anxious about that."

"Then skip it," suggests Eleanor matter-of-factly.

"Oh, stop it. It will be good for me. Put it this way, it's a better alternative than being talked into one of those *Mommy and Me* classes." Mariah pauses for a second, her voice sounding more like a confession. "I guess part of my hesitation with meeting up with people from work is that some of them are still working for the firm in some capacity. Honestly, I'm kind of jealous that I don't have the stamina to do both."

It had been over three months since Mariah had stepped foot

in her office. She had spent the last few weeks of her pregnancy resting and nourishing her weak body. However, after the baby was born, she had brief periods of fantasy about going back to work. It wasn't so much the impulse to leave the house and be among her peers, the way so many new mothers craved that opportunity. For Mariah, the desire to go back to work came from a place of self-love. She misses the rush that comes from engaging her mind fully in a case with nothing else to divert her attention. She had been so good at it. She misses the fulfillment that comes from solving problems that impact people's lives.

A twinge of guilt sits in the pit of her stomach that forces her to reflect on how fortunate she is. Most new parents, if given the choice, would love to stay home and take care of their child without the distraction of work. Perhaps there is a happy medium somewhere, Mariah reasons. Maybe her body would soon stop playing this morbid game and set her free.

"What about a nanny?" Eleanor asks gingerly.

"Yeah, maybe," Mariah offers, unable to admit she'd contemplated that notion more than once.

Secretly, Mariah had considered the idea of hiring a nanny. Surely people at work would have heaps of suggestions about what agencies were best. Over the years, she had heard plenty of conversations in the lunchroom about agencies and how they competed by offering options, from attractive young Swedish women to the French college students to older, dark-skinned Caribbean grandmother types with their strong island accents. "Our nanny speaks only French to our kids," she remembers someone saying. It had sounded boastful at the time, but now Mariah realizes the appeal of that decision.

It wouldn't have to be full time. She is sure her mother would want to help with the baby if Mariah were to go back to work. Perhaps her parents could do a day, Mariah reasons, mentally settling on that plan for the time being.

"Jake made a photo book for his mother," Mariah says, describing the beautiful cover.

"He is a good son, that Jake," Eleanor says.

"And a good husband," Mariah nods.

"And a good Daddy," they both add in a singing voice.

"WHAT IS IT?" JAKE MOVES closer to Mariah to inspect the card in her hand as a sad expression glosses over her face. If there is one thing Jake is exceptionally good at, it is reading people. This skill has proven particularly useful when it comes to assessing Mariah's moods as she navigates through her medical ordeal.

He can tell by the tone of her voice in the morning whether she had a good night's sleep. Her half smile midmorning is not an indication of contentment, but rather a sign of exhaustion. The soft kisses she plants on the knuckles of his hands while he spoons her at night are not so much an indication of love, but a resignation of lust.

"It's just a card from a girl at work." Mariah turns the card over and stacks it on top of the rest. She had been reading through the dozens of well wishes that came in this morning, accompanied by an oversized basket of fresh fruits. *A little something from your work peeps*, reads the small card attached to the exuberant, sparkly ribbon.

A couple of months ago, Mariah's health took a turn for the worse. It landed her in the hospital with persistent diarrhea and severe facial inflammation.

"Your immune system is just not cooperating," the doctor said while prescribing a stronger medication to treat the back pain.

The chronic fatigue made it impossible for Mariah to continue working, and so she had decided to go on sick leave. The new medication is helping manage the back pain, but her body continues to reject any new treatment to address the weight loss, her immune system shutting down as if following its own rules.

It has been difficult for Mariah to adjust to the increased dependency on Jake and her parents to help care for her while they also help care for her one-year-old daughter.

"Why does your face look like you had just sucked on a lemon?" Jake asks, reaching for the card.

"Have faith in God and He will cure you. He is a merciful God if you give Him a chance," Jake reads in disbelief. "And who in the world is this Trish? Is this some kind of psycho reborn nonsense?"

"Jake, stop." Mariah brings her hand to her face and massages her temple. Her eyes meet his. She sees the angry red patches that flare on his neck travel slowly up to his checks, like an ancient world map.

"She means well. They all mean well. They care and want to help," she offers with a pleading stare, knowing that his rage is not entirely directed at the sender of the card.

"Help by making you feel like you deserve this? Like it might be all your fault for not believing in God?"

Jake's voice continues to rise. He walks over to the sink and turns the faucet on, letting the water run as if the rest of the task at hand has failed to materialize in his brain. He leaves the water running and goes back to the stack of cards. "Are there any more of those religious psychos in there?"

"Jake, please, don't," Mariah says, unable to complete her thought.

"Don't what?" He picks up the card and reads it again, "*Have faith in God and he will cure you. He is a merciful God if you believe in him*." He throws the card onto the pile and returns to the sink. He looks at the cascading water as if he had just noticed it was running. "Ughhh," he sighs, turning the water off, the natural coloring of his neck slowly returning.

The room goes quiet. Mariah looks up and reads the sadness in his eyes. He had accepted her fate. How long had it been since he had given up, she wonders?

Was it the recent rush to the emergency room to treat the allergic reaction to the new medicine? They had left the rest of the family behind to finish celebrating her daughter's birthday.

Mariah pulls out one of the cards from the bottom of the pile and reads it out loud:

"Dear Mariah, I just learned of your condition. I can only imagine how hard it must be for you and for your loved ones. Please know that you have a big team at work cheering for you. And please do not hesitate to reach out and to let us know how we can be helpful. You have always done so much for others. May your strength and positive outlook help you meet this challenge head on and win this fight.

My thoughts and prayers are with you.

Sincerely, Patty"

Jake watches her reach for the dark purple envelope and pull out a clay owl figurine. She sets it on the counter and stares at the silent statue that is accompanied by a card from someone whose name she does not recognize. The card is filled with a beautiful story about the significance of the owl; how ancient Babylonians believe that owls serve as an amulet to protect women during childbirth. And how they are viewed as protective spirits among some Native American nations. The story also explains how, in the Japanese culture, owls are a symbol of good luck and protection from suffering.

"I don't even know who that person is," Mariah mutters. She tries to think of someone from the office who might fit the profile. The sender had written *Muy buena suerte,* right before her signature. Mariah understands the Spanish words to express a good luck sentiment.

"I wish I could open up my chest and show you the void of loneliness pooling around my heart. I am tired, Jake. Tired of being a fucking burden. And you are not helping."

Mariah gets up and walks away, leaving the rest of the unopened envelopes behind.

*T*HE SUN SMILES BRIGHTLY, feverish at the warm blast of July. The pleasant breezes had blown away, leaving behind a trapped heat, the vicious type that draws people outside without much convincing to find refuge in air-conditioned stores or coffeehouses.

Mariah and Max stroll down the cobblestone sidewalks, not far from the Ugly Building. Her eyes dance gleefully from the faces of the fellow passersby to the window displays in the small shops. Even the rows of parking meters seem to share in her enjoyment this morning. Mariah stops and leans in against the storefront window where a vintage beach cruiser has caught her attention. She cups her hands around her face to block the glare and pauses for a brief second to inspect the collection of gourds filling up the woven rattan basket.

"I could see Luna riding one of those," Mariah says to Max, gesturing to the light blue Schwinn.

"Totally. You know, she still has her kid-size bike at her parents. It's one of those Huffy banana seat bikes. I mean, we all had one of those, but who keeps that stuff around this long?" Max asks, a sense of amazement speaking louder than the judgmental tone the question was meant to carry.

Mariah turns around to check on her daughter. Lucas is pushing the carriage a few steps behind. He smiles, his eyes full of warmth and devotion. A vision of her father teaching her daughter to ride a bike flashes across her mind. She beams at the possibility, remembering her own thrill at learning to ride a bike.

"Luna is redecorating our place," Max offers. "We're talking about getting married."

Mariah reaches over, linking her right arm snuggly to his left.

"That is the best news ever, Maxwell!" Her eyes, staring at him, press for more details.

He explains with a broad smile, "Down the road, of course, once she is done with her Ph.D. But still, she brought it up."

Mariah stops before crossing the street and checks behind her to wait for the rest of her company. She breathes heavily.

"Do you want to turn around?" Max says.

"I'm fine. Let's see if I can make it a couple more blocks to that cute baby store. I want to get Lil' Boss some new hair clips. Her hair is so fine that nothing stays on." She fingers her hair. "Rafa sent her a package with the most adorable outfit. I want to fancy up her hair for a picture to send him."

"Do you think Rafael would ever move his research back to the States?" Max asks.

"I doubt it. Remember when he worked for that company out in Cambridge right after college? The one with that fucking director who refused to approve the project manager position for Rafa because she thought that his accent was too thick? What fucked up shit. Not that he had planned to stay there long anyway. God, he was so disillusioned by the pressure to create drugs just for treatment. And now with the government chopping research funding ..."

"Yeah, that has to be frustrating. I remember that company," Max says. "It was not interested in finding cures. Permanent solutions were not profitable."

"Right. And Rafael did not go into science for monetary gains. He has never been interested in making medicine a profitable endeavor. To him, having affordable drugs available to all was the goal. So that's when he left Big Pharma for nonprofit research."

Mariah shares her own frustration with the multi-billion-dollar drug industry which focuses on generating sizable profits for itself instead of developing medicines to cure illnesses and save lives.

"These companies will manufacture a pill for ten cents and then turn around and sell it for fifteen dollars. That's just an abomination," Mariah says.

"And they go on and justify the monstrous prices for research, development costs, and marketing. I don't blame Rafael for getting fed up with all the avarice and bullshit," Max adds. "Many drug companies go as far as to pay off generics to hold back on releasing cheaper alternatives. And don't forget about the countless cases of companies that bribe chemists to manipulate data to highlight positive outcomes."

"Right," Mariah says. "Remember that famous research out of Harvard years back about fat being bad for you? Then we found out later that the sugar industry had paid for the research so that the focus was not centralized on how bad sugar was for your health."

Max nods. "It's unthinkable the kind of crookedness that goes on which could be reduced considerably by more governmental regulations. They know the large majority of those companies don't care about legality. They are fined a few million, but that's like a slap on the wrist. What are a few million to them, but pocket change?"

"And then you add the many shady doctors to the corruption mix," Mariah says. "But I blame the system. How is it even allowed for doctors to receive personal favors when choosing to prescribe certain drugs?"

"I agree," Max says. "Doctors should be mandated to tell their patients about the generic version when it's available."

"And to declare any gifts and monetary compensation from drug companies. My God, it's a conflict of interest all the way. And who is getting shortchanged?" Mariah asks, thinking about her own personal experience.

Max had taken over all legal aspects of Mariah's illness, specifically dealing with the back-and-forth disputes with the health insurance companies.

"Not everyone is lucky enough to have a Max for a friend," she adds, squeezing his arm just a tad firmer.

*J*AKE CARRIES HIS HAPPY TODDLER to their bed for a few minutes of play before her bedtime. Mariah positions her body to welcome the fun-loving bundle who had been babbling away, pointing at things while announcing happily "ist!" The proud parents were convinced she was asking for the lights to be turned on, until they began to notice that she was also calling her food "ist!" The eighteen-month-old had been fascinated with ordinary things, ignoring her toys for more regular household had items like hair brushes, pots, and pans.

Her eyes light up at the sight of her mother, and she bounces from her dad's arms and into the bed, her arms open, calling, "ma-ma."

"Come here, you silly girl. You have been telling Daddy all about your busy day, haven't you?" A shower of giggles fills the room.

"She's a jumping bean! I just can't believe she can walk up the stairs," Jake comments. "We'll need to put up those safety gates pronto."

The new parents delight as they watch their baby reach each new milestone. It used to be so hard to keep her entertained for long periods of time. How astonishing it is that now she can choose her own toys and laugh at those clapping hand games. Her biggest amusement is looking out the window at passing dogs, her body jiggling up and down.

Mariah holds her daughter up. The one-piece footed pajamas accentuate Lil' Boss's protruding round belly. Mariah plants a kiss right in the middle of her belly, aiming at the belly button. The baby's strong grip around Mariah's fingers makes her smile with delight.

"She is so strong." Mariah sings a catchy song and the baby bounces with glee.

"Alright, little lady, time for bed," Jake announces. He is aware of the fatigue this simple interaction had brought Mariah.

Mariah kisses the chubby cheeks of her baby girl. "Night, night sweetheart," she whispers.

Jake can feel her watching them as he walks away with their daughter perched up on his shoulders. *We are going to be okay,* he whispers to his daughter, knowing that Mariah believes the same thing.

Jake lays the sleepy child down in her crib. She turns her head to look up at him, her thumb already in place. He smiles, knowing that in a few minutes she will be fast asleep.

"Sweet dreams," he whispers and makes his way across the room. He taps the music pad on the wall and the gentle sound of ocean breezes comes to life. Jake flips on the nightlight, steps out into the hallway, and goes back to Mariah.

"She is such a good girl, isn't she?" As he climbs back into bed, he pulls Mariah a bit closer.

"Yeah. I love to watch her walk around in her walk-run style," Mariah smiles. "That kid went from crawling to running in no time."

"She's looking so grownup since those first molars came in," Jake says.

"She has been doing great with all the new food we're introducing. Did you see the videos we sent?"

Jake laughs with delight, remembering the videos Eleanor had sent him earlier in the day as she and Mariah tried feeding their toddler stir-fry chicken with squash and brown rice. He had been watching the baby eating her lunch each day, their virtual lunch together. Today Jake was stuck at a meeting that ran late, so he missed the lunch date with his girls.

"Did she actually eat any of it? There seemed to be more squash puree on her face than in her mouth."

"It's hard to tell, but the look on her face was priceless. She pushed the puree out with her tongue, but kept stuffing chicken pieces into her mouth like a little chipmunk."

"What's on the menu for tomorrow?" Jake asks.

"We're making quesadillas with black beans and avocado. Eleanor is picking up some super ripe bananas from her store to make banana and yogurt pops to eat outside. That's going to be fun to watch!"

Mariah smiles and gives her pillow a couple of fluffs, indicating that it is time for her to turn in. Jake hands her a glass of water and takes out an assortment of pills from the collection of medication bottles standing at attention on her nightstand. She takes them all one by one and hands the glass back to Jake with a grateful smile.

He doesn't need to know that each pill feels like a gigantic ball of fire rolling down her throat. He doesn't need to know that for the first half of the night those pills will sit in her stomach and she will hear the angry arguments between them. Who would dominate the night? she wonders.

She hopes the good pills would win the battle tonight. Those would let her sleep into the early morning. The party animal pills keep her up all night. They usually win the fight. She prays for the sad pills to stay away. They haven't won in quite a while. Those are the ones that visit her in her sleep and accuse her of being a bad daughter for doing this to her mother and a bad mother for doing this to her daughter. The wet pillow in the morning is evidence of the sad pills' victory.

Jake pulls the covers over Mariah and lies down closely next to her. He kisses her hollow eyes and encloses her with his arms. He whispers words of love while stroking her thinned-out hair. On the night stand a new stack of books sits, their unread pages waiting patiently to be deciphered.

Jake feels the exhaustion hugging him tightly, suffocating him. He feels the anger lurking at friends who keep sending books accompanied by notes of *here is a little something to brighten your day*. Then there are the phone calls asking the same irritating question: *How is she*? As if they really want to hear about her nauseous body and leaky bladder that forces her to wear an adult diaper to bed. He'd say, "She is a trooper. She is taking each day as a blessing and spending lots of quality time with our daughter." He has to take a deep, dry swallow each time someone calls before he is able to give them the answer they want to hear.

Mariah's soft breathing lets him know she has fallen asleep. Jake makes his way into the bathroom where he plugs the tub drain and turns the hot water on. He looks at the extravagant tub, a source of many joyful moments. He had made love to Mariah in this tub more times than he could remember. Now it fulfills a different role.

Jake undresses and steps into the tub as it continues to fill up. The sound of the running water welcomes his weeping.

EG HELD HER GRANDDAUGHTER in her lap. She had been hesitant during those first few months to even come near the child, afraid that the mere air around her could possibly cause the child harm. But her granddaughter had pulled her out of the sea of fear like a humanoid talisman.

She giggled as she hid the rubbery toy giraffe behind her back for Meg to find.

Meg reached over to retrieve the toy. "I found it!" she said and handed it back to the happy toddler, knowing that in less than a minute she would be trying the same trick again. It was her favorite game. From time to time her granddaughter lost interest in the game, in the toy giraffe, and instead reached up, her small hands tracing her grandmother's face with interest.

"Yum, yum, yum!" Meg declared to the happy child, "What delicious little fingers you have." She pretended to eat her grand-daughter's fingers with soft kisses. The toddler pulled her hands away with loud chuckles.

Some parents consider the sound of a sleeping child to be the most beautiful sound. But Mariah listens to her daughter's joyous laughter and decides THIS is the best sound a parent could hear from her child.

Mariah meets her mother's eyes. She can read the fear so easily spelled out. Those eyes have been more accustomed to tears; not the happy ones, but the heavy ones that cascade, forcing the heart to constrict, to wrinkle beat by beat.

Mariah mouths a tender "*I Love You Momma*" to her mother,

who receives it with a smile, hugging her granddaughter a little tighter. Mariah remembers the terror in her mother's face when she gave them the bad news about her medical condition, still an unknown beast. She had remained hopeful with the illusion of a sharing-the-bad-news-followed-by-the-good-news kind of deal. But, it had turned out, there was only bad news to be delivered.

They had been sharing a glass of wine around the kitchen counter when Jake excused himself with the pretext of needing to make a call. Mariah had wanted it to be just the three of them, wanting to lock in the intimacy of the moment.

Her parents had stood there for a while, speechless, like two ancient pillars absorbing the weight of a temple upon their outstretched arms.

The word terminal had woken her up last night. It had flashed on a bulletin board surrounded by blinking lights inviting all to see as if it was a Broadway premiere. *You might be terminal, but I am not ready to give up just yet*, she had muttered to herself as she willed a new dream to come.

Mariah feels a gentle squeeze of her shoulders and a kiss on the top of her head. She recognizes the loving gesture from a childhood ritual. "Don't worry kid. Our girls will be OK," her father whispers.

His words feel like a refreshing mist, a sacrosanct promise. There are days in which Mariah feels like she is drifting away in one of M. C. Escher's intricate labyrinths, lost in a surreal world of possibilities, hope or terror just waiting around each turn. But there are also moments when the guilt of being a burden on her family is forced to stay away by the love surrounding her. She curls her legs up beneath her on the armchair and tips her head to the side. Her right arm reaches up to better nuzzle her father's embrace. Mariah breathes a peaceful sigh. She looks at her happy daughter, a beautiful healthy sprout. *I am breaking my mother's heart, but I am leaving her the best of me*, Mariah reassures herself.

*T*HE HOUSE IS QUIET. Jake left for the office early after dropping the baby off at her mother and father's house. The nurse would be coming in soon. She would help Mariah get out of bed and wash up. It had been Max's idea to hire her, "just to have an extra pair of hands to help keep track of the meds." And, of course, he was right. Over the two weeks since the nurse had started coming, Mariah has felt an immense sense of relief. It is not an easy task to maintain a record of the various medicines she needs to take each day, and to track her food intake in order to ensure that she is consuming the necessary calories. The nurse takes care of all of that, even going as far as determining when it is necessary to supplement her intake with artificial nutrition.

On some days she is glad that the strain has been lifted off Jake's shoulders. Yet there are days when she resents him for handing her over as an inconvenience, a mass of damaged goods.

"Selfish son of bitch," she mutters, her eyes pooling with hot tears. The phone rings and she ignores the familiar tone.

"Sons of bitches, all of you!" she sobs, refusing to pick up the call.

She knows her refusal to see her friends angers Jake.

How could she explain that their attention sends her into silent episodes of rage, and yet their presence is an upsetting reminder that they will still be here, going on with their lives, after she is gone?

"Why don't they go and die with me?" she sobs, remembering Eleanor's last visit a few days ago.

"The weather is just beautiful. Maybe we can try to get you outside soon," Eleanor said.

Mariah stared at her moving mouth, struggling to make sense of the flow of her words. The crash of the large Venetian bowl at Eleanor's feet surprised them both. Eleanor stared at her friend and then back at the shattered pieces of glass sitting in place as if they, too, felt astounded by the rage that sent them there.

"I am so sorry," Eleanor whispered as she crawled onto the floor to pick up the porcelain pieces as if to erase the evidence of a crime scene.

"Just go! Leave it and go!" Mariah commanded, afraid of what else her anger might unleash. Her piercing screams followed Eleanor out into the hallway.

Mariah's eyes fix on the ornate high ceilings. The glossy silver leaf backdrop add an extra touch of class to the already elegant room. She glances at the ceiling light, a glass drop chandelier above the end of the bed. Its crystals cascaded like giant teardrops, their sparks bouncing back into the room.

"Stop!" she yells at the renewed ringing of her phone, and then pushes it under her pillow, unwilling to face the caller.

Mariah lies there, shaking, listening to her shameful sobs pounding her chest like sharp claws. She struggles to decipher the instinct, the nagging idea of going off to die alone, much like a wounded animal would do. Would it be viewed as courageous or merely cowardly? It is nature's way in the animal kingdom. She is but one speck of dust among the infinity of living souls. She hears the small internal voice mocking her: *Why trouble your loved ones with your brokenness? Why not reach out to a merciful doctor for some assistance the way people do for their beloved pets, to put them out of their misery? Isn't that a reflection of kindness and true love?* If it were up to her, she would opt to surrender her body, to be a fresh meal to hungry scavengers without shame or morbidity the way nature instructed it to be.

"Not even the wolf would touch this fucking chemically

saturated body," she says out loud with a sad laugh. "I am a poisoned meatloaf."

It has been a good life, Mariah reflects, trying to convince herself that drifting off to a forever dream is just the next logical step.

Her shaking hands retrieve the phone. The message, "*I love you and I am here for you*," stares back at her and settles warmly deep inside. She returns the call, holding the phone close to her ear, welcoming the familiar voice on the other side of the line.

MAX COMES OVER ARMED WITH cream cheese, tomatoes, avocados, and a generous bowl of fruit salad. Mariah had asked him to help her plan a surprise birthday brunch for Eleanor.

"Oh, Maxwell," Mariah embraces Max in desperation as he steps out of the elevator. Max holds onto her frail body, a quiet duet of sorrow, until she is ready to let him go. Mariah breathes in and holds the breath for a second longer. She exhales with all possible force, as if the desolation inside will flow out with the used-up oxygen being released.

"Thank you," she utters. "I needed that."

Max is the only person Mariah is able to commiserate with. It is Max whom she calls whenever she feels like drowning in fear or self-pity. She doesn't have to put up any pretense with him.

"Where are your people?" Max asks.

"Jake is still not back from his long morning walk with Lil' Boss," Mariah says as she leads him into the kitchen.

Mariah had ordered Jake a backpack carrier for his walks in the woods with their daughter. He had been hesitant to use it at first, worried that if something were to happen to the child he wouldn't be able to see her perched up behind him.

He had carried their daughter around the house in the backpack, just to please Mariah. The excitement of the child while riding in the pack had convinced Jake. The backpack was designed with extra padding for a comfortable fit around his hips. It also came with storage pouches for snacks and other necessities, so they could be away all day and have everything they need.

"Remember how scared he was to use it? Now he loves the

backpack. Actually, they both do. Even when the weather is lousy, they just head out to the mall for some backpacking adventure. She calls the backpack 'bady.' At first we thought she was making up a new version of Daddy, but then she went and dragged the pack out of the closet and told Jake, "Daddy, let's go bady!"

"That's pretty funny." Max laughs as he sets out the spread. He hands Mariah a pile of napkins to fold. Her parents, Eleanor, Andrew, and Gus would be arriving soon.

Mariah watches her friend setting up the platter of food to be brought up to the roof garden. Jake had decorated it with balloons and streamers early this morning. Mariah watches the careful way Max lays out each item. She loves him for being so kind and thoughtful, for seeing past her decaying body and treating her with such dignity. He knows it gives her pleasure to put out a beautiful arrangement for Eleanor.

"Did you look through the *Better Homes and Gardens* magazines for ideas?" she teases.

"I did not, but Luna did give me some helpful pointers," he laughs, garnishing the cream cheese with a few petals of edible flowers.

"And how is Luna feeling?" Mariah asks.

"She is still fighting that nasty cold. It's been over three weeks now. Apparently everyone at work has it, so now they just keep reinfecting each other. I've been sleeping in the guest room," Max offers as a way of getting Mariah to chuckle. They both know that nothing would really keep Max away from sleeping next to his Luna, though.

"She made me make the fruit salad. She didn't want to even touch the fruit, afraid of sending along some of her germs. I know, she's crazy," Max adds warmly. "And she made sure I added extra raspberries for you." Max rolls his eyes, pretending to be annoyed.

Mariah leans in to look at the contents of the bowl and smiles a borrowed smile from two years back before her body declared open war.

"Tell her that this is the yummiest looking fruit salad ever. Those are some juicy looking raspberries. Would you please tell her that I ate some?" Mariah asks, knowing Max would have done so anyway. Her discomfort in swallowing, dysphagia Dr. Patel called it, is worse now. She had explained that if the medication didn't help control the pain, they would need to consider feeding tubes to provide the necessary nutrition.

"And what's going on with you?" Max asks, sitting next to Mariah. "Give me the full account."

"It sucks. I suck and we all suck," Mariah comments with frustrated sniffles.

"You know, when Dr. Patel called last week to tell me that I don't actually have stomach cancer, I was relieved. But then again, I wish the test had come out positive. I just need something to direct my anger toward, even if it is just a label," Mariah growls in frustration.

"It sucks big time," Max says, and guides Mariah's head to his chest.

"I know that sometimes it helps to know what you don't have. But for God's sake, what exactly *is* wrong with me? Rafa says all the stuff he is finding points to cancer. He saw those deformed cells light up one day, but now they are copying themselves onto the image of healthy cells, camouflaging and hiding like cowards. I feel my body's rejection every day I wake up. I look at myself in the mirror, at this shrinking body mocking me.

Her eyes dart around the room. She reaches over to the tissue box and grabs a handful, rolling them between her hands. "I am so sick and tired of feeling that I am letting everyone down. I am tired of keeping a brave face and being all positive and upbeat.

Fuck brave face and being Mrs. Positivity. Fuck upbeat. And fuck enjoying every fucking moment of my fucking living time. And make the best of it can also go and fuck itself. What is that anyway? People say every day is a gift. What am I supposed to do with that? Each day I feel bullied by life."

She places the pile of tissues on the table with a sigh.

"I want to give up, Max: the physical therapy, the occupational therapy, all of it. Even the speech girl who is the nicest person I know. I just want to tell her to get the hell out of here."

"You can, you know," Max says. "Yell at all of them. It will not change what is happening to your body, but I bet it will feel very satisfying. Here, let's practice. GET THE FUCK OUT OF HERE AND TAKE MY FUCKING DYSPHAGIA WITH YOU!"

"Stop it! You'll turn into Eleanor if you aren't careful," Mariah laughs, bringing a gentle slap to Max's forehead. She pauses and takes a deep breath.

"I'm just worn out," she says. "I'm exhausted from grieving my body. Dr. Patel keeps saying I need to find a place for my sickness in my life instead of allowing it to become my entire life. How is that even possible? This sickness *is* my life. It keeps me from being the mother I want to be. It prevents me from making love to my husband and enjoying good wine with my friends or sipping a creamy cup of coffee at my favorite coffee place. It robs me of walking down the street to get ice cream with my dad or taking my mother out to get our nails done. This is it Max, terminal is what Dr. Patel said this fucking whatever it is that is attached to me."

"Well, Eleanor would tell you to tell Dr. Patel to fuck the hell off too," Max says, and they both burst out laughing. Not because the comment is funny, but because they can each picture Dr. Patel's reaction to this profane mandate.

"WHAT'S THAT RACKET downstairs?" Mariah asks as Jake steps into the room. She had been hearing whispers and furniture being moved around.

"It's Eleanor. She's hired a group of masseuses for the afternoon. It looks like we are all getting massages today, including Lil' Boss!" Jake laughs, clearly delighted at the lit-up expression on Mariah's face.

"She is crazy! I have nothing but protruding bones. What's there to massage?" Mariah declares, loving Eleanor just a bit more for bringing in the possibility of such fun, a mirage of normalcy.

"And guess who is leading the troop! Your gazelle," Jake adds with a twinkle in his eyes.

Mariah beams at the prospect. It had been over a year since her last dreamlike massage under the hands of her gazelle. She remembers her first visit and how much she had enjoyed the experience. That one occasion had turned into a biweekly affair. Sometimes Eleanor joined her, but most days she went alone. And she had been secretly glad to have the gazelle all to herself.

"I just left them downstairs setting up. The gazelle is adamant about doing this for you free of charge as a Christmas gift, but Eleanor is insisting that she charges at least for making the arrangements and the rental of the equipment. I figure I'll stay clear of those two."

"Smart move," Mariah declares with a smile.

The inharmonious sound continues to travel up the length of the steps and into the bedroom.

"I think it will take them a bit to finish setting up," Jake says.

"Want me to draw you a bath to get ready?"

"How can you possibly read my mind like that?" Mariah shoots him a wondrous gaze and asks, "Would you add ..."

"... a few drops of lavender oil," they chant in unison.

Jake leaves the room to get the bath ready. The vertical tub has proven to be of great use given Mariah's physical restrictions.

Back in the bedroom, she sits up and scooches closer to the edge of the bed as she awaits his return. She smooths the cotton fabric of her long-sleeved nightgown, reaches up, and traces her hand along the delicate edge of the V-neck adorned with needle-point patterns. Mariah likes the softness of the fabric fine, but it is the medieval vintage style with its three-quarter sleeves puffing up midway that she loves. She traces the high waist ribbon bow. She has been determined to preserve the sense of intimacy even if just for appearances. Neither this sickness nor this bony body would keep her from attempting to look her best for her husband. *Such vanity*, she hears her inner voice utter, more as praise than reproach.

Mariah touches her head tentatively. Her curls, once abundant and vibrant, have dwindled now, leaving behind uneven strands of frail ringlets. She pats her scalp, fingering the French braids Eleanor had managed to engineer this morning. Mariah had asked her to pin on a single gladiolus flower from the bouquet her mother left last night by her night table. Mariah had awakened to find the beautiful orange bloom sitting in a teacup on her breakfast tray.

Like the Roman gladiators, you speak of strengths, Mariah whispers to the orange petals, gently rubbing the bloom's pastel yellow center. *Yet, all I want is to flee, to shade away this broken body and to disappear into nothingness.*

Mariah grabs the flower from her head and plucks each petal out into her hand, "Bullshit of a gladiator you are," she whispers, rolling the soft petals between her hands.

Jake reenters the bedroom holding her fleece bathrobe, a glorified hospital gown, Mariah calls it. He walks around the bed to meet her, laying the bathrobe next to her. He brings his hands to her shoulders and then up to her face, causing her to look up. She holds his gaze, taking in this vision of her husband towering above her like a protective god. He bends over to kiss her, first her forehead, then her eyelids, and finally her lips, where he lingers a few extra seconds.

"Can you give me a hand with this?" Mariah asks, pointing to her nightgown while wondering if he can taste death on her lips.

"Gladly," comes his affirmative response, and he lifts her gown over her head as effortlessly as a Caribbean islander climbing a palm tree. Mariah reaches for the bathrobe, too self-conscious of her exposed nudity. Jake kisses the top of her head encouragingly. She lifts one arm and guides it through the arm opening of the gown and then does the same with her other arm, but that is as far as she can manage. Jake pulls back the front of the gown and the Velcro fasteners hold it securely in the back.

Mariah stands, the bamboo floor feeling cold under her bare feet. She breathes in the moment, happy to be out of bed even when the ache of her body conspires with gravity and her own legs are incapable of doing their job.

"Ready?" Jake asks, and seeing her nod, he lifts her tenderly in his arms the way he had carried her, his new bride, not that long ago.

Part Six

a sweet melody
an encased love
hold it close
watch it grow
a rose answers to no one

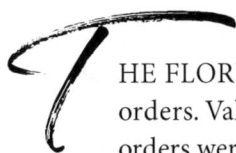

HE FLORIST at Flowers Beyond reviewed the daily orders. Valentine's Day was just around the corner and orders were flying in faster than she could handle. She was contemplating outsourcing some of the regular orders. She much preferred to focus on the part of her business that served as a personal florist representative of the deceased.

When she created this online service a year ago, she had underestimated its potential. The idea came to her after the loss of a close friend. She liked the notion of helping loved ones you leave behind grieve by passing a message of love through notes and flowers, a symbolic warm hug from the other side.

Her eyes moved to the bottom of the invoice form, a place for the sender to write a message or include a photo attachment.

Her client had attached a note that included a dozen sentiments. She had asked for each note to accompany a small bouquet of blue irises to be delivered once a month.

Blue irises speak of faith and valor, the florist reasoned.

She read the list of sentiments one by one, a sad smile lingering on her face.

"Gratitude notes," she whispered.

Her customer had signed each note,

Your Lady Rose.

"WHAT IS IT WITH you this morning? What is that smirk on your face?" Mariah asks with difficulty, her slurred words fighting their way through her unresponsive tongue.

Max had placed the birthday cake shaped like a number two on the kitchen counter. The *Happy Birthday Little Boss* rainbow frosting letters neatly surrounded by an arrangement of colorful jellybeans.

His brows shoot up in surprise. "My God! You don't miss a thing. Do you?"

"Well, you have kind of made it a bit obvious," she teases, her eyes admiring the colorful cake she had ordered for her daughter's birthday dinner that evening.

Max is driving Mariah to the local clinic run by the Department of Rare Diseases. She maintains her commitment to her weekly visits even now that her body requires the assistance of a wheelchair to move. She is part of a new trial treatment and uncertain of whether she is receiving a placebo. Still, it is all she can do in the absence of a treatment for this unknown disease that feasts on her insides.

"There are some things I just found out about Eleanor that will make you very happy, but she doesn't want you to know. It's something she has been doing for a few months now and has kept from you."

"So, go on." Mariah waits in anticipation.

"You really think I should tell you, though?" He looks conspiratorially at her.

"Why do you think she doesn't want me to know?"

"I think she is doing this as a way to honor you and, by not telling you, she probably feels her deed has more meaning."

"OK then, I give you permission to tell me."

"But you have to promise not to say anything. And if she decides to tell you, promise me you'll pretend to be surprised. You know she will never speak to me again if she finds out I told you, right?"

"I will do a stellar fake-out performance. Cross my heart," Mariah offers, bringing her frail hand to her chest to seal the promise.

"Well, I met with her and Sean last week. You know he's back together with Pete, right?"

"Yes, Gus told me the other day," Mariah confirms, adding how happy she had been to receive the news. Sean is completing his internship at the end of the year and she is certain he will land a job in her firm once he is done with law school. Everyone is so impressed with his work ethic and dedication.

"Anyway, Sean has been involved with that prison program you used to work with. He's been giving free legal advice and guidance to fathers from that group. Kind of what you used to do."

"That's great. But why didn't Gus tell me about that?"

"I think because he was afraid of spilling the beans that our dear Eleanor... are you ready for it?" Max smiles at Mariah. She loves suspense, so he gives it all he has.

"Our dear Eleanor has been running a chef training program there. As a matter of fact, she has been doing it for over a year now. She started it soon after you got sick. Apparently, it was Eleanor who enlisted Sean. It's all legit and everything. I mean those guys are graduating with diplomas and all. Eleanor is running a culinary school for your inmates."

Mariah brings her hands to her face in an attempt to wipe away her tears. The sensation of crying is there, but her eyes are no longer able to produce consistent tears, a side effect of the medications. She pictures the young faces swaying in her memory, the darker the shade the more severe their sentence.

"I can feel your happy tears," Max tells her, "even if I don't see them falling."

When they arrive at the clinic, it is quiet as usual. Max rolls the wheelchair to the check-in desk. The receptionist hands him an old clipboard. "Can you please verify the highlighted information and then initial it down here?" She points to the bottom of the form.

Max turns around and hands the clipboard to Mariah. He knows she is unable to see the small fonts clearly, so he places a finger on the place requiring her initials. He looks over the information and hands the clipboard back to the receptionist, who in turn hands him back another form indicating the various tests. Max looks at the list and reads them to Mariah. The clinic had originally hoped to collect traditional biopsy samples, but they discarded the idea due to the invasiveness of the procedure, given Mariah's poor health. They had opted for the liquid biopsy option instead, hoping to detect any traces of DNA mutation material that might be present in her blood.

"Wow, only ten checks. Today is your lucky day. Let's go, your favorite vampire is waiting."

"Max? Thank you for doing this with me," Mariah says with heartfelt gratitude. Jake had initially accompanied her to these visits, but his low tolerance for blood to the point of almost fainting had made Mariah reach out to Max to step in. Jake had resigned without a fight.

Max wheels Mariah into the small cubicle. She places her arms on the armrests almost on impulse. She stares at her outstretched arms covered with dark bruises. Her slim upper limbs seem so foreign to her.

The shy phlebotomist with "Luis" on the nametag pinned to

the pocket of his scrubs greets her kindly. But Mariah doesn't need the visual reminder; she knows his name by heart, just like she knows the names of the other four phlebotomists that volunteer at the clinic.

"I'm sorry," Luis says apologetically while trying to fit his oversized hands into a pair of latex medical gloves. "My hands are sweaty from the heat. It makes it harder to put these things on."

"You know, they should invent a machine, much like those automatic hand dryers where you could just stick both your hands up," Mariah motions her flat hands facing in, "and boom! The gloves are forced onto your hands by air pressure." She offers an encouraging smile.

"That would be a nice invention," he says, giving her a conspiratorial grin.

ELEANOR IS IN THE KITCHEN brewing turkey broth to feed Mariah, who can only manage to ingest meals in liquid form. Her ligaments, joints, and cartilage had ceased to comply with mobility, forcing her to spend most days in bed. Two nurses are with her at the moment, their time overlapping for a couple of hours. They rotate during the day, checking in on Mariah periodically, but they are conscientious about keeping in the shadows to give the family their own space and privacy.

Eleanor adds a tablespoon of tapioca powder to thicken the broth to the desired consistency. Gus walks in, the aura of sadness surrounding him so dense it could be sliced with the edge of the sharp blade resting on the counter. He reaches over and helps Eleanor pour the mix into a small ceramic bowl on the bed tray. She gives him a sad smile and heads out of the kitchen.

Eleanor balances the tray as she makes her way up the flight of stairs to the spacious master bedroom. She remembers how relieved Jake was when Mariah had decided to make this apartment their home. The Ugly Building apartment is a perfect fit for them.

A large floral arrangement of colorful irises sits on the drop-leaf accent table by the tall bay windows, brightening the room. Eleanor wanted to keep fresh flowers in the bedroom for Mariah. She called Jake for suggestions and was impressed by his quick response. *"She would love roses, yellow ones, but they have too strong a fragrance. Go for irises, but an assortment of colors. She will like that."*

Eleanor had planned to send over a large bouquet of lilies or lilacs. She smiles now, glad she had thought of checking in with Jake.

A small fire burns lazily in the white marble fireplace, keeping the room warm and cozy from the November chill. A set of wingback style chairs face the fireplace, adding not only a feeling of elegance to the room, but a magical and dreamy aura.

Jake sits with the newspaper on his lap. He looks up to meet Eleanor's eyes, and then their gazes travel to the large bed where Mariah rests peacefully, her head propped high on the soft faux fur pillows. She looks so small against the king-size bed, that the vision makes Eleanor's heart constrict. The upholstered platform bed had been Mariah's wedding present to Jake. She loved the gray fabric headboard with the silver nail trim. It had an air of sophistication that matches Jake's personality so well.

"How is Chica doing this morning?"

Eleanor knows the effect it had on Mariah to hear Rafael's pet name for her. Eleanor calling her Chica brings a splash of happy feelings; a joyful memory of a time when they all felt inebriated with life and only dreamed of grandiose possibilities.

"You will help Jake watch after the baby?" Mariah addresses Eleanor, clearing her throat.

Eleanor is watching Mariah's hands, her thumb and pinky fingers pointing awkwardly as she speaks. This mannerism—Mariah's talking hands—is one of the few physical traits that remains loyal to her body. It takes great physical and mental effort for Mariah to articulate words, for the morphine that keeps her comfortable also keeps her from being fully lucid. Eleanor's eyes fill up with tears.

"Stop that type of talk or I will call Gus to come up and lecture you."

Mariah smiles weakly at her dear Eleanor. She had organized a rotating schedule so that two friends would be at the house each day to try and keep her alert with personal tales and news of current events. *Dear Eleanor, how sad will my leaving make you?* And Gus and Max, their mixed-matched friendship finally congealed. She pictures how Gus and Max had been like contrasting colors on a color wheel. Although their own peculiar luminance and saturation forced them to clash, when it came down to it, they'd learned that they did, in fact, complement each other, just like the blue and orange colors sitting opposite each other on the color wheel. She remembers how Eleanor had joked about it at the time, but it turns out that Jake had indeed brought Gus and Max together.

"I am so sorry," she tries to say, but the words get lost in the labyrinth of her vocal cords.

Mariah remembers the tall eighteen-year-old blond with the beautiful smile sitting behind her during orientation week. She talked to the people next to her the entire presentation. She fought the urge to hush her. She shifted in her seat uncomfortably, trying to remain attentive in spite of the distraction emanating from the back.

Eleanor had come over after exiting the chapel where the orientation was held to introduce herself and to invite her to join her for lunch. Their beautiful friendship was sealed that one wonderful day.

Mariah obediently opens and closes her mouth while Eleanor's steady hands feed her, trying to hide her discomfort as the thick, gelled broth navigates its way down her throat.

Eleanor begins to retell her latest yoga saga.

"So, there we were stretching on our mats waiting for Doreen. You remember Doreen, right? We used to call her the terminator. She is one hard ass. Remember how she was doing headstands and firefly pose while she was pregnant? Shit, I couldn't concentrate on my pose thinking that she was going to pop that baby right out. She was so good to you, remember?"

Mariah smiles, glad Eleanor acknowledged that.

Eleanor had accompanied Mariah to yoga. Although Eleanor was an advanced practitioner, she had happily agreed to accompany Mariah to a beginner's class. The teacher, Doreen, taught a prenatal class, but the time conflicted with Mariah's weekly checkups. Doreen had been very accommodating, making adaptations for Mariah.

"Remember how she ended each practice by giving you a back massage while the rest of us were napping away through shavasana?" She looks at Mariah lovingly.

"Anyway, so there we were ready for Doreen, and who walks in but the yoga sub from the black lagoon," referring to the popular children's book *Teacher from the Black Lagoon.*

Mariah's eyelids feel heavy. Eleanor's voice becomes softer, but she continues on with her tale. As she nods off to sleep, Mariah delights in the sound of her voice.

$\mathcal{J}$AKE SITS NUMBLY AS THE limo driver pulls away from the cemetery lot. Eleanor is next to him, her head resting on his shoulder.

"It was a nice service. The snow couldn't have been more fitting," she offers. "So beautiful, as the flakes fell on the leis of colorful orchids decorating her casket."

"Mariah's kisses," Max had whispered to the friends as he stretched out his arm toward the clear sky, the soft frozen petals landing on his eyelashes as if forcing them to stay shut.

The minister had spoken about Heaven, inviting the listeners to view the promised paradise not so much as a final destination, but as a motivator to practice compassion while dwelling among the living. "There is hope in eternal life," the reverend had preached in his closing sermon. A notion that would have made Jake flinch with disapproval a year ago, now feels hopeful and reassuring.

The vibration of the moving vehicle lulls Jake to dream. His memory takes him back to Mariah's old apartment, her hesitation to leave a place she had loved. He had waited for her. He would have waited forever, if that's what it took to be with her.

They were celebrating their third Valentine's Day; the wedding was but three months away. Jake had presented her with a small box. He cherished the expression on her face whenever he presented her with a gift, no matter how simple or elaborate.

Mariah had opened the ornate box to find a bracelet charm in the form of a miniature glass bottle no larger than a jellybean. Inside the bottle sat a delicate origami rose.

She added the charm to an old bracelet that had been her grandmother's. She wore that charm until her wrist was too weak and too frail to accommodate the miniscule additional weight.

A couple of months later, Mariah had handed him a large red envelope for his birthday. He tore it open in one swipe to find the classified ads. She prompted him to look on. Jake turned the pages. His eyes traveled to the real estate section where he noticed a large red mark encircling a for sale listing, her decision made.

Jake pulled her closer and kissed her, a sense of relief washing over him.

"Let's make a baby in this apartment. Right now," he had pleaded, and she complied.

Jake returns to his body, to the awareness and numbness. He stares at his wedding ring, a simple gold band. He had asked Mariah to help him choose between gold and platinum.

"Gold goes nicely with your warm skin," she confirmed.

The cruel scene of his wife weeping in her sleep as the reality of her fate sank in loops over and over in his mind. His reassuring kisses and gentle rubs had failed to stop the nightmares from visiting her night after night. Her rose gold ring had slipped off her finger one day, rejecting her small bony fingers.

Jake's sobs break the silence and his shoulders shake as he weeps uncontrollably into his hands.

*M*EG STARED AT THE small clear Mason jar sitting on her dresser. It was one of the few items she would take if they should ever need to evacuate their home. It looked like a collection of knickknacks to unknowing eyes. A feather of a sparrow with reddish brown streaking along the edges; what fate had the Canadian visitor endured? Meg wondered. A foggy and chipped glass marble, no longer a complete sphere, yet with its own story.

The piece of turquoise sea glass stared back at her, as beautiful as the water of the Caribbean Sea. One single Mermaid Tear, a legend of long ago.

A daisy, its crinkled-up petals still attached to its core, the home of its ovaries. Meg marveled at the sense of protectiveness displayed by the daisy, a flower that speaks of new beginnings.

Meg felt the urgent pounding of her heart at the whispering from within the jar. The trapped memories reclaim their own stories, demanding to be set free.

She walked into the kitchen holding the jar. She opened the cutlery drawer and a knife made its way to her shaking hand. She stared at the blade approvingly and walked into the backyard, feeling a pull toward the small patio where the playground had stood decades ago.

Meg heard footsteps following closely behind her. *Lucas*, she thought, always there as if summoned by her emotions. She sat down on the far corner of the patio, put the knife by her side, and began to remove the tower of small rocks Mariah had put there as a teenager, her attempt at a rock garden, a Mother's Day surprise.

Meg removed rock by rock with care, the way a merchant would sample a pile of precious cargo. She could feel Lucas's measured movements behind her, his eyes studying her. She reached for the knife and hesitated for a moment.

"Can you dig a foot-long hole?" she asked, her voice a soft whisper.

Lucas glanced at the small glass jar sitting in Meg's lap. He took the knife and began to dig, his lips sealed. He understood.

The soft May ground gave easily. Meg opened the jar and took out the brittle daisy by tipping the jar into Lucas's open hands. The dried-up petals remained faithful to its core.

"The hike to the old fire tower," Lucas offered tentatively. Meg laid her head on his shoulder as Lucas continued to narrate the story. He paused hesitantly at the part of the story describing their oldest daughter's excitement when Lucas presented her with the flower. *Look at this daisy*, he had said to his curious toddler who was holding trustingly to her mother's hand.

"You called the flower tenacious for finding a way to survive among the rocks." Meg wiped her tears, and then placed the daisy gently into the empty space. "She was tenacious, and so was her little sister."

Meg held out the jar and Lucas's long fingers reached in for the sea glass. He held it to the light, and its beautiful calming hue transported their memories simultaneously to a small beach up the coast of Maine where they had rented a cabin for a week just a few minutes' walk from the beach. Mariah was a couple of months old, and her big sister was feeling strong, the result of a new treatment. Lucas had stayed at the house while baby Mariah napped that morning.

"It was hard to tell which of you was more excited!" Lucas kissed her forehead.

"She thought we had found a piece of treasure and I thought we had found an omen, a sign that the new treatment was going to work." She let her tears fall. She knew there would be more.

"Here is the marble one of the kids dug out of the sandbox and gave her when she was in preschool." Meg handed Lucas the small object. Her daughter had called it a magic fairy egg. She had kept that marble securely inside a small shoebox.

"She put a few dried berries and a tea cup with water in the box in case the baby fairy hatched and wanted something to eat."

Meg remembered, her eyes following the items at the bottom of the small pit.

The last piece of treasure remained alone in the jar. Meg gave the jar a gentle tap, expecting it to pour its contents into her open hand. The feather lingered in the jar as if uncertain about its immediate future. Meg gave the jar another tap, and the feather had no choice but to descend into her hand. It, too, joined the collection now complete, awaiting the weight of the dirt.

"She loved to listen to the chirping of sparrows so much. Remember how worried she was when she found the feather in the yard? She thought that the bird had gotten hurt, but you eased her worry and told her that the sparrow had left the feather for her as a gift," Meg said.

Meg and Lucas worked quietly to rebuild the rock structure.

"It's time to put the house on the market," Meg announced as she stood up, holding the empty small glass jar in her steady hand.

RAFAEL SITS AT HIS DESK staring at the small frame. It is a picture of Mariah holding a rosy-cheeked toddler whose spirited, young soul radiates from her wide hazel eyes, her mother's eyes. The picture shows a happy but tired Mariah. Her skeletal body is silent evidence of the horrific illness that has won the wrestling match, robbing her of her life one day at a time.

Tucked away somewhere at his apartment there is a large box of Mariah's pictures dating back to their college years. Still, it is this picture he treasures most. The expression of triumph and joy in Mariah's eyes send a clear message to the universe that she is at peace, yet those eyes also hold a direct plea for it to watch over her daughter, her most precious offering.

Rafael appreciates the holiday pictures from Jake and the stories he includes with the photographs over the years since Mariah's passing. They help him stay connected by watching her daughter grow. Her mischievous acts during the terrible twos. Her onstage delights while performing a piece from the *Nutcracker* with her fellow ballerinas. She had stopped middance to wave furiously and blow kisses at her dad and then called out, "Hi, Titi Eleanor!" with pure joy.

Tears cloud his vision as he imagines Mariah's body morphing into that of a Luna moth. He imagines her large, bright green wings with delicate tail streamers flapping in useless effort, trying desperately to stay alive, knowing that at the end, nature's unbending rules would prevail. Just like a Luna moth that emerges as an adult for the purpose of mating, their one-week life span makes their sole reason for existence, to give birth. *How cruel can nature be; to rob a mother of seeing her offspring grow,* he laments.

Rafael walks into his lab and turns the corner toward Mariah's section. He had dedicated a special wing of the lab to Mariah. He had promised her that he would continue his research. The *Chica files*, he had named that section of the lab. He has six large cabinets filled with data and test results. Rafael recently added the ten volumes of journals that Jake and Mariah had kept with a detailed day-by-day narration of her symptoms and the various treatments.

The small group of four researchers he had employed seven years ago to work on Mariah's case had grown to a team of fourteen.

Rafael had been collaborating with the Department of Rare Diseases since Mariah's enrollment in their program. She had made the right call on that even if at the time it was hard for him and Jake to accept her decision.

Over the years, Rafael's team had reviewed the data of over five thousand women who exhibited similar conditions to Mariah's. They are currently following twenty-three of those women worldwide.

A substantial amount of data suggests a shift in these women's DNA at the time of their first menstrual cycle. A possible correlation had emerged with the way a female mosquito's DNA switches at the time of its first bite. The team is investigating why the disease in women doesn't materialize until later. Why does it wait until the first pregnancy and then detonate with such force?

There is also unsettling data suggesting the possibility that some of these mothers transfer a faulty gene to their daughters, but that has occurred in less than 0.2 percent of the cases.

Rafael pulls out one of Mariah's files. He takes out the colorful chart and then pulls out another. His heavy brows dip in fierce concentration. He stares at the mother and daughter genome mapping.

*E*LEANOR PARKS HER FRESHLY WAXED SUV, relieved to have found a space so close to the building. The elegance of the vehicle does not match the *Eat my Chive!* inscription on the bumper sticker. Eleanor wobbles her way out of the car, trying to balance on her three-inch platform heels while holding a gift and an assortment of animal balloons. She takes a quick glance at the parking meter. *Whatever*, she mutters and gives the door a side bump with her hips. She will just have to risk getting a parking ticket.

She glances up and down the street impatiently. "Come on! I'm standing at a crosswalk, you idiots! "she shouts to the oblivious drivers. There is a small pause in the traffic and Eleanor goes for it. She makes her way across the street and up the front steps. She grabs the railing to stabilize herself as she rings the doorbell of the brownstone building.

"Hello!" Eleanor knocks on the door, hopeful for a listening ear on the other side. She rings the bell one more time, but still no response from the inhabitants.

Eleanor squints to read the message written on a post-it note at the base of the door. "*We are out back,*" reads the note in Jake's handwriting.

It was Meg's idea to buy a small apartment closer to town, closer to their granddaughter. The condo, although a bit snug, came with a small backyard just big enough for a swing set.

Eleanor maneuvers her way down the steps, onto the sidewalk, and then around the corner to the back entrance of the building.

Today is her goddaughter's birthday, which means the traditional family dinner. Tomorrow she'll get to have a birthday party with her friends at the Make Your Own Pottery studio. She had gone back and forth between the pottery place and the indoor trampoline park. Eleanor is grateful for the final choice.

Eleanor had helped Meg with planning and arranging the party. She will have to get there early to set up the goody bags. Jake is in charge of the cake. Lil' Boss had asked for "an animal cake." Eleanor is sure that cake would be nothing short of sensational, knowing Jake.

The birthday girl had invited her whole class to the party. She will have to remember not to call her Lil' Boss in front of her friends. There will be nineteen youngsters and some lingering adults waiting to be entertained.

Note to self: *Remember to wear sensible footwear for the party tomorrow*, Eleanor cautions herself.

The loud clanking sound of the heavy metal door startles Maddy. She emits a warning bark that sounds more like a whimper. Although officially a senior dog, her alertness remains intact.

Meg and Lucas are sitting on the Adirondack chairs sipping their fresh berry smoothie concoction. They look up as Eleanor approaches and quickly walk over to assist her. She releases the balloons into Meg's hands, and Lucas takes hold of the oversized gift box. Eleanor gives each a warm kiss and follows them. She stops abruptly and opens her shoulder bag to check that she had remembered to drop in the delicate pastry box. She smiles, pleased with herself. She had made a fresh batch of maple toffee for the birthday party tomorrow, but decided to bring over a few samples for her goddaughter, who is just as big a fan of the sweet maple treat as her mother had been.

Eleanor enters the backyard and is greeted by musical words. "Titi Eleanor! Watch me!" the sweet voice sings out as Jake pushes Rose on the swings. His six-year-old pumps her small legs with determination and delight.

ACKNOWLEDGMENTS

I am deeply indebted to my first readers: Bobbi Paris, Jennifer Capute, and Marilyn Barrett for their honest feedback while enduring my grilling questions about the story as I desperately tried to grab it out of the *Pensieve* of my mind and onto the judging screen of my laptop. Your personal connection to the characters and genuine curiosity about the plot gave me the impetus to move forward. *If I can capture their interest, I might be able to capture others*, I reasoned, since you are some of the most amazing readers I know!

Lauren Carroll, ¿Qué te digo? You give a new definition to friendship. You grabbed my hand and dove into the story head-on. Ideas? You got it! Feedback? You got it! Facts? You got it! Title? You got it! Thank you for reading and rereading the manuscript, each time pushing me to dig deeper into the plot. Thank you for caring so much for Meg. You understood her beyond what I was capable of expressing. Then you pointed me to our fellow knitter, the clever, hawk-eyed Mrs. Bigda. Ania, to you I give my utmost gratitude for your keen eyes. For letting me know that you wouldn't be a good friend if you couldn't be totally honest with your feedback. What would have looked like an editing nightmare to one of your students was an incredible generous gift to me. Your feedback came from the lens of your generation, a valuable asset for the plot. I love your alliance to Eleanor!

To my parents for their incredible love and for the many personal sacrifices they endured so that their seven children could get an education. My mom, born ahead of her time, who embodies the meaning of strong (*¡mujeres al poder!*) and my dad for teaching us to love and respect nature and all living things. To Joe and Marilyn, yes, our angels. You took our family under your wings over fifty years ago and have kept us there, close to your hearts.

To my children, who are truly the center of my universe. And finally, I acknowledge my husband; my biggest ally whose love and loyalty inspired the character of Lucas. Thank you for being an equal partner in this journey of parenthood and for gifting me the space and time to write.

A NOTE FROM THE AUTHOR

The characters Mariah and Meg have accompanied me on solitary sleepless nights and haunted me in my waking hours for many years. Although there were changes to their personal narratives from time to time, the essence of their personae remained the same. I have tried to honor that in presenting their personal tale the way they told it to me. This is their story.

Anyone interested in learning more about the language of flowers should read *The Language of Flowers* by Vanessa Diffenbaugh. My mother-in-law, who shares the same love of gardening, gave me a copy of this book several years ago. I loved that story for many reasons, but mainly for the idea of people communicating through the language of flowers. It reminded me of growing up in the Dominican Republic, where flowers are also known for speaking a language—not so much the romantic "Victorian" language as in Diffenbaugh's story, but a medicinal language.

I remember as a child being sent to a neighbor's house to ask for a clump of gardenia to treat insomnia; grabbing the spiky branches of a pomegranate tree for a handful of blossoms to treat upset stomach; and picking wild roses by the road to treat anemia or to dip it in water to drive away bad luck, the way my tía Tatica had done. From my mother I have learned to grow sage to alleviate menstrual cramps, oregano flowers to add to a bath to bring down a high fever (nature bath, my children called it), and hibiscus flowers to combat the flu.

When I began to write this story, my intention was to use their medicinal language, but I quickly abandoned the idea. The flowers spoke loud and clear; they chose their own language.

READING GROUP DISCUSSION QUESTIONS

What was your initial reaction to the book?

At what point in the story did you realize the connection between Mariah and Meg?

Discuss Mariah's decision to enroll in the Rare Disease Program.

What's your opinion of Jake and did it change as the story evolved?

Did race play a role in how a character navigates the world?

Did the underlying theme of flowers help you understand/ connect with the characters better? Why? Why not?

What is your understanding of the timeline? Mariah's story vs. Meg's story?

Which characters did you really connect to? Why?

Discuss Meg's struggle since the death of her firstborn. Why do you think her name was never revealed?

In what ways did the death of her sister impact Mariah's life?

What do you think about Jake's decision to conceal his illegal dealings in Singapore and his financial contribution to Barrett's campaign from Mariah?

What connects Mariah and Rafael?

Describe a memorable moment in the story.

What IF Mariah hadn't agreed to go out with Jake that first time they met? How might the story have been different?

How did the characters change throughout the story? How did your opinion of them change?

How did you feel about the ending? What do you wish had been different?

What questions do you have?

ABOUT THE AUTHOR

Tanya Paris is a native of the island of Hispaniola. She has been a classroom teacher for over two decades. She enjoys immersing herself in fantastical worlds whether of her own creation or imagined by others. She is happiest when riding upon dragons, scheming with fairies, or concocting potions of mischievous outcomes. She lives in the Boston area with her husband and their two teenagers. And yes, she loves to garden.

Visit her at tanyaparis.com

Tanya is also the cofounder of Las Margaritas Foundation, a nonprofit organization working to educate underserved children in the Dominican Republic.

Made in the USA
Middletown, DE
09 November 2020